The Miller's Wife

A.D. 1725

"A Colonial Pennsylvania Novel About Henry and Anna Funk"

Elwood E. Yoder

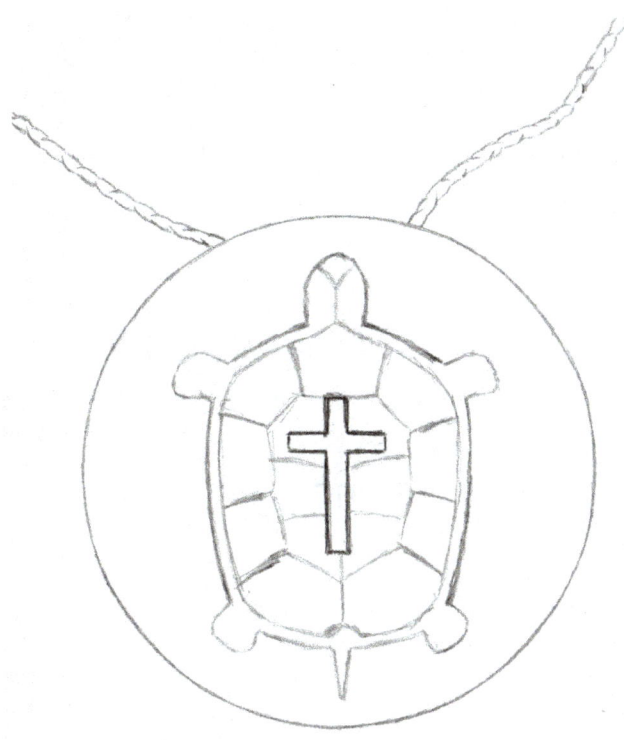

i

PLOWSHARES PUBLICATIONS
HARRISONBURG, VIRGINIA, USA

The Miller's Wife, A.D. 1725

"A Colonial Pennsylvania Novel About Henry and Anna Funk"

Elwood E. Yoder
©2017

ISBN: 978-0-9905559-1-9

Historical fiction

"By the Spirit we are brought to believe in God with a firm faith, to love Him ardently with our whole heart, above all things—to put our hope in Him, and trust in Him patiently in all the afflictions and tribulations that may come over us in His providence."
Henry Funk, in *A Mirror of Baptism*, about 1740

Legacy Print Series includes three books:
    Margaret's Print Shop, 2005
    The Black Tulip, 2014
    The Miller's Wife, 2017

Preface

The Miller's Wife is historical fiction, set in eighteenth-century colonial Pennsylvania. The story is based on events that took place during 1725.

Henry Funk was an actual minister, author, and leader among the Pennsylvania Mennonites, the son of German immigrants to colonial Pennsylvania.

Many of the characters in *The Miller's Wife* are fictitious, including Anna Meyer Funk, but over thirty characters are based on actual persons from the early 18th century. *The American Weekly Mercury* newspaper and all the books mentioned in this novel are actual historical documents.

The Notes section at the end of the book contains historical comments and clarifications of what is history and what is fiction. A list of characters, historical and fictional, also appears at the end of the book. The historical interpretations in this novel are those of the author.

The author acknowledges editing help from Joy Yoder, Max Driver, and Susan Melendez. Maps were created by the author and Max Driver. Sketches on the back cover and on the Title Page are by Micah Riddle.

The Miller's Wife is part three of the *Legacy Print Series*, written by Elwood Yoder. The first book in the series is *Margaret's Print Shop*, Herald Press, 2005, and the second book is *The Black Tulip*, Plowshares Publications, 2014. Elwood Yoder, the author, lives in Harrisonburg, Virginia.

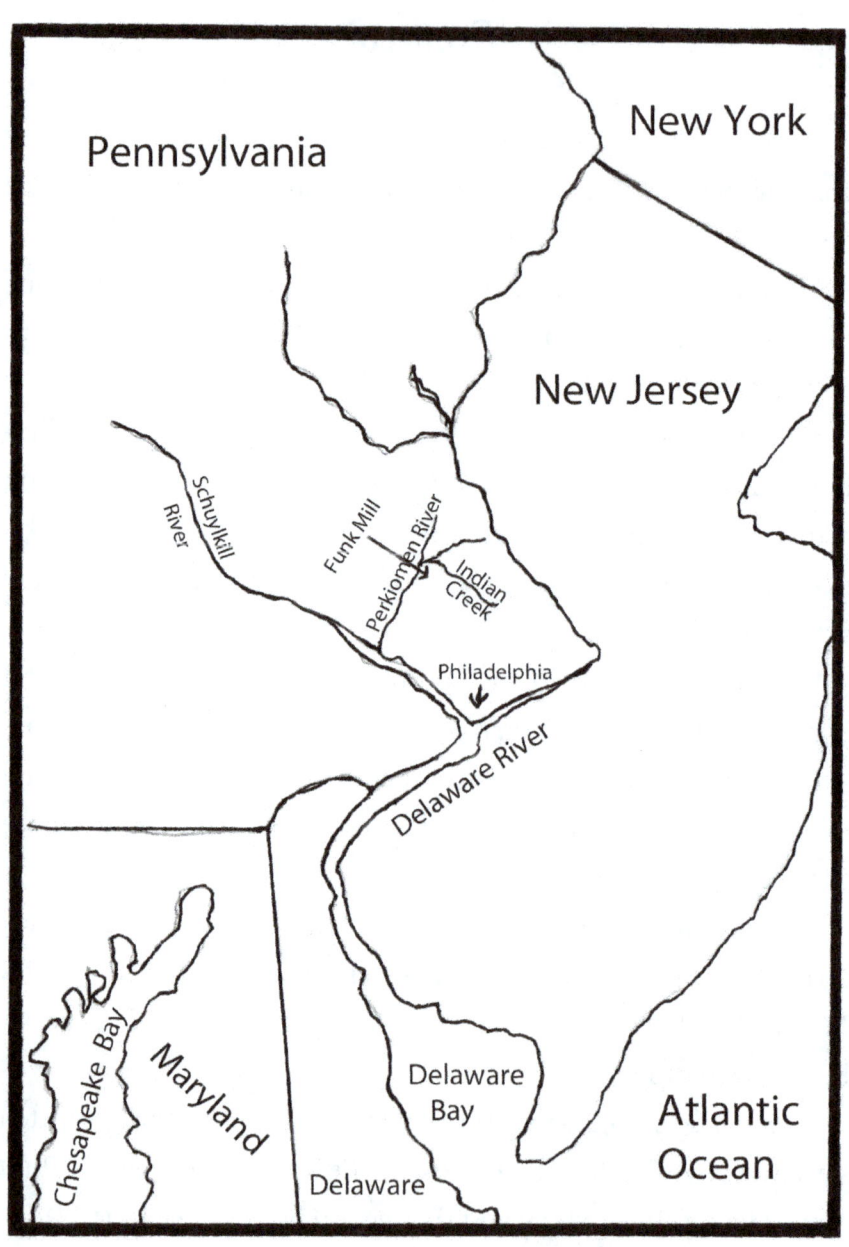

Pennsylvania

New York

New Jersey

Schuylkill River

Funk Mill

Perkiomen River

Indian Creek

Philadelphia

Delaware River

Chesapeake Bay

Maryland

Delaware Bay

Delaware

Atlantic Ocean

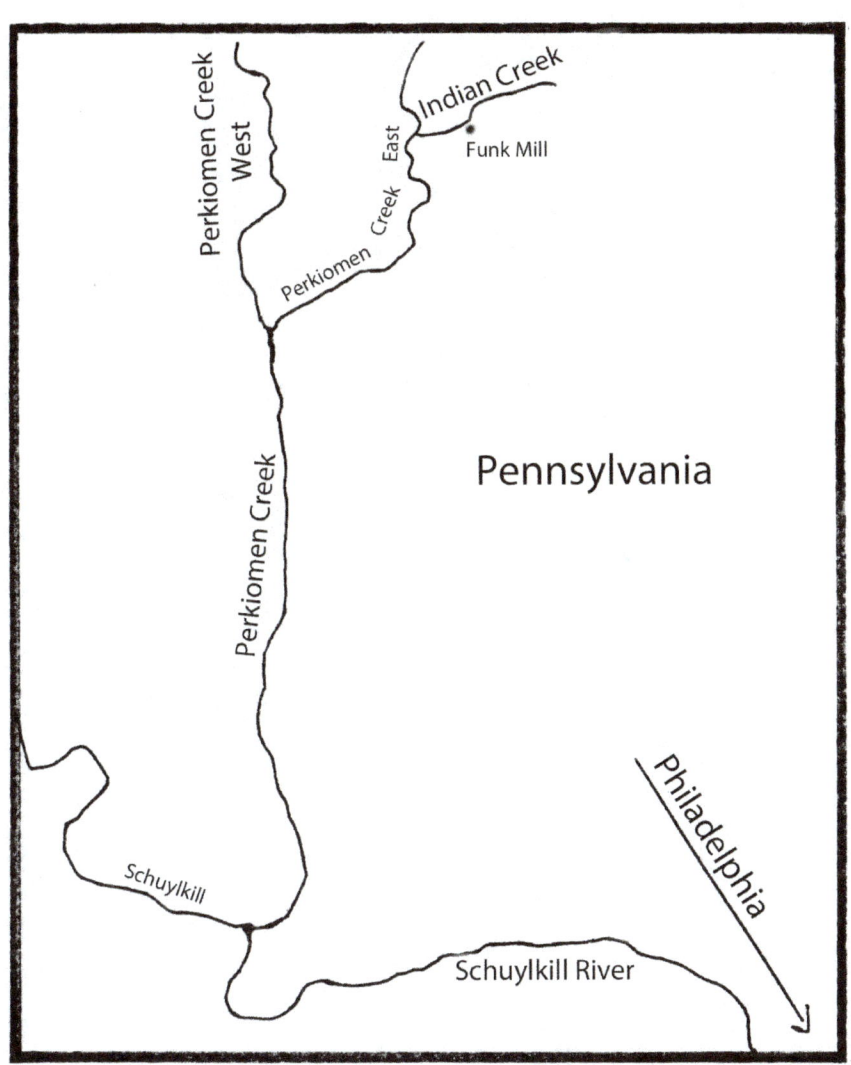

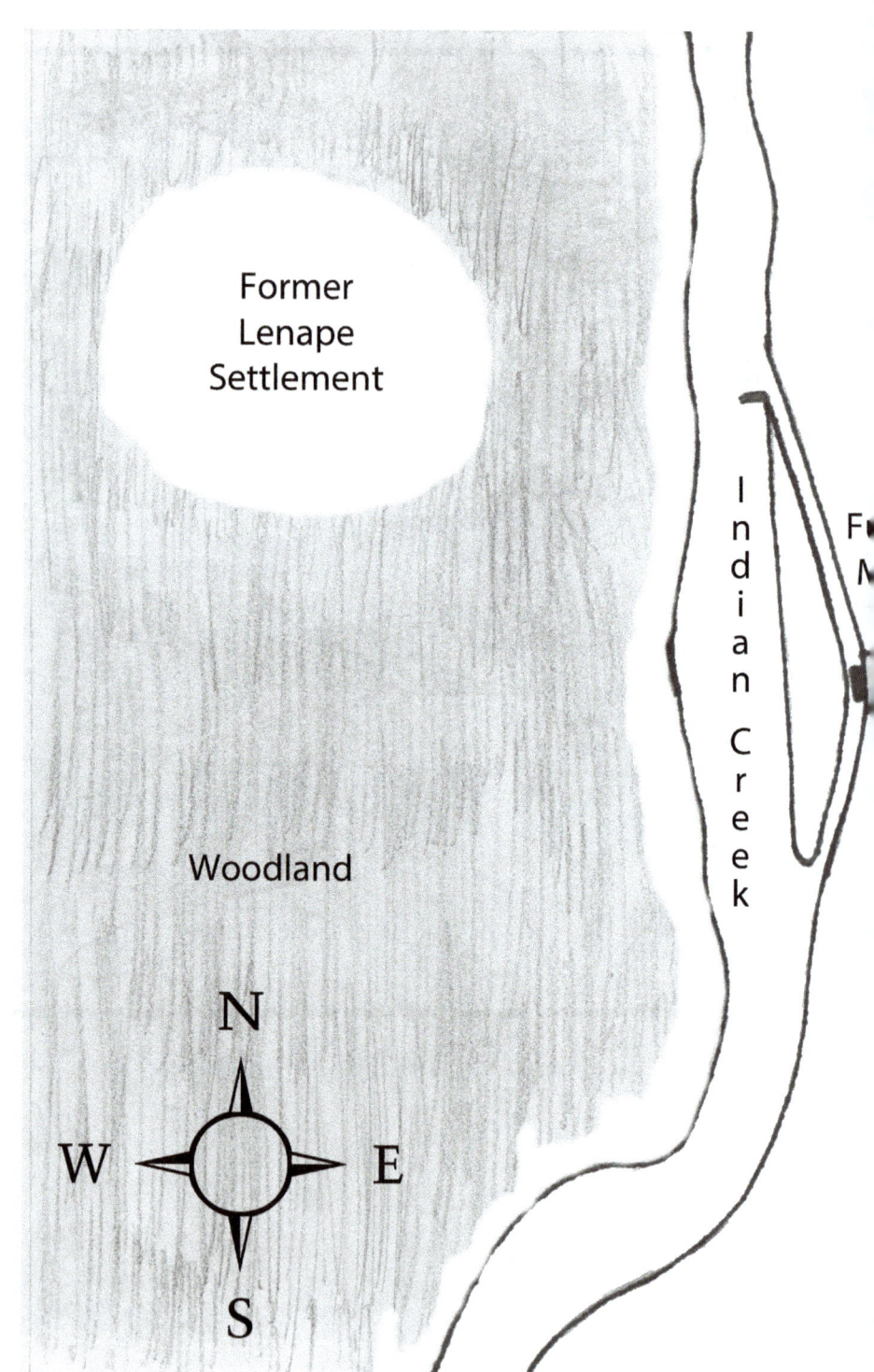

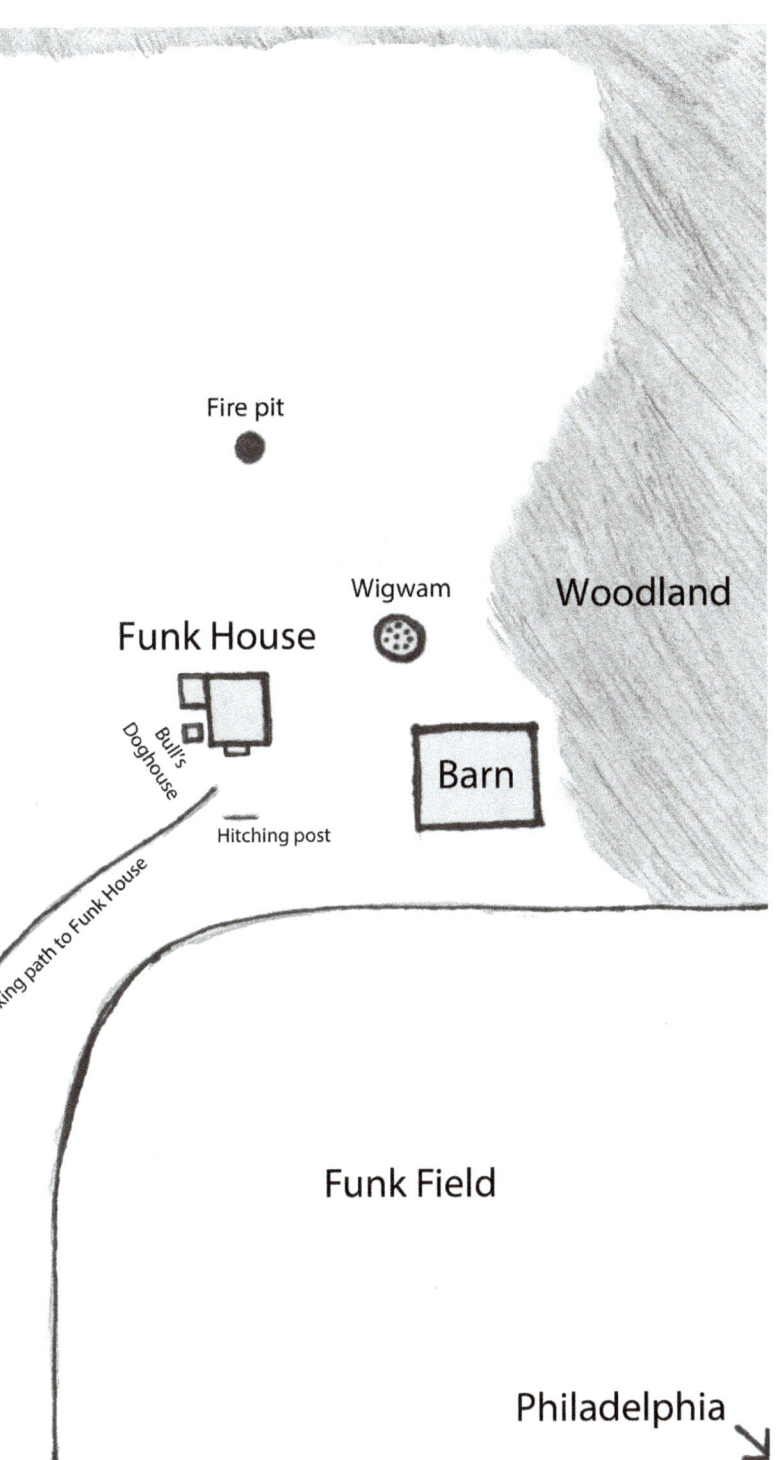

Fire pit

Woodland

Wigwam

Funk House

Bull's Doghouse

Barn

Hitching post

Walking path to Funk House

Funk Field

Philadelphia

1

Announcement
January 1725

A plea for help inside the Mennonite meetinghouse in Philadelphia startled Henry Funk. Grietje De Visscher Meyer, granddaughter of the renowned Dutch printer Jansen Visscher, spoke to the Germantown congregation about her predicament.

"We're looking for our daughter," Mrs. Meyer began. "We think she may be living in Philadelphia or somewhere in Pennsylvania."

Jolted from his thoughts, Henry listened to Mrs. Meyer's appeal and realized that he knew her daughter. In fact, he was in love with her.

Mrs. Meyer explained to the churchgoers, huddled together near the stove for warmth, that her daughter Anna had landed in Philadelphia the previous spring, on her way to Amsterdam to visit relatives.

"There aren't many eligible men around Anna's age in Aruba," Mrs. Visscher continued. "We wanted to give her a chance to find a husband in Amsterdam, but we haven't heard from her in nine months. Her ship stopped here before sailing for Europe."

Henry Funk remained silent while Mrs. Meyer unraveled her dilemma about Anna. Henry knew that Anna kept herself hidden among the Lenape near his farm. He had first noticed her the previous summer, mysteriously living among his peaceful Indian neighbors. She was clearly European, and he had fallen in love with her. She thrilled him, made him laugh, and had stolen his heart. It hadn't mattered to him where she came from. Until now.

Henry Funk, thirty-five, had come to Philadelphia to pay taxes on the 101 acres that he owned on Indian Creek, about thirty-five miles northwest of Philadelphia. Henry had built the roof on his mill the previous year and hoped to install a water wheel and gears by the fall. A bachelor, Henry took two business days in the city to pay his taxes, check in at the factory he had ordered mill gears from, and visit a print shop.

Mrs. Meyer's announcement at the little church in the northern part of Philadelphia the day before weighed on his mind, and he was eager to get back to Indian Creek and find Anna. He wondered how she would respond to the news that her parents were searching for her.

"Morning, Henry," Andrew Bradford called out. Busy printing his newspaper, the first one produced in Philadelphia, Bradford was working when Funk came in the door.

"Good morning, Andrew," Henry responded.

"What can I do for you today?" Andrew asked.

"I came to hear your story. Is it true you went to jail for a couple of days?"

"Yes, Henry. The governor put me in jail for writing about liberty and our civil duty. Take a look," Bradford offered.

Henry Funk read the line aloud that had gotten Bradford in trouble. "*To be friends of liberty, firmness of mind and public spirit are absolutely requisite...we are not born for ourselves alone, nor our own private advantages, but principally for the good of others and service of civil society.*"

"A quote from the Roman writer Lucan," Funk observed.

"Yes, Henry, Lieutenant Governor Keith is not like our first Governor William Penn. Politics have declined into self-interest and squabbling between rival groups. Mr. Keith doesn't understand the need for a free press."

"How long were you in jail, Andrew?"

"Two days, but now my newspaper is selling more copies, and we're making money because readers support me in speaking out against corruption in politics."

"Did the Governor think you were challenging him?" Henry asked.

"He did, and I was," Bradford replied. "I used Lucan's call for civility and seeking the good of others to make it clear I thought Governor Keith was out of line."

"Changing the subject, Andrew, would you print a book for Mennonites?"

"Certainly," Bradford responded. "Bring me your manuscript, and I can do the job for you."

"I'm writing a book about baptism," Henry replied. "I'll need someone with your printing skills to make copies."

"Good," Bradford answered. "Take a newspaper along."

Henry enjoyed holding the paper and he glanced at the headlines from *The American Weekly Mercury*.

At the courthouse in Philadelphia, the growing capital of Pennsylvania with about ten thousand people, Henry ran into the Meyer couple again. He did not want to talk to them. Mrs. Meyer marched in and announced her search to the officials at a big desk in the middle of the room.

"We're looking for our lost daughter," Mrs. Meyer exclaimed.

"When was she last seen?" the manager asked.

"March of last year."

Turning from the manager, Mrs. Meyer spotted Henry across the room.

"Weren't you at the church yesterday morning?" she nearly shouted.

Seeing no way to escape, Henry nodded in the affirmative. Mr. Meyer quickly rounded the big desk and blocked Henry's attempt to escape out the door.

"Yes, I was in church yesterday," Henry blurted.

"Can you tell us anything about our daughter, Anna?" Grietje demanded.

Glancing at a copy of *The Mercury* under Cornelius Meyer's arm, Henry changed the subject and asked about their printing business. He had heard enough in church the day before to know about the Meyer family enterprise.

"My people here in Pennsylvania are looking for a press to make a book or two for our young people."

"We could print for you," Mrs. Meyer answered.

"Have you seen our daughter?" Cornelius cornered.

"I hope you find her, and have a good day," Henry hastily concluded, while quickly heading toward the front door.

Before Henry could leave, Lieutenant Governor Keith stopped him and asked to talk with him privately. In a side room, Keith got right to the point.

"My daughter is thirty-two and unmarried, Henry. She would make you a good wife."

Henry felt trapped in front of the highest official of the commonwealth. He had never seen the Governor's daughter, nor did he especially want to.

"I'm actually courting a woman from Indian Creek," Henry stammered in response.

"I can set you up with a very nice house and good land," the Governor continued.

When Henry didn't respond favorably, the Governor asked if Henry could come to his house for dinner that very Tuesday evening, the 19th of January.

"No, I need to go home, work on my mill, and visit the lady I'm pursuing," Henry replied.

Henry hurried to the inn, grabbed his bag, paid his bill, saddled his horse in the neighboring stable, and rode out of the city. "Some brotherly love in this city," he scoffed. "What would Anna have to say about all of this?" he wondered, urging his horse northwest on the familiar road home.

Henry's path lay along the mighty Schuylkill River. At the point where the river made a big bend to the southwest, Funk stopped at the Freedom Inn for the night. The road to his farm turned to the north at the inn, away from the wide river. At the inn, Funk ran into Adam Miller, a Mennonite man a dozen years younger than him.

Miller was muscular and a fearless traveler, filled with wanderlust who rarely sat still. He had just returned from a trip into the western part of the Virginia colony. Around the dinner table at the inn, Miller told a group of men about his adventures in Virginia. He had been inspired by tales of Alexander Spotswood's trip into the western part of the colony, especially the Shenandoah Valley.

"I'm moving there," Miller exclaimed. "Funk, why don't you go with me? Marry that wild woman you're interested in, the one who lives in the woods with the Indians. Bring her along, and let's move to Virginia."

"When are you going?" Funk asked.

"At the end of this year," Miller answered. "After harvest, we'll move, clear land and plant in the Shenandoah Valley soil next spring. I need help—who's with me?"

Henry Funk had sailed across the Atlantic Ocean on the same ship with Adam Miller several years earlier, and the two had that dangerous journey in common. Now Miller, twenty-two, was ready to strike out and move into the uncharted frontier of Virginia.

"There are Indian trails up and down the Valley," Miller explained. "I heard directly from one of the men on Spotswood's expedition. The deer are plentiful, land almost free, and walnut trees are plentiful, meaning good soil."

"I'm not afraid of living on the frontier, Adam, but no Mennonites live there."

"Ever heard of a place called Elkton?" Miller asked, ignoring Henry's rebuttal. Not a man around the table had. "It's at the foot of a great mountain called 'Massanutten,' " Miller explained, "with bear, deer, squirrel, and cheap land."

"And Indians, I'm sure," one man warned.

"We'll make peace with them," Miller countered, "and get them on our side."

When Henry looked away, Miller tried again.

"Funk, bring that squaw you're chasing. She knows German and the Lenape language. She'd fit in well."

"You want to move in December?" Funk pondered.

"Yes, that's enough time to sell your land and turn over your mill to someone else," Miller concluded. "And enough time to get married in front of a preacher."

The men laughed when Henry responded by saying that he was a preacher himself.

Thinking about Adam Miller's offer, Funk remembered the Meyer couple he had run into in Philadelphia and he pondered their circuitous journey around the Atlantic Ocean to find their daughter. "Adam," he asked, "what are you searching for?"

"Searching for!" Miller exclaimed. "I want freedom to live my own way, freedom to make money, and freedom from this civilized world here in Pennsylvania that's corrupted with greedy politicians and dishonest tax collectors."

"That's reasonable," Funk answered. Thinking of beautiful Anna living in the woods with the Lenape, having run from her parents, he asked further, "What's freedom?"

"Freedom is why we sailed to this land!" Miller blurted. "People are coming by the hundreds almost every day, you know. Soon Pennsylvania will be so full, you can't piss in the open without someone telling you to be modest."

"Who would buy my grain at Elkton?" Funk asked. "There aren't many settlers in those parts."

"Other settlers will follow," Miller replied. "The roads between here and there are good, and your grain, Henry, could be shipped up and down the Valley."

"I've got freedom here," Funk replied. "Freedom to build my mill, plant in the spring, and attend church where I choose."

"William Penn's sons are the scourge," Miller replied. "They don't follow in their father's good will with the Indians. From England, they're forcing the acting Governor to be tough on the Delaware Indians. All hell's about to break out between the Lenape and English soldiers under the command of Lieutenant Governor Keith. There won't be any peace treaty like there was a few years ago between the Indians and William Penn."

Every man in the dining room knew Miller was right. Times were changing in colonial Pennsylvania.

Henry Funk told the men about Andrew Bradford at the print shop in Philadelphia. He read them the eloquent quote about civility and contributing to the public good, and the men nodded in agreement. They all understood why the Governor had thrown Bradford in jail.

"That's not all," Funk continued. "I ran into a Dutch couple from Aruba in the Caribbean, and they're looking for their daughter who disappeared."

After a pause, Miller grinned and looked straight at Funk, saying "That's your Indian woman, isn't it?"

"I need to check with her, but I'm pretty sure that's who it is," Funk smiled.

"She's found her freedom in the wilderness," Miller concluded. "Just like I want to do in Virginia. Now get married to her, and bring her along to Virginia in the fall."

Henry pushed back his chair from the table. He did not make decisions quickly, but when he decided on something, he was determined to follow through on what he had chosen.

"The search for freedom is what we're all looking for," Henry said. "It appears that I have to figure out, Adam, whether I'll find freedom on my farm along Indian Creek, or with you in Virginia, or with Anna who lives among the Indians."

2
Pursuit
January 1725

The next morning, Henry Funk rode straight to the Lenape settlement that Anna Meyer had joined. His Delaware Indian neighbors had lived just across Indian Creek, within sight of his log cabin. The wigwams, however, were gone. Anna had vanished, and so had all the others in her Lenape tribe.

Almost a year earlier, Anna had sailed into Philadelphia, like hundreds of others seeking new lives in Pennsylvania. She never went back to her ship when it sailed for Europe, nor did the captain wait on her.

A group of Lenape had visited Philadelphia the day Anna got off the boat, and she left the city with them, settling into their Indian Creek village.

"I felt completely comfortable among them," she had explained to Henry. "They were like the natives I grew up with in Aruba. You're the strange one," she had smiled at Henry.

At a harvest dance the previous fall, Henry and another man were talking in German when Anna, donned in Indian dress, beads, and paint, stepped out of the circle and began talking to the men in their own language. She had stunned Henry and his friend. German was Anna's second language, after Dutch, but she had a good command of it.

"Why don't you join the dance?" she had invited.

Speechless, Henry had mumbled something like, "I can't dance."

"I'll teach you, come on," Anna had invited.

Still dumbstruck, Henry stalled and stumbled for words. How could a woman who knew Dutch and German be in this harvest dance of Lenape Indians and their European friends from the surrounding community?

Anna was happy to talk with Henry later, and they struck up a friendship, which quickly turned to attraction, then romance, then love. In the early eighteenth-century frontier region of Pennsylvania, it did not seem strange to anyone that an Indian woman was noticed and courted by a mountain man.

Except that almost everyone knew she wasn't an Indian. Anna acted like one, however, and quickly learned the native language.

Standing in the abandoned Delaware Indian clearing, Henry wondered which way to turn. He had to find Anna. He looked around to see if there were any messages for him, but he found none. They had left in a hurry, it appeared.

On horseback, Henry galloped to his mill less than a mile away to check on things and get help locating Anna. A trusted neighbor had fed three chickens in his barn while he was gone, as well as his pig and goats. It dawned on Henry that his neighbor, William, who looked after his place while he was away, might be able to help him.

His grizzled neighbor met Henry at the door about a half mile south of his mill.

"How are you William?" Henry asked.

"Doing fine, Henry, come in."

William's father had been English and his mother Delaware Indian. Years ago, in 1683, his mother had been under the elm tree in Philadelphia when William Penn made a peace agreement with the Indians to live together in harmony in Pennsylvania. William had been named in honor of the great founder of the colony.

William's wife Jubilant, a Lenape Indian woman, offered Henry rabbit from their evening meal, which he devoured.

The three spoke in English since their mother tongues were all different.

"What happened to Anna's settlement?" Henry asked.

"I've no idea where they've gone, Henry, but I could take a look."

"We've got an hour of sunlight left. Can we go now?"

"It would be better in the morning, Henry. Most likely they left a sign you couldn't read or detect about where they went."

"I need to find Anna," Henry insisted.

Jubilant smiled and remarked, "You two need to get married."

"I agree with you," Henry smiled.

"Will you get a Mennonite preacher to marry you, or the Indian chief?" Jubilant asked.

"Maybe both," Henry answered.

"That would be a good idea," Jubilant responded.

At the crack of dawn the next morning, William spotted a message in the clearing that Henry had missed. Two marks had been scrawled inside a partial circle.

"They write with pictures," William explained. "This indicates 'west to the big river.' "

William and Henry could identify the tracks of several dozen Lenape Indians who had departed a few days earlier, but the trail soon grew unclear and William had to work to follow it.

Before too long, William and Henry arrived at the Perkiomen Creek, presenting them with a challenge.

"How did the whole village get across this?" Henry asked.

"They found the shallows," William answered, pointing. "Right here where the water isn't as deep and it gets wider." Their horses easily made their way across. William soon found the Lenape trail on the other side of the creek.

Just beyond the Perkiomen, with the sun high above them late in the morning, William and Henry rode into a clearing where the Lenape had pitched their tents. Two braves met them and recognized both William and Henry.

"I've come to find Anna," Henry stated in broken Lenape.

A brave pointed in the direction of a tent. Henry dismounted, and quickly walked toward it. It was a cold enough day that most women and children huddled inside whenever they could.

"Anna," Henry called. "Are you in there?"

Out of the tent door popped Anna, exclaiming, "How come it took you so long to get here?"

"You gave me no warning and very little by way of directions."

"Come inside and get warmed up—both of you," Anna invited.

Glancing around at the watching eyes, Henry said, "Let's talk by the fire."

"Why did you leave?" Henry asked while they ate and soaked in the warmth of the flames.

"Lenape Mother felt we were too close to the English settlers, people like you."

"Will you go on a walk with me?" Henry asked.

"Yes, but not for long–it's cold. I grew up where it's warm."

"It will be short, Anna, but I have something important to tell you."

Keen eyes watched their every move, but since Henry was known by the braves, they didn't mind seeing the two walk amongst the wigwams.

"Your parents are looking for you," Henry explained.

"How do you know?"

"They came to Philadelphia looking for you and I met them. Grietje and Cornelius—sound familiar?"

Anna stopped and stared at Henry. "You met them, and they were looking for me?"

"They came to church and made an announcement about their lost daughter, and the next day I ran into them in the Philadelphia Courthouse."

"Are they still here?" Anna asked.

"More than likely. Do you want to meet them?"

"No. Henry, I've been missing you. Did you miss me?"

"I came looking for you, didn't I?"

Henry gathered Anna in his arms. "I missed you. And I have more to talk about than your parents."

"What else?"

"I met Adam Miller, and he wants me to move with him to Virginia to start a new settlement."

"Where do I fit in?"

"Well, first, I have to ask you something else," Henry interrupted. "Will you marry me?"

The world stopped for a moment while Anna thought. It was a cold Pennsylvania day in January, far from her home in the Caribbean. She had only met Henry Funk last fall, her parents were looking for her, and now Henry proposed marriage.

"Henry, my only reservation is that you took so long to ask me."

"You know I take time to make up my mind, but when I do, it's settled."

"You want me for your wife?"

"Yes, without a doubt! I want to talk to Lenape Mother and ask her permission."

"She'll agree; I just wonder what my mother would say."

"We could go ask her," Henry offered.

"My answer is 'Yes,' Henry. I say we get married and then maybe tell my parents."

Lenape Mother was wise enough to be watching, and she came to inquire. "I want to marry Anna," Henry stated in the best Delaware words he could muster.

"What can you offer?" the wise woman asked.

"I have over a hundred acres, a mill that I'm working on, a small house, and a barn."

"That doesn't impress her," Anna stated. "That's exactly why we moved west, to get away from German immigrant farms."

"Okay, then what I have to offer is myself and my life. I will always care for her and protect her. I want to marry Anna, with your permission."

Lenape Mother let out a whoop and everyone knew what it meant. By late evening a large fire had been built, a deer roasted, a meal cooked, and the village celebrated Anna and Henry's engagement.

Anna from the Caribbean and Henry from Germany communicated with each other in German. Anna had learned Lenape and could talk with the villagers. This was William Penn's dream for Pennsylvania—a peaceful settlement where people lived together in harmony and friendship.

While the Indians celebrated and ate, and while Anna taught Henry how to dance around the fire, William watched from the edge of the circle. Wrinkled and weathered from years of living along Indian Creek, he sensed trouble ahead, but he didn't exactly know what kind of trouble.

From the edge of the circle came a short man covered head to foot in a bearskin costume, with a red and black painted mask. He came to bless the marriage of Anna and Henry and to scare the children, but William wondered if he also brought a curse.

Only time would tell. Tonight they ate and drank to the good fortune of Anna Meyer and Henry Funk's marriage.

3
Ambush
February 1725

William spotted the trouble first. Raised with Indian and white teaching, William understood why the Governor's surveyors measured land plots and pounded boundary stakes into the ground. He also knew why Lenape braves pulled them out and threw them into the woods.

Angry surveyors complained to the Governor, who sent out soldiers to stop the Indians from pulling out stakes. Anna's people had moved, knowing that Pennsylvania's colonial government intended to push them off the land and sell it to new settlers who were streaming off ships in the Philadelphia harbor, looking for cheap farms.

On the first Wednesday in February, the Lenape people had visited the Funk farm and were examining their old settlement, when James Logan arrived. Logan was the current political face of Philadelphia, holding more offices than you could count on two hands, all legally acquired, and he had come to inspect his Indian Creek properties.

When Logan threatened those who pulled out stakes, Anna spoke up, not intimidated by his wig, sweating horse, or regal British bearing.

"You need to get on that horse and ride back to Philadelphia," Anna insisted.

"What are you doing out here among the natives?" Logan asked, his men listening and snickering. "You belong with your mother."

"My Lenape people moved because of your dishonest officials," Anna replied.

"The surveyors are marking out my land before we sell it to new settlers and you are in the way," Logan responded.

The heat in this disagreement brought the frontier conflict into the open on a cold but bright day. Six soldiers waited patiently on James Logan to negotiate with the Indians and settle the situation one way or the other.

"I want the braves who tied up my surveyor to come here in front of me," Logan insisted.

"Our braves are far to the west, hunting deer," Lenape Mother responded. "Your traders switched from demanding beaver pelts to deer skins for trade. The herds are thin here and our men are gone. We don't know who tied up your surveyor."

Soldiers grew restless while the inquiries went nowhere. William grew alarmed about the growing crisis, while Henry stood in the circle and tried to think of a solution.

"The braves who tied up your man could have been Iroquois rather than Lenape," Anna declared.

"The Iroquois are working with me, Anna, not against me," Logan replied.

"When was your man ambushed?" Henry asked.

"Two weeks ago," Logan answered. "Where were you, Funk?"

"In Philadelphia, paying my taxes and checking on the progress of my mill gears."

"William, did you see any suspicious braves in these parts?" Logan asked.

"They moved in the middle of January," William replied. "Lenape Mother answers truthfully that their braves are hunting deer to the west. There were no Indian men here to tie up your surveyor."

"Then who did it?" Logan persisted. "My surveyor insists that it was Indians."

At the edge of the empty clearing, where the Lenape had lived three weeks earlier, stood two Indian boys watching but trying to avoid being seen.

"Get them," Logan ordered. Half his men galloped in the direction of the fleeing boys. Three men on horses chased down two frightened Indians, grabbed them, and tied them up. When they faced James Logan, he looked at the surveyor and asked, "Are these the Indians?"

"Yes," the surveyor responded.

"He never saw who tied him up," Anna jumped in their defense.

"How would you know?"

"Because if Indians had tied up your surveyor, he would never have seen them."

Looking again at his surveyor who nodded in the affirmative, Logan stated, "I have a witness who saw these two boys. March them to Philadelphia," Logan ordered.

"Justice Logan, these boys aren't who you're looking for," Henry pleaded. "They're scared, they're too young, and they wouldn't have done something like this unless they had a man to help them."

Anna moved quickly and began to untie them, pushing the soldiers away.

"You're obstructing justice," Logan growled. "If you don't stop, you'll go to jail with them," he warned.

"They didn't do anything," Anna snapped, busy with the ropes.

No one budged until Henry spoke up.

"You can't throw three innocent people in jail," Funk glared.

"Watch me," Logan answered. "This is my land and I'm selling it to new English settlers. And these three aren't innocent."

"This is not what William Penn wanted," Henry exclaimed.

"I believe I'm more of an authority on what Mr. Penn wanted in this colony than you are."

"You should think about the consequences, Mr. Logan. Do not throw them in prison."

"Justice must be done," Logan answered.

"Anna and I will be married this spring, and these boys are needed to work in the village," Funk gestured west to the new settlement.

"Bring me ten deer skins apiece," Logan announced, "and they'll be turned free."

Anna didn't respond in order to protect the boys. Two soldiers hoisted her on the extra cargo horse they brought along from Philadelphia, arms tied but with hands able to grip the reins. The boys had to walk.

"Come see me when you get the skins," Logan said. "Just announce yourself in the Courthouse."

Logan turned and his small army rode away.

"Wait," Henry shouted. Jubilant had given Henry a blanket for Anna's cold ride to Philadelphia. He placed it around her shoulders and put the ends in her hands.

"I'll come for you soon," Henry promised. "Be strong." All he got in response was Anna's glare, directed at James Logan, who was stern and unmoved. Logan flicked his reins and urged his horse toward Philadelphia.

It started to snow, hard. James Logan's little entourage took refuge in the Freedom Inn, the familiar stop along the Schuylkill River where Henry had talked to Adam Miller. "Put the boys and girl in the barn with the horses," Logan ordered. Logan's men had the inn to themselves, though some of the soldiers had to sleep on the floor. Meanwhile snow piled up outside.

After Logan rode away, two braves appeared from the trees to speak with Lenape Mother in her tent. She explained to them what had been said and what the boys were charged with. After a bite to eat, the braves slipped into the cold, snowy night, and headed down the main road south toward Freedom Inn and Philadelphia. They knew the way well and didn't take long to catch up.

Logan had the horse barn door padlocked on the outside, with one soldier inside. The braves peeked through a crack in the boards and saw the boys and Anna inside on the hay. To get them out of the snow, the horses had been packed inside.

Anna noticed when the braves pushed open a small vent window. She stood on the hay and reached up to slowly pull the hatch all the way open. If the horses stirred too much, they might wake the guard and the men next door asleep in the inn.

Before the guard could react, he was gagged and tied to a post. The braves moved quickly to help the boys and Anna scoot through the vent and get outside. The horses didn't make much of a commotion, though the guard watched all of this take place, unable to do anything. Before slipping away into the snowy night, one brave, a Lenape chief, turned and shot a single arrow into the wooden door of the barn, where it stuck, as a message and warning.

James Logan was furious the next morning, but the heavy snow made him decide to keep going to Philadelphia. He'd return to the Lenape settlement and discipline them. He kept the arrow for evidence.

At the same time, Henry Funk heard a knock on his door. He jumped to his feet, pulled on his britches, and opened the door a crack. There stood Anna Meyer, shivering in snow nearly reaching her knees.

"Come in," Henry insisted.

"There are four of us," Anna replied. "Can we all come in?"

"Sure, it'll take me a minute to get the fire going."

After stoking the fireplace embers and adding a log to warm the travelers, Henry used the outhouse and surveyed the pristine morning snow covering his land, small house, barn, and mill. He hoped to begin grinding in the fall, once he got the wheel and gears installed. For now, deep snow covered his property.

Henry stoked wood in the fireplace to get his house warmed up. One brave had gone to the Lenape settlement, but the boys and a brave were with Anna.

"You were rescued?" Henry asked.

"We slipped out the barn vent at Freedom Inn," Anna answered. "Have you met Chief Lapowinsa?"

"No," Henry replied. With flames dancing Henry could see distinctive black marks on Lapowinsa's forehead.

"My father helped make peace with William Penn," the chief spoke in German, one of his several languages.

"Thank you for helping Anna," Funk responded.

"You are welcome," Lapowinsa answered.

"How can I repay you?" Henry asked.

"Will you go with me to Philadelphia to visit James Logan?"

"You want to talk to Logan?" Henry asked.

"Yes, we must negotiate peace, Henry, like my father did with the 'Great Miquon', William Penn."

"Peace?" Henry inquired.

Chief Lapowinsa nodded and added, "My people are looking for a missing gold medallion which I must ask Logan about."

"When the snow melts and before spring planting, I can go with you," Henry agreed.

Chief Lapowinsa and the two boys finished their breakfast and left Funk's house. Henry turned to discover Anna fast asleep in his loft bed.

4

Capture

March 1625

Pennsylvania Chief Justice James Logan was determined to make an example of Chief Lapowinsa. Logan believed the Lenape had been stealing from English settlers throughout the Schuylkill River watershed, including the Perkiomen and Indian Creek regions.

"Saddle up men," he barked. They rode out of Philadelphia to find the owner of the arrow he had pried from the door at the Freedom Inn. He figured Chief Lapowinsa had been at the center of the trouble.

"He goes to jail when we find him," Logan ordered.

At the Lenape settlement west of the Perkiomen Creek, Chief Lapowinsa was not hard to find. In fact, he came out to meet Logan, unafraid, and welcomed him to the Lenape settlement.

"Did you shoot this arrow into the barn door?" Logan asked the chief.

"What is your business with our people today?" Lapowinsa responded.

Logan's horses had muddy hooves from the spring thaw, which had prompted Henry Funk to work hard on his mill, now that a hint of warmer weather lay ahead.

"Answer my question," Logan insisted.

"I did, because you took two of our boys who were innocent."

"Tie him up," Logan demanded.

With most of the braves still to the west hunting, there was little resistance to Logan's men.

Anna sprang to action from her hiding place and ran the well-known footpath to Henry's mill. Gasping for breath, she grabbed him and explained that Logan had captured Lapowinsa and was taking him to jail in Philadelphia.

"Can you do something?" Anna begged.

"I'm not sure," Henry replied, "but let's go."

It didn't take long to find Logan's men. They were coming to Funk's farm.

"Anna escaped and must come with us," Logan announced.

"I'll pay the ten deerskins," Henry offered. Anna clung to Henry's back.

"Bring the skins to Philadelphia, and she'll be set free," Logan replied.

"Logan," Henry answered, "what good will it do you or the colonial government to imprison the chief and Anna? The braves will rally to defend Lapowinsa, and more settlers will be at risk."

"They must learn who is in charge," Logan answered. "We serve on behalf of King George I of England, with the full force of colonial law behind us. You are all subjects of the British Empire."

"You must go, Anna," Henry finally agreed, eyeing Logan. "I'll find the deerskins somewhere and get you out."

Henry could only buy eight deerskins from the nearby Lenape Indians. To get two more needed skins, Henry rounded up his brothers from neighboring farms, and they helped him hunt. Two days later they had two more, and ended up at the mill frustrated, worn out, and exasperated with the silly distraction this hunt had brought into the midst of their preparations for spring planting and building.

"I'm not wasting any more time," Henry declared to his brothers. Three days after James Logan took Anna to Philadelphia, Henry headed to the capital with a pack horse carrying the deerskins and a determination to bring Anna back.

After a full day's ride, Henry took a room at his usual Philadelphia inn and waited for the courthouse to open the next morning.

James Logan met Henry as the first visitor of the morning. "Mr. Funk, welcome to our capital."

"I've brought the payment for Anna," Henry replied.

"Let me see."

"They're outside on the horse," Henry directed.

Checking on Funk's deerskin payment, Logan returned.

"They look good," James Logan indicated after slamming the door shut. "Come with me."

In the back of the courthouse, Logan took Funk to the prison and unlocked Anna's cell. Logan vanished out the door and went up steps to his office, while Henry embraced Anna. "Let's get out of here," Anna insisted.

"Where's Chief Lapowinsa?"

"Down the hall."

Henry Funk and the Lenape chief met at the small, iron barred window which provided light and air for his cell. "Can you get me out of here?" Lapowinsa asked.

"I don't know how," Henry answered.

"We'll get your braves involved and force James Logan to release you," Anna offered.

"Be careful, Anna," the chief responded. "My braves will know what to do. I want to talk to James Logan about the gold medallion," the chief requested. "Can you arrange for such a meeting?"

After an inquiry by Funk, through the chief justice's court administrator, Logan grudgingly agreed to a brief meeting with the chief in the courthouse conference room. Logan kept Funk and Lapowinsa waiting for a while before arriving.

"Pieter Alricks served under the Dutch and then under William Penn, the 'Great Miquon,' " Chief Lapowinsa began.

"When my grandfather lived on Manhattan Island, Alricks gave my grandfather's sister, Tender Vine, a gold medallion as a sign of good will. This was before Tender Vine had married. Two years later, Alricks' bullies came back and took the gold medallion from her, after violating her so badly that she died."

Chief Lapowinsa, still stoic, paused and looked at Logan. "When my father negotiated with William Penn for land and peace under the big tree in Philadelphia, the 'Great Miquon' promised to investigate and see what happened to the medallion," the Chief summarized. "My people do not have the gold medallion yet."

"What do you want from me?" Logan frowned.

"To find the medallion, which means so much to my people."

"Why does it mean so much to you?" Logan asked.

"Because it had been a promise of peace to Tender Vine and the Lenape, and because it had a great turtle on the medallion, a sign of our peoples' heritage, and a cross on the other side," the chief answered.

"Two braves avenged Tender Vine's awful death," the chief continued. "When Pieter Alricks became enraged that Lenape braves had killed two settlers, he captured one brave and executed him."

"I have no idea where the gold medallion is," James Logan replied. "Is that the end of the story?"

"Returning the gold medallion to the Lenape of the Delaware region will help in building peace and good relations between your settlers and our people," explained the chief.

"Guard, take this man back to the cell," Logan ordered. Rising, the leading political force in the city strode out the door and was gone.

The first of two stops Henry and Anna made before leaving Philadelphia was at the mill factory. Across the regions beyond Philadelphia, to the north and west, grain mills, like the one Henry was building, were springing up in many local communities. Settlers relied on local mills in their region to grind wheat and corn into flour that they could use in cooking.

A factory had prospered in the capital, making the water wheels and massive gears needed to turn the grindstones that removed the outer shell from the corn or wheat. German immigrants formed a bee hive of men who sawed, turned, screwed holes, and made the big wheels with cogs that would power the grindstone. It was the two big grindstones, with the top one turning within a small finger's width of the lower one that helped feed the tens of thousands of European immigrants in the distant regions of the commonwealth, but also in neighboring New Jersey and Delaware.

Henry had ordered a water wheel and a set of interior wheels, along with the big shaft, from the Philadelphia factory. His brothers and parents had invested money along with him, expecting to be paid back once Henry turned a profit from selling flour. The Funks were confident they could make money from the enterprise. Henry was industrious, even inventive, and knew how to make things work. He believed a grist mill on Indian Creek would help him succeed.

"I need a wife to help make the mill turn a profit."

"Is that the reason you want to marry me?" Anna smiled and patted his balding head.

"No, I love you, and I get lonely in my house sometimes."

"We better get a preacher lined up," Anna smiled. "Come on."

The Mennonite pastor in northern Philadelphia wanted to talk with Henry before getting to the topic of marriage.

"I hear you're starting a fellowship at Franconia," the pastor began.

"We're holding monthly services and building a log meetinghouse," Henry answered.

"Where will the marriage take place?" the pastor asked.

"At my farm," Henry responded.

"And we'll have the Lenape join us," Anna added.

"Lenape?" the preacher inquired.

"She's gotten to know most of them," Henry explained.

"They're my family," Anna explained.

"Where are your parents, Anna?" the preacher asked.

"I'm a recent immigrant," Anna quickly responded. "I'm here in Pennsylvania by myself, except for Henry, of course."

So many had sailed to America on their own that Anna's answer didn't seem unreasonable. Some came for adventure, some to find a job, some as indentured servants for a few years; and others lost their families at sea on the difficult voyage across the Atlantic Ocean.

"Are you living together?" the preacher inquired.

"No," Henry responded.

"I'll move in with him when you marry us."

"You're ordained, right Henry?"

"Yes, last year."

"Good, when do you want me to come to your farm for the wedding?" the preacher asked.

Henry glanced at Anna before answering.

"How about next week?" Anna asked.

"Slow down, Anna. When can you come?" Henry asked him.

"How about the last day of March, in three weeks?"

"We'll plan on March 31st," Henry concluded.

"There's one more detail to discuss," Anna added.

"What's that?" the gentle pastor wondered. Only twenty years old, it seemed like anything might come from Anna's mind.

"I'm going to invite all the Lenape in the area," Anna announced.

"But I'll be doing the ceremony, right?" the pastor asked.

"Lenape Mother's been my substitute mother," Anna explained. "I want her involved."

"What will she do in the wedding?" the pastor asked.

"Give us a Lenape Indian marriage blessing."

"What does that mean?" the pastor asked.

"The Lenape believe in invisible forces that live in the trees, the rocks, the water, the animals, and the moon. She'll bless me with the nature forces that her people understand, so we can have children."

"God gives couples the blessing of children," the pastor responded.

"Your people here in the city can come for the celebration."

"Are you prepared to pay for all the food?" the pastor inquired.

"Yes," Henry replied, "with my brothers and their families, and my parents, we'll be able to host a large celebration with food for all."

"Will you join the Christian community that Henry belongs to?" the pastor asked.

"Yes, but I have Lenape friends that I want to keep."

"Their religion is nature worship," the pastor explained. "Ours is the Christian faith. I will marry you in the name of the Father, Son, and Holy Spirit, and start you in a God-centered home."

Before leaving the next morning, Henry asked if the pastor could speak to James Logan about Chief Lapowinsa who was jailed in the Courthouse.

"I see Logan occasionally; perhaps I can say something," assured the pastor.

"I'd like to have the chief at our wedding," Anna added.

"Would it give you a reason to ask Logan if we invited the chief to our wedding?" Henry asked.

"Why don't you invite Logan himself to bring Lapowinsa to your wedding?" the pastor countered.

Anna wasn't sure she wanted Logan at her wedding, but she nodded in agreement. "If that will get the chief there, then sure, invite both of them."

"There's trouble ahead as long as the chief sits in jail," Henry warned. "His braves will be restless while he's behind bars."

The pastor nodded in understanding ascent.

"I'll do what I can."

Anna wondered why Henry beamed while riding north out of Philadelphia, then she spotted the evidence. He had purchased the latest edition of his favorite newspaper, *The American Weekly Mercury*.

"Hold on Henry, give me a chance to catch up!"

5

Speech
March 1725

Six Lenape Indians came to inspect Henry and Anna's work on the race for the mill. The race diverted water from a dam Henry had built on Indian Creek and channeled the water into a small canal that turned a big wheel that created power to turn gears in the flour mill. A pond near the mill stored the water that could be used as needed.

The Lenape wondered how the dam would change Indian Creek. No more than a big pile of rocks and dirt, it was easy to observe how the dam would direct water in a different direction when the mill wheel was ready to operate. It appeared that over half of the water would go down the race, while overflow would spill over the dam and keep the creek running.

Indian Creek was a sacred part of the Lenape tradition, sustaining wildlife and creating harmony in their lives. Fish were the primary concern of the Lenape as they talked with Henry and Anna and watched them work. Would the fish be able to navigate over the dam, and if not, how would that affect their lives in the settlement? Was this one more encroachment on their way of life from the English settlers?

The Lenape visitors on the Funk farm saw that when the dam was completed, Henry could divert the water he needed to run the mill, leaving Indian Creek with some water, but in dry seasons it may leave the level of the water low, and so affect the fish in the stream. Henry did his best to help the Lenape understand what he was doing, but the concern on the faces of his visitors was obvious.

Henry's mother, Mrs. Funk, lived on a farm about three miles from Henry's mill. She welcomed Anna into her home, and they began making a wedding dress for the special day that was coming soon. Sewn by hand, Mrs. Funk worked on a dress in the old style fashion from Germany, where they had migrated from only seven years earlier. Anna had attended weddings in Aruba, but had not paid much attention to dresses, and the Caribbean styles were very different from Palatinate regions in central Europe.

A spring rain pounded on the roof while the women worked.

"What was your home like in Aruba?" Mrs. Funk asked.

"My father and mother operate the Visscher family printing press," Anna replied. "Years ago my great-grandfather married and settled on the island. He had grown up in Amsterdam."

"Why did you leave?"

"My parents sent me on a trip to Amsterdam to meet young men and to find a husband."

"Not many eligible men in Aruba?"

"There were plenty of men, but not many my parents approved of."

"Did you have a boyfriend?"

"Oh yes, a couple of them. I grew up fast," Anna chuckled.

"Did your family attend church?"

"Most of the time, what church there was. It was small and not many attended. Seems the faith of my great-grandfather didn't transfer very well to Aruba."

"Do you have faith in God?"

"Sure, but it's not that big of a deal to me. Why is a wedding dress white?"

"To show purity and emphasize holiness," Mrs. Funk responded.

"I'd prefer bright colors," Anna quipped. "I'm not sure about all that holiness stuff."

"Do you want children?"

"Sure," Anna answered. "That would be nice."

"I believe Henry will want a big family," Mrs. Funk added.

"To have help in the mill, I suppose?" Anna asked.

Anna wondered aloud if she could sew a colorful band around the middle of the dress. "That's what I remember from Aruba," she explained.

"I don't see why not," Mrs. Funk answered. "We'll have to look around and find something. Mennonites don't much use colorful fabric."

"I know where to get something colorful!" Anna exclaimed.

The bride-to-be bounded out the door, jumped on her horse, faced the rain, and galloped toward Henry's farm. She kept right on going, however, until she reached the Lenape settlement by Perkiomen Creek.

Finding Lenape Mother, Anna asked for colorful fabric. About the same age as Mrs. Funk, it didn't take long for Lenape Mother to find something bright for Anna's dress.

With the rain ending, the Lenape woman and Anna glanced up to see a sparkling rainbow, or at least part of one. "A man and woman come together to make a complete arch," Lenape Mother explained.

At the edge of the clearing stood a brave, watching.

Both women noticed him. "He wanted you for his wife, Anna."

"I know."

"Are you sure the farmer on Indian Creek is the man you want?"

"Yes, but tell the brave he's a nice man. I've discovered that I fit more into Henry's world than that brave's plans for me."

"I will do that for you."

"Everyone is invited to the wedding," Anna exclaimed.

"Including him?" Lenape Mother motioned to the brave.

"Yes."

When Anna returned to Mrs. Funk's farm, Anna stated, "Let's sew this band around the waist of my dress."

"Certainly," Mrs. Funk replied, "if this helps you remember your Caribbean family."

"But it also shows the color I gained by living among the Lenape," Anna concluded.

"Have you informed your parents about Henry?"

"No, but I want them to meet him, sometime, I guess."

"We usually don't let the groom see his bride's wedding dress before the wedding," Mrs. Funk explained.

"Has Henry courted girls before?"

"Yes, a couple of them back in Europe. None of them seemed to work out for him. You're special, Anna."

"I think Henry is special! I've invited the entire Lenape settlement at Perkiomen Creek to attend the wedding."

"That's going to be a lot of people," Mrs. Funk answered. "We always invite everyone in our community as well."

"You mean all the Mennonites?"

"Yes."

"Your people sure have lots of babies."

"And we hope you and Henry can have children."

"Sure, but I've got something to talk to Henry about."

"We'll finish another day," Mrs. Funk assured her.

"Henry, did you see the slave working in the Philadelphia mill factory?" asked Anna.

"I did," Henry answered.

"While you talked with the men about your order, I chatted with the slave. He's from Aruba."

"You knew him?"

"Sort of, at least I knew people on his plantation that he knew. I don't think we ever actually met on the island. But we're a lot alike, having grown up in the same place."

"Where's this going?" Henry asked.

"Could we invite him to the wedding?"

"A slave?"

"And have you invited the men who work at the factory?"

"Adam Miller works there. We should invite him. It wouldn't hurt to invite the owner and the other men making our wheels. It would sort of be a business trip for them, I guess."

"Henry, your farm and mill are like a grand search for freedom," Anna summarized.

"Profound, Anna."

"You found freedom in America, the Lenape want freedom to live their way of life, but the slaves in this colony don't have any rights."

"Let me show you something, Anna." Henry turned to a desk in the corner of his house. He reached for a single sheet, copied by a Philadelphia printer. "This is a statement our people made about forty years ago, speaking out against slavery."

"Then can we invite him?" Anna pressed.

"A wedding with Europeans, Indians, and a slave from Africa?"

"From Aruba, not Africa," Anna corrected.

"But a few generations back his family was from Africa," Henry observed. "Our wedding's two weeks away—how are we going to get an invitation to them?"

Anna was closely in touch with nature in the Indian Creek woods.

She had grown up learning to hear the heartbeat of the indigenous people of Aruba. She empathized with slaves who worked on her island, and she had become a part of the Lenape, feeling their concerns, fears, and hopes.

In the Schuylkill River watershed, braves who returned from hunting deer in the west grew increasingly restless about Chief Lapowinsa being locked up in Philadelphia. Anna sensed a growing determination among the Lenape to get him back.

It was the full moon that helped reveal the movement among her people, but it felt like a bad omen. Anna entered the Lenape settlement to hear, to listen, and to talk with the braves. She learned that they were ready to move and get the chief out of prison.

"Do you have deerskins for James Logan?" Anna asked the brave who had shown interest in her.

"We're going to free him with no deerskins in payment."

Alarmed, Anna confided to Henry about the anger and rising tension between the braves and the colonial government under James Logan. "It was sharp," she explained, "and could burst into violence."

Henry, busy with building his dam, canal, and mill pond, listened carefully to Anna. "Who can intervene and negotiate between the Lenape and James Logan?" Henry inquired.

"You can," Anna answered.

"No, you'd be the best at this, but I doubt James Logan will listen to you."

"That means you need to go to Philadelphia."

"I've been there twice already this year. It takes the better part of three days to make the trip, tend to business, and come back."

"Henry, we may not have peace at our wedding unless you do something to talk to Logan about the chief."

After work, Henry turned to his place of refuge. At his desk in the corner, Henry handled his books and papers. It's where he turned for reflection and renewal when life seemed overwhelming.

Henry had been writing a small book about Christian faith, written with his people in mind, but it was the rolled up document from 1688 that he now turned to and pondered. The phrase that had worked into his mind was the opening line that the Mennonites and Quakers had been "opposed to the traffick in men-body." It had been written thirty-seven years earlier, two years before Henry had been born in Europe.

"Traffick in men-body" was what he saw around him in colonial Pennsylvania. Founded by the venerable William Penn, who had a vision for peace and harmony in his Pennsylvania New World colony, the traffick in men-body had increased since Penn left and went back to Europe twenty-five years ago. The Lenape and other indigenous groups felt threatened by the ships that kept unloading European immigrants who came seeking farm land.

The problem of slavery persisted and showed no signs of decreasing. Men, women, and children from Africa and Caribbean islands had been shipped to Pennsylvania to work as slaves on farms and in factories.

It was hard for Henry to reconcile his tremendous opportunities in this free land, with the slavery of some, and the subjugation of others. Henry turned to Anna, who patiently waited on his response.

"I guess every era has its conflicts. Ours is slavery and the defeat of the Lenape," he reflected.

Anna listened, realizing that her comments may not add much to Henry's ideas.

"Anna, we can make a difference," Henry observed. "You're half Lenape, half Aruban, and soon you'll be my wife. We're the people with power, I guess."

"So can we go?"

"It'll put me back a week, with planting and work on the mill."

"We have to go," Anna responded gently.

"Have to?"

"I mean, if you really believe in peace, which I've heard you preach about at the Mennonite church, then we need to do what we can to stop the coming conflict."

"Do you think the warriors will attack the courthouse?"

"They're restless and angry," Anna replied. "I talked to the braves yesterday, and I sensed it in the full moon."

"The full moon?" Henry asked. "You sense things in the moon, and in the trees, and the birds?"

"I'm half Indian," Anna answered. "I can't deny it."

"But you're also the great-granddaughter of the famous printer from Aruba."

"Did you know he was a pirate?" Anna asked.

"I didn't know that. Tell me that story on the way to Philadelphia. Get ready to ride, Anna. We'll swing by my parents to ask them to look out for the farm while we're gone."

"Henry, when you think about your farm, I think about my people. We need to tell the Lenape we're going to negotiate for Lapowinsa."

"Reasonable."

"Essential. You've got the beliefs about peace, but I know something about the practical way to settle differences. If they don't have one or two of their braves along to witness what we do, it won't help things much."

"So we ride to my parents, then to the Lenape."

"Henry, I think this marriage thing is going to work out," Anna concluded.

Henry wanted a kiss, but Anna bounded up the ladder to the loft. "Catch me!"

Henry chased Anna into the loft, laughing. When he got there, she surprised him with her sensuous strength, rolling him onto the bed, and kissing him with abandon, her roving hands passionately slid around his body, not wanting to release him. "Love me, Henry."

"Two weeks, Anna, two weeks."

Henry rose with reluctance and, like putting down a cup of cool water on a hot day when drinking it all would be so satisfying, Henry declared, "Let's ride."

The Pennsylvania colony had around fifty thousand settlers, about twenty percent of whom lived in Philadelphia. Henry, Anna, and three Lenape braves galloped past an occasional farm in the open countryside on the way to the capital.

During a break at the Freedom Inn, Henry inquired about Adam Miller. Henry gave an invitation to the manager and asked him to invite Miller if he came in anytime soon.

"Your great-grandfather was a pirate?" Henry asked.

"He left Amsterdam to find his freedom," Anna answered.

"Did he find it?"

"He found a pretty girl named Griet and fell in love with her," Anna grinned, "and she was from Aruba, where they settled."

"Have you ever seen an iguana?" Anna continued.

"Never."

"We have them at home, a huge lizard. When great-grandpa Visscher first came to the island, he and his men had to fight giant iguanas."

"They had to fight iguanas?"

"Ever had to deal with a momma bear in these parts?" Anna asked.

"Once, and that's one time too many."

"We don't have bears, but we have iguanas that fight like a momma bear."

Glancing behind at the following braves, Henry observed, "Hope we don't have to fight like a momma bear to get Lapowinsa out of jail."

"Maybe not, but we better be as tough as one," Anna responded.

At the mill factory, Anna spotted a mastiff puppy litter. The momma dog looked on with interest but little response. "They're such cute puppies," she squealed.

"But they grow up to be huge dogs," Henry responded.

"I want one," Anna begged.

The factory manager noticed Anna's interest. "They're great guard dogs, good companions, and they eat a lot of food," he commented.

"Can you come to our wedding?" invited Henry, shifting the topic. "And bring your workers—it'll be a big event."

"It would be good for my men to visit your mill and measure the dimensions again. Just to make sure we're still building exactly what you need."

"My great-grandpa had one of those dogs," Anna told Henry and the manager. "It saved his life."

James Logan wouldn't meet Henry when he inquired at the courthouse. "He says you were here recently, and unless you have thirty deerskins, he doesn't have time to visit with you," an aide at the desk reported.

"Why thirty? May I leave him a written message?" Henry inquired, which the aide agreed to.

A Pennsylvania colonial government meeting was in session, which Henry wandered into, not quite knowing what else to do. James Logan was in attendance.

A small group of visitors sat at the back listening to about twenty men discuss the political matters of the colony. Lieutenant Governor William Keith presided over the deliberations.

"Our last agenda item is to give guests a chance to speak," Mr. Keith announced.

Anna punched Henry so hard he almost gasped out loud. "Speak, Henry, here's your chance."

When no one else rose, Henry stood and asked for permission to address the council. "What is your topic?" Mr. Keith inquired.

"Indian affairs on the Perkiomen and Indian Creeks."

"Come up front," Mr. Keith directed. "Your name?"

"Henry Funk, farmer and mill owner from Indian Creek."

"How many acres?"

"We have 101 acres."

"Who is 'we'?" Mr. Keith asked.

"I'll marry Anna Meyer in two weeks," Henry answered, motioning to the back, "and I work with my parents and brothers who also own land."

"Religion?"

"Mennonite," Henry responded.

"Tell us about the Indian affairs you mentioned."

"Within another full moon, the braves on Indian Creek will cause trouble for settlers and attack them if Chief Lapowinsa is not released from your prison at the courthouse."

Mr. Keith shifted to look at James Logan, who didn't flinch.

Anna had pulled the braves into the doorway for the council to see their traveling companions.

"Anna has lived among the Lenape for the better part of a year, and she tells me the braves will use force to get their chief out of jail. You can avoid this, Honorable Council, by freeing Lapowinsa."

Mr. Keith turned to James Logan and asked, "What has the chief done?"

"He tied up one of our soldiers and illegally released two Indian prisoners," Logan responded. "I have the arrow that he shot in the door of the Freedom Inn barn."

"Mr. Keith," Henry explained, "with all due respect, Chief Lapowinsa rescued two frightened and innocent Indian boys from Logan. The boys hadn't done anything—Logan couldn't find the men he wanted, so he took the boys."

Anna nudged the braves further into the room so that everyone could see their war paint, feathers, and fierce countenance.

"Anna and I have come to help avoid conflict and death," Henry continued. "These men are prepared to defend their chief. Anna tells me they will go on the warpath before the next full moon."

James Logan shifted to look at the braves in the council room. Light came through the windows and reflected the war paint on their faces.

"Ask them how many braves will go to war," Logan responded.

"Anna talked to the men in Lenape and then translated into English. "Every brave in the Schuylkill watershed will fight for Lapowinsa."

"That's not very many men," Logan glared.

"Every English and German family will be at risk," Henry remarked.

"Anna and I are building a mill. We can hardly be safe with braves on the warpath. For the good of the economics, politics, and well-being of this Commonwealth, release Chief Lapowinsa."

Council members reflected on this with a long Quaker-like silence.

Mr. Keith finally banged his gavel and barked, "Meeting adjourned."

6

Friendship
March 1725

Five ships full of immigrants arrived in Philadelphia Harbor on the day Henry spoke to the council. Riding a wave of refugees fleeing Germany, up to half of the settlers on each ship were Mennonites. The German emigrants were pushed by hardship, war, and persecution to leave Europe, and pulled to America by the allure of cheap land, new lives, and religious freedom.

Henry and Anna watched the busy harbor overflow with people desperate to get off their stinking deathtrap ships. The Lenape braves from Indian Creek had never seen anything like it. They watched the spectacle from under the huge elm tree where William Penn had negotiated a peace agreement with the natives in 1683.

It was dusk, but small boats transporting recent immigrants streamed to the shore full of excited and wide-eyed young families. Some were sick, and it appeared many had only one parent, probably lost at sea during the trans-Atlantic crossing.

Abraham and Elizabeth Schwartz, a couple in their early twenties, stumbled ashore with two small children. They stepped out of a wooden transport boat, sloshed to dry ground, and looked around for where to go next. At the processing room, an English official wrote down "Swartz," which Anglicized their German name and gave the family a new identity. Listing their names was the only government procedure. With no particular destination in mind and no one to welcome them, they bumped into Henry and Anna.

Elizabeth appeared weak and delirious. Anna noticed and helped her take a seat, wrapping her in her own warm shawl.

"Funk is my name," Henry offered.

"Swartz is ours," said Abraham.

"Where are you from?" Henry inquired.

"The Palatinate, in Germany. We left seven weeks ago, and stopped in London on the way."

"How can we help?"

"Elizabeth is sick. She needs food and rest."

"Let's try the church," Henry said. "It's not too far from here."

Henry and Anna helped Elizabeth lie down on one of the backless wooden benches with a blanket underneath her.

"We lost our baby at sea," Abraham explained. "Elizabeth's milk dried up, and we couldn't feed the child."

The children, Jacob and John, looked hungry.

At the market, Henry brought bread and dried venison slices, which the family devoured. Henry also bought milk, which Elizabeth gulped down.

"We have some money," Abraham offered, "but we couldn't buy good food on the ship, and I'm afraid Elizabeth is not doing well."

Henry wanted to get back to his mill and farm on Indian Creek, but he realized it was his turn to help immigrants, like others who had helped him when he arrived a few years earlier.

"Thank you for helping us," Abraham stated. "*Friendship* was the name of our ship, and you're our first friends in America." Elizabeth tried to smile, but her pale and drawn face revealed a difficult journey.

"I rented a room at an inn just up the road," Henry announced. "You can clean up there, and they'll offer you soup and bread."

"Thank you, Henry. Would you help me buy a horse, wagon, and a farm tomorrow?"

Henry glanced at Anna. The braves waited patiently outside, and Anna went to talk with them.

"They'll wait a day and help us take this family to Indian Creek," Anna offered.

After baths for the family of four new immigrants, who were glad to be on land again, they all collapsed in the small bedroom that Henry had rented.

At the courthouse the next morning, James Logan spotted Henry but avoided any conversation with him. "We'd like to purchase land in the Franconia area," Abraham remarked to the manager.

"We have a fifty-acre plot," the manager offered.

"I'll take it," Abraham replied. When asked to sign the deed, the new immigrant hesitated to write his name, realizing that he really was now a "Swartz."

It didn't take too long to find a horse and flatbed wagon to purchase, which Elizabeth and the boys rode in. The Swartz's had only one small trunk of belongings.

Henry and Anna left Philadelphia on horseback with three braves and a family that needed help. Because of the wagon, they took the easier Germantown road north out of the city, rather than their usual route that followed the Perkiomen Creek.

Elizabeth grew weaker as the wagon rattled along the bumpy road. Henry grew concerned and asked Anna what they should do.

"We'll camp for the night, build a fire, and give her a break. At this rate, she won't make it to our farm."

"Our farm?" Henry tested.

"Yes, I'm starting to think about it that way. Less than two weeks till our wedding, and we're in the middle of nowhere with a wagon, two kids, and a sick mother."

"A fire sounds good, Anna. Will the braves hunt for game? And we *are* somewhere—in Philadelphia County."

"Sometimes you act so smart," Anna stated with a teasing smirk.

Despite the rabbit roasting over the fire, Elizabeth grew weaker by the hour. Anna told Henry that it didn't look very hopeful for Elizabeth.

"Will she make it through the night?" he asked.

"I doubt it."

Abraham Swartz told Henry that he had already lost one wife during childbirth in Germany. Elizabeth was his second wife, and they both realized that things weren't improving for her.

Elizabeth closed her eyes and seemed to lose the will to live. "Take care of the boys," were her last words as she squeezed Abraham's hand.

In a final teary embrace with his wife, Abraham said, "I love you, Elizabeth. I will see you on the other side."

Wolves. They smelled death, and the braves were the first to spot them in the darkness creeping closer to the fire. Three silent beasts waited patiently in the woods with terrifying silvery eyes. The Lenape advised Anna about the dangerous situation and said they needed to build a roaring fire and keep it hot all night.

With the moon to light their work, five men kept a watchful eye on the wolves in the thicket. Even the Lenape braves worried. "Keep the boys close to you and the fire," one of the men instructed Anna.

No one slept, and the men went in pairs to look for wood for the fire.

"My great-grandfather once had to fight wolves when he was a pirate," Anna told Henry in the middle of the night.

"You have so many crazy stories."

"It's true. While he was in New Amsterdam he and some friends had wolves threaten them. Know what saved them?"

"The sun came up," teased Henry. "Or did your great-grandfather fight them with his bare hands?"

"They had a big dog like that mastiff we saw at the factory," Anna explained. "I'm not kidding you. The dog scared the wolves away."

By the early hours of the morning, at the darkest time of night, it was hard for the adults to keep their eyes open. The three-year-old boy, Jacob, got up to relieve himself and went beside the wheel of the wagon.

Before anyone could react, the wolves struck, sinking their teeth into his legs, the ground stained with crimson blood. The screaming boy was drug away in an instant. There was little that the braves or anyone could do. The wolves left the campsite completely, and in spite of the shock, everyone except Abraham collapsed for a couple of hours of sleep.

When the sun rose, Abraham wrapped Elizabeth in a blanket and laid her fragile body in a shallow ditch the men dug with sticks. They covered her grave with fresh dirt and leaves, and Henry made a cross, stuck it on top, and offered a prayer.

The braves helped with the horses and got the wagon back on the road. Abraham remained in shock, unable to talk much to anyone. His grief at losing his wife and son was overwhelming. One-year-old John rode in the wagon leaning against the family trunk.

Abraham and John Swartz moved into the mill. Abraham tried to stay out of the way, because he knew about the upcoming wedding, but Little John seemed most comfortable in the house with Anna. She slept in the loft bed while Henry slept on the floor below.

Henry soon spotted damage at his Indian Creek dam. Someone had pushed over the top row of stones and smashed the height of the structure by half. Spring water rushed over the dam, leaving Henry to realize that a large part of his work on the stone wall would have to be redone. It was clear that it wasn't the strong current that knocked it down; rather, someone had maliciously destroyed his work.

During a powerful thunderstorm, Henry sat down with Abraham in the mill. They looked at three books in his travel chest.

The first was a *Froschauer Bible*, printed in Zurich during the 1520s, a favorite German translation of the Bible for Mennonites. Henry had a similar Bible in his collection.

The second book in the Swartz chest was a Dutch copy of *Martyrs Mirror*, printed in Amsterdam, the Netherlands. Henry admired the care of printing carried out by the Visscher press in Amsterdam. "I'll be right back, Abraham."

With John in tow, Henry brought Anna from the house to examine the printer's imprint in the front of *Martyrs Mirror*. "Visscher Press!" she exclaimed. "My great-great grandparents printed this, Henry!"

"That's what I thought," Henry agreed.

Abraham Swartz looked at Anna, and wondered how she could be in colonial Pennsylvania, engaged to a man from Germany. "Aren't you Dutch in background?" Abraham asked.

"Yes, I grew up in the Caribbean to a family who printed, and we're related to the Visschers in Amsterdam."

"Maybe you should turn this mill into a printing press," Abraham suggested.

Henry looked around and was pleased with the new idea. His mill had a basement for the big wheels and shaft, the second floor for the grinding, and the third floor upstairs to store the flour. "This really could be turned into a print shop," Henry declared.

"You don't know anything about printing," stated Anna.

Jolted from his dreaming, Henry laughed. "Guess you're right, Anna, I'm a farmer and miller."

"What's your third book?" Anna asked.

"A copy of Flavius Josephus' account of the first century Jewish Wars," Abraham replied, "translated from Latin into German by Caspar Hedio."

"I think I know who printed the book," Anna remarked. Coming from generations of printers, Anna knew where to look for that information. Turning to the very back of the book, she read "Beck Press."

"The Beck Press was Margaret and Balthasar Beck's press in Strasbourg, Germany," Anna remarked.

Henry looked at her with amazement. "And what does this mean to you?"

"They're my four-time great-grandparents, and they printed this book in 1539, about 186 years ago."

As before, Henry was stunned with what he learned about Anna.

"Soup will be ready soon, come and eat." Anna turned and carried John back to the house.

The men followed but turned to look at the full rainbow in the eastern sky following the ferocious thunderstorm that had just passed. The rainbow glimmered in the sunlight, thrilling the foursome. Little John squealed, while Abraham breathed a prayer for Elizabeth and promised her in his heart that when he was able, he would return to her grave and give her a proper burial in the church cemetery. Perhaps he could also put up a marker for Jacob next to his mother, both of whom he was badly missing.

"Does your meetinghouse in Franconia have a cemetery?" Abraham asked.

"Not yet," Henry replied. "We're still working on the building."

"Could my Elizabeth be the first in the cemetery?" Abraham inquired. "I don't see why not."

Early the next morning Abraham left the Funk farm with his horse and wagon and retraced his steps toward Philadelphia. As agreed to the previous evening, Henry joined Abraham at the Franconia meetinghouse in the afternoon. Not far away they dug a grave for Elizabeth, mother of Jacob and John. With head bowed, Abraham wept and stated to no one in particular, "She was a good woman; I don't know what I'll do without her."

With a lantern lighting his desk, Henry Funk finally had time to read the last weekly newspaper from Andrew Bradford's press that he had purchased in Philadelphia, *The Mercury*. Four stories stood out, and he commented on each one to Anna, who seemed genuinely interested.

"Peter the Great of Russia died, Anna. The Romanovs have been in power for over a hundred years. I wonder if Mennonites will ever move to Russia. Look at this. Seems that white men, now for the first, have scalped Indians in a northern colony."

"I'd guess it was retaliation," Anna offered.

"Ever heard of Johann Sebastian Bach?"

"Nope."

"He's a composer in Germany, a man about my age. He has an orchestra performing *St. John's Passion*, in Leipzig, Germany. It's an oratorio, which means there are lots of solos and singing."

Continuing, Henry pointed to another story. "It says here that in China they wanted to print a big history book so they had to craft over 250,000 moveable type characters."

"You have to put the characters on a tray upside down and backwards," Anna replied.

"Anna, you seem to understand the complexities of using moveable type on a printing press," Henry remarked.

"It will take a while to explain all that to you, Henry. Let's go for a walk."

It ended up being a very long walk. Anna led Henry on an adventure around most of the farm, all 101 acres of it. At one point, on a rise, they could see the house, barn, mill, and Indian Creek.

"Any idea who knocked down the dam?" Henry asked.

"Not really, unless it was the brave who wanted to marry me," Anna replied. "But I doubt it was him."

"You had an Indian who wanted you for his wife?"

"Several of them, Henry. I could have had a baby by now if I'd have taken the first one."

Henry embraced his fiance. "I want you for my wife, Anna, and I want to have babies for our little house down there."

"To help you work, I guess," replied Anna.

"You sure know how to get me. I still can't believe what I've learned about you, what with printing being in your family history back to the Reformation."

"My parents did a good job teaching me about our family history," Anna remarked.

"Know what one of my dreams is, Anna?"

"Ten kids?"

"I want to get that *Martyrs Mirror* book translated into German and printed for Mennonites here in America."

"That will take time and determination to accomplish."

"But with your understanding of how printing works, I'm marrying the right woman."

"Do you like me, or my knowledge of history and printing?"

"You, Anna. I went to Philadelphia with you, didn't I? Your knowledge and skills just add to all that makes you attractive."

"I appreciate what you do for me. But I'm asking if you like just me, Anna Meyer, from Aruba?"

Henry kissed Anna, but a loud commotion in the woods interrupted their special moment. A desperate animal came running straight toward them and clawed its way up into the oak tree they were standing beneath.

"Raccoon," Anna noticed.

Hounds barked in the distance, and soon the lanky beasts surrounded the tree, barking loudly. A neighboring farmer showed up with his gun to kill the pest. A shot rang out, and the dogs tore the toppled animal to bits.

"Name's Moyer," the hunter began. "Is this your bride, Henry?"

"Yes, can you come to the wedding in ten days?"

"Planning on it. Bringing the family," Moyer responded.

"Might want to watch your back," Moyer continued. "I saw Indians tearing down your dam the other night. Me and the dogs were out for a run, or they might have torn it all down. We scared them off."

"Much obliged," Henry responded.

"Home," Moyer yelled, and the well-trained dogs turned and loped toward their master's barn.

"You want to kiss again or go back?" Anna teased.

When a lone wolf let out a blood curdling howl at the moon for no apparent reason, Henry said, "Go home."

7

Petition

March 1725

"I talked to Bentura, the slave in Philadelphia," Anna told Henry when they were safely indoors.

"You went to look at the puppies again, didn't you?

"Yes, when you were buying land and a horse for the Swartz family," Anna nodded.

Henry hadn't seen Anna this agitated before. "Where's this going?" Henry asked.

"He asked me to help him."

"You're even more beautiful when you get agitated, Anna."

"Be quiet and listen, Henry. You came to Pennsylvania for freedom, the Swartz's came for the same reason, and people are getting off boats in swarms, all looking for opportunities. Mr. Bradford wrote in his newspaper about liberty and service to society, whatever that means."

"How does Bentura want you to help him?"

"He wants me to buy him passage on a ship to Aruba, his home."

"If you help him, you'll be in trouble. He's someone's property, Anna."

"What kind of trouble?"

"You could end up in jail."

"I've already been there," Anna replied. "Your *American Mercury* newspaper prints ads every week asking for runaway slaves to be returned. That's not right."

"Slavery's been around for a long time."

"But your people wrote a statement against it, remember?"

"A written document is one thing, but to change an entire institution is much harder."

"Look at this ad, Henry. A slave owner from Maryland wants his mulatto slave returned. It says he's about forty, has had smallpox, and is in company with a white woman. Gives their names and everything. If you turn in this slave to the owner, you get fifteen pounds as a reward."

"Why are you so worked up?" Henry asked.

"Because Bentura's great-grandfather delivered an anti-slavery petition to the King of Portugal."

"How do you know?"

"He told me, and I heard that story from my family in Aruba."

"Anna, we can't just march into Philadelphia and free him."

"Why not?"

"Well, because I'm a farmer from the countryside, and because my money is invested in a mill, in spring seeds, and in maintaining this farm. It's your farm now as well, you know."

"Okay, but if we have any extra money, I want to spend it to free Bentura, and get him a ticket to Aruba."

A dense fog had settled over the Indian Creek region in the early morning hours, making it difficult for Henry and Abraham to see the land Swartz had recently purchased. An eerie silence made them pause and listen.

"This is Indian burial ground," Henry stated. "You bought sacred land where they bury their dead."

"Do you think that's a problem?" Abraham asked.

"It might be. I doubt the Lenape will like this," Henry answered.

"So I've been taken advantage of?" Abraham asked.

"Looks like it."

"A fresh grave," Abraham noticed.

"They believe the spirits of the dead live in these parts. They likely won't like this land disturbed."

Fear crept into the men's hearts when a tree creaked, groaned, and crashed down. The piercing early morning sounds made them wonder if the spirits of the dead were watching them.

When two braves stepped out of the soupy fog and looked at them with a cold glare, Henry and Abraham froze, unsure of what to do next.

One of the braves slowly raised his tomahawk and threw it at a gnarled oak next to them. As the tomahawk turned end over end, Henry and Abraham watched in slow motion, filled with terror. It struck and stuck with a loud thud that reverberated across the misty woods.

Henry and Abraham crept backwards, still facing the braves. It didn't take long in the soupy fog to lose sight of the Lenape men who watched them like graveyard sentinels.

Little John was playing at Anna's feet when the men returned to the house at the Funk farm. At first neither man was able to talk to Anna about their trip.

After some time, Henry finally said, "Burial ground, Anna, that's what the colonial government sold him."

"Two braves met us and chased us away," Abraham added.

"They do watch their burial grounds," Anna explained.

"We know," Henry replied.

"You've got a problem, Abraham," Anna stated.

"Abraham, you can work for me," Henry offered. "Oats and corn need to be planted, I've got a dam to rebuild, and a mill to finish. You can live on the third floor until we get it running this fall. Maybe by then you can renegotiate your land in Philadelphia, or find a corner of the property where you can build your own house. Looks like Little John's not wanting to leave Anna's side, anyway," Henry concluded.

"Sure, live in the mill," Anna agreed. "But your name's too long—from now on you're 'Abe.' "

When Abe agreed with a nod, Henry gave directions to his new employee. "We need to get ready for the wedding. We need to clean out the mill and get ready to butcher a pig. Have you ever butchered before?" Henry questioned.

"Yes, in Germany," Abe responded.

"When you get the mill cleaned out, I'll be ready to plant. I think it's dry enough to get an early oats stand in the ground."

"I've done that as well."

"We better get this in writing, Abe." Reaching for paper and quill pen, Henry dipped in his ink well and wrote, *"Room and board, but no pay, through the end of the year. Friday, March 26, 1725."*

"That's fair," Abe answered. "What about Little John?"

"You will find a new wife," Anna answered. "There will be plenty of German and Lenape Indian girls to choose from at our wedding."

"It might be a little soon for that," Abe answered.

"Life's short and things happen in these parts," Anna reflected. "You can get married again—that's what Elizabeth would have expected."

After a moment of thinking, Abe asked, "Can I trap on that land I bought?"

"I think if you talk to Lenape Mother and get the braves to agree it might be okay," Anna answered.

"That way I can at least make a bit of money from my farm," Abe stated.

"Beaver furs aren't worth much these days—the fad in Europe and colonial cities has turned to deerskins for clothing. But we've got a wedding in five days, folks—let's get busy," Henry concluded.

On Monday, just two days before the wedding, Adam Miller rode onto the Funk farm and found Henry and Abe planting oats in one of Henry's fields.

"How's the bachelor?" Adam greeted Henry as he and his partner rode up. Strong, muscular, and single, Adam cut an impressive figure atop his horse.

"Good, Adam, what brings you to the farm today?" Henry responded.

"Your wedding, of course, Henry. Why else would I ride out here to Indian Creek?"

"So you got my invitation?" Henry responded.

"Yes, we're not here to stay with you now, though we will come to the wedding on Wednesday."

"Look, it's time for noon meal. Let's go to the house and get you something to eat and catch up," Henry offered.

"I accept that offer," Adam replied. "Is there enough food for my partner?"

"Certainly, come to the house."

"Do you have a child already?" Adam asked Henry in the house.

"This is Abe Swartz and his son John," Henry explained. "Abe's wife died about two weeks ago, just after getting off a ship in the harbor. And who's your friend, Adam?"

"This is Ben. He writes a column for *The American Mercury*, and wants to see where the Germans live in the regions beyond Philadelphia."

"Henry always buys a copy when he can," Anna informed Ben. "Look in the corner at his pile of papers."

"Thanks for supporting *The Mercury*," Ben responded. "It helps pay my wages."

Anna couldn't help but notice Ben, a tall, handsome man with an outgoing, gregarious personality that made everyone feel comfortable.

"Are you German?" Ben asked Anna.

"No, I was born in Aruba to Dutch parents," Anna responded. "Where were you born?"

"Boston," Ben replied. "I've moved to Philadelphia and now work for Andrew Bradford in his Second Street Print Shop. *The Mercury* is the only newspaper in town, though I hope to start a competitor newspaper soon," Ben answered. "Have any of you read the 'Busy-Body' essays?"

Henry looked up from eating and nodded. "Do you write those?"

"Yes, do you like them?"

"He reads everything in the paper, Ben," Anna remarked.

"So you're a writer and a printer?" Henry asked.

"You could say that," Ben answered.

Changing the subject, Adam Miller asked Anna if Henry had asked her about moving to Virginia.

"Well, he talked about it, but he hasn't seriously asked me to move there," Anna smiled.

"I'm gathering a group of settlers to buy land around Elkton this fall. Property is cheap."

Henry glanced at Abe. "Where's Virginia?" Abe wondered.

"The Virginia colony is south of here. There's lots of game, strong rivers, and cheap fertile land," Adam explained.

"Well, since the colonial government of Pennsylvania sold me Indian burial ground, I wouldn't have much to lose by moving to Virginia."

"What about Little John?" Anna asked. "You need to find a wife before you move, because there sure won't be German women in Virginia for you to marry."

"Tell me more about the German people," Ben asked. "Why have you come to Pennsylvania?"

Henry looked at the young man like he asked something that was extremely obvious. "Didn't you see the fertile topsoil Abe and I were just working in? This land reminds us of home in Germany. Don't you understand how cheap it is to buy good land in this commonwealth?"

"And to get swindled," Abe added.

Henry continued, "Ben, don't you understand the religious freedom we Germans gain when we leave war-torn Rhineland? The effects of the Thirty Years War are still widely felt in Germany. Entire cities were destroyed. We Funks moved because the economic situation in Germany about twenty years ago was devastatingly depressed. We couldn't buy land, the land we did have had been trampled underfoot by legions of marching soldiers who flattened the land for four generations, and the government in Germany just didn't care about us. So we moved."

"Did you move for religious or economic reasons?" Ben inquired.

"Good question," Henry answered. While he pondered how to answer, Anna piped up.

"Both, Ben. Henry's family is here because they can have their own church, but what they really want is the chance to farm and make money."

Ben startled the lunch table in the Funk home by declaring his opinion that the Germans were taking over the English colony of Pennsylvania. "You folks have so many babies that in no time, you'll be the majority ethnic group," Ben summarized.

"God has called us to be fruitful and multiply," Henry responded.

"Our British families have two or three children, while your German families have eight or more children. Why?"

"We're happy for children in our homes," Abe offered.

"I have Little John, though I've had three children and two wives, all who have died."

Ben was startled by Abe's admission. "You've had two wives die and two children pass away?"

"Yes, and with Anna's help, I'll be looking for a wife at the big wedding this week on the Funk farm."

"Do you send your children to school?" Ben asked.

"If they're available," Henry answered. "School happens every day on our farms and homes, practical training—we teach our children how to read and write in our homes."

"Do you have a school for your children?" Ben asked.

"Yes, there's a Mennonite school in Philadelphia, and we started one here last year."

"Do you have trained teachers?" Ben pushed further.

"Our teacher is Chris Dock," Henry answered. "He's a very capable young man."

After the meal, Ben pulled his notebook out and recorded as much of the conversation as he could remember.

"What's that for?" Anna inquired.

"I'm learning about the German people, with Adam as my guide and host. I know English customs and culture, but because there are so many of you coming to Pennsylvania, I wanted to learn more."

"Ben," Henry offered, "you're welcome to come back in two days for the wedding. Will you still be traveling with Adam?"

"Yes," Ben answered.

"What's your last name?" Anna inquired.

"Franklin."

"Much obliged for the meal," Adam concluded as he and Ben rose to ride off on their tour of German farms in the Indian Creek area.

Later that evening, Henry rode to William and Jubilant's little house on their small farm south of his. The couple welcomed Henry to their home, though Henry was startled to find a black man sitting in the room with them.

"He's a runaway slave," Jubilant informed him. "We do this occasionally when they need a place to stay on their way north."

Henry didn't know what to say about the slave, so he turned to his reason for visiting.

"I want to make sure you are both coming to the wedding on Wednesday."

"We are," William replied.

"Could you help with the skewered pig over the fire?" Henry asked.

"Sure thing."

"We'll get the fire going early in the morning, and if you keep watching the fire and turning it, I would appreciate it," Henry replied.

"How can I help?" Jubilant asked.

"Could you help with Little John?"

"Sure, I'll take care of him so you two can enjoy the day. There's one more thing, Henry," Jubilant added. "It looks like this slave could have an outbreak of the pox."

Terrified, Henry looked closer at the runaway, cowering in the shadows.

"Please don't turn me in," the slave pleaded.

"If it's the pox, he'll be contagious, and that's a problem for spreading it at the wedding," Henry responded.

"I'm not sure what he has," Jubilant responded. "It might just be some rash or some dry skin disease that's broken out."

"Okay, could you bring him wedding food here and not bring him to the festivities?" Henry asked.

"He doesn't want to leave our house, anyway, Henry. He might get caught."

"Henry," William added. "Let's roast two pigs. I have one in my barn that I'll add to the one from your barn. I'll be there tomorrow to build the roasting spit and get the fire ready."

"You are my good friends," Henry concluded. "I'm glad you can help at the wedding."

At Henry's desk, Anna had written a petition. It was the first time he had seen Anna's handwriting.

"I worked hard at this," Anna explained. "English is not my first language, but I can handle it."

Examining the document, it was a short but clear request to the Philadelphia Council to free Bentura from the mill factory. Not a long document, but to the point, and easy to understand.

"Good job," Henry commented.

Little John had already gone to sleep, and Abe stayed at the mill.

"Two days, Henry, and we'll sleep in the same bed up there," Anna motioned toward the loft.

"God's been good to me," Henry commented.

"Don't preach, Henry. You're just lucky I didn't get back on that ship a year ago, or I'd be in Amsterdam, getting married to a Dutch man."

"Yes, I'm lucky, Anna. But so are you," and they tumbled onto the rug on the floor, entwined in love and eager to hold each other.

A crack of lightening caused baby John to stir, and Henry jumped when the rain started to pour on their roof.

"Henry, don't be so skittish. Come here," and she wrapped him in her arms, pulled a blanket over them, squeezed him tightly, and helped him forget about the March storm swirling outside on Indian Creek.

8

Wedding
March 1725

Guests starting showing up around noon on the last day of March. William butchered two pigs the previous day which he hung on spit roast rods with tripod stakes on each end. He planned on turning them slowly over a fire all day to feed the big crowd that was expected, providing everyone plenty of pork to eat. William and Jubilant had knives ready to slice meat for guests after the ceremony ended.

Just before noon, ten men from the Philadelphia factory arrived on the Funk farm, including the owner. They went straight to the mill and begin examining the building and taking new measurements. Through a window, Anna noticed that Bentura had come along.

Mrs. Funk waited inside the house with Anna, insisting that Henry not see her or the wedding dress before the service started. It just about drove Anna crazy to not be outside greeting visitors.

Funk's community of Mennonites began arriving shortly after noon, with some sitting on logs that had been placed near the house where the wedding would take place. The pastor from Philadelphia arrived and talked with Henry about details for the service.

The arrival of a distinguished Indian Oneida Chief on his horse surprised almost everyone. With fifteen feathers in his colorful headband, Chief Shickellamy had been sent to the wedding by James Logan. The chief worked for the Philadelphia government and the Iroquois Confederacy, keeping an eye on Indian affairs in eastern Pennsylvania. The government of the commonwealth did not want the Lenape and other tribes leaning favorably toward the French, who continued to make advances in the western parts of the colony. As another shock, James Logan rode in on a horse beside Fifteen Feathers Shickellamy. To Henry, Logan's powdered wig looked comical next to the distinguished headdress of the Oneida Chief, but Henry could never voice that opinion aloud. It appeared his written invitation left at the court house had worked, though Logan was probably here to keep an eye on his land, rather than join in the fun of a wedding.

Anna's people, the Delaware Indians of Perkiomen Creek, began arriving after noon. Henry guessed that around forty Lenape had come for the festivities. Absent, of course, was Chief Lapowinsa.

Abe Swartz managed two long tables for the food that had been prepared by the Funk families. Gifts were placed at the end of one of the tables, such as there were. The German families came with practical gifts, a common practice in the European homeland, and the Lenape brought moccasins, hides, baskets, and preserved food.

The invitations, mostly verbal, had simply included the general start time of early afternoon. When the owner of Freedom Inn rode up and tied his horse at the mill, it appeared to Henry and the pastor that all the guests had arrived and that it was time to begin. Lenape Mother, however, came to Henry to talk about the ceremony, and the start was delayed. When details were agreed to, the pastor called everyone to gather around and sit on logs, or stand in a big circle. The weather was brisk but bright, with a promise of warm sun later in the afternoon.

"Welcome to all," the Philadelphia minister began.

Henry knew his land well enough to notice several Delaware braves standing along the banks of Indian Creek beyond the mill. They were watching the event, but it didn't look like they'd be coming to the farmhouse hill for the ceremony.

"We've gathered to join Henry Funk and Anna Meyer in Christian marriage," the preacher continued.

"Welcome now to the bride," the minister motioned to the front door of the house. Jubilant, with Little John, went to the door and opened it, being the sign that Anna was waiting on. She came down the front steps in her white dress and colorful blue fabric around her waist. Little John clapped and cried out in joy. Henry gasped at her beauty, with hair fixed up and sparkling wedding dress. Guests smiled at the womanly radiance of Anna Meyer.

Among the many witnesses at the wedding, Henry noticed that Adam Miller and Ben Franklin had come back to witness the wedding and eat the food. He chuckled inside, but when he saw Andrew Bradford, the Second Street printer from Philadelphia, he was truly surprised. It seemed that about everyone he knew had come to the wedding.

"Marriage is a sacred institution," the minister declared. After a short devotional from the Scriptures and a prayer, the minister invited Lenape Mother to say a few words.

While the wise Lenape leader spoke in her native language, Anna interpreted. "She says a good spirit has come on this land. She sees the spirit of children, of harmony, and hope for the future. As with every marriage, there will come storms," Anna interpreted. "She believes that children will be abundant in this marriage and that the bad spirits will be swept away by the good." When Lenape Mother turned toward the east, she began a chant which every Lenape rose to recite with her, a ritual repeated many times for at least a thousand years: "*We carry the spirit of Tamenend in the land of the Dawn.*"

When she was finished, the minister stepped back in and came to the part Henry and Anna had been eagerly anticipating.

"I now pronounce you husband and wife, Mr. and Mrs. Henry Funk!"

When Abe Swartz fired his gun in the air, the celebration began in earnest.

What happened next changed Henry Funk forever. The harmonies in the music of the Lenape Indians were different from what he had grown up with. His own people sang in unison, but the Indians broke out in harmonies that thrilled him.

Henry had never heard anything like it before. He would think about it and play it over in his mind many times in the years ahead. It had been elusive, surreal, and marvelous. Henry's experience with music on his wedding day would actually change his people, the Mennonites, forever. The harmonies he heard were beautiful, and why couldn't his people use them in their worship services?

It didn't take long for a short Indian in a bearskin costume with a red and black mask to come and join the dancing. With harmless good fun, he came to chase off the bad spirits and welcome the good spirits.

The Lenape, with Anna in their circle, danced around the Germans and others who watched. Some of the single men, like Adam Miller and Ben Franklin, were pulled into the circle.

But they sang with harmonies, naturally, like it was supposed to be that way. It was beautiful and drew him into the dance circle. Anna grabbed his arms and away he went, basking in the warm March sun, the music, and the bright reds and greens of the Lenape outfits.

Anna danced with energy, abandon, and a feminine charm that few had ever seen. Ben Franklin kept jotting notes in his journal so he wouldn't forget the experience, Henry presumed.

Henry left the dance circle and encouraged guests to eat food. Along with the pork, they could have butternut squash cooked in a large pot over a fire, corn bread with butter and honey, milk to put on dried berry pie, and hot sassafras tea. Henry's brothers and their wives hosted the food table and made sure everyone had enough to eat.

Anna squealed when the mill factory owner came to the dance circle with a surprise. A mastiff puppy bounded toward the new bride and jumped into her lap. "He's yours," the owner beamed. "I hope he has a long life on this farm."

"Henry, take a look!" Wheeling around, Henry scooped up the puppy and held him. "His name's Bull," Anna declared.

"He'll make a great guard dog on your farm," the mill owner told Henry.

"Thank you very much," Henry responded. Watching Anna with the puppy, Henry wondered aloud to the factory manager if she was more excited about marrying him or getting the mastiff dog.

Henry noticed that a few of the Lenape braves that had waited at the Creek had edged into the dance celebration, and they also helped themselves to food.

Henry spoke with the Mennonites who had come for the wedding. Hardworking and plain people, they had taken off from spring planting preparations to celebrate with Henry and Anna.

When Abe Swartz asked James Logan whether he could trap on the land he purchased, the Philadelphia political leader's first response was that he didn't see any problem with it.

Irritated, Lenape Mother had a different opinion. Speaking through a brave who had a good command of English, the language of the discussion, she said, "Our burial grounds are sacred and should not be used to trap beaver."

"I purchased the land from the Colonial government in Philadelphia," Abe countered. "Doesn't that make it my land?"

"The officials shouldn't have sold our sacred lands," Lenape Mother responded.

Oneida Chief Fifteen Feathers tried to intervene and find a middle ground. Looking at Abe he said, "Certainly part of your fifty acres must be outside the burial region," the Chief wondered. "Could you trap there and leave the burial site untouched?"

"Why do you officials sell our sacred land?" Lenape Mother asked Logan.

"The King of England gave this land to William Penn, who in turn paid tribes for it," Logan answered. "Abe Swartz's land is his, and it does not belong to the Lenape."

Lenape Mother wished Chief Lapowinsa could be there to speak in her place, but she forged ahead anyway. "We don't recognize the authority of the King of England," she challenged, "and our burial ground is sacred."

Anna sensed a dispute growing, and came to intervene. "Abe can trap on our land along Indian Creek."

An older brave stood next to Lenape Mother and encouraged her not to give in. "We received a promise from the 'Great Miquon', William Penn," Lenape Mother insisted, "that we would always own the land a mile on either side of the banks of the streams and rivers where we live."

James Logan shook his head and responded. "I have heard this argument from other natives before, but none of your tribes can produce the written documents to verify that claim."

The brave who knew English came and stood beside Lenape Mother. "We in the Lenape tradition place little value in written documents. Instead, our stories of history and treaties are passed down from one generation to the next by stories. Chiefs tell their memories, received from their grandfathers, to their own grandsons. We know that the 'Great Miquon' promised us land a mile on either side of waterways throughout the Lenape territory."

"That was an event from over forty years ago," James Logan responded. "With no written treaty to verify, we can't honor your memories. Abe Swartz owns his land and can do with it what he wants to."

The brave stood tall and challenged Logan and Henry on another point. "The mill that Mr. Funk has built is within the one-mile limit for waterways. The dam he is building comes onto our land and will stop fish that try to swim upstream."

"I purchased this land six years ago," Henry responded. "No one has ever raised this issue with me before."

"You are a good neighbor," Lenape Mother added, "but the dam you've installed threatens our way of life."

"You've moved," the Oneida Chief inserted. "You moved to Perkiomen Creek."

"Mills are springing up everywhere," Lenape Mother responded. "Wherever we move, mills are being built."

"We'll grind the corn you grow," Henry replied, "and we'll provide you with flour."

"We have ground our flour for hundreds of years with hand-powered millstones for as long as the Lenape have lived in the east," Lenape Mother answered. "Our ancient methods are good for our young people."

"I intend to use the power of Indian Creek to turn a large millstone and produce our flour. The bread you ate today was from flour ground at a water-powered mill near Philadelphia."

"We are not impressed by your new methods," Lenape Mother thoughtfully answered. "Our way of life is threatened by your ways."

"It's time for the races," Anna yelled. "It's a wedding tradition of the Lenape."

Young men came forward from both the Mennonite and Lenape communities to test their speed against others.

"Line up here," Anna pointed. "You'll race from the big oak tree to the mill and back. You have to touch the mill before you turn around and come back."

Adam Miller and Ben Franklin ran in the first race, against two stout and eager braves. People cheered and watched the foursome run for all they were worth. It looked like Adam Miller would win until the endurance of one of the braves helped him gain at the end and cross the finish line first.

"Next four runners," Anna called. "Bentura, get over here!"

The second race featured a slave from Aruba and one of the men from the Philadelphia mill factory, pitted against two more Lenape braves.

It was obvious to everyone at the wedding that the slave could run fast. Bentura dashed to the mill, turned, and ran neck and neck with the fastest brave. At the end, though, the brave's stamina outdid Bentura's initial burst of speed and the brave won.

"Girls?" Anna asked. Two young Mennonite women stepped forward and one Lenape. Soon the crowd urged Anna to run. In spite of the wedding dress, Anna lined up. All four women had to hold their dresses when they ran.

The Mennonite girl who won ran like the wind. The men noticed her striking figure as she ran. After the race Anna found her talking to Abe Swartz. "Can you introduce her to me, Abe?" Anna asked.

"This is Annie Beth Kolb," Abe answered.

"You're fast," Anna replied.

Annie Beth beamed a smile at Abe and Anna. "Guess so."

"Anna, look at the gift I brought for you," Abe pointed at the gift table.

In a burlap sack he had rescued from the day he cleaned out the mill, Abe had wrapped a present for Anna and Henry.

"The Beck Press book from 1539," Anna exclaimed. "Henry, look at this!"

"Are you sure you want to give this to us?" Henry asked.

"Yes, it's the least I can do for what you've done for me."

"Come to the house, Annie Beth," Anna insisted.

Leading Annie Beth and Abe up the steps, Little John came bounding out and jumped into Anna's arms. "This is Abe's boy," she said and handed the child to Annie Beth.

"Abe, show Annie Beth your room in the mill," Anna insisted, and the threesome walked toward the creek.

As the afternoon merged into evening, most of the men migrated to the mill, to see what Henry Funk and his brothers had been working on. A simple three-story wooden structure, the mill was functional and nearly ready for the new waterwheel that was being built in Philadelphia.

Five additional gears had been ordered, and the factory owner described to the men how they would work, taking power from the big wheel outside to interior gears, eventually turning a large horizontal millstone.

"Here's where the work gets done," the factory manager explained. "All the energy from the water wheel gets transferred into power to turn the runner stone, which rotates above a lower bedstone." Illustrating with his hands, he explained, "The runner stone, which is the upper stone, is slightly concave, while the bedstone, the lower stone, is slightly convex. While the upper stone turns, the flour from the corn or wheat can be channeled to the outer edge, where it can be gathered up and sold."

"Where will you get the stones?" the pastor from Germantown asked.

"We import them," the manager answered. "The finest and longest lasting quartz stone comes from France, where they bind pieces together for use in American mills. I hope Henry's millstones are on a ship somewhere in the Atlantic."

"Can you get everything installed by this fall?" Funk's father asked. The elder Funk had invested considerable money in the gears and millstones and was curious when the work might be completed.

"Yes," the manager replied. "We're on schedule to get everything running by this fall. Then you can test the gears and learn how to operate it. By next year you'll grind flour for customers in Indian Creek."

Anna walked into the mill with Bull following on her heels. "There's still food up at the house, men. Help yourself."

Upstairs in the mill, Abe Swartz and Little John showed Annie Beth Kolb where they slept. Abe opened his small trunk to show Annie Beth his entire store of worldly possessions.

Annie Beth asked about the dress in Abe's trunk.

"My Elizabeth passed away just after we got off the ship," Abe explained. "This was her one dress. By the end of the trip across the Atlantic, it was worn out."

"Was she pretty?" Annie Beth asked.

"She was beautiful," Abe answered.

A rustling in a wooden barrel in the corner caught Annie Beth's attention. "What's that?" she asked.

"Raccoon babies," Abe answered. When I moved up here, a momma coon had already moved in and had babies. I've decided not to mess with her home or litter. She comes and goes at night while I sleep."

"Does that scare you?" Annie Beth asked.

Little John looked at the baby coons in the barrel and squealed.

"Annie Beth, after crossing the ocean, not much scares me."

"I was born here, seventeen years ago," Annie Beth replied.

Little John grew restless and wanted food. Holding the squirming boy, Abe asked, "Can we come visit you in your home next week?"

"I'd be pleased if you did," Annie Beth smiled.

9

Negotiation
April 1725

There was a reason Anna had kept rum away from her guests at the wedding celebration. While living with the Delaware Indians, she had seen its devastating effects. Alcohol caused them to act in ways that were irrational, harmful, and further weakened their own communities.

Though they had lived in the Delaware River basin for centuries, the Lenape had only recently consumed rum. Introduced by European traders, peddlers, and hucksters, they discovered that the Lenape would give away almost anything to acquire more of the addicting drink.

Anna was aware of Atlantic trade dynamics enough to understand where rum came from. Produced from molasses, which had been extracted from sugar cane grown in the Caribbean region, rum was distilled in colonial America, and then often used to purchase more slaves in Africa to work the sugar plantations in the Caribbean. It was a deadly cycle of slavery, intoxication, and then purchasing more slaves from merchants on the west coast of Africa. Few had seen the complete cycle of the sugar-to-rum product like Anna.

Raised on Aruba, a slave island, she had seen the horrible conditions of slavery. Now having lived among the Lenape, she knew the terrible effects of rum on Indians who came under its spell, which had been sold to them, often in exchange for their land or hunting rights. The only part of the equation she had not seen was the purchase of slaves in Africa, but she could imagine kegs of rum being hoisted off ships along the African coast, eagerly received in exchange for more slaves.

Intoxicating love. That's what Henry and Anna Funk drank during their first week together after the wedding. In their own house, with few interruptions, they erupted with ecstatic cascades of sheer delight. Both hoped that it would never end. Anna put Henry under a mesmerizing spell, offering charms of irresistible delight that kept him wanting more. He barely left his house for seven days, only occasionally working. He returned to her captivating beauty again and again.

A knock on Henry and Anna Funk's door a week after the wedding surprised them. It was the first outside contact they'd had since the wedding. Abe Swartz had worked on the mill dam and done some planting, mostly by himself, while keeping Little John with Jubilant or Henry's mother.

The insistent rapping left them both puzzled. Their home was pretty much in the middle of nowhere. There really wasn't a major road that led to their farm, plus you had to know where they lived. Further, it was springtime and every farmer in the Schuylkill River valley was busy with planting and the spring routine. Who had come to visit them?

From the loft window Henry noticed two horses outside. Perhaps ministers had come to their house to seek counsel on church matters. He had mentioned the possibility of getting the *Martyrs Mirror* book translated into German—maybe the visitors were from the Second Street print shop in Philadelphia, seeking work. Or, had the searching parents from Aruba discovered the whereabouts of their daughter and come to inquire? Henry went to the door.

"Logan?" Henry dropped his jaw.

"Hello Henry," the chief justice and agent of colonial government responded.

"What are you doing here?"

"I need your help," James Logan responded.

"Who's with you?" Funk asked.

"A deputy of the governor," Logan answered.

"Come in," Funk offered. "Tie up your horses at the hitching post," Funk directed the deputy.

"Hello, Anna," Logan said.

Anna was wary of James Logan coming unannounced to their new home so soon after her wedding. This was the man who had tied her up and put her in jail. He brought the full force of the law with him. She wondered why he was here, now.

"Get some food ready for our guests, Anna," Henry suggested.

"That's a kind offer," Logan began.

"What brings you here?" Henry asked.

"I've come to speak to both of you," Logan continued.

Still wary, Anna pressed Logan, "Both of us?"

"Anna, I understand why you may be suspicious of me coming here so soon after your wedding. But please, give me a chance. I need you and Henry to help me."

When the deputy sat down, Logan began.

"Two years ago Governor Keith invited a group of around thirty families to move from New York to the Tulpehocken Creek area, here in Pennsylvania. Have either of you been there?"

Anna nodded and indicated that she had visited the region. "Our braves hunt there."

"It's a day's ride west of here, in the Schuylkill River watershed, like Indian Creek," Logan explained.

"How do you need our help?" Henry pressed.

"The families we invited to Pennsylvania are Mennonites, Henry, like you."

"Okay," Henry continued, "so what's the problem?"

"They've settled on Delaware Indian land," Logan said. "As we offered them originally."

"And now the Lenape people don't like it?" Anna guessed.

"Exactly right," Logan answered. "The problem is that the Mennonites are good farmers. They are clearing the land, building houses, and a church. They are industrious."

"It's taken two years for the Indians to fight back?" Anna said.

"Yes," Logan responded.

With hot cakes in front of the men, Logan continued. "Governor Keith and I believe you two make the perfect negotiators to work out a solution between the Mennonite settlers and the Indians," Logan continued.

"Because I'm a Mennonite and Anna's practically an Indian," Henry looked at his new bride to make sure she wouldn't be offended.

"Yes," Logan answered. "Henry, you understand the Mennonites and have a command of German. Anna," turning to her, "you know the Delaware customs and ways of thinking as well as anyone."

"Will it be negotiation or coercion?" Anna asked.

Logan paused and realized that Anna understood the situation perfectly. "The Indians will need to leave and move to other land further west," Logan concluded.

"So you want me to tell them to move off their land," Anna pushed.

"We need you to negotiate a solution that they agree to, but yes, they must move off the land."

"What do you want from the Mennonites?" Henry asked.

"That remains to be seen," Logan replied. "That may emerge in the negotiations. But you will be able to communicate with the Mennonites better than my deputy or myself."

"Are you acting on behalf of Lieutenant Governor Keith?" Henry asked.

"Oh yes," Logan answered. "What we negotiate with the Delaware and the Mennonites carries the authority of the governor's office."

Henry and Anna were hesitant to agree. "Could the deputy and I sleep in the mill tonight?" Logan asked. "You'll have until the morning to decide if you'll help us. It might take three days of your time, and we can offer fifteen pounds apiece for your help."

"I'll take you to the mill and show you where to sleep," Henry agreed.

Abe Swartz talked to James Logan about trapping beaver.

"I can't catch them," Swartz explained.

"How are you trying to get them?"

"I've made two wooden traps, and I've waited on them to come up from their dams," Swartz replied.

"Europeans seldom have any luck trapping beaver," Logan explained. "You'll have to hire the Indians to catch them. They bring a group of hunters and tear the dam apart to get them."

"Looks like I'm out of luck with trapping," Swartz concluded.

"Build a house and farm the land," Logan replied. "We're taking over this colony, and the Indians are going to have to move west."

Little John warmed up to the deputy, and cried "Coons!" James Logan and his assistant climbed the mill stairs to peer in the barrel.

"Guess you could trap these," Logan said.

That night wolves howled outside the mill, and the men were relieved that they had four walls around them and a roof over their head for the night.

After breakfast in the Funk house, James Logan and the governor's deputy waited on a response from Anna and Henry.

"I've written a petition," Anna began. "I want you to release Bentura, a slave who works in the mill factory in Philadelphia." Anna laid the document she had penned in front of Logan.

"If we help you negotiate with the Delaware Indians, will you help us get this slave freed and on a ship to Aruba?" Henry asked.

Logan looked at Anna and then Henry. "So we're working a deal," Logan concluded, drumming his fingers on the table. The chief justice had taken his wig off and actually had normal hair on his head.

"Yes," Anna replied. "We can help achieve your goals, if you'll help me with what I want."

"It will take an action of the governor to get a slave released," Logan added.

"Your deputy can see to that," Henry nodded to Logan's traveling partner.

"Your petition is addressed to the council," Logan observed. "You'll probably have to come and make the request in person."

"Do we have a deal?" Anna persisted.

Tucking the petition in his coat pocket, Logan nodded. "We do, Anna. Can we ride to Tulpehocken Creek today?"

Looking at Anna, Henry said they could, though he would need some time to clarify with Abe what to do on the farm for three days.

At the Freedom Inn, Henry and Anna learned that Logan had prepared to negotiate with or without their help. Two men were in charge of a large quantity of trade goods that the Lenape would value. They had waited patiently at the Inn until Logan returned, with two carts full of supplies. The foursome from Funk's farm stopped long enough at the Freedom Inn for food and to give instructions for the two men to follow them to Tulpehocken Creek.

Henry and Anna found the situation as James Logan had described. A large group of German families had migrated from the Palatinate region about fifteen years earlier, before the Funk family had come to the New World. New York hadn't worked well for them, and they found the Quaker environment in Pennsylvania ideal for their families and farms. They had chopped down trees, cleared the land, built houses, and were planting spring seeds. A small meetinghouse had been erected in the middle of the colony, similar to the Franconia meetinghouse being built in Funk's community.

The Lenape, a larger group than Anna's on Indian Creek, had camped just upriver on marginal land. The men hunted for game, while the women foraged for nuts, berries, and roots in the woods. It didn't take long for Anna to find the Lenape leader of the Delaware settlement, traditionally a woman. Anna spoke with her in her own tent and finally got her to agree to hold a general meeting around their fire the next morning. Anna slept in the woman's tent that night, while Henry found a family in the Mennonite community that he was related to, and they invited him to stay with them for the night.

In the morning sunlight, Anna noticed the blatant signs of rum addiction in the Lenape settlement. A half-dozen men had collapsed and lay in disheveled heaps around the tents. Empty gallon rum containers were strewn about the site. Even with limited life experience, at twenty, Anna wondered if the rum would lead to the downfall of the Lenape community, a once noble people who populated these forests for hundreds of years before the Europeans arrived. The devastating impact of rum on her people, the Delaware Indians, had seemingly not registered sufficiently in their own community. European traders and government officials, however, recognized this weakness and often took advantage of it.

Negotiations began when James Logan, his deputy, Henry, and two Mennonite men came and sat on logs around a fire in the middle of the Indian settlement. Anna could see that Logan's trade goods from Philadelphia had arrived, and his men waited patiently at a distance.

"This woman says her people have lived on these lands for as many generations as anyone can count," Anna began.

"Can you explain to her that King George I of England is now the supreme ruler of this land?" Logan asked.

A brave who appeared to have authority came to the circle and sat down. "They have not met your king," Anna responded, "but they do have a memory of William Penn, who negotiated with their parents."

"Please explain that we have brought many gifts for the Lenape," Logan offered. "If they will agree to move further west, we will give them all the goods in our carts."

"The Mennonites agree that the Indians can always hunt in the woods beyond their fields," Henry offered. "The Lenape are welcome in this region, but the farms that are already established are here to stay."

The Lenape woman and the brave with authority considered this offer from Henry and the two Mennonites.

While the Indian leaders considered how to respond, Logan motioned for his carts to be brought into the clearing. Pulling back the coverings, he showed the Indians what he brought. In his crates were shirts, hats, blankets, ribbons, looking glasses, coats, shoes, stockings, brass kettles, and guns.

After the Lenape had looked at the items offered from Logan, Anna announced to everyone that she and Henry had been married a week ago. "All the Lenape of Perkiomen Creek came to our wedding," she exclaimed, moving to stand next to Henry. "We are learning how to live together in peace," Anna continued. "Henry is building a flour mill, and we have an understanding with the Indians about how this will work in the future."

"Anna is my squaw," Henry chimed in. Anna looked at him without smiling. In the Delaware language, Anna explained that she was Henry's wife. "He knows very little about Indians," Anna stated, and the braves around the fire laughed.

It was the barrels that Logan revealed in his carts that drew the most interest, especially from the braves. "Explain to them that these are theirs if they sign this agreement," Logan waved his document. "In addition to the other goods, we offer fifty pounds of money and twenty gallons of rum."

Men drew round and examined the five gallon wooden barrels, and soon excitement began to build. The Lenape leader realized she had to act fast because her braves were eager to begin drinking the rum. The chant, which Anna and Henry heard recited at their wedding was declared by the Lenape: "*We carry the spirit of Tamenend in the land of the Dawn.*"

Anna helped the senior woman and the eldest brave sign the document, though what they wrote looked more like scribbles. After the signing, bedlam broke out as the gifts were distributed. Braves opened the first barrel and began to consume the intoxicating rum.

"It won't be long until they are drunk, and then they beat their wives and fight each other," Anna reflected. "They were sober, but the desire for rum led them to drink their land away," she told Henry. "It's best if we leave."

When Henry rose to speak in the Mennonite meetinghouse along the Tulpehocken Creek, he found a ready audience. Logan and his men were long gone, but the Mennonites gathered to hear from Henry.

Ordained and now married, Henry brought greetings from the Franconia Mennonites. Henry talked about the Germantown Mennonites, and the way many of them had been assisting recent immigrants. Henry related the story of Abe and Elizabeth Swartz and their boys, including the older boy's grisly death, a story readily understood by these frontier pioneers in an untamed wilderness. Henry then told them about his marriage to Anna, from Aruba. He explained that her great-great-grandfather, a Dutch printer from Amsterdam, had been one of the first to print a collection of martyr stories, and how that collection evolved into the *Martyrs Mirror*.

"I will need your help to get the book translated into German, for our people in Pennsylvania," Henry explained. "I may have a printer in Philadelphia who will help us with the project."

"I'm also writing a book about baptism," Henry continued. "With so many religious groups from Europe streaming to Pennsylvania, we need to explain what we believe about baptism."

Early on the third day away from the Funk farm, Anna took off on her horse, making Henry ride hard to catch up.

"What's the hurry?" Henry asked.

"My puppy," Anna responded. "I've got to see him. And you, Henry, have to build him a dog house."

10

Building

April 1725

"A house for Bull?" Henry asked the next morning.

"You build all kinds of things on this farm," Anna responded. "Why not a house for our puppy? It won't be long until he's huge. The mill manager said he'd get three feet tall on all fours. You don't want him sleeping and living in your mill, Henry, because you want to sell flour without animals in the room. Your customers may not appreciate seeing a dog lying on their sacks of flour."

"True," Henry responded. "But nobody builds houses for their dog."

"I don't want Bull living in our house," Anna insisted. "A puppy is one thing, but not a dog that's almost as big as I am."

"I've never seen a dog house, Anna."

"Henry, there's a lot of things you've never seen, but you build them. You built this log house without a written plan, but it's perfect. You and your brothers made the mill without a diagram—it came out of your head, Henry. And you built a barn, but that's not where I want Bull to stay."

"We've seen houses and mills before, Anna."

"Okay, a dog house will have a roof and sides, and be a place where Bull can get out of a storm or sleep at night when it rains. He'll be an outdoor dog."

"He's a part of our family," Anna responded, cuddling Bull on the front step of their little house.

"Okay, Anna. If you want a place for Bull to sleep, I'll build it."

"Henry, there's something else. Did you hear the conversation when the Lenape woman I stayed with at Tulpehocken Creek asked James Logan about the gold medallion?"

"I missed that, Anna."

"The Delaware Indians are persistent in looking for that medallion, and it might help my people if we can find it for them."

"But it's lost," Henry responded.

"I'm guessing it's in Philadelphia," Anna replied. "If we can find it, I think it would help build peace between the colonial government and the Delaware people."

"So you want me to go looking for it?" Henry asked.

"Well, where do you think it is, and how can we find it? Logan is staying completely silent about it."

"I'm not sure he knows where it is," Henry replied.

"If he put pressure on people in Philadelphia, I think it could be found."

"Guess we missed our chance to talk with him about it."

"Yeah, it slipped my mind when he was here, with everything else going on," Anna sighed.

"Bull, go find the gold medallion," Henry asked, and the puppy started running around like he was looking for something.

"Maybe Bull is the way to find the medallion," Anna remarked.

"So how would that work?" Henry chuckled.

"If we can train Bull to sniff out gold, maybe he can detect it someday."

"Anna, is this dog going places with us?"

"Why not? Bull can go with us on trips, including Philadelphia. Let's find something gold plated and start teaching him."

"There's nothing that valuable on my farm," Henry remarked.

"The Lenape get trinkets from traders all the time—I know where to find something," Anna announced. With a jump she headed for the Lenape camp at Perkiomen Creek.

"Don't you think the puppy should go along?" Henry asked.

Anna called and Bull followed her, leaving Henry alone at the house.

When Henry's father came to the farm that afternoon, he and Henry and Abe worked at leveraging big stones into place for their dam in Indian Creek. Their goal was to position enough stones together, tightly configured, to divert some of the water into the race. They found rocks, both upstream and downstream, for the dam.

By dinner time, Henry rummaged up some food in the house for his father and Abe.

Inquiring about what happened on the farm during Henry's three days away, about the only thing unusual, according to Abe, were a couple of black bears that nosed through the property.

"Always keep the mill door closed," Henry instructed. "I don't want bears in there looking around."

"The meetinghouse has a roof on it," the elder Funk commented. "The preacher from Germantown Mennonite Church is coming this Sunday to speak," he concluded.

"Can you men tell me about the Kolbs?" Abe asked.

"They're a very good family," elder Mr. Funk offered.

"Going for a visit, Abe?" Henry asked.

"Tomorrow evening," Abe answered.

"Annie Beth's a nice girl," Mr. Funk added.

Finished eating, Abe rose, thanked Henry for the food, and concluded, "I'll be gone now, to get Little John at Jubilant and William's house."

A sound like a woman screaming in the woods startled Henry and his father. Bolting outside Mr. Funk commented, "Bobcats." Another screech in the distance made the hair on Henry's neck stand straight up.

In the distance Henry heard Bull barking, and he saw Anna running out of the shadows toward the house.

"Are you okay?" Henry asked.

"I am now," Anna answered. "Bull scared the bobcats away. He's a good guard dog." Bull continued to bark into the darkening woods nearby, aware that the cats were out there.

"I better stay here this evening," the elder Funk concluded. "Can I sleep in the mill?"

Alone in their own house, the newlyweds heard Bull whimpering outside their door. "He's not coming in," Henry declared.

"Then I'm going out," Anna said.

"Okay, bring him in here, but before you do, I want a little privacy with the miller's wife," he kidded, grabbing her in a flourish of desire which she did not resist.

The next morning, Anna stepped outside and told Henry to watch her new trick with Bull. Showing Bull her newly acquired gold colored trinket, she threw it as far as she could and Bull raced to find it. The eager dog picked up the treasure and brought it straight back to Anna's hand, begging for another go.

"Bull and I are going to find the gold medallion," Anna declared.

"About that dog house, Anna. I think I'm going to use the leftover lumber from the house and the mill and build a shed."

"You're a builder, Henry."

Looking at his mill, Henry did not disagree. "I wish the Philadelphia factory would finish the parts we've ordered. I'm ready to get this mill working."

After a day of building and planting, Henry looked up to see two black bears meandering through his property. At about the same time, Bull spotted the bears and ran after them, barking.

Anna and Henry watched the spectacle. The bears turned and looked at the agitated dog, then ambled off into the woods.

"He's a guard dog, Henry."

At the same time the Funk's watched Bull chase bears, two braves quietly opened a door at the courthouse in Philadelphia. One warrior stepped in and crept down the hallway to talk with Chief Lapowinsa, while the other brave watched near the door.

In their native language of the Delaware Indians, the chief spoke with his brave. A dozing guard woke, heard something, and came to look. A warning whistle from the waiting brave quickly brought his partner. When the braves slipped away, the guard saw them in the shadows.

Alerting James Logan that two braves had come to visit the chief, Logan ordered a guard to watch him at all hours of the day and night.

"If he gets out, you will take his place in the cell," Logan threatened.

Philadelphia in 1725 was not a city that Indian braves walked about on their own in daylight. They could be captured and sold into slavery, or worse.

Logan consulted with Governor Keith the next morning about the heightened danger from Indian unrest.

"We forced the Delaware on Tulpehocken Creek to move west," Logan reported. "Henry and Anna Funk helped ease them out."

"Are we at risk of an Indian uprising?" the governor asked.

"I'm not sure," Logan answered, "but it's possible. Two braves tried to free the chief last night."

"Keep him well-guarded," ordered the governor.

"Governor, the Delaware keep asking me about a gold medallion. Do you know anything about it? They tell me that William Penn promised to help find it, and they say it has a turtle imprinted on one side."

"I have an idea where it might be," the governor answered. "Just keep them in the dark when you get asked about it."

"Okay."

"Logan, did you read that young reporter's article in *The Mercury* about the Mennonites?"

"I did," Logan answered.

"Do you agree with him?" the governor wondered.

"He's only nineteen, Governor, barely old enough to know anything," Logan responded. "He came to the Funk wedding. I didn't know he was so opposed to the Mennonites."

"He wrote that the German immigrants are going to out-populate the English settlers," Governor Keith continued. "That unless we Quakers get busy, by either having more children or bringing more settlers from England, the Mennonites will soon be in the majority."

"Governor, I wouldn't worry much about the Mennonites. They're harmless and most believe in nonviolence. They won't fight," Logan assured him. "Those families we resettled along Tulpehocken Creek are industrious, hardworking, and they mind their own business. They're builders, traders, and merchants. Their industrious spirit will strengthen the economic foundations of our colony."

"Franklin thinks the German immigrants are fundamentally inferior to English stock," the governor noted. "And he doesn't like their pious religion, their prayers, or their simple faith in God."

"Franklin is a deist, Governor, and doesn't much hold to faith in God. The Mennonites are harmless. The only thing to watch out for is that they may side with the Indians if there is an uprising, which there very well may be."

"You mean since we caught two braves in the jail, you think there's a chance of a fight with the Indians?" the governor probed.

"Yes," replied Logan.

It would be several weeks until Henry Funk purchased a copy of Andrew Bradford's newspaper and read Ben Franklin's critical column about German immigrants.

The slave that Henry saw in Jubilant and William's home a day before their wedding died.

"Probably the pox," Jubilant explained to Henry.

"Where should we bury him?" William asked.

"Next to Elizabeth Swartz at the church," Anna recommended.

"I'm not sure we should use the church cemetery," Henry cautioned.

"We buried a slave out in the field last year," William mentioned. "We could do that again."

"No," Henry said. "The church cemetery is fine. But we won't invite anyone else, because it's the pox. Just us four."

"And Bull," Anna chimed in.

They put the slave's body on Henry's cart and walked to the cemetery not very far away. It was a simple burial, with a shallow grave that William and Henry dug. They laid the slave next to Elizabeth Swartz's unmarked but freshly dug grave. Henry prayed a simple prayer, they covered the body with dirt, and they returned home by dark.

When Bull barked at a skunk on the way back to the farm, Henry chased the varmint away. "The dog needs to learn about skunks sometime," he commented, "but not now."

Amidst planting and work on the Indian Creek dam, Henry built a shed with leftover wood he had on the farm. It wasn't very big, with room to keep a few tools in storage. Henry created a door for Bull, using leather straps to make it swing in and out so the dog could use the shed as desired.

The Funk Farm now had five buildings, including the mill, house, outhouse, barn, and tool shed. Only a few years earlier, Henry's farm had been claimed by the Lenape Indians for their settlement and for hunting. Since then, Henry and his brothers had cut down numerous trees and cleared the land for planting crops.

Henry was keenly aware that his economic prosperity had come at the expense of the indigenous people who had lived there for centuries. He had been one of the early German immigrants to Pennsylvania in 1719. In the harbor in Philadelphia, boatloads of immigrants from all over Europe, and from many religious backgrounds streamed to the Quaker colony, in a new wave of immigration, seeking economic prosperity and religious freedom.

Henry looked over his shed. The boards had been cut and planed in Philadelphia, and hauled to his farm across primitive but acceptable roads, all of which were signs of progress. This "progress," of course, Henry realized, was defined in European terms. It wasn't considered progress by the Lenape Indians of the Schuylkill River basin. Henry liked order, symmetry, and a well-planned farm, all virtues that Governor Keith and James Logan counted on for the economic development of their colony.

The Kolb home, on a farm not too far from Henry Funk's mill, was simple and functional. Abe was invited in and met with the entire family. Annie Beth seemed happy to see Abe again.

"Little John was born in Germany," Abe explained. "His mother and brother died when we arrived in Philadelphia."

"The Funks helped you?" Mr. Kolb inquired.

"They have," Abe responded. "They helped my wife and me when we got off the ship." Revealing the colonial American understandings that life could be brief and uncertain, Abe said, "But Elizabeth died, and she is buried at the church."

Mrs. Kolb expressed sympathy to Abe, but then changed the direction and invited, "Let's eat." Everyone gathered around the table.

After supper, seventeen-year-old Annie Beth Kolb went for a walk with twenty-two-year old Abe Swartz, while eighteen-month-old Little John stayed in the house with Mrs. Kolb.

Annie Beth asked Abe about Germany, the land her parents came from, but a place she had never visited.

Abe Swartz asked Annie Beth about how her family had moved to the Indian Creek area, and how they made a living.

"We raise corn and wheat, like most others," Annie Beth answered.

"Annie Beth," Abe began, "I need a companion for me and a mother for Little John."

"I like children," Annie Beth responded.

"I've been thinking about selling my land here at Indian Creek and moving with Adam Miller to the Virginia colony."

"Where's Virginia?" Annie Beth asked.

"Far to the south of us," Abe explained.

Almost business-like, Abe explained to Annie Beth that if she was at all interested in him and Little John, she should be aware that he was thinking about moving away to a distant place.

"Adam Miller talks about Elkton, Virginia, and I may end up there," Abe concluded.

"I'm not afraid of new things," Annie Beth responded.

Back at the Kolb house, Abe thanked Mrs. Kolb for the meal and for watching his son, told Mr. Kolb he'd like to call again, and headed home with Little John. When the bobcats screamed, Abe held his son close and hurried along the path.

At the Funk farm, Bull barked and the bobcat screams seemed to retreat further into the dense woods beyond the recently planted fields. Bobcats had been known in the Indian River region to challenge wolves, so every adult on the Funk farm understood that barking from an oversize puppy hadn't frightened the night cats away.

The mother raccoon ran from her nest when Abe and Little John climbed the stairs in the mill.

"Henry, your father told me that the Mennonite pastor is bringing a visitor to church on Sunday who promotes baptism by immersion."

"Immersion?" Henry asked.

"Is that a problem?" Anna wondered.

"It depends on what he says," Henry answered. "We practice baptism by pouring."

"I'm not sure it makes much difference," Anna concluded.

Henry looked at his papers on the desk and determined to spend more time on his writing project that explained his beliefs about baptism.

11

Mirror
May 1725

One of Anna's wedding gifts continued to amaze her. Someone had given her a simple mirror, of poor quality and inexpensive, but yet it had opened up a whole new world for her.

She had looked into a mirror before while living in her parents' relatively affluent home in Aruba, but in the frontier region of eighteenth-century colonial Pennsylvania, not many people had mirrors.

Annie Beth, at a stop at the Funk house while going to church with Abe, gawked at the image she saw in the mirror. In seventeen years of living, Annie Beth had never seen her own reflection in a mirror.

"Here's a comb, Annie Beth," Anna offered.

"I've never seen myself in a mirror before," Annie Beth replied.

"If you comb your hair and pretty yourself up, Abe might like you even more," Anna suggested.

"I think he likes me the way I am."

"Yes, he does," Anna replied. "I know the mirror is distorted, but it's fun to see what you look like, don't you think, Annie Beth?"

"I guess, but it only shows what your face looks like," Annie Beth responded.

"What do you mean?" Anna asked.

"Well, this mirror shows your face, but it doesn't really reveal what's in your heart. It just shows the surface."

Anna realized the profound insight. "Let's see if the men are ready to go. We can show them our faces and who we really are."

Annie Beth, Anna, and the women sat on the opposite side of the Franconia meetinghouse from the men. The benches were just flat boards, without backs. It was Sunday morning, May 16, 1725, and warm sunshine promised summer which lay just ahead. The meetinghouse shutters had been opened halfway.

After the minister's sermon, he introduced a visitor from Philadelphia. Thirty-four-year-old Conrad Beissel rose to greet the small audience in the tiny log meetinghouse.

"I come to you from a sister Anabaptist group in Philadelphia, the Dunkers. We baptize by immersion, and our numbers are few but growing. Most of our other beliefs are similar to yours. On Saturday next, we will hold a baptism service in the Indian Creek, where it flows into the Perkiomen. Please join us. We will baptize seven that I know of, possibly more."

After church Beissel explained to Henry Funk that he had recently been immersed by the Dunkers in Philadelphia. A new immigrant from Germany, Beissel was a mystic and spiritualist, and he wanted revival among the German speaking people of Pennsylvania.

"Why did you join the Dunkers?" Henry wondered.

"They showed me from the Scriptures where they found the practice of immersion."

"But the vast majority of Scriptural verses about baptism confirm the pouring method that we use," Funk concluded.

"You and I disagree," Beissel concluded. "Come to the baptism next Saturday and see for yourself."

"Do you have a place to eat dinner?" Anna inquired.

"Thank you, but I'm eating with the Kolbs today," Beissel answered.

On the way home from church, Anna asked if Annie Beth had been baptized yet.

"I don't think so," Henry responded.

"Do you think Beissel might convince her to be baptized by immersion in the river?" Anna asked.

"I hope not," Henry responded.

"Does it really matter which way a person is baptized, Henry?"

"Well, Anna, I think you know what my answer to that question is, don't you?"

After Sunday dinner, Henry sat at his desk and noticed the mirror that Anna had left there that morning. "A Mirror of Baptism," he mumbled.

"Did you say something?" Anna asked.

Fingering his papers, Henry commented, "I need to finish my book that explains what we believe about baptism."

"What good will that do?"

"People can read it and understand our beliefs."

"Do you think a book is going to change anyone's opinions on baptism?"

"It might," Henry concluded. Looking into the mirror, he grinned and said, "At least now I have a title."

A rider showed up at the Funk farm just before noon on Monday, having stayed at Freedom Inn the night before. The man informed Funk that his water wheel was finished and would be delivered from Philadelphia in two days.

With that good news, Henry and Abe worked hard to make sure everything was ready for the big arrival. They cleaned out the pit where the wheel would turn and checked the entry shaft box they had built.

When three wagons rolled onto the Funk farm Wednesday at noon accompanied by four men, Henry realized his dream of building a mill was becoming a reality. Like many others before, Henry's spirit was enlivened with hope for the future as his dream turned into reality.

"How's the miller's wife?" the mill factory manager inquired.

"Doing great. I love the puppy you gave me," Anna responded.

"He's not much of a puppy anymore," the manager observed. "He's grown from a puppy to be very large. These dogs slobber over everything."

In the eighteenth-century frontier region of Philadelphia, a water wheel represented progress. A functioning mill meant trees had been cut down, fields cleared, and wheat and corn planted. Farmers needed a local way to grind unprocessed crops into the flour they used to make food. The German immigrants might debate the mode of baptism, but they were unified in the enterprise of building mills.

For the Delaware Indians, the mills being built along streams everywhere were changing their lives. Most of the Lenape were moving further west into more remote tree-covered regions. They had lost their gold medallion, they had lost the promises given to them by William Penn, and they were losing their way of life at the hands of the devil's potion, rum.

Anna, between the two worlds, watched the men, including Henry's brothers and father, assemble the pieces of the wheel into one unit and position it into place. It was an engineering marvel, similar perhaps to the progress represented in the print shop of her parents in Aruba.

Anna missed her parents, though she wouldn't admit that to Henry or anyone. She wondered how they were doing, how the printing business was going, and how her friends on the island were faring. Had any of her girlfriends gotten married, she wondered?

It became clear to Anna that the four men from Philadelphia would be here for a couple of days. Anna knew that Henry wanted to attend the Dunker's immersion baptism on Saturday, but she wondered if that would be possible because of work on the mill.

"What are you thinking about?" Annie Beth Kolb asked.

"You startled me," Anna sputtered.

"I came to see the progress. Abe talks about it all the time."

"Are you two seeing each other?"

"He comes to my house twice a week for a visit, and I've learned to love Little John."

"Do you think Abe wants to marry you?"

"I'm not sure, Anna, but I hope so."

Abe and Henry had built a race that brought water from the mill pond reservoir and poured it on the water wheel, turning it to create power for the mill. It was a simple concept, but complex in monitoring the flow of water that powered the wheel. A strong flow of water was needed at first, to get the wheel started, but very little water was needed to keep it turning. A lever inside the mill allowed the miller to adjust the amount of water flowing onto the wooden wheel.

"Why doesn't that Beissel fellow hold his dunking baptism in your mill pond?" Abe asked.

"I wouldn't let him," Henry responded.

"The Dunkers are gaining converts in Philadelphia," the mill manager informed.

"That's because they're a new denomination, formed just a few years ago. New movements often get a lot of attention," Henry countered.

"Did you know the Beissel guy believes in celibacy as the highest virtue, and that he's taken a vow of poverty?" the mill manager asked.

"Celibacy?" Henry asked.

"He believes it shows your complete dedication to God when a disciple keeps away from the opposite sex."

"How will his church add members?" Henry wondered.

"Lots of others will have children," the manager added. "Then his church baptizes them, and they join his eccentric movement. He's living with a group of single men who think like him."

"He explained his beliefs and practices to the Kolbs last Sunday after church," Abe noted.

"Did he make any converts?" Henry wondered.

"Annie Beth is interested," Abe responded.

"Annie Beth?" Henry quizzed. "She's Mennonite."

"But not baptized yet," Abe added.

"Oh my, I hope that she doesn't let Beissel baptize her in the river!" Henry exclaimed.

Abe replied, "Well, I agree with you, but it's her decision."

By Saturday morning the water wheel had been installed and the men from Philadelphia left. It was exciting to watch it turn when water from the race poured over the top. Inside the mill, the shaft wasn't connected to anything, and the Funks had to wait on their five gears and the grindstones to begin making flour.

In a secluded spot on Indian Creek, Henry and Abe cleaned up and got themselves ready to head to the Perkiomen Creek for the baptisms. There were five adults who left after lunch, including Henry's father, Abe and Annie Beth, and Anna and Henry. Little John would spend the afternoon with Jubilant and William.

Conrad Beissel invited seven candidates to wade into the cold Perkiomen Creek with him. The water in May was still frigid, but the baptism wouldn't take long, Beissel promised.

Beissel immersed each of the seven, pushing them forward three times under the water in the name of the Father, the Son, and the Holy Spirit. On the shore, family members gave them towels, and they quickly found a spot behind trees to change into dry clothes.

After the last one, Beissel turned to the small crowd on the shore, and asked if there was anyone else who wanted to be baptized. He looked cold but he was patient and willing to immerse others.

When Annie Beth Kolb took a step toward the river, Henry tried to block her. "Annie Beth, we practice baptism by pouring. We can baptize you next Sunday at the Mennonite church if you are ready."

"This is her decision," Anna intervened.

Abe stood by without saying anything. He had been baptized in Europe, a necessary rite to becoming married to Elizabeth, almost four years earlier. Henry had been baptized in Germantown, and Anna had not received the ritual.

Annie Beth stepped into the water and waded out to Conrad Beissel. Without hesitation, Beissel pushed Annie Beth forward three times, saying, "Upon your desire to be baptized, we do so in the name of the Father, the Son, and the Holy Spirit."

Beissel had brought an extra towel to the event, and he gave it to Annie Beth, the only additional candidate to be baptized. In her joy, Annie Beth Kolb shivered in the brisk May air, cold, but happy in her decision. With little else to do, the five travelers from Indian Creek got on their horses and headed home. Annie Beth continued to shiver but she was determined to be strong and not complain about feeling cold.

Back in their house that evening, Anna noticed Henry's dour attitude and sullen countenance.

"How could she have done that?" Henry demanded.

"She was ready, Henry, just accept it," Anna consoled.

"But her parents are Mennonite, and we have taught about baptism by pouring," Henry argued.

"Now she can get married to Abe, because she's baptized, right?"

"I guess so," Henry replied.

"Don't make such a big deal out of baptism, Henry. It's just water—what does it matter if you get poured on or get immersed?"

Henry looked at the mirror on his desk. "In our faith, we try to mirror the beliefs of the Bible," he replied. "We seek to mirror our practices and community life on what we find reflected in Scripture."

"Then you better get busy and write your book," Anna encouraged. A moment had arrived, Anna realized, in Henry's life, where he needed to write his beliefs on paper, for himself and for his church. And for their children, and their descendants who would come later.

"What's your title again?" Anna asked.

"*A Mirror of Baptism*," Henry replied.

"How will you organize the book, Henry?"

"Around the three baptisms of the Holy Spirit, the water, and the blood, from 1 John 5:7-8," Henry answered.

After Henry had been laboring for several hours, Anna begged, "You've been working a long time. Come to bed."

Henry glanced up into the loft, and with only the dim lantern light on his desk to battle the darkness, he couldn't help but smile and be drawn away from his writing and study by Anna's invitation.

"I have something to tell you if you come up here," Anna coaxed.

"Let me finish this sentence," Henry answered, "and I'll come."

Henry had few study resources on his desk in the corner of the house.

He had his Bible, with no concordance, and a copy of *Martyrs Mirror*, but few other books of significance. Henry had to find his Scripture references for the book he was writing on baptism from memory or by searching through the pages of his Bible.

Henry's memory of the Bible he had studied for years helped him locate the references he wanted to include in his book. He wrote in German, and his handwriting would need to be transferred to a printing press that used individual letters if his manuscript would ever become useful to others. That would take time and money to accomplish.

After Henry climbed into the loft, Anna asked, "Did you notice how pretty Annie Beth was when she came out of the river today?"

"Well, sure, I'm guessing every man there noticed."

"Her wet dress didn't leave much to your imagination, did it Henry?"

"I'm not sure how to answer that, Anna."

"Abe Swartz will be a lucky man if Annie Beth agrees to marry him," Anna commented.

"I suppose so," Henry answered.

"But you're luckier, Henry."

"Why?"

"Because you know what?" Anna pressed.

"What?"

"Well, at least guess," Anna insisted.

"Okay, is today our six-week anniversary?" Henry guessed.

"Close, but that's not the right answer. Try again."

"Well, did Abe ask Annie Beth to marry him?" Henry wondered.

"That's not the answer yet, Henry. Try one more time."

"Anna," Henry said, settling into her arms. "I'm not much for guessing. Just tell me."

"Okay your guesses were on the right track. Think about our six-week anniversary and marriage," Anna smiled.

"Well, your birthday's coming up soon. Is that what you want me to remember?"

"No, Henry, something else, much more important than my birthday," Anna replied. "Okay, Henry, how much do you know about babies?"

Looking at Anna, Henry began to understand. "Are you pregnant?"

"I am, Henry, I am. At least I'm almost sure that I am. You better get ready, because you're going to be a papa."

"That is good news, Anna. Now hush your talking and come here."

12

Fire

June 1725

Anna went to visit the Lenape of Indian Creek. What she found there was an outbreak of smallpox.

Lenape Mother showed Anna the sweat lodge where they placed their sick. It was believed that when water was poured on hot coals of fire and produced steam, that it would drive sickness out of the person. The sick person, sweating from the intense heat and steam, would then be thrust into cold water to close the pores and keep the evil sickness from returning. Finally, they were wrapped in a blanket to rest.

The disease struck randomly, Lenape Mother explained, and neither young nor old was immune from the deadly pox. "Our people are dying every day," Lenape Mother stated. "A deadly disease that we do not understand is destroying us."

Anna watched an herbalist apply natural remedies from roots, bark, and plants, but they didn't seem to help. Another Indian woman used herbs but also tried to drive the evil spirits away from the sick with chants and incantations.

"Since your people have come from across the sea," Lenape Mother explained, "our people have been perishing."

Anna talked with Lenape Mother and several braves about Chief Lapowinsa. "Are the braves planning to get him out of the jail in Philadelphia?" Anna inquired.

Two braves explained to Anna and the others how they had tried to break into the jail and free their chief but failed.

"What will you do next?" Anna pressed.

"Our braves may begin to burn buildings of the settlers from across the sea," Lenape Mother explained.

"You mean houses and barns?" Anna asked.

The braves nodded.

"We need to get the attention of Mr. Logan, the city-man who was at your wedding," Lenape Mother commented.

"But he will probably send soldiers out and chase you away or take your braves to jail," Anna responded.

"Our chief must be released," one brave responded. "We will succeed."

After her day-long visit, Anna rose to leave. The brave who had wanted to marry Anna came to talk. Anna's ability to use the Lenape language was good enough for her to both understand the words and the heart throb of the man.

"Will you marry me?" the brave asked boldly. He had attended Anna's wedding, but still he asked.

"No, I will not," Anna answered, "but I am doing everything I can to get your chief released and to help your people find the gold medallion."

Rebuffed, the brave stalked away.

"Anna, come to our burial grounds this evening," Lenape Mother invited, "and bring along Henry and the man who lives in the mill."

With Bull at her side, Anna left the Lenape settlement where she had lived for months, a place she had called home. Her dog was both admired and feared. He seemed friendly enough, but would growl at danger and was growing so fast that most of Lenape shied away from trying to get close.

Anna explained to Henry some of the issues the Delaware Indians faced.

"They're fighting smallpox, Henry."

"It was likely spread from the slave we buried," Henry responded. "It's very contagious."

"They use a sweat lodge to try and cure their people when they get sick."

"What are they thinking about the chief?" Henry asked.

"They mentioned burning houses and barns, to get Logan's attention."

"They're starting to feel desperate," Henry concluded.

"Henry, they invited you, me, and Abe to a burial this evening."

"Oh my," Henry pondered. "They've invited us to a sacred burial?"

"Yes, and we should go. This invitation means we've earned their trust."

"Aren't you worried about the smallpox?" Henry asked.

"Yes, a little, but still we must go."

"All right," Henry concluded, "we'll go."

It was the first full week of June. The Lenape tended to growing their crops of the "three sisters," corn, beans, and squash. These crops would feed them during harvest time later in the summer. The Indians knocked kernels from dried corn cobs picked the previous summer, and then ground them by hand, a difficult job.

Henry's mill would make the task of grinding corn kernels easier and produced at a much greater volume than the Indians could achieve. The rapid production of grain was one reason the German immigrant population grew so quickly. With dozens of ships arriving in the Philadelphia harbor weekly, bringing thousands of new immigrants from the Rhine River Valley to the Schuylkill River Valley, the Lenape died off daily from the ravages of disease and heartbreak.

Since she had previously participated in a burial ritual, Anna knew there was little hurry to get to the Indian burial ground much before dusk. Bull tagged along.

When they arrived, Abe, Henry, and Anna sat on a log in the circle of Lenape mourners who had come to bury two of their dead, struck down by smallpox.

Braves called on the Great Spirit *Kishelemukong*, whom they believed had created the world. Those spirits opposed to the Great Spirit brought evil, sickness, and death. The Delaware shaman uttered incantations.

In slow procession around the dead, the shaman called out to the Great Spirit, and in a low voice threatened the evil spirits that lurked in the trees. For a time, the Indian men entered a trance and circled the new graves in a slow death walk, releasing the spirits of the dead to the underworld.

The ritual changed when two men brought out tobacco pipes. The Lenape used a native wild tobacco plant and rolled leaves for their pipes. The pipes were smoked by each man in turn, including Lenape Mother.

After the braves had smoked, a pipe was offered to Anna and the two men. Anna didn't hesitate, with the fire declining, the shadows lengthening, and the evening turning into nighttime. The animal sounds of the forest began in earnest.

Henry hesitated to smoke the pipe, but Anna encouraged him, counseling that if he refused, it would be extremely rude and an affront to their hosts. Henry took the pipe, but Anna had to show him how to hold it and smoke the tobacco. The aroma was far more pleasant than what Henry tasted when he took his first puff.

Henry held the pipe and asked Lenape Mother a question, which all the braves listened to. There was no hurry to go anywhere, and the braves would sit all night if necessary, keeping vigil against the evil spirits that lurked in the dark.

"Can you tell me the meaning of the marks on Chief Lapowinsa's face?" Henry asked. "He has distinct lines that I don't understand."

"Lapowinsa's marks come from his grandfather and father," Lenape Mother responded. "Lapowinsa was destined to be a chief, and the marks reveal the heritage of our people, carried from one generation to another."

"But what do they mean?" Henry asked again.

"After Chief Lapowinsa's father met with the 'Great Miquon', he made marks on his son's forehead and cheek to remind all of the peace between the 'Great Miquon' and the Lenape."

"They're peace marks?" Henry asked.

"They are," Lenape Mother sadly replied. "But James Logan and Great Miquon's sons have forgotten the peace treaty."

"I do not understand the meaning of the title 'Great Miquon,' " Henry continued.

"Let me try to explain," Anna interjected. Having heard the story before, she spoke first in the Lenape language, and then translated into the English of William Penn. "When William Penn tried to explain the meaning of his name to the Indians in Philadelphia, he held up a goose feather, most commonly used as a writing instrument, or a 'pen.' The braves then exclaimed, 'Ah...mi-quon,' which is Lenape for goose feather."

There was a pause in the discussion, giving time for more puffs on the peace pipe and incantations from the shaman. When a raccoon ventured near to investigate, Bull barked and chased it away. The men laughed, and the seriousness of the burial ritual dissipated.

"Henry is a 'miquon' man," Anna told Lenape Mother. Knowing the Lenape couldn't understand writing with quill and ink, Anna explained, "He is writing a book with a goose quill pen. He dips the quill into ink and puts marks on paper."

The men laughed again. They had seen such a quill pen, but they had not watched a man make marks on paper with pen and ink.

"Would you like to see my miquon's pen and paper?" Anna asked.

Several braves nodded in the affirmative.

"Henry is writing a book about religion," Anna continued. "You use water for cleaning, bathing, and to put out a fire, but his people use water as a religious ritual to the Great Spirit."

None of the braves had seen a baptism in the Mennonite meetinghouse, but one of the braves had watched the baptism by immersion the previous week. When the brave explained the way a man pushed people under the water three times, all the braves laughed.

"When can we see your 'miquon' write with a quill pen?" one of the braves asked Anna in the Lenape language.

"They want to see your pen and paper," Anna translated to Henry.

"Okay," Henry agreed. "When?"

Anna asked the brave when he would like to see a demonstration. Laughing, she translated for Henry, "Right now."

"I guess now is as good a time as any," Henry said.

After returning to their house, Bull got agitated and growled when twenty braves and Lenape Mother traipsed into the Funk log home.

Because he barked and frightened the braves, Abe put Bull in the shed and blocked his escape door. There was a bit of light from the moon, but not much.

With his only lantern burning as brightly as possible, Henry pulled out his papers, his ink well, and his goose quill feather pen. He began to make marks on the paper, showing the braves how to write, a procedure they gawked at.

"You write on paper," Lenape Mother observed, "while we write on the faces of our men. We have made peace tonight. Now braves, it is time to go."

After the Indians left, Abe turned to go to the mill, but commented to Anna that the brave who she had stilted did not join in the spirit of the other Indians. He had waited patiently outside. "You may want to keep an eye on him," Abe advised.

The next morning Anna and Henry talked about a trip to Philadelphia. Henry wanted to check on the progress of his mill gears. Anna wanted to ask James Logan about the petition to free Bentura the slave, and they both wanted to talk with Chief Lapowinsa.

"And you can get a copy of *The Mercury*, Henry. Your favorite thing to read," Anna quipped.

"Anna, the Bible is my favorite thing to read," Henry replied with a grin.

"That's not true," Anna replied. "Your little newspaper is the real reason we're going, I believe."

Before leaving the farm, Henry talked with Abe about managing the farm in his three-day absence. "Please keep an eye on our buildings, Abe. You know about the danger to barns and homes in our community."

"Sure, Henry, but I need to advise you that I will probably be moving to the Virginia colony in a few months."

Henry asked, "Will you take Annie Beth along?"

"I hope so," Abe replied.

On the way out his door, Henry reached into his desk and pulled out the deed for the land he had purchased from Governor Keith.

"Why are you taking that along?" Anna inquired.

"I have an idea," he answered. "Let's ride."

At the inn where they usually stayed in downtown Philadelphia,

Anna had to negotiate a place to keep Bull, who had loped alongside the horses to the colonial capital. The owner agreed that the dog could stay in the barn with the horses.

The next morning Henry and Anna called on James Logan, who agreed to meet them.

"Can we get Bentura the slave freed?" Anna began.

"I'm not sure we can do that," Logan grumbled.

"But you agreed to it when you visited our house," Anna demanded.

"Okay," Logan responded slowly, "I'll write a letter you can take to his owner."

"I thought you said we'd have to speak to the city council," Henry countered.

"No, not just to free a slave. I can take care of that."

After writing out a release for the slave, Logan stamped his seal on the paper, representing his office as chief justice.

Pushing the paper toward the couple, Henry continued. "Mr. Logan, I have here the deed to my 101 acres on Indian Creek, with a seal from Governor Keith. Look, it has three ears of corn and shows many grapes, a sign of the abundance in the Indian Creek region."

"What's your point?" Logan inquired.

"Seals and images, like the one I have on my deed, and like the one you just put on this paper, have meaning, especially for those who receive them."

"Yes," Logan responded.

"When Pieter Alricks gave the gold medallion to Tender Vine years ago it had a turtle imprinted on one side and a cross on the other side."

Logan, annoyed, growled at Henry and said, "And you want me to find it and give it back?"

"Yes, Mr. Logan," Henry insisted. "That medallion may be the key to the colonial government's ability to make peace with the Lenape Indians."

"I don't know where it is, Mr. Funk. I've told you that before."

"We understand," Henry replied, glancing at Anna. "But we wanted to ask again."

"May we talk to Chief Lapowinsa?" Henry asked.

"Briefly," Logan allowed. "You'll only be given a few minutes."

"Thank you," Anna answered.

Stuffing the release form and his deed in a pocket, Henry and Anna rose to leave.

In the courthouse lobby, where Bull had patiently waited, the dog bounded to the door when Anna and Henry came from Logan's office. But he quickly turned and sniffed at the big counter in the middle of the room, with two city workers, before he began to bark.

"Not now, Bull," Henry scolded.

"He's found something," Anna replied. Turning to a worker inside the counter, she asked, "Is there something in your desk that's gold or silver plated?"

Though Anna received a strange look, Bull wouldn't stop barking at a corner of the desk. "Do you have a gold watch or trinket that's gold-covered in this desk?" Anna asked again.

Glancing at the other worker, the man finally reached under the counter and found his gold watch which he laid there while he worked. With Bull satisfied and Henry embarrassed, Anna apologized and they headed out the door.

"I told you that Bull could help us find the gold medallion," Anna exclaimed outside. "He found that guy's gold watch!"

"That was terrible," Henry replied. "Let's go."

"Wait, we have permission to meet the chief."

In the narrow hallway outside Lapowinsa's cell, Anna and Henry talked with the chief while a guard listened.

"We showed Mr. Logan the corn and grapes seal on our deed," Anna mentioned in Lenape, "and explained that you wanted the turtle and cross medallion returned to you."

"Can you get me out of here?" the chief responded.

"No, not today," Anna replied. "Some of your braves are restless and have threatened to burn barns and houses."

Without a direct response to the burning threat, the chief asked Anna to inform Lenape Mother that he was doing well, had enough to eat, and was not harmed.

The guard figured that was enough time, since he couldn't understand a word of what had been said anyway.

Henry visited with Andrew Bradford in the print shop and bought the latest copy of *The Mercury*. "Don't be offended by what Ben Franklin wrote about 'dumb Germans,'" Bradford advised. "He's trying to make a name for himself as a writer."

At the mill factory, Funk discovered it would be September until his gears would be ready. When he gave the emancipation document to the owner, the manager gave Henry a quizzical look, but soon got Bentura and brought him to the desk. "You're free to go."

A startled Bentura did not know what to do next.

"Come with us," Henry offered, "I can use your help on the farm."

That night, on Indian Creek, the smell of smoke awoke Abe Swartz. Rising, he rushed downstairs to the door on the second floor, looked toward the house, and saw flames.

13

Stone

June 1725

Abe Swartz had few options when he came out of the mill after he got dressed. In the black of the night, he could only watch flames tear through the wooden rafters and shingles on the Funk house.

None of the Funk neighbors lived within eyesight of the farm, and he could only hope that perhaps the smoke would awaken someone, like it had him. But even if all the farmers around the Funk farm came immediately, there would be nothing they could do to stop the inferno.

Abe Swartz had lost two wives and two children. He had experienced persecution in Europe, and the difficulty of the trans-Atlantic crossing, but he had never stood by helplessly watching a fire consume a house. The logs were ablaze and burned hot, meaning it would be well into the next day or two until the ashes cooled down.

Abe wondered what Anna and Henry would think when they returned from Philadelphia. It was well past midnight, and they would probably arrive at evening of the same day. The fire would still be burning.

When the roof collapsed through searing flames, and a wall fell out from the heat, Abe saw Henry's writing desk crumbling in fire and ashes. Nothing would be left for the Funks to recover, including Henry's cherished books.

While their house burned, Anna and Henry slept well in each other's arms at the Philadelphia Inn, still newlyweds on a bit of a vacation from work on the farm.

Around the breakfast table, two German Amish immigrants met Anna, Henry, and Bentura. Zug and Joder explained how the customs office had renamed them Zook and Yoder. "He didn't like the sound of our names and just changed them," Zook stated.

The men had come to scout out Pennsylvania, see what it was like, and return to their homes in Germany. Their people in the Rhineland were ready to move to America if their reports came back positive.

"Where are you folks from?" Zook inquired.

"Indian Creek, a day's ride northwest of here," Anna answered.

Zook glanced at Bentura, and Anna explained. "Yesterday Bentura was released to live as a free man. He will go home with us today to work on our farm."

"You're welcome to come to Indian Creek and meet with the Franconia community this Sunday," Henry offered.

"We're members of the Ammann division," Zook replied. "Will that make a difference?"

Henry had heard of the contentious splintering of Jakob Ammann's followers from the Mennonites, which had taken place about thirty years earlier in Europe.

"No, that won't matter," Funk replied.

Zook glanced at Yoder and informed the Funks that they wanted to see the Lancaster region, where news had come to their German community that land was cheap and excellent for farming.

"Why don't you come to Indian Creek, then go to Lancaster next week?" Henry asked.

"We have three weeks to look around," Zook replied. "Where would we stay on your farm?"

"We have a mill, though it's not operating yet. You can sleep there, with another man and his boy who work on the farm."

"Are you men married?" Anna wondered.

"Neither of us are married," Zook answered.

"We have pretty girls in Franconia," Anna smiled.

"We'll work for our keep," Zook offered. "We're not here to live with you unless we can work."

"That we have plenty of," Henry smiled.

"How are we going to get to the farm?" Bentura asked.

"We have two horses, a dog, and five travelers," Henry observed.

"Six," Anna corrected.

Henry smiled at his pretty bride and agreed, there were six travelers.

"Bentura, could you find your way to the farm?" Anna asked. "You came for the wedding."

"I'm not sure," Bentura answered.

"I'll draw you a map," Henry offered. "You men could walk while we ride on ahead." From a piece of paper and a crudely made lead pencil he retrieved from the Inn's owner, Henry sketched the route to his farm on Indian Creek.

Bentura's confidence did not increase by looking at the map. "What if someone decides to sell me into slavery again?" he asked.

"Guess this paper won't mean much if that happens," Henry replied, showing them the emancipation document.

Zook looked at the document, but handed it to Yoder who was able to read a little English. "He's the scholar," Zook stated.

Henry realized he had a man worried about being resold into slavery and two travelers who could barely read English, the language of the colony. "We'll take our time and all walk," Henry concluded. "We have a reliable man on the farm who can take care of things until we arrive this evening. Can you men walk fast?"

Outside in the plaza, with two horses, a dog, and six travelers, Anna confided with Henry that she didn't feel well and may need to ride home.

"Ever heard of a woman's sickness in pregnancy?" she asked.

"Do what you need to," Henry answered.

"And we may need to stop for a bit at the Freedom Inn for me," Anna replied.

When the troupe left Philadelphia, it took some time before Bentura trusted Bull enough to pet him. In contrast, the German men were used to dogs and warmed up quickly to Bull.

Bull survived on scraps of food from whatever table he was near. He ate about anything thrown his way and had caught rabbits in the woods, which he ate. Bull was growing fast, but would never have an ounce of fat on his body, because he was constantly foraging and looking for whatever he could find to consume. Henry paid little attention to what his dog found to eat.

Along the way, Bull lunged into the nearby woods, chasing anything that moved.

"I had a shepherd dog in Germany," Zook mentioned. "He kept the wolves away from the animals on our farm."

"Bull keeps the critters away from our farm," Henry replied. With plenty of time on their hands, Funk explained what he knew about the lost medallion, and how Anna had trained Bull to find it.

"The Saint Bernard dogs in Switzerland, where my people came from," Yoder replied, "would help to find those who were lost in the snow."

Atop her horse, Anna tried to mask her sickness, struggling to keep from throwing up. She was relieved to get to the Freedom Inn and lie down in private for a moment.

The proprietor at the inn questioned Henry about Ben Franklin's article that disparaged the German immigrants. "He called you 'dumb Germans,' " the owner commented.

"I'm not sure why," Henry responded. "Franklin came to my farm, ate a meal with me, and came to our wedding. He seemed to enjoy the visits."

"He says that the English culture is superior to the German culture." Noticing the plain clothes and unkempt beards of the men who traveled with Funk, the owner asked, "Germans?"

"Yes," Henry answered. "Just got off the boat yesterday."

Assessing that only Yoder knew any English, the manager scowled at the two travelers and replied, "Maybe Franklin was right. Why are men like this coming to Pennsylvania? This is an English colony."

"My people seek religious freedom," Henry replied.

"No, your people want to get rich," the owner insisted. "You Germans just want to make money. You claim religious persecution drives you out of Germany. I'd say the black topsoil of Indian Creek and Lancaster pulls you Mennonites here, like deer to a salt lick. 'Dumb Germans' might be just about right," the owner concluded, staring at the two plain men. "They can't even understand what I'm talking about. That's why the tensions in Indian Creek are rising."

"The Indians are the restless ones," Henry responded.

"No, there are too many Germans," the owner answered.

By noon, Henry's parents had arrived on Indian Creek, followed by a number of neighbors.

"This is tragic!" Jubilant exclaimed.

While the logs still burned, Mr. Funk stated that Henry and Anna could live in the mill or move in with them until they built a new house.

"It's okay," Annie Kolb consoled Abe. "There's really nothing you could have done about it."

"I wish I would have awakened earlier."

"You were in your deepest sleep part of the night," Mr. Kolb stated.

"We'll have to all pitch in and help them rebuild."

When the travelers got close to the farm, they made their last turn onto a dirt road that led into the heart of Indian Creek. Bull charged ahead, recognizing where they were.

Abe Swartz walked out to meet the Funks when he saw the mastiff arrive.

Abe stopped Henry and Anna and announced, "I have very bad news."

The Funks stared after Swartz told them about the fire.

"Our house burned?" Henry finally said.

"Just after midnight I smelled smoke, and by the time I got up and looked out, the house was in flames."

It was a very somber finish to the Philadelphia trip when Henry and Anna came to the smoldering ruins of their former house. Anna, still sick, slumped on the ground and wept.

Henry sat with her on the grass, shadows lengthening in the dusk which settled on their Indian Creek farm. Henry could only bow his head and pray to God who had been his source of living and direction for thirty-five years. Henry's mind swirled with thoughts of the Great Spirit that the Indians had called out to at the burial recently. He remembered the prayers offered for him when he had left Amsterdam seven years earlier. With good times always came bad, Henry pondered. The evil forces that the Indians tried to scare away seemed more powerful than the good spirits. Even when people tried to work in the power of God, it felt like evil often overwhelmed the good.

Henry pondered the meaning of his life verse, in which the apostle prayed that his readers could work in God's power and so live in dreams and hopes inspired by their faith. Henry had attempted to build a home, a marriage, a church, and grow his dreams. Turning, Henry noticed his mill, fully intact. The thought of his wooden gears arriving in the fall seemed far away and small in light of the prospect of rebuilding his house.

Jubilant came and sat on the ground next to the couple, and Little John bounded into Henry's arms. "We're so sorry," Jubilant consoled. "By the time you rebuild, you'll have your own baby."

Henry turned to the Indian woman who had become like a second mother to him. Jubilant had cared for him ever since he had begun to carve out a farm on Indian Creek. She had been so gracious, and now she knew just how to speak and what not to say.

"Well, folks," Henry began, jumping to his feet. Around him were his brothers, his parents, the Kolbs, William and Jubilant, Abe, Little John, Anna, Bentura, and the two men who had climbed off a ship just two days earlier. Even in the midst of sadness, he couldn't help but notice the pretty Annie Beth Kolb. Women, he thought, always his temptation.

"I still have our deed!" Henry declared.

Reaching into his pocket he retrieved the deed to the Funk farm. "We took it along to Philadelphia," Henry exclaimed. "We still have Governor Keith's seal on our deed—corn and grapes."

"Folks," Henry continued, "This is Bentura, now a free man. Along with us are Zook and Yoder, from Germany."

"Where shall we begin?" one of Henry's brothers asked.

"With the house?" Henry asked.

"Yes, we're ready to begin tomorrow."

Looking around in the evening shadows, Funk pondered how to respond with everyone waiting for his instructions. Glancing at the dam in the creek, now barely visible, Henry declared, "Stone."

Anna glanced up at him with a puzzled look.

"Our next house will be built with Indian Creek stone," Henry stated. Stone houses were built in Philadelphia, but few this far out from the capital.

Turning to the group around him, Henry asked, "Who's a mason?"

No one responded until Zook stepped forward. "My father is a mason in Germany. I've helped him and learned the basics of masonry."

"Anna needs a bed," Henry concluded, "and it's been a long day, but Zook, I want you to think about whether you will build our stone house."

"Give me the night to think about it," Zook responded. Glancing at his traveling partner, he said, "It changes everything for us if I build your house."

"We'll talk in the morning," Henry concluded.

"There's too many men in that mill tonight," Jubilant told Anna. "You come to my house. William, you'll sleep with the horses."

Four days later, after the fire had gone out and after cleaning away the charred ashes of the log house, what seemed like a small army of men dug at a new foundation for a stone house. The new foundation followed the outline of the log house, only bigger. Bentura, Zook, Abe Swartz, and the Funk brothers used the tools they had and clawed at the ground to dig a foundation deep enough. Zook took depth measurements and told the men to keep digging.

During a lunch break under the trees by the creek, Zook and Yoder had a discussion with Henry.

"In the hymnal we used at your church yesterday," Yoder began, "there's a song of hope for you."

"You know the hymnal?" Henry asked.

"It's the same one we use in Germany," Yoder answered.

"Henry, look!" Anna called out, "pelicans!"

Everyone turned to see two white pelicans gliding into the stream. They came occasionally to fish in Indian Creek, and when they arrived, with their wide wing span and graceful flight, everyone looked.

"Number seventy-one in the hymnal talks about our prayers in the midst of difficult times, like the burning of your house. The lyrics express that God will hear our prayers, like the Pelican's young when they trust in their parents to bring them fish."

"I'll have to look at the hymn when I get a chance," Henry answered. "My copy of the hymnal burned, but my parents have a copy."

"On our barn in Germany we painted a family crest," Yoder responded. "It has a pelican and stalk of wheat. With trust in God, you'll be restored."

"I'm not sure about God's work here," Henry stated. "I'll be restored with hard work, it seems to me. Let's get back to the trenches, men, and dig."

Zook, Yoder, and Funk had drawn up an agreement. The scouts would go to Lancaster to see the farms and test the soil. They wanted to see what opportunities there were in that region. Their community had paid their way, and they wanted to follow through on their assigned tasks.

But Zook agreed to come back in a week from Lancaster and spend the summer and fall helping to build the foundation and walls. "When you get to the roof," Zook said, "you have others who can build."

"I'll pay you well," Funk responded.

"Yoder will return to Germany in a few weeks, as planned," Zook concluded.

"Any idea what the Funk family crest is?" Henry wondered.

"I have no idea," Zook answered.

When the pelicans took off for another place to fish, Bull began to bark.

The Lenape Indians walking up the trail halted in their tracks. They did not like the big dog.

Anna, not feeling very well, saw the Lenape coming up the farm trail, but walked as best she could to meet Lenape Mother and her braves.

Henry hoped they had come in peace. He'd have to wait to find out, because Anna sat down under the trees and talked with her people. Henry returned to digging a foundation.

14

Foundation

June 1725

The Lenape visitors to the Funk farm included a young woman who had joined a dozen braves and Lenape Mother. The young woman's presence puzzled Anna.

Seated under a large tree along the trail, Lenape Mother expressed sadness at the loss of Anna's house.

"Thank you," Anna replied. "We have no idea how the fire began. There was no lightning, we had extinguished our lamp, and there was no stove fire."

"We are so sorry," Lenape Mother continued. "We heard of your bad news and came to encourage you as our friends in Indian Creek."

"You are our friends," Anna replied.

"If someone started your house on fire," Lenape Mother insisted, "it was not one of my braves."

Looking at the pretty squaw, Anna asked, "Why did she come along?"

"My scouts noticed that the black man is among your workers on the farm."

"Bentura is a free man," Anna answered. "He hopes to return to Aruba, his home."

"Anna, Cool Water met the black man at your wedding, they liked each other, and loved," Lenape Mother smiled.

"Are you here to see Bentura?" Anna smiled.

"I am," the girl responded.

"She wants to marry him," Lenape Mother added. "We have come to see if the black man wants to marry her."

Henry helped dig for a while, and realized it was inconsiderate of him not to join Anna and their neighbors. Wandering into the circle, Henry greeted Lenape Mother and inquired about their reason for coming.

"They're here to express sorrow at our loss," Anna interpreted.

"Do they have any ideas how it started?"

"No," Anna replied. "They've told me none of their braves would have started a fire at our house."

Henry looked at the eyes of every brave in the circle and believed them. The thought crossed his mind that he had been far too trusting in the past, so he hoped that his conclusion about the braves' sincerity was not naive.

"They've come for another reason," Anna smiled.

Henry had noticed the very pretty Indian woman with the men and Lenape Mother. Henry usually noticed women; it was just something that happened.

"Why has she come?" Henry asked.

"She and Bentura met at our wedding. She likes him and they've come to see if he'll marry her."

"Marry him?"

"They've made love, Henry, and she likes him."

"What? How can you just come and ask to get married?" Henry asked.

"What's wrong with that?" Anna quizzed.

"Don't you have to court, or get to know the families, or do things together before you get married?" Henry wondered.

"In your land, maybe, but here in Indian Creek marriage is a community event, and is about having children."

"He's black and she's Indian," Henry replied.

"That's not a problem here," Anna continued. "Black men have married Indian women before in the Schuylkill River region. He's a strong man, able to be with a woman, and she likes him. What else matters?"

Henry looked up the hill at his workers digging a foundation and noticed Bentura glistening from sweat in the hot June sun. "Let me talk to him," Henry said.

"Bentura, a squaw that you met at our wedding has come to see you."

The recently freed man smiled at the small crowd gathered under the big tree.

"Do you want to see her?"

"Yes!"

"Go get cleaned up in the stream," Henry continued. "You don't want to smell bad when you meet her."

"Okay." Bentura sprinted to the mill, grabbed a change of clothes and ran upstream to a private spot where men waded in and washed. The speedy Bentura had been noticed by the Lenape under the tree.

"I want to go to him now," the squaw said, standing.

"Wait," Anna cautioned. "He'll come to you soon."

As the men dug for a foundation, Little John fell in the trench and everyone laughed. He cried out, but he soon began to investigate the dirt, picking up a worm.

Bull barked when the Lenape came to the job site, but Henry chased him away and demanded silence from the dog.

It didn't take long for the young Indian woman and Bentura to meet. In Indian Creek, courtship often did not take very long. Bentura and the squaw smiled at each other.

Anna got right to the point. "They've all come to see if you want to marry her."

Bentura was the kindest man one could ever meet but he was thoughtful and reflective. His muscular arms and strapping biceps were attractive to any woman, but especially the eager young squaw who stood by his side.

"Let's all go to the stream," Henry called out. "I'm hot and hungry. We welcome our guests from the Perkiomen Creek," Henry concluded.

Mrs. Funk, Henry's mother, had chicken pot pies ready for everyone in the shade. She'd make them stretch for the additional guests. In the pies were onions, potatoes, carrots, eggs, and chicken. Though they had added a dozen people, there seemed to be enough food for all.

"Bentura says he will!" Anna exclaimed.

Everyone in the circle understood what Anna meant, and they clapped.

"Tonight," Henry stood and talked, "we'll marry Bentura and his squaw." A rumble in the distance turned heads. Storm clouds were moving their way, and it would soon rain.

"We need two things to happen before our evening celebration of Bentura and Cool Water," Henry continued. "Lenape Mother tells me a man who marries a Lenape woman needs to kill a deer, which Bentura has never done. Two braves will go with him into the woods to hunt and bring us venison for the celebration." A cheer went up from the workers and the Lenape.

"Second, I've realized for a time that I have very few trees on the Funk farm, except on the forest at the edges. We cut them down to clear our land for farming. I want an elm tree to plant at the celebration to mark the marriage of these two. Who can find a sapling in the woods to bring this evening?"

Two braves stood, told Anna they could do that, in Lenape, and took off for the woods.

Rain fell on the Funk farm, and except for the hunters and the two braves finding an elm, folks quickly took cover in the mill. Rain soon pounded on the wooden shingles.

In Philadelphia, Fifteen Feathers met in the city council conference room with James Logan and Governor Keith.

"Three farm houses across the Schuylkill have gone up in smoke," Logan began. "Are the Lenape on the warpath?"

"They're probably lone wolf attacks," Shickellamy responded. He had not taken off his fifteen feather headband and carried a commanding presence. "The Lenape braves are not ready to fight yet," he concluded.

"Your task is to keep the Delaware Indians in place," the governor stated, "and if possible, moving to the west."

"The Iroquois Confederacy is fully in charge," Shickellamy answered. "If the Lenape go on the rampage, we will know, and we can pressure them to stop."

"The farmhouse burning events are troublesome to me," Logan reflected. "German settlers are going to get worried about building on the frontier."

"Henry Funk is building a stone house to replace his log house that burned," Fifteen Feathers answered. "That will encourage settlers, not discourage them."

"You have an amazing network, Chief. You know details long before we know them in the capital," the governor reflected.

"My men are situated throughout the Schuylkill region," Shickellamy answered. "I hear news in hours, while it takes days for your news to be delivered."

"He's being paid well," Logan informed the governor. "He should know what's going on. Should we talk to Lapowinsa?"

"We don't need to," the chief answered. "I have things firmly in control along Indian Creek."

"Governor, did you hear the story about the gold watch Funk's wife found in the Courthouse?"

"I did, James. I'm not sure what William Penn ever did to try and find the medallion," Keith answered.

With a stone face that came from many years of ordering braves around and seeing some killed, Shickellamy responded, "Peace is kept with an iron hand of force, not some silly medallion."

Governor Keith and James Logan, both Quaker, looked at the chief with surprise, not having heard him talk like this before.

"Logan and Keith, the Iroquois Confederation is more powerful than all your colonial governments combined. If the Iroquois decided to take control of Pennsylvania forests again, we could. Not even your king in England could prevent that."

Governor Keith pushed back his papers and rose to leave. "Logan, I have other work to do."

Six months after inquiring in Philadelphia about their missing daughter, Grietje and Cornelius Meyer landed back at their home in Aruba. In Santa Cruz, the capital, they explained to their family that Anna was nowhere to be found. No one in Philadelphia or Amsterdam had seen or heard from her.

"She was always ready to try new things," Anna's mother lamented. "She may have married an Indian."

"Or a pirate," her father added.

"Well, maybe she married a Mennonite like my mother did," Anna's grandmother concluded. "Anna's a little wild, but she's smart."

In the mountains above the Meyer print shop in the Dutch provincial capital, Bentura's family also wondered what happened to their son. When he had been sold, it was completely uncertain where the ship had gone. They too could only hope that one day they would see him again.

Bentura's hunt for a whitetail deer was unsuccessful at first. He carried a gun, as did the two braves with him, but he felt clumsy with the weapon since he had never hunted. During the downpour, they tried to stay under trees, but still they got wet. The trio sat under an imposing oak, but nothing was moving in the rain.

When the rain subsided, they walked toward the west. The braves knew where the salt lick was located that they used to draw in deer. The braves noticed that Bentura walked loudly, scaring off anything that heard them coming. Of course the further they got from the Funk farm, the longer it would take to return with the venison.

On a ridge where they looked back and could still see the Funk farm, the braves motioned for Bentura to sit and wait. The men operated mostly with sign language, as they had no common language to speak.

When the storm moved away, and the sun came out, Bentura became hopeful that he might spot a deer. If they walked down the other side of this ridge, carrying the kill to the farm would become difficult.

Bentura's guides sat still for what seemed like a long time, but then a buck appeared to the men. If he moved, Bentura figured, the deer would bolt, so they sat motionless. When the deer lowered its head to eat, Bentura raised his gun and fired, wounding it.

The gunshot stirred other braves who had been watching them, and while Bentura and one brave chased the fleeing deer, the third warrior pursued the braves who had been hiding in the bushes.

Bentura and his guide soon located the fallen deer, and the Lenape warrior cleaned the animal with ease, having done the work many times before. By the time Bentura was ready to hoist the carcass on his shoulders, the second brave returned and spoke in animated terms to his partner, which the soon-to-be groom could not understand. They looked concerned.

"Why do you want an elm tree?" Anna asked Henry.

"This little tree," Henry responded, "represents the peace treaty between William Penn, the 'Great Miquon,' and the Lenape Indians from forty-two years ago."

"Are we going to sign a peace treaty?" Anna grinned.

"No, but we are going to marry Bentura and Cool Water. Why not recommit to the peace terms of an earlier generation?"

"We need Chief Lapowinsa," Anna declared. "His father was there."

"They met under an elm tree," Henry continued. "This is my statement to work at peace on the Funk farm."

"It will take years for this sapling to grow," Anna responded.

"Peace takes a long time, even generations." Patting her little baby bulge, Henry commented, "I hope our children and grandchildren will enjoy the shade of this tree."

William and Jubilant got the fire going, expecting they'd have venison to turn over it soon. Excitement rose when Bentura triumphantly marched onto the festive farm with his kill. A wedding was going to take place!

Lenape Mother and Henry huddled with Bentura and Cool Water.

"Can this be an Indian ceremony?" Lenape Mother asked. Bentura nodded his approval, caring little about how the event unfolded.

"Just get us married," Bentura said. "I don't care how you do it."

"We'll have a big dance," Lenape Mother continued. "You need to dance for us," she explained looking at Bentura. "When someone from outside the Lenape comes in, we watch them dance."

"Okay," Bentura agreed.

"Do you want a Christian blessing?" Henry asked the couple. Neither claimed to be Christian, though Bentura indicated it would be fine. "I've never been baptized," the Aruban concluded.

"Bentura, will you continue to work for me?" Henry asked. "I need your help."

Bentura looked at Cool Water before responding.

"If I work for you, where will we live?"

"They can build a wigwam on our property, right Henry?" Anna offered.

Cool Water curled up next to Bentura, looked into his eyes, and purred, "That sounds fine to me."

"And it's okay with our people," Lenape Mother added.

Henry looked around his property, wondering where to build such a wigwam.

"How about next to your little elm?" Anna wondered.

"The venison's ready," Jubilant interrupted.

"Let the party begin," Henry announced.

A dozen Lenape warriors began to dance around the fire. They wove into the food area, taking bites of the venison, then moved around the fire in a rhythmic, hypnotic fashion.

Henry began to hear musical harmonies again. It was the most intriguing sound he had heard in Indian Creek. He loved to sing, and did so with the community at church, but always in unison. He heard something different, so unique that it brought him great joy. Voices singing other sounds that united with the main voice—he was enthralled.

Before he could have further profound thoughts, Anna pulled him into the dance circle and Henry had to try. He gave it his best, but his upbringing in Germany had not included training in dance.

Eating venison and other food items from the table and the fire at the marriage of Cool Water to Bentura made events on the Funk farm a celebration of black, white, and red. A special unity of three cultures met in such a way that the relationships were open and strong.

Late into the night, with the fire dying, Lenape Mother whispered into Bentura's ear. He looked puzzled but did not refuse her request.

With her nod, each brave felt Bentura's black skin, which had been so rare in the Indian Creek region. They squeezed his skin to ensure that his black color wasn't painted on, and that Cool Water's husband's skin felt like their own.

Another whisper from Lenape Mother left Bentura even more puzzled, but still agreeable. With a signal from the older woman, the men danced with Bentura in the lead.

"This is a Lenape tradition," Anna whispered. When Bentura's marriage dance ended, Cool Water whisked him away and all clapped.

The two warriors who had accompanied Bentura into the woods to hunt for a deer sat down with Lenape Mother, Henry, and Anna.

Anna understood the men to say that they were being watched, which she relayed to Henry. "They're not sure if the braves they saw were Oneida or another tribe of the Iroquois Confederation."

In the dark, Henry looked toward the ridge where the men pointed. The Native American presence on Indian Creek apparently included more than Lenape Indians.

"I'm tired, Anna. Let's go to our little corner of the mill."

William put out the fire while the braves peered deep into the woods to see if there were eyes looking back at them.

15

Feathers

July 1725

"You spend a lot of time with that Bible," Anna stated.

"It's the good book," Henry answered. "Look what I found."

"Okay, amaze me with your wisdom."

"It says here to 'write it in a book,' Anna. This verse gives me inspiration."

"You've got a problem, Henry. You don't have a desk, paper, or a pen. How are you going to write?"

"I don't have an inkwell, either, Anna. Somehow we'll get those things again."

"Henry, you should write in a book about what's happening here."

"What are you talking about?" Henry responded.

"We have an African man helping to lay up stones for our house. We have German builders and an Indian woman who lives in a wigwam next to our new house. That's three cultures on our farm."

"Which of those are you, Anna?"

"I'm not sure, Henry. Maybe I'm a combination of all of them.

"Know what's amazing?" Henry asked.

"What?"

"You are, Anna. I just wish we had a place to go where we could be alone, so I guess we better get this house finished."

Other than the Lenape, Abe Swartz was the best hunter along Indian

Creek, and Anna turned to him for help.

"I want goose feathers for Henry to write with, Abe. Can you get some?"

"Probably, but the birds are practically sacred to the Indians."

"I need the biggest feathers," Anna continued.

"Getting them will be a challenge," Abe responded.

"See what you can do, Abe. I'd appreciate it."

Bull had followed Anna and Abe to Indian Creek, and scared the geese away that they were looking at.

"Take that dog back to the house with you, Anna," Abe laughed.

"Have you seen what he does?" Anna asked. Turning, she threw her gold trinket up the hill toward the stone house.

"You still have that?" Abe quizzed. "Your house burned down."

"I had it tied around my neck when we went to Philadelphia."

When Bull returned with the gold trinket, Abe remarked, "I should teach that dog to hunt."

"He already does, Abe. Bull's hunting for the gold medallion."

Anna met Henry's father in his small log workshop.

"Can you make a new desk?" Anna began.

"Your husband certainly needs one," Mr. Funk replied.

"Yes, and either I find someone to build one, or we need to purchase a desk and haul it from Philadelphia."

"I may be able to do something for you," Mr. Funk answered. "It'll take me a few weeks, since we're in the middle of harvest."

"I'd be very grateful."

"Anna, may I ask you a personal question?"

"Sure."

"Have you been baptized?"

Anna had wondered how long it would take until someone in the Funk family asked her this question.

"Yes, in the Santa Cruz chapel."

"You were a baby, I presume?" Mr. Funk asked.

"Yes," Anna answered. "Our family had a heritage of Mennonite belief, but the only church in my hometown was Catholic, and I was baptized as a baby."

"That's what I had guessed," Mr. Funk replied.

"You'd like to see me baptized again, wouldn't you?" Anna inquired.

"Well, perhaps. You think about it and anytime you want to talk more about it, let me know."

"Right here is where I'm going to write my book about this place," Henry remarked to Anna.

"This place?"

Seeing her piercing eyes, Henry corrected himself. "Our place, Anna."

Standing in the middle of their home, with stone walls rising outside wood interior walls and a wooden floor, Henry pointed out where their two bedrooms would be, his study, their kitchen, and living area.

"What if we have a lot of kids?" Anna asked. "Where will we keep them?"

"There will be a big open loft area that should be room enough for children."

Abe Swartz and Bentura worked at the interior walls and floor, while Zook worked on the stone exterior. The novice mason worked patiently, using stones from Indian Creek, but also bringing stones in from a more distant limestone quarry that others had used to acquire stone. The Funk home would not be the first Indian Creek house to be built of stone.

With a playful push, Anna challenged her husband, which she knew he enjoyed, coming from her. "Get your book written about our place."

Henry looked around and laughed. "No desk, no pens, no ink, no..."

"Okay, write it in your head until you get some paper."

James Logan galloped to the Funk farm on the third Wednesday of July. With him came two sweating law enforcement officials.

Ignoring pleasantries, Logan got right to the point. "The chief escaped, Henry. His braves broke him out. Have you seen him?"

"Not around here," Henry answered.

"Can you ask the men who work for you?"

"I can," Henry answered. Looking around, Logan saw men working at various places on the Funk farm.

"I meant right now," Logan insisted. The chief justice rode without his usual wig, and he growled his order the moment he got off his horse.

"Anna, can you gather the men?" Henry asked his wife.

With a glare at Logan, Anna turned and began rounding up all the workers.

Bentura took the Philadelphia rider's horses to be watered at the mill pond while others gathered round.

"Chief Lapowinsa's out of jail and we're looking for him," Logan lectured. "Has anyone here seen him?"

No one moved or volunteered any information to the Philadelphia official. The men stood in the July heat and sweated, patiently listening.

"Mr. Logan, none of these men have been away from this farm in several weeks," Henry explained.

Logan stared beyond Henry at the young Indian woman behind him. "You had a wedding about three weeks ago for the slave and an Indian, Henry. Is this the woman?"

Henry turned and noticed Cool Water. "This woman married Bentura, a free man. They live in the tent beside our unfinished house."

Logan turned to Anna and instructed her to ask the Indian woman if she knew anything about the whereabouts of the chief.

"You can talk to her if you want to," Anna retorted.

Fuming, Logan repeated himself. "Ask her," he demanded.

Anna slowly walked to Cool Water and said a few words in Lenape, which Logan could not understand.

"She knows nothing about the chief," Anna seethed.

"What did she say?" Logan demanded.

"Why didn't you listen to what she said?" Anna responded.

"Anna Funk, you will get on your horse and ride with me to the Lenape village," Logan demanded.

"Ride with you?" Henry interrupted.

"You can come along if you want to," Logan replied.

"She's my wife and we have work to do here."

"I've put her in jail before, and I can do so again," Logan sneered.

Bull sensed trouble and began barking at Logan and his men. The Philadelphia men backed up when Bull challenged them and stood at his full height. No one did anything to stop the dog, and the three visitors weren't sure if they were going to be attacked by the guard dog.

Bull continued to bark at Logan until the justice asked for help from Anna and Henry.

"Show me what's in your pocket," Anna countered. "Bull and I want to see what's in there," pointing to his vest.

"My watch," Logan offered.

"Bull's looking for the gold medallion," Anna declared. "And you're looking for the chief. Good thing I've got Bull to protect me."

"Get our horses," Logan ordered one of his men.

"Show us the watch," Anna insisted.

Logan glared but revealed his watch. Bull waited for a signal from Anna, but none came.

Henry broke the tension. "Mr. Logan, Anna and I will ride with you to the Lenape village. But I'd prefer you ask rather than order us around."

Logan watched his man bring the horses, and softened a bit. "Henry, would you and Anna ride with us?"

"Logan, do you know Anna's pregnant?"

"I thought so," Logan replied.

"Will you take it easy on the ride, since she's with child?"

"I will."

It caused a stir in the Lenape village of about fifty people when Logan, his men, and the Funks rode in. The mastiff bounded in along with the horses, and the Indians kept an eye on the dog at the same time they watched Logan and his men.

Anna quickly explained to Lenape Mother and several braves what Logan was there for, and they turned to glare at him.

"Do they know where the chief is?" Logan asked, in a considerably softer tone than when he had started on the Funk farm. Logan knew he was totally at Anna's mercy to translate for him.

"They don't have information for you," Anna replied.

"Do any of them know where he is?"

Anna turned and talked to Lenape Mother. "Logan, they don't know where their chief is today."

"Well, then where is he?" Logan yelled in exasperation.

Bull barked at the Philadelphia visitor.

"Let's ride," Logan ordered. With that he and his men wheeled and galloped away.

Henry and Anna were invited to stay and eat, and they accepted.

During the meal Lenape Mother, the braves, and Anna speculated how Chief Lapowinsa got out and where he was.

Anna informed them that Cool Water was doing well and seemed to love Bentura more each day.

"Would your braves let one of my workers take a goose from the creek so I can get feathers for Henry to write with?"

"Miquon Funk!" one of the braves rose and exclaimed.

"They laugh at your desire to write, Henry."

Henry smiled and didn't object to the joking at his expense. Lenape Mother, however, stood and snapped at the men, and they sat back down, wiping the laughter from their faces.

"Good thing you have me here," Anna winked at Henry. "Otherwise you might not get out of here very easily."

Turning to the braves, Anna told them she had a trick to show them. "Bull's helping us look for the medallion," she explained. "Watch."

When Bull exploded in pursuit of the trinket that Anna threw, the men gawked. They had not seen a dog trained in this way. With the trinket back in her hand, covered with the dog's slobber, the braves began to smile.

"We can find the medallion," Anna explained, "if we can get Bull into the area where it's hidden."

"Do it again," one of the braves begged.

"You throw it," Anna offered the brave.

When the Lenape warrior rose and threw the trinket, Bull just looked but didn't move.

Henry watched the unfolding saga and wondered what would happen next.

When Anna retrieved the gold piece and threw it over the heads of the seated braves, Bull practically leaped over the cowering men, who turned to watch the dog pick up the cheap object and return it to Anna, begging for more.

Anna laughed, Henry began to laugh, and so did the braves.

Wiping the dog's slobber from it, she hung it around her neck again, said goodbye to Lenape Mother and the braves, motioned to Henry, and they mounted their horses and rode back to their farm.

"Good thing you have me," Anna offered. "Ever heard what they do to white men when they capture them?"

"No, tell me."

"If I did, Henry, you'd faint. Just ride."

"Anna, some men get drunk on rum, and they go crazy. You know what I'm drunk on?"

Looking at the German farmer riding on a horse next to her, Anna, from the Caribbean, couldn't figure out where this conversation was going.

"Anna, I'm drunk on your love."

She was twenty, with child, two thousand miles from her parents, and riding through the woods in colonial Pennsylvania. First she blushed, and then she cried.

Stopping, Henry embraced his bride.

"Henry, we have no privacy, we're newlyweds, and we're working so hard to build a house. When do we get time for each other?"

Judging why Anna had tears, Henry ventured a guess. "You miss your parents, don't you?"

"A little," Anna acknowledged.

A gentle July rain began, kept safely away by the big trees over them with massive branches and full foliage.

Henry reached in his saddlebag and pulled out a blanket. The horses fed on grass, and Bull guarded the trail while Henry and Anna fell into each other's arms. Wrapped in the blanket, they became entwined in the glories of the love between a man and his new bride.

At the Freedom Inn, Logan asked the owner if he knew anything about the escaped chief. None of the men there, including Adam Miller, who seemed to live at the inn, knew anything.

"How did the Indians break him free?" the owner asked.

"No one saw anything—he just vanished," Logan reflected.

"Where would he go?" Miller wondered.

"I wish someone could tell me the answer to that," Logan responded. "The governor is not going to be very happy with my lack of results on this mission."

"If I was you," a frontiersman listening in offered, "I'd put dogs on his trail and track the Indian. If the hounds can get his scent, he'd get caught."

"You think so?" Logan wondered.

"I've got two dogs," the man responded. "They can follow a trail."

"Can I hire you?" Logan asked.

"Be glad to try and catch an Indian," the man offered. "The Indians killed a man who hunted with me in the woods a while back."

"Can you meet me at the courthouse tomorrow?" Logan asked. "Lapowinsa left a couple of things in the cell. Maybe your dogs could pick up a trail from that."

"I'll be there."

At noon the next day, a roughly dressed and unshaven woodsman with two hounds came into the courthouse in downtown Philadelphia. Logan and the governor met him.

"Here are his things," Logan offered.

"Let's take the dogs into his cell as well," the dog's owner suggested. "Anyone else stayed in here since the chief was here?"

"No," Logan replied.

The dogs looked hungry, which is the way good hunting dogs were kept in the rugged frontier of colonial Pennsylvania. It made them eager for a chase.

"Go!" the man hollered outside the door, and the hounds took off with a flourish, picking up a trail that headed due north.

"I just came from up north," Logan complained to the governor. Mounting quickly, he gestured at the dogs and the hunter who had already headed out of town. "Let's see what those howling mutts can find."

16

Hunt

July 1725

Early on Friday morning, Bull began to bark.

When the dog wouldn't be quiet, Henry had to get up from his bed and take a look. The first rays of the sun peeked through the darkness while Bull barked into the woods.

Henry heard dogs in the distance, two of them, coming toward the farm. By now he had been in the colonial American woods long enough to recognize the distinct baying of coon dogs. Farmers would keep the dogs to track raccoons and other animals. The farmer would listen to where the dogs went and could usually tell when the prey had been treed.

What was unusual about this early morning hunt was that woodsmen rarely worked at this time of the day. The middle of the night, when it was dark, was the best time to track raccoons.

Bull continued to bark and loped to the edge of the clearing, as it became clear the tracking dogs were going to run right by the Funk farm. Henry was puzzled by the early morning hunt but he also noticed that the hounds looked up from their trailing long enough to notice the huge mastiff barking at them.

There was something different about these hounds than the usual coon dogs he had seen before. They had huge heads, black snouts, and a determined gait that told everyone they were on a hunt.

Henry had a chilling thought that these dogs may be chasing a person, perhaps a slave. Or maybe the escaped chief.

A short time later, in the quiet of the morning, Henry heard horses that he believed were likely trailing the dogs, two or perhaps three of them. Henry came to the edge of the clearing with Bull to see who would come riding by.

Henry turned to see Bentura coming toward him, having also been awakened by the commotion. The Aruban's eyes were big and wide-eyed with concern. "What's going on, Henry?"

"Not sure, looks like there's a hunt going on," Henry answered. "I'd guess they're chasing a person, not a coon."

"You think it might be a fugitive, Henry?"

"Could be, Bentura. More likely they're chasing Lapowinsa."

James Logan wheeled on his horse and pulled the reins hard on his sweating horse. "We're chasing the Indian. Do you know anything about him coming through here?"

"No, I don't, Logan," Henry answered.

Without a further word, Logan turned and flicked his reins, and the trail dog owner and another deputy charged after the baying dogs.

By now, Abe Swartz had been roused from his sleep and came to join the men. Little John trailed along.

"Want to ride with me?" Henry asked.

"What's going on?"

"Logan and two men are chasing blood hounds that are apparently trailing Chief Lapowinsa," Henry answered.

"Bentura, can you and your wife look after Little John?" Abe asked.

"Sure."

With that Abe and Henry each grabbed a couple of pieces of bread, their hats and guns, and saddled up their horses as fast as they could. Hearing the dogs baying in the distance, they rode off into the woods, with Bull right beside them.

It didn't take very long until it seemed like the hounds up ahead had treed their prey, whatever or whomever it was.

Abe and Henry heard shots fired in the woods, which seemed to come from the land Swartz had recently purchased from the Pennsylvania colonial government. This hunt was taking place on his land, and both men figured they had a right to find out what was going on.

When more shots rang out, Henry urged his horse on faster, and Bull just stretched out his gait a little longer to keep up.

Logan stood underneath a tree and was loading his gun when Henry and Abe Swartz rode up and dismounted. A dead Indian warrior lay nearby in the weeds. Up in the tree was Chief Lapowinsa, with his distinctive face markings, having climbed the tree out of desperation to get away from the howling dogs.

"You can't just shoot him," Henry hollered.

"Watch me," Logan growled.

Lifting his gun, Logan became distracted by a vicious dog fight. The hounds were not pleased with the mastiff's intrusion on their hunt. The fight turned so violent it literally shoved Logan away from his spot under the tree. The frontiersman and Abe Swartz waded into the snarling dogs to try and separate them, while Logan and Funk watched both the dog fight and the chief in the tree.

"Just catch him, Logan, and bring him to my farm until you can take him back to his cell," Henry bargained.

"We chased him all night, and he's a fugitive from the law."

"He's a chief and if you shoot him, the entire Schuylkill River region will erupt in flames. Every home of both Germans and English will be at risk of attack. You're not going be able to defend killing the chief in front of the governor. You need him alive," Henry insisted.

Abe finally managed to shove the mastiff away from the angry hounds. He used his gun crosswise to keep the barking Bull away from the hounds. It was completely unclear to the men trying to stop the fight which side had the upper hand, but none wanted the dogs to fight to the death, which they very well might do.

Logan eyed the chief in the tree, who had few options in terms of going higher or coming down. Logan would be entirely within the law to gun his fugitive down right here, since he had escaped and fled.

"Logan, if you take him alive, Swartz and I will help you get him back to the jail. I have a rope in my bag and we can tie him up. Make him walk to the mill and we'll tie him to the hitching post."

"If any braves along Indian Creek see him tied up, it will be worse than if I just shoot him here," Logan grunted.

A hail of arrows shot through the air, landing all around the men and dogs. A half dozen braves stood on the nearby ridge and were aiming at them.

"Let them have it," Logan ordered. The deputy and frontiersman turned their guns and began to fire at the Indians.

When the braves retreated from the blazing guns, Logan ordered Funk to get the chief on his horse fast and tie him up.

The chief understood enough English and German words to realize that he was supposed to get on the horse, which he did. Swartz and the blood hounds' owner kept the dogs away. With Lapowinsa in Funk's saddle, the deputy tied him up tight. Logan kept his gun trained on the ridge in case the braves returned.

They did. Another barrage of arrows rained into the area while the men milled around the horses and dogs. Henry Funk ducked behind a small tree and Swartz flattened out behind a fallen tree trunk. The deputy collapsed in his tracks and bled badly from a direct hit, his life oozing out of his wound. Within seconds he stopped breathing.

Logan and the dog owner fired again, and the braves retreated.

"Why don't you and Swartz fire your guns at them?" Logan complained.

"I'll explain some time," Henry responded. "You better get out of here now while you have a chance. I'll bury this man later."

"We'll ride hard to Freedom Inn. I want all you men to go with me on the main trail—that way if we're seen, we have a better chance of getting through."

"I'm not going with you," the owner of the dogs declared.

"What?" Logan retorted.

"You hired me to catch this man, and my work is done."

"I need you to help so I don't lose the chief along the way," Logan replied.

"Pay me now," came the woodsman's stern response. "The longer we stand here, the more likely we get hit with arrows again."

Logan realized he had little bargaining power. He reached into his pack and pulled out the agreed upon wages. While the rough hunter counted the coins, a hail of arrows sliced through the trees again.

The blood hounds' owner got his dogs and horse out of range quickly, but an arrow struck Abe Swartz in the back of his right shoulder, puncturing the bone and flesh. Swartz screamed and slumped over his saddle.

"You've got to hang on, Swartz," Funk declared. "We'll get you back to the mill as quickly as we can."

Logan, Funk, the chief, and a bleeding Swartz rode toward the mill and the main trail.

At mid-morning, the men rode onto the Funk farm and took Swartz off his horse, dragging him up the steps and laying him on his mat.

"Get the doctor," Henry told Anna.

The doctor, such as he was, untrained and with few remedies, came by early afternoon. Abe still had the arrow stuck in his shoulder and lay unconscious.

The only option the doctor had was to pull with all his might and jerk the arrow out of the man. "Get some water and rags," he asked. "We need to clean the wound."

"Henry," Logan insisted, "I didn't shoot the chief because you promised to help me get him back to Philadelphia. We need to ride now."

"I wish you would stay out of our lives," Anna scowled at Logan.

"What I want to know is why that chief came straight for your property when he escaped," Logan barked.

"Come on Logan, let's go," Henry insisted. With a glare at Anna, Logan turned to follow Henry.

"Keep the dog here on the farm," Henry instructed Anna.

Anna took up the task of nursing Abe Swartz's deep wound, which festered and looked bad. Anna's mother-in-law guessed that he might die.

Annie Beth Kolb came and took up watch almost around the clock in the mill, applying poultices to his fevered face. Annie Beth and Jubilant looked after Little John and tried to keep him away from seeing his struggling father. All anyone could do was wait and see if the man was strong enough to pull through.

On the main trail to Freedom Inn, Henry met a messenger from the mill factory in Philadelphia.

"Two of your gear wheels are coming on Tuesday next week," he announced.

"Great," Henry mused aloud, "Abe is sick, I have to ride to Philadelphia with Logan, and you're bringing me gears."

"Logan, could I pay this man to ride with you back to the jail, so I can go back to the farm?"

"No," Logan replied. "I'm holding you to your promise." Turning to the messenger, he said, "I order you to ride with us and help protect this chief from harm."

Logan and the men rode on into Philadelphia, getting there after dark. With the chief still firmly tied, Logan pushed him back into the cell where he had been before, but this time, Logan would have more security on hand. None of the guards had any idea how the Indian got out in the first place.

On Saturday morning, Henry stopped in to see Andrew Bradford, the printer he always went to see.

"What's new in *The Mercury*?" Henry wondered.

"Here's a copy," Bradford offered. "Is it true you had a fire?"

"Yes, my house burned, but we're rebuilding," Henry remarked. Turning, Henry noticed the collection of writing supplies that Bradford offered for sale.

"I need an ink well and quills," Henry remarked, "and paper."

Bradford wrapped Henry's supplies in a small package to add to his saddle bag.

"Wait, Andrew, I didn't realize you sold Bibles."

"Lost yours in the fire?" the printer asked.

"Indeed. Include this German Bible and the King's English version in my package," Henry replied. Examining the new British Empire's Bible, he said, "I need to start reading the Bible in the language of the Pennsylvania commonwealth."

Back on the job site Monday morning after riding from Freedom Inn, Henry learned that Abe was still breathing. He was very happy to see Anna again. Zook had a question for Henry. "Who were the Indians that tried to kill Logan?"

"I sure don't know," Henry replied. "We didn't get a good look at them because we ducked and tried to avoid their arrows."

Looking at the dog lying in the grass, Henry remarked, "Bull probably kept the chief from getting shot. When he picked a fight with the hounds, it distracted Logan long enough for me to convince him not to gun the man out of the tree."

"Why did the chief come to Swartz's land?" Bentura wondered.

"That's a mystery that only the chief can answer," Henry replied. "But he's not talking."

When Henry's brothers brought another long straight log to the farm, which they would use in the roof system, he told them that two mill gears were coming Tuesday morning.

That evening, in their little corner on the second floor of the mill, Henry opened his package for Anna to see what he had purchased. Anna beamed when he opened the package to reveal the ink well, the quills, and the two Bibles. Holding the paper, she said, "Now you can start writing your book about this place."

"Anna, I'm not writing a book about this place. Do you remember what I was working on before the fire?

"Something about baptism."

"And do you remember how I got my book title?"

"My mirror," Anna responded.

"I've got one more thing to show you," Henry continued.

"You bought me another mirror!" Anna beamed.

Anna was learning to love this man more each day. Having skipped the trip to London to find a husband, Anna had taken a chance in the untamed frontier region of colonial Pennsylvania. She had fallen in with the Lenape Indians, with braves who recognized her beauty, and one who wanted to marry her.

But she had ended up on a German farm, married to a Mennonite minister. He was more than a minister, though; he was a writer, and he believed in peace. Henry had told her the story of how Logan wanted him to shoot at the Indians, but he had refused.

Henry wanted to publish books and write them. But he was also a farmer, a mill owner, and a businessman.

"Henry, you're the sweetest man I've ever met."

"How many men have you met?"

Anna sassed, "You think I'm just a young girl who hasn't been around much. I should tell you about the boys and men in Aruba who wanted me. I could have had any man I wanted, Henry, but I want you."

"Did I ever tell you that Governor Keith wanted me to marry his daughter?"

"Well, why didn't you?"

"Because I wanted you, Anna. Now can you give me that mirror?" Henry asked. "Let's look into it together."

"Where's this going?"

"This is our place, Anna, for both of us. This farm is ours, the mill is ours, and my books get written because of your love for me."

"Henry," Anna reflected, "Do you remember that quote you liked so much about liberty and public spirit, from *The Mercury*?"

"Sure, but it burned in the fire," Henry replied.

"I remember it," Anna continued. "I don't know much about the Romans, but Lucan said that we live the noblest when we give ourselves to others, for the good of society."

"Great memory," Henry said. "Now what's your point?"

"I'm saying you're pretty lucky I talked to you at the harvest dance,"

Anna stated.

"Okay, but I pursued you at the Lenape village, remember? And I had to come sit next to you and get your attention away from that brave who had stolen the twinkle in your eyes," Henry replied.

"You did not, Henry! I turned to talk to you first!"

"Come here, Anna. Stop talking and kiss me. This is our time," Henry whispered. "The mirror is nice, but I like to look at your beauty without that silly thing in the way."

"Or anything else, right, Henry?"

"Right, now come here and love me."

On the wooden floor of the new Funk stone house, in the black of the night, two braves crept quietly along the walls, inspecting the structure. Not even Bull heard them.

On a faraway island in the Caribbean, Grietje De Visscher, Anna's mother, awoke in the night, worried. Was her daughter okay? She wondered. Had she met good people or bad? Where was she? Was she even alive?

On Indian Creek, Anna awoke when the baby inside her kicked, now four months along. Anna was happy and seemed to see her mother's face in the dark. "Momma, don't worry," she whispered.

All at once Bull barked and chased something away from the farm. Anna figured it was just a midnight varmint of some sort. After a bit he quieted down. All was well with the world, Anna smiled, and she went back to sleep next to Henry.

17

Nation

August 1725

The wooden gears for Henry's mill fit perfectly and turned steadily. It was fun to crank the lever that allowed water to push the wheel forward. He needed only the last three gears and the grindstones, and he would be in business.

Because of ample rain, the wheat and corn crops in Indian Creek had produced a bounty. Farmers had to cart their grain to other mills, however, at some distance and cost. When Funk got his mill going, he was confident of having plenty of business.

By mid-week, when the men from Philadelphia had returned, Abe Swartz regained consciousness. Annie Beth smiled when he opened his eyes.

"You're going to heal and get better," Annie Beth encouraged.

"I need water," Abe begged.

Anna came back with Annie Beth and brought him a cup and pitcher of water.

"We need you to heal and go with us to visit the Lenape," Anna began.

"Why?" Abe asked.

"The arrow," Anna began. "No one in these parts recognizes it."

"What do you mean?"

"Our braves don't use the arrow we pulled from your shoulder."

Abe grimaced and rolled over.

"We're going to a meeting at Perkiomen Creek the first week of

August, and Chief Shickellamy will be there. You need to come along."

As soon as Henry had come home from Philadelphia the previous Saturday evening, he and two men buried the deputy and the Indian who had died in the skirmish. Henry kept the hanging claws that had hung around the brave's neck and the distinctive woven belt the man wore. They were unlike anything he'd seen in the Indian Creek region. The burial was not a pleasant task, but Henry dug graves for the two men where they had fallen in the woods.

On Tuesday, during the first week of August 1725, Henry laid out the claws and the woven belt in a circle for all to see. Anna added the arrow that had been pulled from Abe Swartz's shoulder.

Anna spoke to Fifteen Feathers. "No one recognizes where these come from."

Lenape Mother and her braves waited patiently for the visiting chief to speak.

"They are Mohawk," Shickellamy began. From under his distinguished fifteen feather headdress, the chief decided to be forthright and direct.

"The Mohawk are among the six nations who make up the Iroquois Confederation. Your people, the Lenape, are subject to the Iroquois."

Waiting just a minute to let the truth sink in, the chief continued. "We work with the British to establish order and independence in Pennsylvania. The Lenape need to accept our authority and that of the British government."

"How did Chief Lapowinsa get out of jail?" Anna asked.

"Mohawk warriors broke in, something your own braves failed at."

Everyone in the midday council along Perkiomen Creek realized the secondary status of the Lenape Indians. They were focused on hunting, raising crops, and moving from one place to another, while the six powerful nations of the Iroquois were peace-loving but always ready to act with deadly force.

"Why did Chief Lapowinsa come by our farm?" Henry asked.

"Our braves were taking him to New York, our Great Council meeting."

"What for?" Anna asked.

"To meet at the Tree of Great Peace," Fifteen Feathers responded. "At the Great Council, we sit with chiefs from other tribes and outline our laws and understandings. If the Lenape obey the Great Binding Law of the Iroquois Confederation, then they shall be welcome to take shelter beneath the Tree of the Long Leaves."

"How can there be peace if you conquer and rule over other tribes?" Anna asked.

"For many years," Shickellamy continued, "The Iroquois have banded together in a confederacy. We have governed in such a way to work together, to maintain peace, and to rule over other tribes. At the top of the Tree of the Long Leaves is an eagle who is able to see afar, and he can warn of approaching evil or danger."

"What is the eagle warning of today?" Henry inquired.

"The British, with their new ways and demands of land and submission, are a threat to the Iroquois Confederation. We believe the French are more sympathetic to the Indian way of life."

"For much longer than the Iroquois Nation has existed," Lenape Mother responded, "the spirit of Tamenend lives in the Delaware region."

A brave rose and continued. "Our people moved here a thousand years ago, and this is our land."

Henry flinched at the thought that he had purchased acreage from the Pennsylvania government, at the expense of the Lenape Indians.

"We are united," the brave continued with the historic chant of his people. When the Lenape rose, they recited with him, "*We carry the spirit of Tamenend in the land of the Dawn."*

Almost ignoring the chant, Shickellamy forcefully replied, "This is Iroquois land."

"Governor Keith says this is British land," Henry Funk replied.

The Indian meeting on Perkiomen Creek ended with tension, realizing that very conflicting interests had collided in the region.

"I will report to the Great Iroquois Council what I have heard here today," Shickellamy summarized. "The good will of peace may turn into the sting of war."

Next to her rising stone and wood house, Anna checked in regularly with Cool Water, living in a wigwam with Bentura.

"We would like to travel to Bentura's home," the young Indian woman announced.

"That's a very long trip," Anna replied.

"It's not too far for us."

"Does Bentura want to live in Aruba?" Anna asked.

"He's not sure, because it will depend on whether he can stay there as a free man," Cool Water replied.

"I can tell you Aruba is a lovely place, with warm temperatures all year long."

"We might go and stay this winter," Cool Water stated.

"You are welcome to live here on our farm," Anna insisted. "Bentura will always have work here, both with the crops and helping in the mill."

Anna and Cool Water watched Bentura shove wooden shingles up to Abe and Henry, high on the roof of their new house. One side of shingles had been installed, and now they were working on the other side.

"You have a very large house," Cool Water observed.

"For our family to live in," Anna replied and patted her pregnant belly.

"I hope you will have many children."

When Bentura came to Cool Water's wigwam for lunch, Anna noticed that Cool Water playfully reached around him and slipped his knife from its sheath without him realizing what had happened.

An idea popped into Anna's mind, and it involved Cool Water and her dog Bull.

"Henry, I need to go to Philadelphia."

"What in the world for?" Henry wondered.

"It's a woman's thing, Henry. Just me and Cool Water are going."

"No man to go along?"

"Bull's going, and he's a boy," Anna replied.

"Are you going shopping?"

"No silly, but I do need an extra horse to take along."

"To bring along home all the stuff you're going to buy?"

"Henry, just trust me. Can I have two horses and three days away from the farm?

"Have you asked Bentura what he thinks about this scheme?" Henry asked.

"He's fine with it, Henry."

With a smile, Henry agreed.

"We're leaving in the morning, Henry." Patting his slightly bald head, she kissed him with a flourish and exclaimed, "I love you so much."

Early the next day, Anna and Cool Water rode toward Philadelphia. Bull marched along in full agreement with whatever the women had in mind.

The Freedom Inn manager couldn't figure out what was going on when the two women stopped in for a meal. He fed and watered their horses while wondering what in the world they were up to, with no men along. Bull kept the man from getting too friendly with the women.

In Philadelphia that evening the women checked in at their usual inn, with the manager also wondering where Henry and Bentura were.

"We're on a shopping trip," Anna lied.

Early the next morning, Anna and Cool Water began to explore the city, with Bull in tow. They turned into a bit of a spectacle in a city where people noticed the unusual and spotted visitors who had come to town. Even Logan looked out from the second story window of his office above the courthouse.

To put on an appearance, the women actually did some shopping, though they bought very little. Store owners kept looking for their men to walk in the door after them, and all they saw was a huge mastiff at the door, guarding the women. But a little money spent here and there, and the shopping convinced Philadelphians that Henry Funk was making some serious money on Indian Creek and had sent his wife with a friend on a spending trip to stores in the capital. Anna wrapped a pretty new scarf around her neck, and the caper was in full swing, lulling the city to sleep.

When Andrew Bradford, the printer, saw the women strolling along Second Street, he waited for them to come in and talk to him. When they passed his door, on what appeared to be a women's shopping trip, he went to talk to Anna and her friend.

"What brings you to Philadelphia?" Bradford inquired.

"We're looking for clothes," Anna replied.

"Who's your friend?" Bradford asked.

"This is Bentura's new wife, Cool Water," Anna responded.

Right behind Bradford tagged his nineteen-year-old reporter Ben Franklin.

"Henry must be making money," Ben said.

"You don't think I have money?" Anna quipped.

"I just thought it was your German husband who was getting rich, and here you are spending it," Ben countered.

"My parents in Aruba are wealthy," Anna sassed. "I bet they're richer than your parents!"

"What's your family business?" Ben Franklin wondered.

"Printing, what's yours?"

"Same as yours," Ben answered. "My family got started in Boston."

"Mine got started four generations ago," Anna stated. "My great-grandparents got rich printing books in Amsterdam."

"Well now, don't we have a shopper with an attitude," Ben replied.

"Ben, go back to work," Bradford demanded. "What can I do for you women today?"

"First, I want a copy of the latest *Mercury*, for Henry," Anna began.

"Sure, what else?"

"Can you go with us to the courthouse to inquire if James Logan will meet with us," Anna innocently asked.

"Anything for my good friend's wife," Bradford responded. "Let me get a newspaper, and then we'll go."

Anna whispered into Cool Water's ear when Bradford bounded into his shop to get a paper. Andrew Bradford did not notice the sly smile on the Lenape woman's face when he came back out the door.

Bull wagged his tail at Bradford, sensing that he was a friend to Anna, which he indeed was. On this bright Friday August morning, Andrew Bradford didn't realize the role he was playing in an unfolding ruse.

"Do you remember that quote about freedom in your newspaper you printed last January?" Anna asked.

"You mean the one that got me thrown in jail?"

"Yes, Henry and I like that quote," Anna stated. "Would you wait here a moment while we shop in this fabric store?"

"Sure," Bradford offered.

Ben watched the unfolding spectacle from the window of the print shop. He suspected something was up, but had no idea what.

Hurrying out of the store quickly, Anna complained to Cool Water about high prices in the store.

"I agree," Bradford offered. "I don't shop in there, or let my wife go in, because they charge too much."

At the door of the courthouse, Anna talked to Bull, deliberately, instructing him to sit still and wait for them to come out. Cool Water surveyed the landscape while Anna distracted Bradford.

When the two women walked in with Andrew Bradford, a few folks turned to look at them, but with little interest or surprise. Bradford came in all the time, and Anna Funk was known in the city.

Inquiring whether Logan would meet with Anna and Cool Water, Bradford made a convincing case for the visit. A guard turned and walked through a door into the hallway where Chief Lapowinsa was kept. Both women eyed his keys, and when he disappeared down the hallway, they winked at each other.

"James Logan is busy today and can't meet with you," the attendant informed the disappointed women.

"You'd think that since the Funk's pay taxes and are productive farmers," Anna remarked, "he'd meet with us."

"He's a busy man," Bradford assured them.

A runaway horse galloped through the city square, frightened by an attempt to nail shoes on the beast. The blacksmith and his son sprinted after the terrified animal. It all seemed so innocent and normal, except that Anna had been at work the night before.

In the square, Anna began her trick with Bull, tossing her trinket into the air, with the dog retrieving it and bringing it to her. After several tosses she began to draw a crowd. Anna's plan was working like a charm.

When the overweight guard with keys on his belt wandered out of his boredom to see what was going on in the square, Anna noticed.

Offering the trinket to Bradford, she encouraged him to try the trick with Bull. Bradford threw the cheap little ornament, but Bull simply looked at him. Everyone laughed at how he had been fooled. Anna ran to get the trinket and the curious crowd leaned in to see what the woman from Indian Creek would try next.

"Here," Anna offered the guard. "You try it."

The guard had seen what happened with Bradford, and tried something different. He got Bull to come to him, leaned over, and got the dog to sniff it.

Cool Water slipped around the back of the guard when he leaned toward the dog, and quickly entered the courthouse. Everyone inside, bored on a sunny Friday, had gone outside to watch Anna and her dog do tricks. An Indian squaw didn't attract much attention.

Anna got into the act in earnest now. "Throw the trinket as far as you can throw it," she yelled at the guard. "If you throw overhand, like this, he'll go after it. Let me show you."

With a strong throw, Bull lunged after the trinket, practically knocking down one of the gawkers. "Now throw it hard, overhand," Anna encouraged.

The guard threw it as far as he could, careful to copy Anna, but the dog just looked at him, turning to Anna for a signal. "Let's try another woman," Anna offered, playing the game for all the time she could get. "A woman might get the dog to chase it." Turning to the attendant who had been at the desk, the woman threw the trinket, but again the dog didn't respond.

By now Logan's curiosity got the best of him, and he nosed out the door to see what was happening.

"Mr. Logan, you try it," Anna exclaimed. "Just throw the trinket as far as you can, and Bull will bring it back to you. When Logan took the piece, however, the huge dog growled. Bull had seen the man before and knew there had been tension and even threats from Logan toward Anna. Bull kept growling while waiting for a signal from Anna, and the game soon ended.

"You folks get back to work," Logan demanded with an eye on the angry dog.

Wiping it clean, Anna soon had the trinket back around her neck and sat along a store front wall holding Bull.

After a bit, Anna rounded the corner, found Cool Water, and they continued to shop while Bradford bid them goodbye and went back to his store. Franklin kept a wary watch on the women, taking a work break to see where they were and what they were doing.

About fifteen minutes later, just before noon, when the guard was going to take a small dish of food to the prisoners, the hapless colonial government employee discovered his missing keys, ran back and pulled the rope alarm, and then stumbled out the back door looking for Chief Lapowinsa. The alarm bell rang loudly while Anna and Cool Water slipped quietly around the corner and back to the inn. There they calmly paid the bill for their room, got their horses, mounted, and rode out of the city.

Bull paraded along beside them, glad to have been in on the trick.

18

Council
August 1725

The Mohawk warrior who had shot the arrow that killed James Logan's deputy, three weeks earlier, heard a ferocious fight near the Freedom Inn. Investigating, he and another brave discovered a large dog challenging two snarling wolves.

The warriors were surprised to find, in the middle of the night, two women trying to stop a death battle between their dog and the vicious wolves. The warriors were amazed at the power of the large dog, the way he fought, and the fact that he hadn't been killed instantly.

The Mohawk warriors had been patrolling Iroquois Nation territory in and around Philadelphia. When they discovered that Lenape Chief Lapowinsa traveled with two women, they were shocked.

The Iroquois Nation Grand Council met on Manhattan Island in the summer of 1725. The Mohawk warriors decided that Chief Shickellamy would be glad to have Lapowinsa to display and judge in that setting. The warriors left the dog for dead, bound Lapowinsa tight, and as an afterthought agreed that the women might also be valuable to the Grand Council. The women had tried in vain to defend Lapowinsa, and they appeared connected to his escape.

Two days later, at the Hudson River, the Mohawk warriors put their three captives in a large canoe and paddled across to Manhattan Island, escorting them into the Grand Council. All fifty chiefs turned to look when their braves brought Lapowinsa and two women into their midst.

Chief Shickellamy rose to speak and described to the council who these three captives were.

"Chief Lapowinsa of the Lenape is from the Schuylkill River region, in the Delaware territory. Anna Funk comes from across the big lake to the east, has lived among the Lenape, and is married to a spiritual leader along Indian Creek. Cool Water has married a freed slave who works on the Funk farm."

A Mohawk warrior explained that the two women had broken Lapowinsa free from his jail cell in Philadelphia. While that prospect amused some of the men, none smiled while the Grand Council convened.

The council discussed Chief Lapowinsa and where he should be taken. Most of the fifty men agreed that to keep a good political relationship with the British government, the Lenape leader should be taken back to jail in Philadelphia. Six of their chiefs had recently sailed to London to meet King George I.

When the Mohawk warriors were ordered to take the three captives back across the Hudson, they were instructed to return the women to their farm, and Lapowinsa was to be taken to James Logan.

Six days after she left Henry, Anna and Cool Water came back to the Funk farm. The Mohawk warriors rode on past without stopping, taking Lapowinsa back to Philadelphia.

"Where have you been?" Henry called out.

"Traveling," Anna began.

"Start at the beginning and tell me the story," Henry encouraged.

"We got Lapowinsa out of jail," Anna smiled. "Cool Water stole keys from the jailer and let him out."

"I'll bet Logan was irate."

"I don't know because we left town fast. When we got to Freedom Inn,"

Anna continued, "Bull got in a fight with wolves. Has he come home?"

"We haven't seen him," Henry replied.

"Then I need to go look for him."

"Can you tell me about the rest of your trip?"

"Two Mohawk braves caught us with Lapowinsa and took all three of us to Manhattan for the Iroquois Grand Council."

"Did they hurt you?" Henry asked.

"No," Anna answered.

"What's happened to Lapowinsa?" Henry wondered.

"He's going back to jail, because the Iroquois support the British, and Logan and Governor Keith are allies with the Grand Council Chiefs.

"Will you go with me to look for Bull?" Anna asked.

With great concern about these new details he had learned, Henry paused, but he saw that Anna's singular focus was to find her dog Bull.

"Sure," Henry replied. "Let me get some work lined up for the men and make a few plans."

When Henry and Anna rode out the dirt path toward the main road to Freedom Inn, Henry asked how all of Anna's horseback riding in the previous week had affected the baby.

"The baby's fine," Anna replied. "I'm halfway through this pregnancy, and our baby seems to like riding horses."

"I think that after this trip, you need to stay put for a while on the farm."

"Henry, I hope Bull is still alive. When the Mohawk warriors grabbed us and took us to the Grand Council, they showed no emotion and didn't care about my dog."

"Maybe the manager has taken care of him."

"It's possible he didn't make it, Henry. It was a vicious fight."

"I saw wolves in Germany as a boy," Henry mentioned. "When cities got destroyed by the constant warfare, wolves moved in and roamed where people had previously lived. It seems like when people build cities and towns and clear the land, it pushes wolves further into the frontier."

"We're still living on the frontier, then, Henry. I'm not sure how the fight started or why, but we woke up when Bull was battling for his life."

At the Freedom Inn, Henry and Anna Funk went inside to ask about Bull's whereabouts.

"Look out in the barn," the manager directed. "He's barely alive. I gave him water twice."

Bull looked up at Anna and his tail wagged, though he couldn't get up. He was a bloody mess, with skin torn up, and a badly scratched snout.

"Bull, I'm here for you," Anna cried. "We're going to help get you back on your feet." As Anna stroked her dog, Bull sparked to life and tried to get up but wasn't able to stand on his own legs.

Kneeling, Anna said, "We're going to help you get better. Henry, find some fresh straw and a bucket of water. And bring a clean rag."

After Anna did her best to clean the dog's wounds, he seemed to regain a bit of strength. Noticing his ribs sticking out, Anna said, "He hasn't eaten anything in a week. Go buy food and bring it to me."

"How are we going to get Bull home?" Henry asked.

"See if the owner has a cart we can pull behind a horse."

Coming back, Henry told Anna that there was a cart they could use to haul Bull. He had paid for lodging, in the barn. "Cheaper fare than staying in a bed," he said.

At the crack of dawn, the next morning, the second Saturday of August 1725, Henry and Anna Funk began their fifteen-mile journey home. They rode their horses at a walking pace to make Bull's ride in the cart as painless as possible. Bull wagged and seemed to be gaining strength, especially with food and water, and love. Anna was confident she could nurse her dog back to health on the farm.

"You're right, Henry."

"About what?"

"Needing to stay put on the farm for a while, Henry. I don't want to travel anywhere until this baby is born."

"Good. You barely looked at our house when you were there. We'll be able to move in a couple of weeks, as soon as we finish a few things inside. But it will be unfinished until we can make it look nice. It's time for us to start sleeping in a house again, and to get out of the mill."

"I agree, Henry."

The walk took all day and Henry asked about the Grand Council that Anna had been taken to earlier that week.

"Women sat around the perimeter of the fifty chiefs," Anna began. "It was clear they weren't supposed to speak out loud, though I saw them talking to the chiefs of their clans occasionally."

"Did you get to speak?" Henry wondered.

"I did, Henry. At one point Fifteen Feathers asked me to explain about building our mill. So I talked to the Iroquois chiefs about your gears, your grindstone, your dam, and the way you would process corn and wheat for people."

"Did you explain how you got Lapowinsa out?

"No, they didn't ask," Anna responded.

"When I stood to speak, I think the fact that I am with child and they could all see it gave me some degree of respect among them. They also valued that I could speak Lenape to Shickellamy who translated into Mohawk."

"Have you ever heard about Malinche?" Henry asked.

"Who?"

"A hundred years ago, when Hernan Cortez invaded the Yucatan

Peninsula and attacked the Aztec Empire, Malinche was a translator for Cortez."

"How do you know this story?" Anna wondered.

"I learned this story from my school teacher in Germany," Henry answered, "when I was a boy."

"You only had one teacher?" Anna wondered.

"Pretty much," Henry answered. "Anyway, Malinche had grown up to Aztec parents and learned their language. Then she was sold into slavery and learned a Mayan language. When Cortez bought a group of slaves to help his men invade the Aztecs, Malinche was among them and quickly learned Spanish. So when Cortez wanted to talk to Moctezuma, the Aztec ruler, he spoke Spanish to Malinche who translated his words into the Aztec language.

"Henry, that's enough history for now. Let's get home."

As the evening shadows lengthened, Henry and Anna Funk came to their farm. They laid Bull in his house in the small shed next to the big house, and the dog seem delighted. He continued to eat whatever Henry could find for him, and he gulped water.

Adam Miller came to the Funk farm the next day and inquired if Henry or Abe wanted to move to Virginia with him.

"I'm leaving at the end of the month," Adam announced.

"You said December earlier," Henry replied.

"Yes, but we need to get moving. I want to get cabins built before the winter sets in, then clear and plant in the spring. I'm going to Elkton. Either of you men want to move with me?"

"Not me," Henry replied. "Anna's with child, and my mill's about finished."

"How about you, Abe?" Adam inquired.

"I'm engaged," Swartz began. Startling Henry with the announcement,

Miller didn't flinch.

"Bring her along, then," Miller continued. "Got a wedding date set yet?"

"No, we don't," Swartz answered. "I also have land to the north here and I don't know if anyone will buy it, because an Indian burial ground is on the property."

Miller had come to the farm on Sunday and talked to the men after they had been to church in the morning.

Annie Beth Kolb came up beside Abe, smiled, and wondered what Miller wanted.

"He wants us to move to Virginia with him, Annie Beth," Abe informed her.

"Better wait and see what happens at the church this afternoon."

Miller looked at Funk and Swartz and wondered what Annie Beth had referred to.

"There's going to be an ordination at the Franconia church this afternoon. Why don't you join us?"

"Church?" Miller asked.

"Haven't been to one for a while, have you, Adam?" Henry asked.

"Almost never," Miller confessed.

"Swartz's name is in the lot for ordination as a minister," Henry explained. "Three men have been nominated, and one man will be chosen."

"When do they start?" Miller wondered.

"Immediately," Funk answered.

"So if you get chosen, you're locked in here?" Miller asked.

"Sort of like that," Swartz answered. "If I get chosen, I'll stay and minister in the community."

"And if you don't get chosen?" Miller wondered.

"Then we could move to Virginia with you."

After Abe described the process of choosing a minister, Miller grinned, "Seems like a lot is riding on the luck of three books. You shouldn't let fate deal with you this way," Miller continued, looking first at Annie Beth and then Swartz.

"I support whatever happens," Annie Beth responded. "The lot shows us God's will."

Adam Miller couldn't help but come to the little log church just over a mile from the Funk farm. This would be a spectacle, he figured, and he might as well see what happened. Either he would get a couple to travel with him to Virginia, or the new minister and his woman were stuck working in the church, where "God's will would be shown," Annie Beth had said.

Miller wondered where the idea had come from that to ordain a man you set up three books, and have them each take one. Just choose the man who felt like maybe God wanted him to do the job; but no, they were going through gyrations of moving books around and hiding a slip of paper, and they were going to call that God's will. Sure.

After a sermon that seemed interminably long to Adam Miller, three books were placed on the pulpit. Each man in turn took a book. Fate rested in the balance, Miller laughed inside. What if a man simply didn't choose a book, then would one of the other men have to choose two books? It seemed like fate or gambling, something Miller knew about and had participated in. At least in gambling you had a chance, you held the cards and had an idea what the outcome might be. Three grown men, Miller kept pondering, had agreed to test the powers of fate and draw a book to see if their life would change in an instant. And each man's woman lined up behind him, supporting him, trying not to cry. They would be brave, Miller was sure.

Now the moment of fate had arrived, Miller observed. The bishop came to the men and began to open each book in turn. He was looking for a slip of paper that would decide a man's destiny. Men should take their own fate in hand and decide for themselves, Miller mused. He had.

The last man with a book was Swartz. After the first and second book didn't have the slip, everyone in the small log church knew it was Swartz. "Run," Miller wanted to cry. Of course, what Miller didn't know is that in the past men had run, to get away from the heavy responsibility of becoming an instant minister.

The bishop read a Bible verse from the slip of paper in Abe Swartz's Bible: *"The lot is cast into the lap; but the whole disposing thereof is of the Lord."*

Adam Miller groaned inside.

"This is from Proverbs," the bishop stated. "Welcome to the ministry."

Anna invited Abe, Annie Beth, and Miller to their farm after the service.

When they came close to their farm house, Bull came limping out to meet them.

"He can walk!" Anna exclaimed.

"What happened to him?" Miller wondered.

"He fought two wolves," Anna answered.

"He's lucky to be alive. What happened to the wolves?"

"They slunk away into the woods when Mohawk warriors broke up the fight."

"I bet they were glad to be chased away," Miller responded. Checking the dog closer, Miller informed Anna and Henry that the wounds on the dog should have killed it. "Wolves don't mess around," he concluded.

"Guess you're not moving to Virginia, now, are you?" Miller asked Swartz.

"God has spoken," Annie Beth interjected. "Abe's a minister in the church now."

"Someday we may come to visit, Adam, but we're going to build a house on my land and begin farming."

"It's soon going to be our land," Annie Beth said.

"That's my girl," Anna encouraged. "Without wives our men wouldn't be able to accomplish very much."

"I stood in the row behind you at the ordination, Abe. But after we get married, we'll stand together, side by side."

"Do you have any prospects for marriage?" Henry asked Adam.

"None," Miller replied.

"I have an older sister who would be perfect for you," Annie Beth blurted.

"She's right!" Anna exclaimed. "Annie Beth, go get your sister and bring her to the farm."

"Now?" Annie Beth asked.

"Now," Anna responded.

When Annie Beth left, Anna showed her trick to Adam. She threw her small gold trinket a short distance away and Bull barked, wagged his big tail, and lumbered over to pick it up.

"He's getting better!" Anna rejoiced.

"Anna, I don't know whether to ride away now or wait and meet the older sister."

"You better stay. Your fate may be in the balance if you don't meet her, just like Abe's destiny lay inside that Bible this afternoon."

"Do I sleep outside?" Adam asked.

"No, how about the floor of our unfinished house?" Anna asked.

"It's a deal," Adam concluded.

19

Teacher

August 1725

The Lenape had taught Anna how to make popcorn, and so the Funks filled their kettle over an open fire. Anna and Henry slept and lived in the mill, but did most of their cooking outside, since their house was not ready.

It was Sunday evening, August 15, and Annie Beth Kolb brought her sister Dorothy to the Funk farm. Seventeen-year-old Annie Beth was more than happy to introduce nineteen-year-old Dorothy to twenty-two-year-old Adam Miller.

While Annie Beth was lively, animated, and eager to try new things, Dorothy Kolb was reflective, thoughtful, and quite comfortable reading a book at home. Dorothy was pretty and not without interests from Mennonite men in the community. In fact, it was the relationship she had been building with the local schoolteacher that came into play around the fire that evening.

"Adam wants to move to Virginia," Anna explained.

"I like living here at Indian Creek," Dorothy stated.

"Adam had hoped that Abe and Annie Beth might move with him to the southern colony," Anna explained, "but with Abe's ordination, that's not going to happen."

"I've been helping our school teacher get ready for classes," Dorothy replied. "He's a nice man."

Miller noticed Dorothy and immediately had interest, but he began to realize that she apparently already had another suitor in the community. He decided to try anyway.

Miller made his case to the lovely Dorothy Kolb. He was a hunter and a trapper, an adventurer, and bold in making decisions. He was not at all afraid to venture into the untamed frontier region of Elkton, Virginia, where there were no cultural refinements. Life would be difficult, he explained to the six young adults around the popcorn kettle.

"When I see smoke from my neighbor's chimney, I need to move further into the wilderness."

"What can you offer a woman who likes books and the refinements of culture that come from a nearby city like Philadelphia?" Anna asked.

"She can bring books along," Miller offered. "But life with me will be primitive, with hunting, skinning animals, raising crops, and living off the land being my way of life."

"I like to teach students," Dorothy replied. "The Mennonites built a log school house last year and parents of young children will send their children in just a few weeks."

"I'll teach my children how to hunt, to survive off the land, and enough English and German to both understand Christian faith but also how to trade in the marketplace."

"What marketplace will you have in Virginia?" Henry asked.

"Remember how I explained to you about the Indian roads?" Adam replied. "The Indians have good travel roads all over the place, including up and down the Shenandoah Valley. My settlers in Elkton won't be stuck there, just isolated."

"Cool Water and I discovered the amazing network of trails the Indians use," Anna explained. "They whisked us off to Manhattan a week and a half ago like it was done all the time. Their trails are different than in Aruba or Pennsylvania, but they're still good to travel on."

"How many years of school do you hope your baby will attend?" Adam asked Anna.

"I haven't thought much about that," Anna replied.

"As many years as we can afford," Henry answered. "Parents pay the teachers for whatever schooling their children get."

"I like to teach children," Dorothy interjected. "When you teach a child, you touch the future."

"You've been spending time with our teacher, haven't you," Anna stated.

"Well, he's a single man and is looking for a wife to support him in his work."

Boldly, Annie Beth interjected, "Dorothy's going to make some man a wonderful wife. She loves children, can cook, and is strong."

In colonial Pennsylvania, among immigrants, the choices for a husband or wife were often limited. Around the welcoming fire at the Funk farm, on a warm August evening, everyone understood that months of courting were often out of the question for young adults. Sometimes decisions about a spouse were made in a moment, with little chance to evaluate the potential partner. Newly married couples hoped that love would bloom in their new marriage.

When her sister called her strong, Dorothy's radiant smile permeated the darkening shadows around the fire. Turning to Adam, she asked, "Why don't you want to buy a farm here and raise a family in a community of support and love?"

"I'm a frontiersman, Dorothy. I like to rely on my own skills and hunches."

"Adam, there's very little you can do on your own," Henry replied. "You can't scratch your own back, you can't harvest corn yourself, you can't have babies on your own, and you can't raise children on your own."

"I know that, Henry. That's why I'm looking for a wife," Adam replied. "I suppose I can't offer a wife very much in the way of material possessions and the finer things of life, but I can offer her adventure and the chance to stake out a home in a new place. In my opinion Indian Creek is getting filled up with people. The young and strong need to keep moving west and south, to frontier regions."

"That's a little the way the kingdom of God works," Abe commented. "Seems it's best when people move and spread out rather than staying all clustered together."

"Wow, Abe just preached his first sermon," Anna stated. "But what you've said is profound. The Funks and Kolbs moved across the Atlantic to start over in a new world."

"I came on my own," Adam Miller replied. "My family didn't cross the ocean with me. I have no other family here." Glancing at Henry, he added, "Yes, I know there's not much we can do on our own, but there were no other Millers aboard my ship."

Dorothy Kolb found Miller's confidence inspiring, and his determination a star she wouldn't mind following. She realized that after tonight, Miller might be gone and her chance with him no longer available. Men like Adam Miller didn't sit in one place very long, waiting on others to make up their minds.

On the other hand, Chris Dock, the local school teacher, had his own farm and house and wanted her to become his wife, or so she believed. Her options appeared to be creating a homestead in Virginia, and rarely, if ever, seeing her family again, or supporting the local school teacher. These two options were real, they were in front of her, and she needed to make up her mind.

Beaming her wonderful smile, Dorothy explained to the group that she wanted a large family. Being Mennonite, like her family, was desired, but not a requirement in choosing a man. Moving around the fire, Dorothy sat down beside Adam Miller, making three couples around the dying embers. Sometimes in colonial Pennsylvania men smelled a little rough, but Adam Miller apparently had cleaned up for this event. "Good for him," Dorothy thought.

"You're a lovely and bright young woman," Adam began, "just like Anna had promised when your sister went to get you. I'll probably leave tomorrow morning, headed to where I'm not exactly sure. I keep talking to folks here and there about moving, and I need to soon go, before the fall and winter set in. I'd be glad to have you join me in Virginia."

"As your wife?" Dorothy asked.

"Yes, as my wife," Miller replied.

Before Dorothy and Annie Beth left for their home, the three women gathered outside the listening range of the men.

"We could get married in the same service," Annie Beth offered. "You and me, just like we played when we were girls."

"I don't have much advice for you," Anna said. "Both Chris and Adam are good men, but your life will be very different depending on which man you choose."

The next morning, Dorothy Kolb walked to the little log schoolhouse at Skippack that the Mennonites had recently built. Chris Dock, twenty-six, worked in his classroom preparing materials for the arrival of students who would come later in the month.

Wearing somewhat tattered but clean clothes, the teacher Dorothy came to see was a man who was a typical colonial American school teacher. Like others, he was paid very little, worked hard, and was wholly dependent on parents to send him students and pay for their children's education.

Unlike other colonial American school teachers, however, the teacher that Dorothy knew was kind, well-educated, and advanced in his teaching methods. Parents in Skippack, south of the Funk farm, knew that their teacher was considerate in punishment and genuinely attempted to help his students learn, unlike other teachers of the time. Dorothy understood that teaching was a calling for Dock, and not just a job.

"Good morning, Dorothy," Dock greeted her.

"Hard at work on a Monday morning?" Dorothy smiled.

"Yes, my farm could use some work, but this is where I'm needed and feel most fulfilled."

Not seeing any students in the school, Dorothy asked, "Do you have any help on the farm?"

"Not much, Dorothy. A single man occasionally gets some help, but everyone seems to have their own farms to tend to."

Getting straight to the point of her visit, Dorothy told Chris about the meeting at the Funk farm the previous evening. Chris had been at the ordination the day before and had seen a visitor.

"His name is Adam Miller," Dorothy informed. "He asked me to marry him last evening."

Waiting to see Dock's reaction, Dorothy kept her winning smile for the teacher.

"Marry you?" Dock asked. Shuffling a few papers on his desk, the teacher came out in front of his desk next to Dorothy.

"I had hoped you felt something for me," he replied.

"I do," Dorothy answered. "I came to see where we stand and what your intentions are."

"Oh my, Dorothy. I had thought I would work a couple of years and try and save some money before asking you to marry me."

"You're uncertain, then?" Dorothy asked.

"Oh, Dorothy, this is something I had not been thinking about recently."

"Okay, Chris, I just wanted to come and see you this morning. Good luck with the new school year."

When Dorothy turned and left, the teacher came to the door and watched her walk away, realizing that his indecision may have cost him dearly.

Dorothy hurried home and joined her family in farm work for a bit. Before noon, however, Dorothy saddled up a horse from the barn and took off for the Funk homestead. Annie Beth watched her go and wondered what was going on.

Dorothy galloped up to the farm and Bull barked excitedly at her arrival.

"Is Adam still here?" Dorothy asked Anna.

"He just left, Dorothy. I packed him some food, and away he went."

"How long ago?"

"Not long—you could catch him if you ride hard," Anna assured. "He wasn't in any hurry going down the trail, and seemed disappointed that you hadn't come back. He kept looking for you."

"Thanks," Dorothy answered. Speaking to her horse and flicking the reins, Dorothy Kolb took off at a gallop.

It took about five miles of hard riding until Dorothy caught up with Miller on the trail that led to the Freedom Inn. Miller wheeled around to look when a lone rider galloped toward him. Always ready, Miller fingered his gun in case the rider was bringing trouble. He soon saw Dorothy Kolb's flapping dress and recognized her gorgeous smile.

Hopping off his horse, he steadied her horse while she dismounted.

"Adam," she spoke, while trying to catch her breath. "Is your offer still good today?"

"Of marriage?" Miller asked.

"Yes, marriage."

Realizing that this might be the luckiest day of his life, he gladly said again, "Yes Dorothy, I would like to marry you. Will you marry me?"

"I will," the beaming woman replied. "I will."

"And you'll move to Virginia with me?"

"I will."

Adam Miller realized that his fortunes had just vastly improved. He took two sets of reins and tied them at nearby trees, then came back to Dorothy.

"I have very little to offer you," Dorothy began. "Only myself."

"That's all I ask," Miller replied.

Adam Miller was a rugged frontiersman, but he naturally understood that a gentle embrace with Dorothy was very much in order.

"Aren't you going to kiss me?" Dorothy finally asked.

Breaking out in the biggest smile that Adam Miller had, he obliged his new life partner, right there in the woods with only the horses watching. It was just the way Miller liked it.

"Can we get married on the same day as Annie Beth and Abe?" Dorothy asked.

"Yes," Miller replied. Looking down the trail toward the Freedom Inn, then back toward the Funk farm, Miller hardly knew which direction to head.

"I want you to meet my parents," Dorothy stated. "Annie Beth and Abe are getting married two weeks from tomorrow."

"Okay. I have a few things to take care of at the Freedom Inn, then I'll go meet your parents."

"I'm not leaving you, Adam. I'm riding with you."

Adam Miller could only offer a big, broad smile. He had discovered a fortune on the Funk farm. "You are a gem," Miller gushed. "How have I become so lucky to win your hand?"

"You won my heart last evening at the Funk fire," Dorothy replied. "Especially since you smelled good when I sat next to you," she chuckled.

"What?"

"I didn't think you'd believe that, Adam," Dorothy winked. "Come on, let's ride. We'll take care of your business, then we've got to go to the Kolb farm so I can get a few things packed and get ready for the wedding."

"Why did you call it the Kolb farm?" Miller wondered.

"Because it's no longer where I live, Adam. I've moving to Elkton, Virginia. With you."

Adam kissed her again, and their love, just a seed, began to grow. It would take root and grow into a mighty tree in the teaming woods of Virginia.

That evening Anna's curiosity led her to ride over to the Kolb farm, where she spoke to Mrs. Kolb about the events of the previous evening. Annie Beth explained to her mother that Adam had proposed to Dorothy.

"This morning Dorothy went to see the teacher," Mrs. Kolb reflected. "When she came back, I could see she was thinking hard and concentrating. Then she left without looking back or saying goodbye."

"When she came to our farm this morning, she took out after Adam Miller, riding hard."

"Momma," Annie Beth said, "I told Dorothy last night that we could get married in the same wedding service."

"I have four daughters, and two might get married on the same day," Mrs. Kolb reflected.

"But that's a good thing, right Momma?"

"Annie Beth, give your mother a chance to think about all of this."

"Adam Miller was a charmer last night, Mrs. Kolb," Anna explained. "But he's a good man, and I believe if that's who Dorothy chooses, she'll have a good life."

"In Virginia," Mrs. Kolb lamented. "I'll never get to hold her babies."

"We'll go to visit," Annie Beth assured.

"We better hold up before making plans," Anna offered. "Let's wait until she gets back before we speculate too much."

"From what you've said of Miller, they may not come back at all," Mrs. Kolb stated. "I haven't even seen him yet."

"Yes you have," Annie Beth assured. "He was the visitor who sat in the back of the church yesterday."

"Oh," Mrs. Kolb responded with a growing smile. "He was handsome. Even I noticed that."

With a laugh, Anna turned to leave. "If they get engaged, we'll be glad to host a double wedding on our farm," Anna offered.

20

Double
August 1725

Freedom of the press in Philadelphia was a concept only slowly growing in acceptance. *The Mercury* was a regular and increasingly established publication. With other cities like Boston having newspapers, government officials were learning not to automatically pitch editors and writers in jail for exposing their weaknesses.

Ben Franklin wrote a scurrilous article about the escape of Chief Lapowinsa from the Philadelphia jail. His article criticized the Logan administration's inability to maintain order in the colonial capital's courthouse. That everyone pretty much figured out what happened was about the only thing that kept Franklin from getting thrown in jail himself.

Further, when Ben Franklin investigated and discovered the circumstances that led to the return of the Lenape chief to jail, he wrote of the inability of the colonial government to keep order. "**Logan had to rely on the Iroquois to do his work**," he penned. James Logan seethed at the public shaming he was getting from the pages of Andrew Bradford's weekly newspaper. This time around, Logan demanded from his courthouse employees that the chief was not to get out under any circumstances.

The third week of August had been dry and hot in Philadelphia. That's when the fire began that tore through the courthouse. The guards had time to open all three jail cells and take the prisoners to another location. Everyone wondered who had set the fire.

No one could figure it out. There had been nothing burning in the fireplace, and the chimneys were not in use. Folks thought maybe the kitchen staff had forgotten about something on a stove, but there had been nothing cooking.

Ben Franklin was on the reporter's beat again, trying to find out what happened. Farmers from the outlying areas, like the Funks, were on their farms harvesting corn and wheat. There simply weren't visitors in the city at the time of the fire. There had even been a lull in ships arriving in the harbor delivering immigrants from Europe.

The courthouse had burned to ashes. Hundreds of city men had rallied to work on bucket brigades and keep surrounding buildings from burning, but the council building was in a heap.

It was a mystery that not even the excellent writer Ben Franklin could solve. His usual suspects hadn't been in the capital. About all the government officials, like Governor Keith and Chief Justice Logan could do, was to begin the arduous task of cleaning up. People knew the fire may have started from entirely natural reasons, but there had been no lightening that week whatsoever.

Franklin knew Anna Funk, and knew of her involvement in the escape of Lapowinsa, so he rode out to the Funk farm to investigate.

"The courthouse burned to the ground," Franklin explained to Henry and Anna. "Any ideas who may have done it?" he asked.

"No," Henry answered. "We've been busy on the farm."

"So has everyone else," Franklin replied.

"Is Logan angry?" Anna asked.

"He's livid," Franklin answered. "I'm surprised he hasn't come out here himself."

"Why here?" Anna asked.

"You and the Indian woman broke the chief out before, and he didn't come after you because everyone knew what you did, and he got the chief back."

"Anna's been here for almost two weeks since she came back from the Grand Council," Henry stated. "I'm not letting her go anywhere. Would anyone think that a woman who's five months pregnant could set the courthouse on fire?"

"Okay, let's change the subject," Franklin replied. "Where's Adam Miller? I haven't seen him in a while."

"He was here three days ago, on Monday," Henry answered.

"Four days ago," Anna corrected. "He was here this past Sunday and met a beautiful girl who he wants to marry."

"So here we go again," Franklin mused. "You Germans keep marrying and producing babies, populating the colony with folks who don't speak English."

"Adam Miller speaks pretty good English," Anna defended. "In fact, he and Dorothy Kolb are getting married and moving to Virginia, an English speaking colony of the king."

"Dorothy Kolb," Franklin answered. "I met her at your wedding. She's beautiful."

"Guess you missed your chance, Ben. Are you seeing anyone?" Anna asked.

"No, I'm not, but I'm glad for Adam."

"Come back on the last Tuesday of the month—we're hosting a double wedding reception."

"Where's the wedding taking place?"

"On our farm," Anna answered.

"Not in the church?" Franklin asked.

"Mennonites don't use the church building for weddings," Henry informed him.

"Is yours a serious invitation?" Franklin asked. Raised with a degree of civility, formality, and respect for tradition, Franklin was skeptical of the German immigrants, but he wouldn't come to a wedding uninvited.

"It's serious," Henry replied. "Come on back and enjoy the food."

"We'll save some pork for you," Anna replied.

"It's a deal. If you see Miller, tell him I'm coming to his wedding. Who else is getting married?"

"Annie Beth Kolb and Abe Swartz," Anna answered.

"Sisters getting married on the same day. This will be a great story for *The Mercury*," Franklin mused.

"This event is not a 'story,' as you say, but two couples getting married," Anna replied.

Ben Franklin, who set a dashing and impressive profile in the saddle, rode back out the trail to the main road.

"Wonder if we could find him a wife here in Indian Creek," Anna smiled. "We could call this place the matchmaker's farm. How many have met here?

"Come on Anna, we have work to do," Henry laughed.

"Bentura, Abe, Adam, and Henry," Anna laughed.

Henry shook his head but admitted that Anna actually might find the young writer from Philadelphia a bride at the wedding.

It had been five months since Henry and Anna's wedding on the farm. William and Jubilant agreed to turn the pigs again on the spit, providing pork for the guests.

"I don't think we'll have many Lenape attending," Anna told Jubilant. "But there will be lots of friends of the Kolbs. Abe's got no relatives around here to invite and neither does Adam Miller."

"So all the guests are friends of the brides," Jubilant noted. As compared to the March wedding, Little John was now over two years old and full of life, investigating, and trying out new words.

The wedding, on the last day of August, was hot and dry. The bishop conducted the marriage ceremony, keeping it simple and relatively short because of the heat.

Before the couples could catch their breath and begin to enjoy the service, they were married, and were announced to the guests as Mrs. and Mrs. Swartz and Mr. and Mrs. Miller. Mrs. Kolb both wept and laughed.

Her daughters had accepted the vision, the goals, and the life directions of the husbands they had chosen. One was now the wife of a farmer and minister, while the other was going to the frontier to build her life far to the south. "May God be with them," Mrs. Kolb prayed.

The most unusual, yet useful, gift came from Mr. Kolb, father of the brides. He purchased the finest muzzle loading long rifles he could afford for his daughters. These were not cheap guns, as they had long barrels and were fairly heavy. "You'll need these in your new homes, girls," Mr. Kolb said. "Learn to shoot them and you can help your husbands hunt, and perhaps the day will come when you need to protect yourselves or your children from danger."

Adam Miller was especially pleased with Mr. Kolb's gift. "This will be very useful in Virginia," Miller remarked.

At this double Mennonite wedding, there was no dancing, as there had been five months earlier at Henry and Anna's celebration. There was plenty of food, though, and Ben Franklin helped himself greatly to the wonderful spread.

Anna pulled Ben toward a bench next to an older sister of Dorothy and Annie Beth. "This is Maria Kolb," Anna explained. Twenty-two, Maria didn't hesitate to chat with Ben Franklin, twenty. The conversation didn't go very far, Anna observed, as Franklin came from a sophisticated Boston family, and he was interested in printing and writing; Maria was from a

German farm family along Indian Creek, and she wanted nothing more than to find a farmer husband.

"Anna, thank you for the invitation. I'll be leaving now," Franklin concluded. "I'm so glad for Adam and his new wife Dorothy."

"Any interest in Maria?"

"No, but I am interested in the youngest sister," Franklin added.

"Agnes?" Anna quizzed, turning to look where Franklin looked at the girl. "She's only fourteen."

"Get in touch with me in about two years, and I'd like to have a chance then," Franklin said brazenly. On the frontier, Anna and others knew that marriage was a serious life event, and sometimes older men actually did wait a few years until a young girl grew up. They would often communicate their interests to the parents of the young woman.

"I'll pass your interest on to the Kolbs," Anna concluded. "Ben, be kind in your writings about the Germans. These are good people."

"I know, Anna."

"Wait, Ben. One more thing. You're a reporter who likes to solve mysteries. Can you help me find the gold medallion?"

"I've heard about it, but I have no idea where it is."

"Keep looking, Ben. It's out there somewhere. I'm searching for it."

The next morning, after his daughters' wedding night, with the Swartz's in the third floor of the mill, and the Miller newlyweds in the barn, Mr. Kolb came to the Funk farm and helped his daughters learn how to shoot their new long rifles. Mr. Kolb had purchased lead balls and powder for them. Abe Swartz and Adam Miller were both good shots with their own guns, and they could greatly appreciate the important gift their wives had received.

"The Pennsylvania long rifle has changed the American frontier,"

Mr. Kolb philosophized. "It is lighter than European models, it shoots straight, and is dependable, meaning the person who shoots the gun is safe from explosions."

"I predict it will make the colony of Pennsylvania independent of Great Britain eventually," Mr. Kolb continued. The men turned to look at the senior Kolb and ponder what he had just said, while the women continued to learn how to load the guns and fire them.

"I want one," Anna mentioned to Henry.

"A rifle?" Henry responded.

"If I have one, I can help you hunt," Anna added.

Bull ran around the shooters, barking each time a gun fired.

It was the arrival of Chief Shickellamy and three Mohawk braves that surprised everyone. They rode onto the Funk farm in almost perfect timing, making most wonder if they had been watching events the previous day. It was Wednesday, September 1, 1725, and Fifteen Feathers had come to inspect events in his Iroquois Nation.

"You have very nice guns," the chief noted.

"They were wedding gifts," Anna explained.

Henry was not sure he was happy the chief had come on his property. Only a month earlier, Mohawk braves had captured his pregnant wife and taken her to the Iroquois Grand Council, without her agreement.

"Mr. Funk, I am here to offer assistance," the chief began.

"In what way?" Henry asked.

"My braves will travel with the newly married couple to Virginia."

Not having any idea how the chief knew that the Millers were going to Virginia, Henry asked, "Why do they need braves to travel with them?"

"It is a long and dangerous trip, and they will travel through many other Indian tribe regions. With Mohawk braves at their side, your newly married couple will make it safely."

Adam Miller had been listening to the conversation, with the main discussion taking place in English, though occasionally he had to seek interpretation for a difficult word from Anna.

"He wants to send his braves with you," Anna explained to Adam and Dorothy.

Miller knew the woods, he had traveled to Virginia and back, and he appreciated the offer. "Tell him that we'll be glad for the escort."

"Our Iroquois nation braves, stationed all along the way, will keep the couple safe," Fifteen Feathers declared. "When should my men be ready to leave with the couple?"

"Tomorrow morning," Miller responded.

"You get two nights with your new husband, here," Anna whispered to Dorothy. "Then you'll travel to Virginia with Indians, and sleep under the stars. Be strong."

Ben Franklin took Mr. Kolb's observations and wrote about them in his next essay in *The American Mercury*. "***This untamed frontier,***" Franklin penned, "***will one day become independent from Great Britain.***" Months from when Franklin wrote his editorial, the newspaper from Second Street landed on the king's desk in London, and from what was reported to Franklin another three months later, the king had not been happy with the essay.

"*Give this frontier enough fine long rifles, such as were given at the Funk farm wedding and combine that with the spirit of independence found in young couples who forge into the frontier, build all of that rugged individualism on the backs of freedom-seeking immigrants from Germany, and this land shall not long be a colony. It will someday be its own country.*"

Ben Franklin's strong essays, written from his own travels and real life experiences, helped the circulation of *The American Mercury* spike in popularity. Now, Andrew Bradford thought, he had to keep his writer out of jail and protected from the ire of Governor Keith. The thought also crossed the Philadelphia printer's mind that Franklin and he could be hauled across the Atlantic to answer in front of the king himself.

Since getting engaged to Annie Beth a month earlier, Abe Swartz had worked hard building a simple log house on his land to the north of the Funk farm. He had invited Lenape warriors to the property before he began. He considered the location of the sacred burial ground while planning use for his land. He stayed away from the land the Lenape claimed along the Creek and staked out the corners of his house without intruding on Indian lands. None of the Lenape protested.

The first night in their new log home, far from any other cabin or farm, the Swartz coupled celebrated their good fortunes. Late at night when wolves howled, Annie Beth picked up her rifle and stepped outside the door.

"You're brave," Abe remarked.

"No I'm not, Abe. I'm afraid. We need a dog like Bull on our property, to scare the wolves away."

To give the wolves something to think about, Abe took Annie Beth's new gun and fired in the direction of the wolves. They grew silent and apparently left the area.

Minister Abe Swartz and his new bride Annie Beth Swartz knelt beside their mat to pray. Abe made sure the door bolt was secured and the window closed before they lay down in their own corner of the frontier to sleep. Here they would live, for better or for worse, as they had promised two days before, and here they would raise a family, they prayed. Little John was fast asleep in the opposite corner on his own mat and had not awakened when Abe fired the long rifle.

Anna and Henry Funk had given their nearly completed house to Adam and Dorothy Miller for their last night to sleep in Indian Creek, perhaps ever. At a distance, three Mohawk braves, some of the finest, slept under the stars, unafraid, resting before the long journey to the Shenandoah Valley of Virginia in the morning.

Henry put out the fire and Anna asked how long it would take to travel to Elkton in order to visit Adam and Dorothy someday.

21

Underground
September 1725

William and Jubilant were up to it again. It was the third time within the past year that they opened their home to a runaway slave.

The slaves in colonial America knew that the further north they could get, the safer they were from being dragged back into their servile conditions. Owners, however, did what they could to get runaways back, including using bloodhounds to chase them.

Joshua Fry, a map maker and adventurer from Virginia, along with his partner, Peter Jefferson, had hired the same frontiersman who helped James Logan trail and capture Lapowinsa in July. Fry had been in Philadelphia working on his map of The Great Road when his slave escaped.

Joshua Fry, twenty-five, and his partner Peter Jefferson, seventeen, rode hard in pursuit of the frontiersman and his hounds, turning north at the Freedom Inn. The dog owner kept close to the baying bloods and listened for when they had their prey cornered, which according to their barking, they had.

Fry and Jefferson reined up their horses outside William and Jubilant's house and banged on the door. When William came to the door, Fry demanded that the elderly couple bring out the slave.

Anna sensed something was wrong when Bull barked and insisted that she come outside. Anna and Henry had moved into their new stone house, and the front door had been recently installed. Anna swung open the door to investigate Bull's urgency.

Listening, Anna heard hounds barking in the distance, coming from William and Jubilant's house. Bull ran circles and begged her to follow him. "All right, Bull, let's go see what's up."

Anna rode to William's house and was startled to see two men questioning William. Bull, now a full-size mastiff, charged the same barking blood hounds that he fought in the woods two months earlier.

An exasperated frontiersman waded into the dog fight swinging his gun at the huge dog that threatened to tear his valuable hounds apart. Interrupting their questioning of William, Fry and Jefferson helped end the fight. Anna had to hang on to her dog while the frontiersman chased his dogs away.

"What do these men want from you?" Anna asked William. With Bull at her side, she stood tall and confident. Fry and Jefferson couldn't help but notice, and they kept an eye on the dog while they talked to the woman.

"They have our slave," Fry began.

"How do you know?" Anna demanded.

"The hounds led us to their house," Fry responded.

Pausing, and looking at William, and then at Jubilant standing in the door, Anna asked for a chance to talk with the couple alone.

Fry and Jefferson hesitated, but agreed when the farm woman's dog growled at them.

"Do you have a slave in your house?" Anna asked William.

"We do."

"If they get him back, the slave may be killed," Jubilant told Anna. "We've seen that happen before."

"How many slaves have you helped?" Anna wondered.

"I have no idea," William answered. "It's something we do, whenever the need arises."

"It's a secret route for the slaves," Jubilant continued. "Somehow our home is known by runaway slaves."

"I guess your location is not so secret anymore," Anna glanced at the waiting Virginians. "What are you going to do now?"

Henry had seen Anna leave with her dog and after finishing a detail at the mill, decided to see where she had gone.

Riding south, Henry soon realized that William and Jubilant had visitors. He noticed two men and then found Anna sitting at the front door of his neighbors' house.

Now that the frontiersman had been paid for his work and left the area, Anna relaxed a bit and came out to greet Henry.

"William and Jubilant have another slave in their house," Anna informed her husband.

"Let me see," Henry asked. Walking inside, Henry soon found the slave, worried and cowering.

"Can you help me?" the man pleaded.

"I'm not sure," Henry replied. "Come with me."

When the slave and Henry came back out, the two Virginians returned to the house.

"He's my property," Fry demanded. "Turn him over to me."

"Hold on," Henry counseled. "Let's all go over to our farm. I want to meet you men and find out what your work is and why you are here."

"We chased our slave to this home," Fry replied. "We're ready to move on."

"They're from Virginia," Anna told Henry.

"We had a couple leave our farm for Virginia yesterday," Henry told the men. "Come to our farm, eat a meal, and we'll tell you about them, and learn more about where you are from."

Fry turned to the younger man, and they agreed.

"It looks like your traveling friend is hungry," Henry smiled to Fry.

"He is, and so am I," Fry replied. "We'd be grateful to eat a meal with you."

With Jubilant's help, Anna cooked up a meal for the three visitors, along with William, Jubilant, Henry, and herself. She managed to find seven stools and chairs for everyone to sit around the table.

"Tell us where you are from," Henry asked the men.

"I live along the Rappahannock River in Virginia," Fry answered. "My home is near where the river empties into the Chesapeake Bay."

"I live in Chesterfield, Virginia," Jefferson answered. "Near the James River."

"What are you doing in Pennsylvania?" Anna asked.

"We're making a map of Virginia," Fry answered.

"So why are you here?" Henry quizzed.

"We're including The Great Road on our map," the young Jefferson answered. Inhaling his food, Jefferson tried to explain that the main road into the interior began in Philadelphia and went west to Lancaster, and then south through Virginia, and finally into the Carolinas.

"Undoubtedly your friends who left for Virginia yesterday are traveling on The Great Road," Fry continued. "That road is full of Germans and Scotch-Irish immigrants."

"It's an old Indian trail, now a road," Jefferson added. "These days you'll find lots of wagons and horses on the road, with immigrants heading into the interior."

"Have you ever heard of Elkton?" Henry asked.

"We have," Fry answered. "It will be on our map."

After the meal, Fry rolled out his sketch drawing of The Great Road, and showed it to his hosts.

"The road goes west from Philadelphia toward Lancaster," Fry explained.

"Zook and Yoder traveled that road," Henry told Anna. "Two scouts from Germany came here this summer, looking for land to the west."

"If the scouts bring their families to America, they'll most certainly travel this road," Fry pointed at his map. "Here it turns, crosses the Potomac River, and follows the Shenandoah Valley into Virginia."

Henry noticed that The Great Road eventually crossed the Blue Ridge Mountains at a river gorge and entered Carolina.

"Let me show you our mill," Henry announced. With an air of gentry from the south, Fry and Jefferson strode to the mill with their slave firmly in tow and examined Henry's enterprise.

"My last gears come next week," Henry explained. "I'm not sure if the grindstones are ready or not."

"Mr. Funk," Jefferson asked, "Why don't you own slaves? Most everyone in Virginia does."

"Mennonites don't believe in enslaving people," Funk answered.

"We need slaves for labor," Jefferson answered.

"We do our own work," Funk responded. "We have lots of children, and they help out with the work," Henry replied.

"My people in Virginia have plenty of children, but we also have slaves do the hard work," Jefferson explained.

"While some in Pennsylvania have slaves, it sounds to me like our colonies operate very differently," Henry responded. "We have many small farms with few slaves, while it sounds like you have large estates with many slaves."

"That's about right," Fry responded.

When Fry, Jefferson, and their slave slept in the mill before departing the next morning, Henry reflected on all the people who had stayed there.

"This is the Funk Inn," he said to Anna.

"I don't like having a slave sleeping in there," Anna remarked. "It's just not right. Bentura's worried the men will take him along with them."

"Your dog won't let that happen," Henry laughed.

"Bull kept those men from barging into William and Jubilant's house," Anna declared.

"Their slave is valuable property," Henry replied. "They want him alive to carry their stuff and do their chores."

Chief Shickellamy's Mohawk warriors led Adam and Dorothy Miller on The Great Road west toward Lancaster, Pennsylvania. It was just as Joshua Fry predicted. The Millers met many travelers, most going west, but a few going east toward Philadelphia. An entire business network had grown up along the road, with merchants selling essential goods for the hundreds of travelers. The British colonies in America were growing and thriving on the backs of swarming immigrants and thousands of hard-working slaves.

The burning of the Philadelphia Courthouse was still a mystery. Speculation centered on the Delaware Indians who may have burned the building to get Chief Lapowinsa released. Officials doubled down on security for the chief, making it difficult for anyone to break the Lenape leader free.

When the mill manager arrived at the Funk farm on Monday, September 6, he brought several men from Philadelphia with him. He also brought a copy of *The American Mercury*. Henry read the news voraciously, commenting to Anna that King George I of Great Britain was not very well liked in England because he spoke German and French fluently, but he spoke very little English. "He'd be right at home with all of us German immigrants in Indian Creek," Henry mused.

The article about the king also noted that the monarch's health was in decline, as he was getting old, at age sixty-five.

The wooden gears fit perfectly, and by Tuesday, the mill was in full motion. There had been a delay, however, in the millstones, which had been ordered from France. "These things take time," the manager explained to Henry.

Henry's father brought him a new desk on Wednesday after the manager left for Philadelphia. It was a wonderful addition to the new stone house. Henry brought out his quill feathers, his ink well, and paper, and began to write. He started over on his book, *A Mirror of Baptism*, since it was destroyed by the fire. Henry's two new Bibles, one in English and the other in German, were his two main resource books.

Abe Swartz had never been able to get goose feathers as Anna had requested. Swartz had been busy with other things, and the delicate task of dealing with Lenape concerns about killing geese for their feathers was never overcome.

Bentura and Cool Water explained to Anna again that they wanted to visit Aruba. Though he had grown up a slave, he would now return as a free man. It would have pleased his great-grandfather, Bentura told Anna, to know that he would live as a free man on the Caribbean island. Five generations earlier, Bentura's ancestor had been a proud chief in Kongo, along the southeast coast of Africa.

Cool Water confided in Anna that she was pregnant. She had become pregnant on their wedding night over two months earlier.

Bentura and Cool Water wanted to work another two weeks and then leave for Philadelphia, purchase tickets, and sail to Aruba and live there during the fall and winter months. It was important to travel now due to the progressing pregnancy.

"I expect we will come back next spring to work on the Funk farm again," Bentura explained.

On the second Friday of September, Chief Fifteen Feathers met with James Logan and Governor Keith. They had to use a rented office building on Second Street for official work.

"We think it was Lenape braves who set the courthouse on fire," Shickellamy began.

"Why do you say that?" Logan wondered.

"My braves around Philadelphia have all been questioned, and their location at the time of the fire was nowhere near the center of the city."

"We have no evidence of Lenape involvement, though, do we?" Governor Keith asked.

"Perhaps the fire began as an accident," Logan mused.

"Lapowinsa's braves are getting desperate," the Oneida leader declared. "Their chief has been in jail for months, and they are willing to try anything to get him out."

"Perhaps we need to move the Lenape further to the west," Governor Keith suggested, "to get them away from Philadelphia."

The weekend on the Funk farm seemed slow and uneventful. The Miller and Swartz newlyweds had moved away, while Bentura and Cool Water had gone to spend time with the Lenape at Perkiomen Creek.

"Henry, it's just the two of us this weekend."

"I'd be glad to sit at my desk, writing and studying," Henry replied.

"What about me?" Anna asked.

Turning in his chair, Henry said, "We've been married over five months, Anna. I love you, but I also feel like I must write for my people, so they understand their faith."

"Can we go on a walk sometime?" Anna wondered.

"Sure, when would you like to go?"

"Oh look, Henry, the sky is turning beautiful shades of evening red. Let's go now!"

Like in March, before they were married, they walked around their property, talking about their good fortune of being able to rebuild, and their hopes for raising a family.

Bull, Anna's constant companion, growled. Peering into the woods and looking around, Henry couldn't figure out what the dog was worried about.

When Bull lunged into the woods, a single Indian brave turned and ran away into the thickest part of the trees. Bull barked but did not pursue.

"We're being watched," Henry remarked.

"Perhaps, but we don't know exactly why that warrior was out here," Anna replied.

Bull barked again, but this time it was a momma coon and her three young following her into the woods.

"Probably the brood Swartz allowed to live in the mill," Henry guessed.

"Let's visit Annie Beth and Abe," Anna begged. "I miss seeing them."

"Okay, but it will be dark when we walk home," Henry advised.

"It's not far from here, Henry."

Bull was the first to arrive at the empty log Swartz home. The lack of any fire or lantern puzzled Henry and Anna. When they knocked on the door, no one answered. The place appeared to be deserted.

Pushing on the door, Henry opened it and peered in. Even in the dark he could see that no one was there.

"Perhaps they are staying with Annie Beth's parents tonight," Anna suggested.

Looking closer it appeared they had been gone for a while.

"Maybe they went to Philadelphia for some reason," Henry guessed. "In our region, though, we tell each other when we go on a trip, so the neighbors can look out for things. We better head back," Henry concluded. "They may be in church tomorrow morning."

"Henry, look," Anna slowly pointed. Henry froze when he saw a sunken tomahawk in a tree near the Swartz cabin, the meaning of which neither he nor Anna could interpret.

22

Runaway

September 1725

Five-and-a-half-months pregnant, the miller's wife hoped she wouldn't have to leave her farm before the baby arrived. Though Anna stayed at home, she couldn't avoid the tensions of her day. The political struggles between the Iroquois Nation, the British colonial government in Philadelphia, and the settlers on the frontier came right to her doorstep.

Two visitors arrived at the Funk farm in late September who each revealed the bigger political struggles of empire. The first came in search of his past while the second came in search of his future.

Anna could tell when Bull's bark meant a stranger had arrived at the farm, and she quickly went to the door to look outside.

"Daniel Trico's my name, ma'am," the silver-haired man announced.

"How can I help you?" Anna responded, glancing out to notice that he rode alone.

"I'm here to meet the great-granddaughter of Jansen Visscher."

"How do you know who I am?" Anna asked.

"I've been doing research for the past nine months, and I'm here to talk with you and explain what I've learned."

Intrigued, Anna invited the older man into her stone house.

Glad for a seat in the Funk house, Daniel Trico began by explaining that he had attended church at the Mennonite meetinghouse the past January in Philadelphia, when Anna's mother had inquired of her whereabouts.

"I talked to your parents after the service," Trico outlined. "Your mother is the granddaughter of Jansen and Griet Visscher, isn't she?"

"Yes, but why does that information bring you here?" Anna asked.

Henry walked in the door, having seen that a visitor had come to his house.

"I've come to your farm, because a hundred years ago two women aboard your great-grandfather's ship helped deliver my mother's first baby." The Philadelphia guest spoke slowly, deliberately, and with great respect for the Funk couple.

"How do you know these details?" Anna asked.

"I am the eleventh and last child of Catalina Trico," the gentle visitor answered. "When my mother gave birth to her first child, your great-grandfather's ship, *The Black Tulip*, had anchored nearby."

"Did he help your mother?" Anna inquired.

"Not directly, but two women aboard his ship helped deliver my mother's baby and probably saved her life. My mother was only eighteen at the time."

"You're the eleventh child?" Henry asked.

"Yes, and there are many Tricos scattered throughout the colonies," Daniel responded. "My wife and I had ten children, though she has now passed on."

"I'm sorry," Anna answered.

"She died this past spring," Mr. Trico replied. "I've been patiently investigating your whereabouts and your connection to Jansen Visscher."

Anna started preparing for their evening meal. "Can you eat with us?" Henry invited.

"I'd be honored." Joking, Mr. Trico added, "Of course, I really have nowhere else to go for a meal, now do I?"

Laughing, Anna encouraged her guest to continue his story.

With potatoes and beans from the Funk garden on the table, and a slice of ham for each, Mr. Trico marveled that Anna had come to live in Pennsylvania.

"Why is that such an amazing thing?" Anna asked.

"We're Dutch," Mr. Trico explained. "My parents were from the Netherlands, and I carry that heritage. You are from Aruba, a Dutch colony."

"She's married to a German farmer," Henry replied.

"I've never thought about my Dutch heritage and living in a British colony," Anna remarked.

"It doesn't make much difference, I suppose," Mr. Trico reflected. "Though it may matter for your children's identity."

"How so?" Anna pressed.

"This is a British colony," Mr. Trico explained. "Dutch and German immigrants are welcome, but it is the English who receive the favored benefits of living here."

"And I suppose the Indians don't get any of the benefits you refer to?" Anna inquired.

"It's true. While they've lived here for centuries, even thousands of years, it's a new era," Mr. Trico replied.

"Would it be better if Anna registered her marriage to me as a German immigrant?" Henry asked.

"Marriages aren't recorded in Philadelphia," Mr. Trico answered. "But immigrants and babies born here are registered. There may come a time in the years ahead where it might be in your best interests to register Anna's German heritage."

"So my marriage to Henry makes me German?" Anna laughed.

"Someday it may not be like this, but in eighteenth-century Pennsylvania, your identity carries with your husband," Mr. Trico answered.

The pleasant discussion with the historian from Philadelphia was interrupted, however, by a galloping horse. Its rider reined up outside the Funk door, horse snorting. After a friendly bark from Bull, a sharp knock brought Henry to the door.

It had been five days since Abe and Annie Beth Swartz, and their son John, had vanished from their log home. Mr. Kolb, Annie Beth's father, stood at the door, out of breath, and told Henry what he knew.

"The Mohawk have captured Annie Beth, Abe, and Little John, and taken them to Fort Orange on Castle Island in New York," Mr. Kolb explained. "Albany is the new British city nearby to Fort Orange."

"The New York Colony?" Henry exclaimed. "Why there?"

"Fort Orange is in the Iroquois Nation," Mr. Kolb explained.

"How did you find this out?" Henry asked.

"The Mohawk sent word to the authorities in Philadelphia, which is where I just returned from. Abe and Annie Beth's capture is part of the Mohawk removal of ten families from Pennsylvania," Mr. Kolb explained. "It seems to be part of a power move by Chief Shickellamy."

"Can you come in?" Henry invited.

"No, I have several more homes from the church to visit with this news," Mr. Kolb explained. "Pray for them," and with that he mounted his horse and rode off to the next farm.

Henry slumped in a wooden chair and turned to Anna and Mr. Trico. "How could Abe, Annie Beth, and Little John get swept up in a game of politics between empires?"

"It's not hard to imagine," Daniel Trico replied. "Governor Keith, James Logan, and Chief Fifteen Feathers are each powerful and proud men."

"Ruthless would be the better word to describe them," Anna replied.

"Anna, does Fort Orange mean anything to you?" Trico asked.

"No, why do you ask?"

"It was in Dutch-controlled Fort Orange where your great grandfather's ship, *The Black Tulip*, lowered anchor in the Hudson River. It's there where two women aboard his ship helped my mother survive childbirth."

"It seems the Iroquois Nation is trying to assert itself against the British," Henry commented.

"True, Henry, but I came to your home not only to tell you the story of saving my mother, but to thank you."

"I'm three generations later," Anna replied.

"But I'm a direct link to a hundred years ago," Trico answered. Reaching into his pocket, he pulled out a gold medallion.

"I know you've been searching for such a medallion," Trico reflected.

Anna gasped in surprise.

"How did you know that?" Anna asked.

"I saw you with your dog and the Indian lady in Philadelphia recently, and I watched you play tricks in the square. I asked around after you left. Everyone knows you're looking for the gold medallion that is so highly valued by the Lenape Indians."

Anna held the bright jewelry piece and noticed the delicate chain that came with it. It had a cross on one side, like the lost medallion, but a stalk of wheat on the other side, not the Lenape turtle.

"It's for a woman to wear around her neck," Trico explained.

"For me?" Anna inquired.

"It's my way of saying thank you, Anna. I owe my life to your great-grandfather's willingness to help my mother."

Anna put the medallion around her neck and reached for her mirror to see a reflection of what it looked like on her.

"It's lovely," Henry replied. "Since it's dark, you should stay the night in our mill."

"Thank you, Henry. One final thing, Anna. You represent the finest of what's taking place in Pennsylvania."

Henry and Anna looked puzzled.

"You are Dutch in background, but you're married to a German immigrant. You lived with and made friends with the Delaware Indians. James Logan and Governor Keith both know who you are," Trico concluded. "You represent the best hope for peace that William Penn dreamed for in this new land," Trico paused.

Anna noticed a tear in Trico's eye, which he wiped.

"My life is now complete, Anna. I have thanked the Visscher family for saving my mother. Now I can go."

Anna shed a tear, and gave Daniel Trico a gentle hug. "You remind me of my grandfather," Anna concluded.

"I'm honored to have met you," Trico concluded. "Now it's time for me to go. I'll be gone at the light of dawn. Come visit me in Philadelphia sometime."

"It won't be anytime soon," Anna stated, patting her belly.

Three days later, on the third Saturday of September, a slave named Sampson arrived on Anna and Henry's doorstep. Of course, Sampson was not his actual name, Anna soon learned.

James Logan, Sampson's owner, had stripped the African man of his real name and his African language. Sampson was the assigned name that Logan gave him. After Logan purchased Sampson from a recent arrival of slaves from Africa, Sampson had worked at Stenton, Logan's mansion and estate north of Philadelphia. The African worked on the farm, contributing to the economic prosperity of the Logan household. He learned the English language quickly and communicated well with

Henry and Anna.

Most recently Sampson had worked for Logan in Philadelphia, and he had seen the squalor and poverty in William Penn's capital, and to Anna's surprise, Sampson had information on how the fire started that burned the courthouse.

On Saturday and Sunday, Sampson told his story to Anna and Henry. They learned of James Logan's desire to turn the Pennsylvania frontier into agricultural gold, not so much for the farmers themselves, but for the colonial treasury and government officials in Philadelphia.

Sampson explained to the Funks about the contrasts in Philadelphia, between the ambitious economic prosperity of the city and the dismal conditions most lived in. There was no police force in Philadelphia, Sampson told Anna and Henry. There were gangs, pick pockets, self-promoters, prostitutes, and visitors who were often scared to walk the streets of the city of brotherly love. Diseases ran rampant, people didn't trust the water so they drank alcohol, and people dumped their trash into the streets, that stunk with human waste.

In the middle of Philadelphia stood a pillory that served to humiliate anyone caught in the cross fires of Logan or Governor Keith. Men, and sometimes women, had their heads and wrists locked in the wooden contraption, and there they stood for days while people mocked them, spit on them, and abused them.

Philadelphians were angry at Logan, Sampson explained, and three day ago he had just run away. He figured that Logan would chase him, and at some point he'd have to run again. His worst fear, he explained to Henry and Anna, was hearing the howling blood hounds who hunted down slaves.

Too near Philadelphia to be safe, he wanted to go to Canada or other French-controlled territory. Would the Funks protect him from being taken back to Logan's farm, or worse? Runaway slaves were sometimes executed or sold and shipped somewhere else. Sampson sat in Anna's house and shook with fear.

"How did the fire in the courthouse start?" Anna asked.

"Several men, angry at having been locked in the pillory, worked together one night to set the building ablaze," Sampson answered. "Fires burn buildings in the city all the time, and there's no organized way to put them out."

"Has Logan found those who started the fire?" Anna asked.

"No one's talking," Sampson responded. "Logan has not caught the men, and Lord help them if he does."

"How did you learn about our farm?" Henry asked.

"Your farm is known among the slaves," Sampson answered. "We don't write anything down, but slaves tell one another that your home and William and Jubilant's home are places where runaways can find help."

When Anna set her Sunday noon table for five, she couldn't help but think of Daniel Trico's assessment that her home was what William Penn had in mind for his commonwealth. She served the runaway Sampson, the former slave Bentura, the Delaware Indian Cool Water, and Henry the German. And herself, well, she was Dutch, but she was increasingly a mix of all of the groups in her community. Perhaps she was just "American."

Henry Funk's two millstones arrived on the farm on Monday at noon. He and Anna had a little celebration which lasted only a moment, since the men from Philadelphia had come to install them, not join a party.

The workers placed the stationary bedstone in position first, with a cross-shaped rind in the middle which supported the runner stone on top. Bentura and Sampson gathered around, and with Henry, marveled at the engineering in the stones, imported from France. By evening, water from the race turned the giant wooden wheel outside the mill, which turned the internal gears, which brought power to the runner stone, which began to turn. The men cheered when it operated successfully.

"Get some corn," Henry ordered. From corn harvested on the Funk farm, Sampson poured kernels into a chute above the bin, which Henry slowly released into the top of the runner stone. Within a few minutes of grinding, the flour from the corn began to come out between the stones, again bringing a cheer from the men.

Cool Water and Anna watched the process as well. Anna brought the men garden tea she had prepared, and they took a break to celebrate. "We've got a small army to feed, Cool Water. Would you help me make the evening meal?"

It did not take long for Henry to notice the mechanical skills that Sampson brought to the mill. "Where did you learn how to work with gears?" Henry asked.

"I was trained as a blacksmith in Africa," Sampson replied. "Then I was captured and brought to Stenton, where I worked in the carriage and blacksmith shops."

"I need you to work here," Henry continued. "Will you help me run this mill?"

"I'm a slave," the tall African answered.

Henry did not know quite how to respond to this observation. Yes, Sampson was a slave, and owned by the most powerful man in Pennsylvania, James Logan himself.

"We'll figure something out," Henry stated. "There's a place for you to live upstairs," Henry added, "where Abe once stayed."

Abe Swartz, Bentura, and now Sampson. Men had come and gone from the Funk farm. Sampson's mechanical skills and his desire to acquire freedom made him a valuable person to work for Henry. At some point, of course, Logan would come storming onto the farm and want his property returned. Henry knew he would have to eventually deal with that problem.

Moyer, the neighboring Mennonite farmer with coon dogs, arrived late on Monday. Moyer came to inquire about whether the mill was ready for use. He had talked with Henry at church the week before, and thought the mill might be operational.

"I'll be your first customer," Moyer stated.

The men from Philadelphia left the Funk farm at about the same time on Tuesday morning that Henry and Sampson turned to see Moyer coming up the trail with a load of corn that needed to be milled. Before Moyer arrived, Sampson confided in Henry.

"Mr. Funk, one of the men from the factory recognized me. He knows I was Logan's slave."

"What does that mean?" Henry asked.

"He's one of the men who spent time in the pillory and joined with other men to start the courthouse on fire. He is aware that I saw him help to start the fire."

"Will he tell Logan where you are?" Henry asked while both men continued to watch Moyer pull his load toward the mill.

"If he does, and Logan comes here, I have deadly information about him," Sampson concluded. "So, I don't know if he'll tell anyone about where I am or not."

"We'll find that out eventually, Sampson. For now, we have work to do at the mill. Our first paying customer has arrived."

23

Tickets

September 1725

It surprised Anna and Henry when the proprietary governor, John Penn, came to see the tomahawk at Abe and Annie Beth Swartz's home. Penn lived in England, but had come to Pennsylvania to inspect his colony.

At the first sight of Penn, Sampson fled to hide among the Lenape at Perkiomen Creek. Lenape Mother welcomed him and promised to keep him safe.

Penn traveled with Lieutenant Governor William Keith and Chief Justice James Logan. William Penn's son was single and at twenty-five, was apparently an eligible bachelor. With the Iroquois Nation challenging the British crown by kidnapping ten families from Pennsylvania, Penn had come to investigate.

The officials found the tomahawk still stuck in the tree where it had been discovered. Nothing had changed at the Swartz farm.

"Is this the way you first saw it?" John Penn coldly inquired.

"It is," Henry answered.

"Did anyone in this region see them taken away?"

"No one saw anything, Governor Penn," Henry answered.

Through clenched teeth, Penn scowled. "Fifteen Feathers must be taught a lesson. Kidnapping families like this needs to cost him."

"We hardly have the soldiers in the colony to challenge him," Logan remarked.

"Then what options do we have?" Penn asked.

"It would take a large army to attack Fort Orange," Keith responded.

"What does Shickellamy want?" the British official asked.

"He wants to reinforce the understanding that the Iroquois still control the eastern woodlands," Logan said.

"In his dealings with the Lenape at Perkiomen Creek," Henry added, "Shickellamy's been generous but firm, though threatening at times."

"I heard he came to your wedding," Penn stated flatly.

"He did," Henry replied, "but it seems that, as more and more Germans and Scotch-Irish come to Pennsylvania, he feels like he may be losing control."

"He is," Penn icily responded. "We must get recompense for kidnapping innocent families."

Throughout the morning, news circulated in the community about the arrival of officials from Philadelphia. By noon, when Logan, Penn, and Keith arrived at the Funk farm to see the new mill, itself a noteworthy event for the visitors, local folks had gathered to see the dignitaries.

Bull barked at Governor Penn and the delicate, indoors-acclimated British inspector flinched. Anna noticed but did little to rescue the man. He seemed detached and elite, Anna observed. When Penn glanced at the pretty Agnes Kolb for a little too long, Anna grew alarmed.

"She's only fourteen," Anna glared. "And she's a Mennonite."

John Penn remained undeterred by Anna Funk's challenge to his interest in the attractive girl. When Anna grew perturbed, Bull sensed it and growled at the visitor, and Penn soon returned to looking at gears and grindstones in the mill.

"You might want to take Agnes and go home," Anna informed Mr. Kolb. "The governor has noticed her."

"He won't try anything, will he?" Mr. Kolb asked.

"He's used to getting what he wants, I'm sure," Anna responded.

"We'll leave after we eat lunch," Mr. Kolb assured her.

"Anna, that's a lovely medallion," Logan offered. It was a genuine compliment, and Logan asked where she got it.

"It was a gift from a visitor who came to the farm," Anna responded.

"Can you tell me who?" Logan asked.

"Daniel Trico from Philadelphia."

"I know him. He lives on Second Street, just down the street from the courthouse, or where it used to be."

"Will you rebuild this fall, or wait until spring?" Anna asked.

"With cleanup and the costs of building, it will be next year," Logan answered. "Could I see the medallion?"

Taking it from her neck, Anna handed it to him and said, "Do you see the cross and the wheat stalk?"

"It's very nice, Anna. May I show this to Mr. Penn and Mr. Keith?" Logan asked.

With her approval, Logan walked from where he had been seated on a log to where his companions sat. Bull followed and barked excitedly. Logan hesitated at the sight of the big dog tracking him but felt confident enough to continue walking.

"Look at this," Logan began. "Daniel Trico, from Philadelphia, gave this to Anna."

"Why does it matter?" Penn asked.

"Have you heard of the lost gold medallion?" Keith responded.

Even though Penn shook his head and showed little interest, Keith continued the story. "Your father promised to look for the medallion. Do you have any idea where it is?"

John Penn stood, ignored the question, and left the group. He walked toward the house, where Anna and the Kolbs ate lunch. Bull followed him.

"Mr. Kolb," the arrogant London visitor began, "May I talk to your daughter?"

Anna flashed alarm across her face. Mr. Kolb noticed and reacted; he stood tall, and said that they had work to do on their farm.

"As soon as my father's estate is settled, I will move to Philadelphia and assume leadership of the colony. I could provide your daughter with a good future." Agnes glanced at Penn, almost twice her age, and quickly looked away.

Aghast at the bold and callous offer to Mr. Kolb, Anna held in her anger at the fact that Penn had not even talked to Agnes.

"I'll be staying at Mr. Keith's home, about fifteen miles from here. I would be glad for you to bring your daughter to the house so I can get to know her."

"I don't plan on doing that," Mr. Kolb responded. "Thank you for the food, Anna. We'll be going now." Agnes, the youngest daughter in the family and as beautiful as her older sisters, followed after her parents, and was smart enough not to look back at the man from England.

Unlike Penn's arrogant approach, Henry chose to look away from the pretty neighbor girl who walked toward her home. It was not good for his soul. He saw her at church most Sundays, and she was very attractive.

After the Kolbs left, Penn, Keith, and Logan prepared to depart. Anna put the gold medallion back around her neck.

"Bull and I are looking for the Lenape medallion," Anna remarked. "We intend to find it."

"Not in your condition, you won't," Penn laughed.

Embarrassed, and then angry, Anna bit her tongue.

"Watch this," Anna retorted. Pulling it off and throwing the cheap trinket, Bull lunged after it, bringing it back with slobber all over the gold colored toy.

"That's how you're going to find the medallion?" Penn laughed. "That's silly."

Henry tried to break the tension and take the conversation in a different direction. "Our baby is due in December, Governor Penn. Will you still be in the colony?" Henry asked.

"I'm not sure," Penn replied.

Without a word of thanks for the noon meal, or the tour of the mill or the Swartz homestead, Governor Penn flicked his reins, and the men rode off.

Henry and Anna sat on the front stoop of their stone house, where Henry surprised his wife by revealing an envelope in his pocket.

"Where did you get that?" Anna asked.

"Logan delivered this to me. It's from Philadelphia," Henry answered. Looking at the outside, Henry showed Anna that it was from Ben Franklin.

Gazing down the trail toward the main road, Henry asked Anna if she thought there would ever be regular mail service to their farm.

"We had mail service to our home in Santa Cruz," Anna replied. "It came once a week."

"Who did you get letters from?" Henry asked.

"From relatives in Amsterdam," Anna answered.

"Anna," Henry switched topics. "You were steaming mad at the governor, weren't you?"

"He was rude, Henry. He didn't thank us for anything, and he made it clear he wants Agnes."

"Do you think he'll do anything further about her?" Henry wondered.

"Who knows?" Anna scowled.

"Anna, I want you to write a letter," Henry stated.

"Why?"

Scanning the letter, Henry told Anna that he had been invited to a

Junto meeting. "It looks like I might be going to Philadelphia," Henry answered.

"What's a Junto meeting?" Anna asked.

Turning, Henry switched topics again. "Anna, I'll tell you more about the letter, but I'm in love with the queen of the Funk farm." Holding her, he kissed her boldly. "I'm glad I'm married to you and that you're not mad at me. Let's go inside."

"Henry, I'm pregnant."

"Hush. Come with me."

Bull whimpered outside when Henry pulled the front door of the house closed. Henry and Anna were alone in the privacy of their own home.

Three and a half weeks after Adam and Dorothy Miller had left the Funk farm for Virginia, they arrived at the deer-crossing called Elkton.

"There's nothing here," Dorothy blurted out.

Turning, she noticed that the Mohawk escorts had vanished. It was just her and Adam in what seemed like the middle of nowhere.

It was a beautiful fall day, with leaves just beginning to turn from green to orange and red. Adam reached for his axe, rolled up his sleeves, and began to chop down a tree.

Dorothy found a place to start a fire and prepare food with the little she had brought along. She turned and looked back at the tall mountain peak they had recently passed. Its prominence and stunning magnificence helped mute the sinking realization that she may have made a mistake marrying Adam. Watching him swing the axe with determination, however, drove that thought away.

Before she lit the fire, she reached for her new gun, loaded it, and went to look for something for dinner. A few minutes later Adam heard a shot, and soon Dorothy emerged from the woods, beaming.

"I shot a deer," Dorothy announced. "Come help me clean it, Adam." Together the newlyweds dressed the venison, lit the kindling, built a fire, and made their first meal in Virginia. As darkness fell, Adam embraced his traveling partner and new bride, and they found a grassy place to lie down and make a bed for the night. Under the Virginia stars and moon, they were home.

Meanwhile, in Pennsylvania, Henry spoke to Anna. "Why don't you write a letter to Chief Lapowinsa. You've known him since you arrived here last year. You helped him get out of his cell last month, and he's locked up again."

"What shall I say?" Anna asked.

"Encourage him," Henry suggested. "Tell him we're still looking for the gold medallion."

"I should tell him about Abe and Annie Beth being kidnapped," Anna added.

"Tell him that Bentura and Cool Water are going to Aruba."

"Are you going to help them get tickets?" Anna asked.

"That's another reason I'm going to Philadelphia," Henry replied.

"Okay, I'll write him a letter," Anna agreed. "But someone will have to read it to him."

Anna had four days to write a letter to the Lenape chief. With quill pen and paper at Henry's desk, she worked at it whenever she got a chance.

After Henry preached at the Franconia Church on Sunday, he announced that he would be taking Bentura and Cool Water to Philadelphia on Wednesday. He wanted to help them purchase tickets to sail to Aruba in the Caribbean. Anna had remained at home, telling Henry that she was uncomfortable; she wasn't sure she could sit on the hard benches for two hours, and she wanted to work on the letter.

On Tuesday morning Bentura and Cool Water took down their wigwam next to the Funk stone house and stored it in the back of the barn. Since their wedding in late June, Bentura had worked three months for Henry on the farm and in the mill. He would miss the work and had come to enjoy the many aspects of farm life, and he hoped to return next spring.

Cool Water wanted to visit her people for a night before leaving for Philadelphia early Wednesday morning. They had one trunk for all their things, and they took it along on the walk to Perkiomen Creek. Bentura hoisted it on his shoulder.

The Lenape Mother welcomed Cool Water and Bentura to their circle.

"We are going to Bentura's home a long way from here," Cool Water explained.

"Bentura is a good husband, and he will help you with your baby," Lenape Mother replied.

"We have to sail by ship, which I am uncertain about," Cool Water confided.

"Do not be afraid, Cool Water. You will find strength for the journey."

"Anna explained that a ship is always moving, and it is easy to get sick," Cool Water replied. "I hope that with my baby I can avoid that."

"Henry, I love you," Anna began. "I wish you weren't leaving for Philadelphia."

Holding his new wife in his arms, Henry said, "Anna, I love you, and I'll only be gone a few days."

"That's too many days away," Anna replied.

"I'll get you something," Henry answered.

"What?"

"It's a secret, but I've been thinking about a gift for you. You'll like it," Henry promised.

"There won't be anybody here at the farm. Everybody's left, Henry. Annie Beth and Dorothy are gone, and Little John is somewhere in New York."

"That's why Bull will sit outside your door and guard you," Henry smiled.

"I want you, Henry. Stay here with me."

"I have to get tickets, and Ben wants me to attend a meeting on Friday evening at the print shop."

"Last night I dreamed about you, Henry. It was a nice dream, but it ended badly and then I woke up," Anna frowned.

"I'll be coming back," Henry promised. "You are my love and my everything. This baby will bring me back, Anna. I can't wait to see if we will have a boy or girl. Where were we in the dream?" Henry asked.

"At the dam down at Indian Creek," Anna replied. "We were kissing as the sun went down, but you fell off the wall, and then I woke up."

Henry held his wife and felt the baby kick. "We have a future here on Indian Creek. See that loft up there?" Henry looked. "I want more children to sleep up there and play on our floor."

"So what are you going to get me?" Anna begged.

"I can't tell you," Henry insisted.

"Fine, here's my letter for Chief Lapowinsa."

"I'll deliver it, promise," Henry replied.

"Now don't get tricked by the pretty girls in Philadelphia," Anna warned.

"Pretty girls? Are you worried about me?"

"We'll, you're handsome and there are plenty of girls who would like to have you," Anna counseled.

"I'm yours alone," Henry consoled.

"Good."

"I have to go," Henry stated. "Bentura and Cool Water are waiting."

When the traveling trio left with Cool Water on horseback, while Bentura and Henry walked, Bull knew that he was supposed to stay at the farm with Anna. The homeward bound Aruban smiled and eagerly carried the trunk on his shoulder.

In Philadelphia, Bentura produced his emancipation document with James Logan's seal pressed on it. It didn't take long for Henry to buy two tickets for passage on a ship that would sail on Friday, October 1. Bentura and Cool Water had a three-day wait in the capital until they sailed to Aruba. They would arrive by the middle of October if all went as planned.

At the courthouse office, now a rented building on Second Street, Henry delivered Anna's letter to the constable who agreed to give it to Chief Lapowinsa.

"Will you take along someone who can read the letter to the chief?" Henry inquired. It was agreed to, and Henry was confident that the Delaware chief would get the letter and learn the contents therein.

At an intersection on his way into Ben Franklin's print shop on the last day of September, Henry witnessed a horrible scene. Three women had their hands tied low on a post, which forced them to lean over, and a man was whipping them on the buttocks, bringing shrieks of terror from the women. Ben met Henry in the square, and told him that this was one of the reasons he had called the Friday evening Junto meeting.

"They're each pregnant illegitimately," Ben explained. "This is their punishment."

24

Junto

October 1725

When the Junto Club met around a work table in Andrew Bradford's Second Street print shop, Ben Franklin outlined how the group operated. Henry was the newest man to join, and the ground rules were simple to understand.

The men around Ben Franklin's table were older than he, but no man was yet fifty. Creases of work-related concern etched their foreheads that had been forged in the crucible of the business world. When the men introduced themselves to newcomer Henry Funk, their professions included a printer, a surveyor, a cabinetmaker, a clerk, a bartender, a merchant, an inventor, and astrologer. The group had only met a few times, and additional men had been invited each time. As the new man in, Henry had been asked to make a presentation to start the second session.

"We are Junto, which means 'civil meeting.' We start by examining a problem in the city for the first portion of our meeting. During the second session one man makes a reasoned presentation, and we discuss it." Franklin explained.

"We listen well to one another," Franklin emphasized, "we debate topics, we seek common understandings, but we do not attack or ridicule another man's ideas."

The men nodded in agreement. Two women brought drinks from the bar next door.

"Our first topic is the problem we saw yesterday in the town square,"

Franklin announced. "What can we do about the whipping of unmarried women who get pregnant?"

While a reasoned discussion of the whippings problem and who was responsible for them took place, Henry couldn't help but notice the voluptuous young women who served drinks and food to the men. The women didn't mind at all when a man noticed them, and they dressed to attract attention. The juxtaposition of men discussing disgraced women that had been taken advantage of as prostitutes in the street with the two provocative women serving them puzzled Henry. He did not have the nerve to raise the topic.

During the first session, Henry mostly listened. The group's purpose was to come up with a reasonable proposal for the city council on how to stop the whippings, but they weren't getting very far. The men agreed that it was the women's problem for why they had gotten pregnant, because they had tempted men who had been lured by their womanly charms. The men did talk about creating respectable jobs for the women in order to help keep them off the streets.

After about thirty minutes, the men agreed to take a motion to the council asking that the whippings stop, but they did not have a good alternative to suggest. The women continued to bring food and drink, and Henry noticed them, and they eyed him.

After a break, Henry launched into his presentation. Using content from the sermon he had preached the previous Sunday, he announced that the topic was *Citizenship*.

"This morning I helped load a former slave and his wife, a Lenape Indian, onto a ship that departed for the Caribbean," Henry began.

"Bentura had been a slave in Aruba and was captured by slavers who brought him to Philadelphia to be sold. James Logan signed and sealed his freedom papers, and now he is returning to Aruba. Which country is he a citizen of: the Netherlands, who claims Aruba, or Great Britain, since his seal comes from the British Crown? His wife Cool Water is Lenape Delaware. Which country is she a citizen of?" Henry asked.

In order to bolster his argument, Henry pulled details from his recent sermon. "Believers in God are citizens of a different kingdom," Henry reasoned. "They owe their highest allegiance to Christ Jesus our Lord."

The men shifted uneasily as Henry developed his topic. Henry had been introduced as a mill owner along Indian Creek, which brought respect from the club. But as he spoke, the men increasingly realized that Henry was also a minister of the gospel. There wasn't much gospel in the room and even fewer churchgoers. Even the women who served sensed how the mood in the room had changed, and they paused their work to listen. When the women looked at him and adjusted their dresses, Henry wasn't sure he could go on.

"The Apostle Paul was a Roman citizen, yet his allegiance lay with God's kingdom," Henry stated. "Christ himself was crucified at the hands of the Roman authorities." One man belched, but quickly apologized.

"We've had slaves come to our farm, seeking freedom," Henry continued. "Where does their citizenship lie? Are they British or African? One out of ten people in Philadelphia is a slave. It's an institution that I wish would end," Henry concluded.

Trying to read the body language of the men around the table, Henry was uncertain what they were thinking, but he could tell they were uncomfortable. The men ate and drank and listened, the women got back to work filling steins, and Henry realized he should quickly finish his presentation.

"I find the Quaker willingness to trade and own slaves a contradiction," Henry declared. "Quakers are a peaceful people, but they harm Africans when they enslave them. That should end. My people do not own slaves,"

Henry announced. "Citizenship brings with it rights, freedoms, and responsibilities," Henry concluded.

"Slaves are property and should be returned to their owner," reasoned the surveyor.

"Their owners bought them with good money," the clerk added.

"In the natural course of civilizations conquering others," the astrologer finished, "one culture conquers another. The conquered are inferior people."

The inventor agreed that the Quakers had a double standard. "The Pennsylvania Quaker government won't raise an army to defend frontier settlers from the Indians, but their people will own slaves. That is a contradiction."

"Your people the Mennonites," the bartender queried, "do they consider themselves German or British?"

"Our first loyalty is to the kingdom of God," Henry answered.

"Will you defend yourselves against the godless Indians?" the bartender pressed.

"The Indians are people like we are," Henry replied. "Some seem to have more of the divine in them than settlers who savagely attack them."

The men at the table remained respectful, but it was clear to the host that Henry Funk didn't fit with the Junto men. "Henry," Franklin asked, "You do believe that Englishmen are of superior value to the Indians, don't you?"

Henry hesitated, sipping on his drink. Every man waited, patiently, to hear Henry's thoughts.

"The English people have a cultured civilization," Henry began. "They have inherited and learned from layers of many civilizations before them. They are refined and learned, with great writings, buildings, and music. But so are the Indians. My wife Anna lived with the Lenape for several months and learned their language. She found them friendly, courageous, and peaceful. Their culture is a world apart from the English, but they are equal to the English as people."

The merchant pushed his cup toward the center of the table and coughed. "Indians cut down my parents in cold blood," he responded. "They are godless and ruthless. Their warriors scalped my father and mother. The Indians are not equal to the British."

Each man challenged Henry Funk's ideas of the equality of the Indians with the British. To get the discussion going in a different direction, Franklin asked Henry to tell the group about his mill.

Immediately the men around the table perked up. These hardened men understood business, work, and efforts to make money. Mills were one of the most significant economic events on the frontier. When they became operational, businessmen in Pennsylvania applauded, for they understood the progress it represented.

At the door, Henry met the women who had served him food and drink. Henry tipped them, but they wanted more. The minister politely declined.

Eleven days after his disappearance, Sampson returned and knocked on Anna's front door. Bull barked but wagged his tail when Sampson spoke to him.

Opening the door, Anna asked, "Where have you been?"

"I had to run when I heard that Logan was coming to the farm," Sampson explained.

"Where did you go?"

"The Lenape on Perkiomen Creek took me in."

When Anna looked outside the door, she spotted a young woman. "Who's this?"

"My new friend," Sampson answered.

"You have a lady friend?" Anna inquired.

"Yes," Sampson grinned. "She loves me."

"Come in," Anna insisted. Anna recognized the young woman from when she had lived among the Lenape.

"That was fast, Sampson. She likes you?"

"She does, and we want to get married. We will need your help."

"What? Another wedding on the Funk farm?"

"If you would be so kind to help us, we would be grateful."

"I must talk to Lenape Mother," Anna replied.

"We can bring her to your house," Sampson suggested. "You do not appear to be in the best condition to travel very far from home."

"Henry comes home tomorrow," Anna told Sampson. "Can you work in the mill?"

"Oh yes, I want to work for Henry," Sampson replied. "Can Pretty Leaves live upstairs in the mill with me?"

When Anna hesitated, Sampson understood. "Pretty Leaves will go back to Perkiomen Creek until Henry returns."

"You can live upstairs in the mill," Anna offered. "We will see what Henry says about Pretty Leaves staying with you."

On Saturday morning Henry went to visit Chief Lapowinsa before leaving Philadelphia. The guard agreed to let him in, and Henry was surprised to find a young Indian woman in his cell.

"This is my granddaughter," Lapowinsa explained. "She's here to help me."

Henry examined the leather pouch that the chief had always carried around his neck. Lapowinsa's granddaughter, from Indian Creek, brought colorful porcupine quills. The quills had been flattened and dyed, and the two were stitching them to the surface of the elk hide.

"Did you receive Anna's letter?" Henry asked.

"I did," Lapowinsa answered. Henry noticed creases in the man's forehead, concern etched across his face. Here he was, locked in a cell in a jail in Philadelphia with a granddaughter helping him stitch quills on a pouch. He's a chief, Henry thought. He should be with his people.

Two times since this past spring Chief Lapowinsa had escaped the jail. The first time Mohawk warriors broke him loose. The second time Anna and Cool Water played a trick with Bull, and he got out. He'd almost been shot in a tree near the Funk farm when bloodhounds hunted him down.

The lines on the chief's face revealed his distinctive heritage. His grandfather's sister, Tender Vine, had been the one who received the gold medallion, then had it taken away in a horrible death. After Lapowinsa's father had made peace with William Penn under an elm tree in Philadelphia, he had been marked on his face as a man of peace, as one who would carry on the peace tradition of the famous 1683 meeting.

At fifty, Lapowinsa appeared to Henry as a tragic figure, like an Old Testament prophet who may have spoken to his own people in exile. The Old Testament prophets spoke words of hope, though, and rarely defeat. Lapowinsa kept his confident bearing about him, not broken in spite of the months in jail.

"What did she write?" Henry inquired.

"She encouraged me, and she wrote of receiving a gold medallion from a Philadelphia visitor."

"Yes, I want you to see it," Henry replied.

"Anna wrote of a couple being taken prisoner by Chief Shickellamy. Do you have any further news about them?"

"No," Henry said.

Two guards came to the door and announced that it was time for the weekly cleaning in Lapowinsa's cell. When a lady entered the room, the three were escorted outside by the guards. In the warm October sun, Henry and Lapowinsa could see the harbor, with ships either unloading or being loaded. They could see the big elm tree next to the harbor.

"You never got to know Bentura, did you?" Henry asked.

"No," Lapowinsa answered.

"He had been a slave, and got his emancipation papers from James Logan," Henry explained. "Two days ago I helped load him and his wife Cool Water on a ship, bound for Aruba."

"Cool Water?"

"Yes, why do you ask?"

"She is another of my granddaughters," the chief answered.

Surprised, Henry tried to tell Lapowinsa about Cool Water, living on his farm, traveling to the Caribbean, and possibly coming back in the spring for Henry to work on the farm.

"My people will need to move west," Lapowinsa announced.

"Say more," Henry encouraged.

"Cool Water went east and south. My people need to go west, to lands beyond the reach of the Penns, James Logan, and the Iroquois Nation."

"Can't we live in peace beside each other on Indian Creek?"

"Your people are taking over the land," Lapowinsa reflected, looking at recent immigrants coming off ships.

"Your people get their names changed," the Lenape chief reflected, staring at the harbor. "My people are getting their names erased, and we will need to move west, back toward the ancient land from where we came many moons ago."

After the cleaning lady dumped water waste from the chamber pot into the street, one guard went in to see if the room was ready.

Henry thought for a moment about trying to escape with the chief, but just then Ben Franklin arrived and greeted them.

"Is this Chief Lapowinsa?" Franklin inquired.

"Yes," Henry said. "Would you help me get him out of here?"

"I'm afraid you wouldn't succeed," Franklin said. He turned to look at guards putting two men in the city pillory for a couple of days. "If we try anything, we might be next in the stocks."

Changing the subject, Henry showed Franklin Lapowinsa's pouch. "Look at this," Henry said. "Two rows of quills, indicating how people should be able to live side by side and together, with their differences, yet getting along."

"That won't happen here," Franklin said. "With John Penn in the colony, the Indians are going to be driven out. I feel sorry for the chief."

"Can you write something in his defense?" Henry asked.

"Maybe. Is Agnes Kolb still eligible?"

"Eligible? Are you interested?" Henry asked in surprise.

"Yes, I am."

"She's too young for marriage," Henry replied.

"I hear Governor Penn doesn't think so."

"Where did you hear that?" Henry inquired.

"After a few drinks, tongues wag in bars around here," Franklin said.

When the guards took Lapowinsa back to his cell, Henry and Ben left. Henry soon had his saddle bags loaded, and coaxed his horse toward the Indian Creek road that led home.

In the back of the Second Street Print Shop, Ben Franklin wrote one of his widely distributed essays.

"The Mennonite minister from Indian Creek is a decent man. He disapproves of slavery. Mr. Funk visited the Delaware chief in prison and has befriended the Indian. Mr. Funk is naive about citizenship, believing that heaven is where his kingdom lies, but he is nevertheless a productive

and upright resident of Pennsylvania. His mill on Indian Creek represents progress and good fortune for the colony."

Ben Franklin was discovering what writers through the ages had learned: write, get your ideas distributed, and you can influence others. Franklin had learned to accept criticism, though, and he was learning how to write so as to express his opinions yet not alienate his readers.

When Bradford's *American Weekly Mercury* landed on Governor Penn's desk, the London visitor seethed. "Mr. Funk needs to be taught who's in charge around here," the Governor lectured.

Though no one was listening to him, it still felt good to say it out loud. He needed to give orders to Logan about Mr. Funk.

25

Citizen

October 1725

After church on Sunday, Sampson came to Henry's door and asked if he had work for him.

"I certainly do," Henry answered. "I need your help to get the mill operating."

"I'm a slave, Mr. Funk. You might get in trouble for hiring me."

"That's a chance I'll take," Henry replied.

"Thank you," Sampson said. "Did you hear of anyone in Philadelphia who asked about me?"

"No one."

"Good. Mr. Funk, did Anna ask you about Pretty Leaves living with me upstairs in the mill?

"No, Sampson, please come in."

When Sampson saw Anna he gasped. "That's a lovely dress, Mrs. Funk."

"Henry bought it for me in Philadelphia, for my birthday," Anna beamed. Simple and deep blue, Henry had found and purchased a special dress made for his very pregnant wife.

"She wore it to church today and everyone noticed," Henry smiled.

"I'm sure they did," Sampson replied. "Mr. Funk, can Pretty Leaves live with me in the mill?"

"Are you married?"

"Not yet. But we intend to get married. We were wondering if you would marry us."

"I can marry you, Sampson, but I prefer you wait until then before Pretty Leaves moves in with you."

Sampson thanked Henry, and then looked at Henry's books. Henry had accumulated a fair number of books. Friends and family had given Henry books after the fire, and he had purchased a few, that now stood on shelves. Sampson pulled one out and admired the binding and pages before he attempted to read it.

Glancing up at Henry, Sampson said that he couldn't read English very well but that he wanted to learn. "Of course I can't read your German books at all," Sampson laughed.

Henry marveled at Sampson's desire to read a book and expand his world of learning. Henry had learned Sampson's story enough to know that he had worked in the largest library in Pennsylvania, and possibly all of the American colonies, the one in James Logan's study. At Stenton, Logan's mansion, Sampson often entered into the three-thousand-book private library room of James Logan, only to be shooed away by his owner. Sampson had learned that the vast library of books was only for white men.

Sampson had mastered the spoken English language, and was learning to read it, when he broke loose one day while working at Logan's farm. Captured by other Africans across the ocean, Sampson had been shipped to Philadelphia in a stinking, overcrowded, death trap of a ship. He was one of the lucky ones who survived the Atlantic crossing.

"What's this big book?" Sampson asked, hoisting the largest in Henry's collection. "It's called *Martyrs Mirror*," Henry said. "Abe and Annie Beth Swartz gave it to me when they moved to their new home. Abe said it would be more useful on my desk than in his family chest. He brought it from Europe."

"What's it about?" Sampson asked.

"They're stories from Europe," Henry said. "Of people giving up their lives for convictions."

"It was printed by my great-great-grandparents in Amsterdam," Anna added.

"I can't read it," Samson said.

"Yes, I know, and fewer and fewer of our German people can read Dutch—I need to get it translated into German," Henry concluded.

"If I'm put to death for running and trying to learn how to read," Sampson pondered, "Will I be a martyr?"

"Good question," Henry replied. "My ancestors were burned at the stake and tortured for their religious beliefs. Martyrs listed in this book gave their lives for their religious convictions."

"I believe in freedom, Mr. Funk. I'll give my life to find it and learn to read."

"I hope you never become a martyr," Henry stated solemnly.

As the sun began to set Sunday evening, Henry heard harmonies again, like those at his wedding. Looking outside, Henry and Anna smiled as practically the entire Perkiomen Creek Indian community came singing and marching toward their house. They knew Henry loved music.

"We're here for you to marry Pretty Leaves to Sampson," Lenape Mother began.

"Right now?" Henry asked.

"Could you?" Lenape Mother replied.

"These two want to be married, and they both have asked for Minister Funk to perform their ritual."

"I'll get my Bible," Henry said. "Sampson, can you help get a fire started?"

Sampson stood tall and wiry next to Pretty Leaves, a petite Lenape woman. Henry noticed Sampson's admiration for the Bible he read from for a meditation. With little ado, Henry pronounced the couple husband and wife, and a party broke out on a warm October Sunday night along the Indian Creek.

Like Bentura three months earlier, Lenape Mother asked Sampson to lead a wedding dance around the fire. It was normal and expected in the Lenape community. Henry and Anna were surprised at how little Sampson wore, despite having seen the same at Cool Water's marriage to Bentura.

Mr. and Mrs. Kolb came calling for a Sunday evening visit and, though surprised by the wedding, they joined in quickly to help Anna make a feast.

"Can you invite William and Jubilant?" Henry asked Mr. Kolb. "They would enjoy being here."

Henry and Anna cuddled near the fire in the clearing outside their stone home. Anna recalled the devastation of the fire which had destroyed their previous log home. They had so much help rebuilding, and when the Zook man from Germany came with masonry skills, she knew they could rebuild with a degree of permanence.

Anna's people, the Delaware Indians from Perkiomen Creek, danced the night away. Between forty and fifty total, she realized that their numbers were dwindling, and that they would soon need to move again.

Bull, sitting next to Anna, patiently surveyed the situation and watched the farm, but bolted when an unexpected man appeared. It was the man in a bearskin costume who came to weddings, as he had at theirs. With red and black paint on his face, the man came to scare off evil spirits, frighten children, and welcome good spirits.

"Henry, do you remember when you asked Lenape Mother if you could marry me?"

"Yes, that man with the painted face showed up," Henry said.

"I guess he scared the evil spirits away," Anna replied.

"Why do you say that?"

"Because we've had a good marriage so far," Anna gushed. "I love you, Henry."

"The evil spirits are trying hard to interfere, I'd say," Henry replied.

"Why do you think that?"

"We can't get Lapowinsa out of jail, your people hardly have any children, and Sampson might be executed if Logan catches him. Seems to me the evil powers of darkness are closing in on the Funk farm."

"Be positive, Henry. We have friends, a baby on the way, we have a house, and your mill is open for business."

"But what of Abe and Annie Beth and Little John who are captives of the Mohawk in New York? Do you think your friend Dorothy has a roof over her head yet in Virginia? Are you prepared for what happens when the Pennsylvania militia marches against the Indians on the frontier and starts a blood bath?"

"Where are your thoughts coming from, Henry? We're at a wedding celebration, and your mind is going over all our troubles."

"It's who I am, I guess. I just keep thinking about these crazy times we live in. Germans are getting chased out of Europe because of terrible wars, and they migrate to these peaceful shores that William Penn established. When they get here, they face Indians, conflict between the Iroquois and the government in Philadelphia, and the rising threat of the French on the frontier. The government will sell you any land, like they did when Abe bought Lenape burial ground."

"Stop your bad thoughts," Anna begged. Fifteen years younger than her husband, Anna retained a positive outlook on life.

"Don't you miss your parents, Anna?" Henry asked. "I miss my grandparents that I left behind in Germany."

"I miss my mother," Anna confessed. "I want her to hold my baby someday."

"Have you thought about a name for the baby yet?" Henry asked.

"Oh sure," Anna replied. "Jansen if it's a boy or Griet if it's a girl."

"Your great-grandparents, right?"

"Yes, they settled in Aruba and gave me a heritage."

"Do you want us to move back to the Caribbean?" Henry asked.

"No, I like it here. You built me a house, we have friends, and this is now my home."

"Stop barking, Bull!" Henry insisted. Chasing Bull, Henry had to intervene to rescue the short Indian man with the bearskin from the massive dog. Bull wasn't challenging the harmless man, however. In the woods beyond, Bull sensed a threat, and he kept barking. Nothing that Henry could say would stop the dog.

Retrieving his rifle from the mill, Henry followed Bull. They ventured into the dark woods that led in the direction of the Lenape burial grounds and the empty Swartz log home.

Henry soon smelled smoke which hastened his steps as he tried to keep up with Bull. He knew it wasn't coming from the wedding fire at his house. Bull barked and wanted to run, but waited on Henry to catch up. Henry turned and noticed two braves following him. "We're here to help," one warrior struggled to say in poor English.

Henry could tell this wasn't about a raccoon on the loose, a bear ambling by the farm, or another varmint in the woods. All three men sensed that something dreadful was ahead of them.

The smell of smoke grew stronger, which hastened their pace. All three men had rifles. Henry had not seen any weapons among the Lenape, as they had concealed them when they came to the farm.

"Use your weapon or perish," had been the unspoken understanding of the European immigrants on the frontier. Henry was discovering the meaning thereof.

At the edge of the woods, it became clear that the Swartz's log house was burning. The men could see flames inside through the open front door. As Henry ran to try and find a bucket to get water from the nearby Indian Creek, shots rang out from the surrounding woods. The braves with Henry turned and fired back in the direction the bullets had come from. Henry hesitated, but ran to get water while the men reloaded.

Bull rocketed into the nearby woods and challenged the warriors who had fired at Henry. Before they could reload, the attackers realized they were going to be torn to shreds by an angry mastiff who threatened to rip their legs off, or worse. They turned and fled, dropping their weapons in order to run faster. Bull kept chase until the men leapt a log, stooped to grab sticks, and turned to defend themselves against the angry dog.

Kicking in the front door, Henry attacked the flames, throwing a bucket of water at the fire. The Lenape warriors joined him, though they could only find two buckets. After several trips to the creek, the men had slowed the fire enough to make them believe it could be stopped short of consuming the house. That realization made them work even harder.

In the woods, without the moon or any other light, two men fought for their lives against a massive dog. Never in their lives had they prepared for or imagined such a situation. Attacking proved futile, and they realized they needed a different option—they were not going to win. Up a tree the two men went, with Bull tearing at their legs. Unarmed and with a terrifying beast below, they settled on a limb to see what would happen next. In the distance they heard men trying to extinguish the fire which they had recently started.

Fire had consumed the furniture inside the house, but had not entered the main logs in the frame. This was fortunate, because Henry and the braves would not have been able to stop a structure fire. Sweating in the October night, Henry and the warriors put out the fire, with smoke all around. They coughed and rested for a moment after they conquered the fire.

Bull's insistent barking got their attention, and the Lenape warriors went to investigate. On impulse, the first Delaware brave to arrive raised his gun and shot into the dark tree, striking with deadly impact. A warrior dropped to the ground with a thud, dead. Bull kept barking into the tree above at the other man.

Pausing in his fight against the dying coals, Henry peered into the glowing charcoal, then turned toward the woods. He wondered if this was anything different than what his grandparents had faced in Europe during the War of the Spanish Succession. Entire German villages had been flattened by thousands of marching soldiers, accompanied by men on war horses that stomped crops flat with massive hooves. Farms had been ruined, disease spread like the plague, and his grandparents had watched their barn go up in flames. No one questioned him and his family when they emigrated away from the destruction of Germany. They had been forced out of Europe.

What faced Henry here on Indian Creek was the occasional threat to life and home, not the decades-long wars in Europe that were fought for no apparent reason, other than monarchs in distant cities wreaking havoc on other monarchs in other distant cities.

With smoke around him, Henry realized he had it very good. Anna was right. He should not complain about anything. God had led the

Funks to cross the Atlantic, and none of them had died. The vision of wolves tearing at Abe and Elizabeth's little boy around their wagon a few months prior still burned in Henry's conscience. There must have been something he could have done to save the boy.

The Apostle Paul had written about the powers of this dark world, of the way evil forces beyond the realm of humankind tore at the universe and did battle with the positive that came from humans and God's good creation in nature. Henry knew he was in a cosmic battle against the forces of evil. One man in one place, however, could make a huge difference. When inspired by God's Spirit, the difference could have long-lasting impact.

Bull had returned to stand beside him. Henry shed a tear at the hilarity and helpfulness of the imposing dog. Anna had begged for such a pup, and after it had been given as a gift, Henry learned to like the dog. Now it had saved a house from destruction. Bull was a symbol of the intersection of man's desires for good and the created order that God had established on the earth.

Kneeling, Henry said, "Bull, we're fighting against the forces of evil in this dark world." Bull licked the German immigrant's face and wiped the tears away. "What did you find, Bull?"

"Crazy dog," Henry thought, "while I was listening to the music at the wedding fire, you were listening to the music of a different sphere. How did you know there was trouble here, while we were at the farm?" The dog just wagged his tail.

With a Mohawk warrior tied up and guarded by two Delaware braves, they trekked back to the farm, carrying two extra guns. Henry reflected on his sermon two weeks prior about citizenship. He recalled the discussion at the Junto gathering in Philadelphia, in which he outlined his ideas about citizenship. The men had told him that he himself was not yet a citizen of the commonwealth, as he not been here for ten years. Sampson, whom he had just married to an Indian woman, was definitely not a citizen of Pennsylvania. Who was a citizen?

James Logan would answer that question with definitive clarity when he learned that Sampson may be at the Funk farm on Indian Creek.

"Get my horse ready," Logan instructed another of his slaves.

26

Escape
October 1725

For the sixth time since February, Pennsylvania Chief Justice James Logan reined up at the Funk farm hitching post, riding with two other men. He had surprised Anna at her wedding, but it had been four months since his last appearance, and the sight of him concerned her. Bull barked but did not threaten the wigged rider. Dismounting, Logan approached the Funk's front door where Anna met him.

"What brings you here?" she inquired.

"I've come to see if you have a slave that I've lost."

"Why have you come to our house?"

"I've heard you may have my slave," Logan repeated.

"Who told you this?"

"I have my ways of finding things out," Logan growled.

Both Anna and Logan glanced up when Henry rode out of the trees into the clearing. Logan saw another rider in the woods turn and go the other way.

"Good afternoon, Logan," Henry began.

"Hello Henry. Were you hunting?" Logan interjected.

"No, I had to bury a Mohawk warrior who was killed two days ago," Henry replied.

"Who killed him?" the visitor inquired.

"Mr. Logan, let's sit down to talk. I'm parched. Anna, what do we have to drink?"

"Henry, I can't sit right now. Who turned and rode away in the woods?"

"I had help burying the Mohawk brave," Henry replied.

"He left in a hurry, Henry." Glancing at his men, he ordered, "Let's find whoever's out there."

Logan's men rode quickly up the Indian Creek, searching. Soon Logan spotted his slave on the other side of the creek, watering his horse. Alarmed at the approaching men, and seeing Logan, Sampson mounted and fled west.

Sampson had learned where to cross the creek at its low point, such that a horse could navigate the stream without fear. Logan and his men, however, had never forded the creek, and they had to study the water and figure out how to get across. By that time, Sampson had galloped away.

With a ten-minute lead on Logan's party, Sampson headed for the Lenape Indian settlement. When he arrived, he let his horse run free and ran for Pretty Leaves' tent. Several braves curiously watched his haste.

Before Logan arrived with his hunting party, Sampson and Pretty Leaves had fled. The braves watched and wondered what was going on. When Logan reined up at the edge of the settlement, they met him and asked what he wanted.

"Where's the slave?" Logan demanded.

Lenape Mother quickly came to negotiate with Logan. Assisted by a translating brave, Logan insisted that Lenape Mother bring the slave to him.

"He's not here," Lenape Mother declared.

"Then where is he?" Logan insisted.

"What makes you think he's here?" Lenape Mother asked.

"His horse," Logan motioned into the woods beyond the settlement.

On another day, without rum in their veins, the braves might have been quick enough to hide the horse, but not today. Rum was causing braves to be careless.

"He's not here," Lenape Mother insisted.

"Inspect the tents," Logan ordered.

When challenged by a brave, one of Logan's men cocked his flintlock pistol and pointed it at the man. The brave retreated, and Logan's men ransacked the place, poking their heads in every tent. Lenape Mother remembered a day when the braves would have fought Logan's men, and won. But not anymore. Demonic rum had weakened her braves and their resolve to fight. She sadly looked into the woods and hoped that Sampson and Pretty Leaves had escaped.

When his men couldn't find Sampson, Logan dismounted, having watched from his saddle as they tore open the tents. Putting his gun in the face of the brave who had challenged him, he demanded someone tell him where his slave had gone.

Lenape Mother sensed that Logan might actually pull the trigger. No one would be able to hold him accountable if he did. She quickly thought up an alternative.

"I can offer you a Mohawk warrior, Mr. Logan."

Logan lowered his gun. "You have a Mohawk?"

"I do, Mr. Logan." With the quick thinking of Lenape Mother, one of the most gracious and gentle women in the Pennsylvania commonwealth, a series of events began to unfold that would eventually bring a semblance of balance and peace to Indian River.

"You'll give him to me?" Logan asked.

"In a trade," Lenape Mother answered.

"For what?"

"For the return of Chief Lapowinsa to our village," Mother Lenape replied.

Logan paused, looked around the village at the forlorn looking band of Lenape, and began to understand the value of the bargain that had been offered to him.

"It's a deal," Logan answered.

"Good, but how can we be assured that if we turn over our captive to you that you'll release Chief Lapowinsa?"

"You'll have to take my word for it," Logan replied. "Now where's the Mohawk?"

"Not so fast, Mr. Logan. I need something from you of value that you'll leave here and then get back when we see our chief."

Logan scanned the village again. The Mohawk warrior was nowhere in sight, and he and his men would never find the brave without Lenape Mother's agreement.

"You will leave your saddle in the Funk barn, and it will be returned to you when we get the chief," Lenape Mother outlined.

Hesitating, Logan again calculated the value of the Mohawk warrior and the bargaining power it would bring him against Chief Fifteen Feathers.

"I accept," Logan replied.

By sunset on Wednesday, October 6, 1725, James Logan and his two men rode back to the Funk farm, but this time they brought a tied up Mohawk warrior with them who walked while the Philadelphia men rode. Two Lenape braves also came along to insure the deal that Lenape Mother had made with Logan proceeded smoothly.

Anna met them at the door of her house.

"Mrs. Funk, I apologize for leaving in such a hurry earlier today. Now I have a favor to ask of you."

Glancing at the tied-up warrior on foot, Anna asked what Logan had in mind.

"I need to leave my saddle in your barn for a while, until I get this man back to Philadelphia. I'll release Chief Lapowinsa and then come back for it."

"You want to leave it in our barn?" Anna inquired.

"Yes, it's a deal I worked out with Lenape Mother. My saddle stays here to assure that I'll release Lapowinsa." The two Lenape nodded in agreement with what Logan had said.

When Anna walked down her steps, Bull perked up and followed her to the barn with the men following.

"Put it in that corner," Anna pointed. "No one will bother it there."

When Logan stepped into the barn the horses spooked from fear at the new man, which led Bull to bark and block Logan's path.

"Take it easy, Bull. Here, give me the saddle," Anna offered. Logan hesitated because of the weight of his saddle, but still was happy that Anna carried out the task. Bull was a guard dog to Anna and all the men noticed. Mess with her, Bull seemed to assert, and you go through me.

"Look," Anna concluded, "I have some potatoes cooked and a bit of venison. Eat with us before you go."

Glancing at his men, Logan knew they were starved, as he was. "We'll take you up on your offer."

Anna spoke Delaware to the braves whom she knew and invited them to stay as well. Pausing to look closely at the dejected Mohawk warrior who was going to eat her food, Anna noticed it was one of the men who had captured her, along with Cool Water and Lapowinsa, the previous spring. "Bring him in," Anna instructed the men.

Henry, working alone in the mill, glanced out his window toward the house, and noticed a group of visitors entering with Anna. Henry tied the last bag of flour he had ground, and headed to the house.

"Henry, your wife is an amazing woman," Logan stated as Henry entered. "She's feeding a small army with no notice."

Glancing at Anna, Henry agreed. "She can cook."

"Anna," Logan offered, "I'm looking for the gold medallion, but no one seems to know where it is."

Turning, Anna countered. "Logan, your flattery is a function of your hunger."

"Henry, your wife is sharp, and understands men well," Logan replied. Laughing, Henry stated that he too was hungry.

"What happened to Sampson?" Anna inquired.

"Logan," Henry turned, "where's Sampson?"

"He got away," Logan replied. "He's probably long gone to the west."

"Pretty Leaves knows her way around in the woods, Logan," Anna replied. "You may never see him again."

"We'll catch up to him eventually."

Anna glanced at the chief justice of Pennsylvania, patiently waiting on a bit of food. Her meal had been meant for two but she added to it in order to feed eight.

Sensing Anna's displeasure with his veiled threat, Logan changed the subject. "One way I can work at commerce and general improvement in these parts is by building bridges."

"Bridges?" Henry asked.

"You need a bridge over Indian Creek to help get travelers across. Your mill is the economic center of this community which is growing with more and more settlers all the time. A bridge for horses and travelers would be good for you and the commonwealth. I'm going to send a team of men to build a bridge over the Indian Creek."

"When?" Henry wondered.

"Next week," Logan answered. "I have a team ready to start on the next project. They'll bring their own tents and supplies and should be able to finish by Christmas."

"Who pays for it?" Anna inquired.

"Taxes," Logan answered. "They're the price of a functioning government."

With the food devoured, Logan's party left for the Freedom Inn. It was almost dark, but the night was mild. Even the moon seemed to cooperate, providing light on the trail.

"Thank you for the meal, Anna. Keep an eye out for Sampson—he's my property and I intend to capture him," Logan called as his party left.

Anna, six months pregnant, slept well past sunrise the next morning. Henry had slipped out quietly and gone to work. She jumped when Bull barked. Glancing out her window, she noticed Sampson and Pretty Leaves running toward the mill. They were looking for a place to hide, Anna guessed.

Anna's gold medallion, a gift from Mr. Trico, lay on her night stand. She examined the stalk of wheat with a cross on the other side. Glancing at Sampson, in a moment of morning clarity, she had an idea.

By the time Anna walked to the mill, Henry and Sampson had terms already worked out. Sampson would live on the third floor of the mill while Pretty Leaves agreed to slip in only at night and leave before sunrise in the morning. She would also avoid being seen in the daylight around the farm. Sampson would have to stay in seclusion to avoid being caught by Logan's spies.

"A good plan," Anna agreed. "I have a project for Sampson."

"A project?" Henry wondered.

"Yes, Sampson, can you press a turtle on this medallion?"

Examining the soft metal gift, Sampson sat down.

"You've had experience working with metal in Africa and at Logan's farm," Anna encouraged.

"I think it can be done," Sampson concluded. "But you'll end up with a turtle on one side, and nothing on the other side. I will have to press it flat before I can make something new."

"It's a Lenape symbol," Anna explained.

"I know. I saw turtles sewn and painted among the Lenape," Sampson replied.

"Get upstairs and be quiet," Henry ordered. "My first customer has arrived."

When the door opened, Henry said, "Good morning, Mr. Kolb."

"How are the Funks?" Mr. Kolb asked.

"Doing great. What can I do for you?"

"I have corn on the wagon for you to grind. I'll leave the wagon here and you can let me know when you're finished."

"Sure," Henry replied. "How's your family?"

"No news from Virginia, nor from Annie Beth in New York, but John Penn visited our house. He's interested in Agnes. I had to send him away, which was odd, considering he's the governor."

"He's an unusual man," Henry agreed.

"What was Logan here for?" Mr. Kolb wondered.

"I guess word gets around when visitors come to the farm. He was looking for his slave," Henry answered.

"Did he escape?"

"Yes, but you know what, Kolb? Logan intends to build a bridge across our Creek."

"Progress on Indian Creek," Mr. Kolb mused. "Let me know when you're finished with the corn. Oh, and take a look at Franklin's latest essay." Tossing Henry the most recent edition of *The Mercury*, Henry noticed the new column.

"Thanks for the newspaper, but it will have to wait until I have time to read it. I'm working alone in the mill these days."

"Maybe you'll have a boy to help soon," Mr. Kolb joked.

"Or a clutch of lovely girls like you have," Henry responded. "I'll be happy with either."

After a day of work, Henry read Ben Franklin's column: "***One of James Logan's slaves escaped recently and is still at large, likely hiding somewhere in the wilderness or in Canada. Perhaps slavery should be abolished in Pennsylvania. Enslaving thousands of Africans does not agree with the freedoms we have as British citizens. The slaves would make a considerable economic contribution to the colony if they were freed, and could work for their former masters as paid employees. Perhaps the former masters would find it less expensive to free the slaves and pay them wages than to pay so much money to support the slaves during their lives.***"

In mid-morning the next day, Jubilant entered the mill to talk to Henry. She walked upstairs to inspect the third floor, where Henry went to chat with her.

"You have a slave living here?" the Indian woman asked.

"Yes, Sampson is married and sleeps over there," Henry motioned. "You were at the wedding. Why do you ask?"

"Because his wife is living with us," Jubilant replied.

"Why do you take such chances by keeping slaves in your home?" Henry asked.

"Many years ago I was cared for by English settlers when my parents died. Then I married William. It is my goal to pass my good fortune on to others."

"Of course, if Logan's men come back to Indian Creek to capture Sampson, you may be charged with assisting in his protection."

"I am not worried about that," Jubilant replied. "The Great Spirit of the Lenape calls us to care for all who are in need."

"And the God whom I serve calls on me to provide refuge for those who are unjustly treated," Henry responded.

"Perhaps we are talking about the same Spirit," Jubilant answered.

Henry did not disagree with the short woman in front of him, who had demonstrated every grace and Christian attribute he had ever preached about.

Anna did not interrupt Henry's concentrated writing that evening in their stone house. Near the end of his booklet, *A Mirror of Baptism*, Henry wrote about Christ's baptism, passion, and death: "***And in this manner also is the affliction and suffering of the disciples and followers of Christ, which they endure for his sake in bearing His cross after Him, called a baptism. Thus is the pouring out of the blood of Jesus and His disciples the perfect baptism of which He spake. And without suffering affliction and bearing the cross, this baptism cannot be accomplished.***"

"Anna," Henry said. "I'm going to write a letter to Logan asking him how much money it will take to free Sampson."

"You'll give yourself away," Anna replied. "He'll know you have him."

"It's a chance I'll have to take," Henry replied.

"How will you get the letter to him?" Anna asked.

"I have no idea, Anna. You may as well go to sleep while I work." Reaching for a quill pen, Henry Funk addressed a letter to the chief justice of the Commonwealth of Pennsylvania, an officer of the British Empire in America.

27

Bridge
October 1725

Logan did indeed send out a work crew the next week to build a bridge over Indian Creek. Ten men arrived on Tuesday morning, October 12, and began digging holes for the posts that would anchor the structure. Henry watched, just to the north of his dam, and it became clear that they had done this before, and each man knew his part in the team. By evening of the first day, they had dug four deep holes for the stoutest of their posts that would keep the structure from sagging in the middle.

The work crew created a buzz of excitement in the community. Folks from far around came to watch, gawking at the tents, the food wagon, and all the supplies that the men brought with them from Philadelphia. Even the Lenape came to watch. Most everyone understood the importance of the bridge in terms of soon having the ability to cross the Creek without getting themselves and their wares soaked.

The men were paid by the bridge, Henry learned. The quicker they got the bridge finished, the sooner they got paid. Economic progress at its finest, Henry mused. He knew there were British philosophers writing about the nature of economic systems in Europe. Henry realized they should come here and watch the motivation of these men to make money.

On the second afternoon of bridge-building, Henry saw to his surprise Chief Lapowinsa riding up the trail to his mill. Henry ran to meet the lone horseman.

"Welcome to my farm!" Henry called to him.

Dismounting, the chief smiled and asked how he and Anna were doing.

"She is healthy and rarely sick," Henry replied.

"Good," the chief replied. "I was asked to leave this horse with you."

"With me?" Henry asked.

"Yes, Mr. Logan gave me the horse to use and instructed me to give it to you until he comes to get it."

"All right," Henry agreed. "Let's take it to the barn. You left this morning?"

"Yes, I left Philadelphia early today."

"Did you know Lenape Mother made Logan leave his saddle here until you arrived?" Henry asked.

"No," the chief responded. "I guess that's why he made me ride bareback," Lapowinsa smiled.

At the barn door, Chief Lapowinsa handed the horse's reins to Henry before turning to look at the bridge building project. After tying up the horse and giving it a bucket of water, Henry rejoined his visitor.

With the western setting sun illuminating the chief's face, Henry couldn't help but notice the distinctive black peace marks on the chief's forehead and cheeks. The creases in his forehead, underneath the permanent markings, revealed to Henry years of concern, worry, and travail for his people. They had been harried from their land by the settlers, including himself, it seemed, but Lapowinsa remained strong and full of resolve. The chief watched work at the Creek with a bridge being built, and Henry thought he looked sad.

"It is time for my people to move west," Lapowinsa spoke to the open area below the barn. He glanced at the sky, the sun, and the trees, and then again at the bridge. "Many years ago my people moved to a new land, and we carried the spirit of Tamenend to the east, and here is where we arrived," Lapowinsa motioned across the region. "Now we must move to the west, back toward the land we came from."

Pretty Leaves suddenly burst out from the woods behind Lapowinsa and wrapped her arms around the chief.

"Welcome home," she cried.

"Dear one, how did you know I was here?"

"I watched you coming up the road," the Lenape woman answered. "I don't have much else to do, so I watch out the windows."

"Will you go with me to our people?" Lapowinsa asked.

"Certainly, but can I take Sampson along, Mr. Funk?"

Henry agreed that another traveler could go along. "I'm pretty sure Anna will want to go too, so we'll close the mill and all go."

Opening the front door of the house, Henry announced to Anna that the chief had arrived, which instantly brought Anna to the door, down the steps, and into an embrace with the Lenape leader.

"Welcome home," Anna gushed. "It's been so long since you've been here. Come in for some food."

"I'm eager to see my people," Lapowinsa replied.

"Then I'll make food for the walk," Anna answered.

"How about for me too?" Henry begged.

"And you, Pretty Leaves?" Anna asked. A nod from the squaw turned the event into a picnic. "We'll eat across the creek somewhere. Give me a few minutes."

Chief Lapowinsa resumed staring at the beehive of workers building a bridge across Indian Creek. "Why are they building it there?" he asked.

"Because James Logan builds bridges wherever there's a need for one near a mill," Henry answered.

"What's the need?" Lapowinsa asked.

"For farmers who will move to these parts to bring their grain to the mill and then take the flour home," Henry replied.

"We've forded this creek on foot for a thousand years," Lapowinsa lamented. "This is what Europeans call progress, I guess."

Henry couldn't help but think about Lapowinsa as one who was in anguish over a turning point in Lenape history. His people had moved in the spring and now a Philadelphia work crew, who had little respect for nature or the life teeming in its banks, had come to tear the creek apart.

"Creeks and rivers are sacred, and they come to us from the Great Spirit," Lapowinsa stated.

"I'm ready," Anna exclaimed when she arrived. "Let's go."

Chief Lapowinsa headed to a spot at the creek south of the mill, which was an alternate crossing point from the one further upstream. He waded in confidently, like braves and squaws had done for centuries. The water came up to their waist, but they were determined to cross. Even the fish, darting as they did, seemed happy to see the chief back in their haunts. Bull splashed across with Anna.

Rain began to fall. Gray clouds had moved in, and in a refreshing fall shower, the travelers got doused with water from above.

"It's like a baptism!" Henry announced.

"Henry, it's not my turn yet," Anna replied.

"When will it be?" Henry asked.

"I'm not sure."

As the four travelers climbed out on the west side, they heard a shout behind them. Sampson had seen them, ran from the mill, leapt into the water, lunged across, and joined them. "I'm going along," he gasped.

"Who is this man?" Lapowinsa asked.

"My husband," Pretty Leaves answered. "I told him we were leaving right away, but he had a job to finish, I guess."

"Very well, let's continue."

"Looks like we have to divide our food to feed Sampson," Anna remarked.

"No, I just ate," Sampson responded. "Where are we going?"

"To the Lenape settlement," Anna responded.

With a gentle but steady shower on Indian Creek, the travelers stopped under a large tree and ate their food.

"Cool Water married Bentura," Henry explained to Lapowinsa, "and they sailed to Aruba."

"My granddaughter, may the Great Spirit give you safety and good fortune in your new life," Lapowinsa stated as he gazed toward the horizon.

"They may come back," Anna said. "Bentura wants to work on the farm next spring, so it's possible we'll see them again soon."

"They may come back to your farm, Anna, but our settlement's time at Indian Creek is over. We need to move west."

"Sampson, will you move with us to the west?" Pretty Leaves asked.

"I'm going wherever you go," Sampson promised.

"Good," his new bride gushed.

"I guess if you get far enough away with the Lenape, you'll be free and out of reach of James Logan," Henry suggested.

"That's what I'm thinking too," Sampson agreed.

Blood hounds. Henry heard them at the same time the others did. There was the familiar howl of dogs on a hunt, loping through the woods, over trails, and following a scent their owner had provided.

"Run," Sampson cried. He sprinted west with Pretty Leaves close behind. Anna, Henry, and Lapowinsa hurried their steps but did not run.

The hounds faced a barrier to their pursuit, though. Bull turned, listened to their approach, and bristled. It was the same dogs Bull had fought before, and now it was going to happen again.

"Leave him," Henry ordered. "Let's get Lapowinsa to the settlement. We're not sure who the dogs are chasing."

Anna and Lapowinsa did not argue. If the dogs and hunter were after the chief, they could not defend him. Henry didn't even have his gun, since they had left in a hurry, and it had seemed like such a peaceful afternoon.

As it happened, Henry, Anna, and Chief Lapowinsa arrived at the Perkiomen Creek settlement just ahead of the hound dogs. Bull waited for them and a violent fight broke out at the edge of the settlement when they bounded into sight. Again.

The frontiersman who owned the dogs came riding in with another man, and they were disgusted to see the dogs fighting.

"Who are you chasing?" Henry demanded.

"The slave," came a rough reply.

"What makes you think he's here?" Henry countered.

"The dogs don't make mistakes," the rider muttered. "Better stop these dogs from fighting," he grumbled. "Maybe I should shoot the big one," and with that Henry waded into the fray to separate the dogs.

"Put your gun away," Anna yelled.

The frontiersman ignored Anna, and everyone else, to save his dogs from being ripped apart by Bull who was on top of both dogs, flinging them away whenever they came at him.

On the other side of the settlement, a couple fled, carrying nothing. It continued to rain, but braves who were sober rallied to the defense of the settlement. They had a chief to lead them, and Lapowinsa quickly took charge.

"Get ready to move," Lapowinsa ordered. "Warriors, chase the men with the dogs away."

It had been a very long time since Lenape braves fought for their way of life and culture on Indian Creek. Lapowinsa's presence helped drive out their fear. Within seconds, a dozen warriors confronted the two riders from Philadelphia.

It did not take long until the frontiersman got on his horse and prepared to leave.

"How did Logan know about Sampson being out here?" Henry asked the men as they saddled up.

"You sent him a letter, remember?"

"Five days," Henry mumbled. "The mail moves faster in these parts than what I expected."

"Leave," a brave ordered, and a warning arrow whistled by the ears of the frontiersman. Fingering his gun, the Philadelphian noticed eleven more arrows pointed at him. Wheeling around, the frontiersman and his sidekick departed with the hounds, glad to get out of range of Bull.

"We'll move west," Lapowinsa announced. "We have no choice."

Every Lenape got busy packing, taking down their wigwams, and collecting their cooking equipment. The light rain did not seem to matter to them.

Anna and Henry soon realized it would be best if they left. Before they got very far, Lenape Mother came to Anna. "Sampson asked me to give this to you," she said.

Looking at the medallion she was handed, Anna smiled at the turtle that Sampson had etched into it. "This is beautifully crafted," she exclaimed. "Henry, look at this."

Pleased at what Sampson had accomplished in his third story mill exile, Henry asked Anna what she planned to do with it.

"Do with it?" she repeated. Glancing at him, Henry's nudge reminded her of what to do.

"Chief Lapowinsa," Anna announced. "I have a gift for you."

Turning, the chief seemed hurried, but yet patient with Anna Funk. "Yes?"

With Lenape Mother at her side and braves circling, Anna placed the gold medallion in Chief Lapowinsa's hand. He smiled.

"Look at it," Anna exclaimed.

Examining the medallion, a tear ran down Lapowinsa's face, visible even with the rain.

Lenape Mother smiled at the chief and then smiled at Anna. Lenape Mother had already seen the turtle, a symbol of their people, a hope for them and for their future.

Turning to his people, Lapowinsa announced, "The gold medallion has been returned to our people. My grandfather's sister, Tender Vine, once had the gold medallion, but it was lost. We have been searching for it."

"Today we have it, and now we can move." Turning his face toward the west, Lenape began the chant that his people had repeated on important occasions for centuries: "*We carry the spirit of Tamenend in the land of the Dawn.*' "

With a gentle embrace of the very pregnant Anna Funk, Lapowinsa turned to help his people pack. The chief placed the medallion around the neck of a granddaughter, who smiled at him, and they scurried to get ready.

The moving time was a sacred event for the Lenape, Anna knew, and it was time for her and Henry to depart. With a tear in her eye, she turned toward the east, toward her home on Indian Creek. They would not take the bridge on the way home, even though the beams had been laid and the boards would have allowed them to cross it.

"Anna," Chief Lapowinsa cried out. "I have something for you."

Turning, Anna wondered what he wanted.

"I want you to have a special pouch," Lapowinsa offered. Taking it off from around his neck, he handed it to Anna.

"Why are you giving this to me?" Anna asked.

"Because you gave me the gold medallion," Lapowinsa answered.

"You understand that it's not the actual medallion," Anna replied. "Sampson etched it for you in the mill."

"That makes it special. Please take my pouch as a gift in return."

When Anna hesitated, Lapowinsa explained. "I make a new one each year, usually out of elk hide. I keep one, but I make one as a gift. I didn't use this one very much because I was locked up in Philadelphia most of the time. I'll make another one this winter."

"The quills are beautiful," Anna said, examining the pouch.

"My granddaughter helped me attach the quills," Lapowinsa replied.

"Thank you, Lapowinsa," Anna replied. "But it might actually fit Henry better than me."

Putting it around Henry's neck, she smiled. "What should Henry put in it?"

"Herbs for healing, maybe a lucky bead, or an eagle's claw. You decide." With that Lapowinsa turned and helped his people pick up their things and move west.

Anna was from Aruba, but she was a citizen of the Netherlands. Married to a German man, however, and carrying his baby, she felt drawn back to the stone house above the mill. She had been called the miller's wife, and now she embraced it. With a final glance at the busy Lenape, she grasped Henry's hand for the return walk. Bull was right beside her, as always.

Headed to the mill, Anna told Henry he looked like an Indian chief with the pouch around his neck.

"I'm not much of a chief," Henry responded.

"You're my chief," Anna smiled.

Ahead, Bull began to bark. They had an unannounced visitor at the mill.

28

Bargain
October 1725

With no one around to stop it, a young bear decided to investigate the inside of Henry's mill. It meandered into the mill through the door that Sampson left ajar when he ran after Pretty Leaves earlier in the day.

The bear, however, did more than investigate. By the time Bull and Henry arrived, flour bags had been torn open, buckets upset, and Henry's small desk for records and bookkeeping had been upended.

Bull charged through the open door, and with only one way out, mayhem erupted. The bear rose up and challenged the big dog, roaring with fright and alarm. When Bull attacked, the small bear went on all fours and used its advantage of being quicker than the dog, running for the door.

The bear ran across the field into the woods to the north. Henry sprinted to get his gun in the house, while Bull chased the bear into the woods beyond. The dog soon gained on the small, frightened bear, who climbed the first tree it could find. The yearling was desperate.

Henry ran to the tree where Bull had the bear treed. With his gun that was almost always loaded and ready for use, Henry looked at the wild-eyed creature above. With the sun going down, and shadows lengthening, Henry aimed carefully and steadied his arms for the shot. After his flintlock's crack, the dead bear dropped to the ground.

The next morning, Henry worked at scraping the bear hide in order to dry it out, planning to make a rug for their house. Henry had taken the cleaned carcass to his father's smokehouse the previous evening in the dark and hung it there until sometime in the coming winter. He and Anna would make bear jerky after the arrival of the baby.

Alone with a tough scraping job, Henry thought about the baby and the coming winter. He jumped when a voice greeted him from behind. Wheeling around, Henry found it hard to believe that Chief Shickellamy and two braves had crept up on him without being heard. "Fifteen Feathers, what are you doing here?"

"Checking on your bear skin," Shickellamy responded.

"You know how to startle a man," Henry replied.

"Good thing I'm your friend," Fifteen Feathers answered.

Collecting himself, Henry welcomed the chief to his farm.

"Here, we'll help you." Turning to the two braves with him, he found another of Henry's scraping tools, and his braves grabbed their knives, making short order of the work. "This is a small bear. When we kill a large bear, it's more work."

"Do I hang it with the fur side out or in?" Henry asked.

"Fur side in," the chief answered. "It will dry this winter, and Anna will like the rug next spring."

The braves helped Henry stretch and nail it to the side of his barn.

"Thank you, Shickellamy," Henry said when they were finished. "Will you come inside and say hello to Anna?"

"It would be my pleasure to see her again."

At the house, two braves waited patiently outside while Henry and the chief went inside.

"Fifteen Feathers," Anna greeted, "what brings you to our farm?" For the third time in the year, the Oneida chief had come to the Funk's Indian Creek farm.

Feathers got to the point. "I've come to make a bargain."

"What kind of bargain?" Anna asked.

"I need your help," the chief began.

"What do you need?"

"I need you to help me get the Mohawk warrior out of Logan's jail in Philadelphia."

"You mean the one Henry caught last week?"

"Yes, Anna, I need him released."

"Why is this so urgent that you've come here?" Anna inquired.

"The Mohawk is the son of an Iroquois Nation chief in New York," Fifteen Feathers replied. "I need to get him out."

"He tried to burn the Swartz house," Henry interjected.

"Yes, but I must release him."

"So what's your bargain?" Anna asked.

"I can get the Swartz family back to their home, if you help me get the Mohawk brave released."

"Their house has fire damage," Henry reminded. "Can you fix the damage?"

"No, I can't do that, but I can get your neighbors released and safely back to Indian Creek," the chief repeated.

"How do we figure into your bargain?" Anna wondered.

"You need to come to Philadelphia and speak to Logan and Governor Penn on my behalf."

"Anna's over six months pregnant," Henry responded.

"Our women travel up until the time they give birth," Fifteen Feathers replied. "On a slow but steady horse, you could make the trip in a day."

"*It's thirty-five miles*," Anna exclaimed. "You want me to ride there?"

"That's what I have in mind," Fifteen Feathers confirmed.

Anna and Henry looked at each other, disbelief etched on their faces.

"You want Henry and me to ride to Philadelphia and negotiate the release of your Mohawk in order to get the Swartz's back to Indian Creek?" Anna summarized.

"That's my bargain," Fifteen Feathers concluded.

"Eat your biscuits and gravy," Anna offered, serving both men breakfast hot off the oven. "Henry, take these plates out to the braves."

Back inside, Henry said, "Shickellamy, I have a mill to clean up from when that bear tore the place apart yesterday. And customers are coming every day with their corn and wheat for me to grind."

"Is there anyone who can run your mill for a few days?" the chief pleaded. "Anna, this was a great meal—thank you. I'll hunt today and will come back this evening, at which time you need to give me an answer." With that, Fifteen Feathers slipped out the door as quietly as he had walked up behind Henry two hours earlier. Henry realized that if the man had been angry, the outcome of his silent arrival could have been very different.

On a mild Thursday afternoon in mid-October, Henry and Anna Funk ate their late lunch sitting on the bridge over Indian Creek. They could see their small dam, the race taking water to the water wheel, and the rest of the farm.

"Do you want to go to Philadelphia?" Henry asked.

"No," Anna replied, "but I will, if that's what it takes to get Abe and Annie Beth home."

"Don't forget about Little John," Henry reminded.

"I can do it," Anna determined. "If we ride slowly and I watch where I lean into the saddle, I should be fine. I may need a few breaks along the way."

"We'll leave on Monday," Henry concluded. "That'll give me time to clean up the mill, and I have to preach at church on Sunday."

"Can Bull come along?" Anna asked.

"Yes," Henry answered.

"Feathers knows what he wants and how to get it," Anna concluded. "I hope we can trust him."

"I suspect he's under pressure from the Iroquois chiefs to get both the Swartz and the Mohawk headaches resolved."

They decided Anna would speak for both of them when Feathers returned that evening. Before she could give their answer, however, the three Indians from earlier in the day dragged a large bear skin to the farm. Bull barked, but recognized the men and didn't put up much resistance.

"Look what we shot," Feathers began. "It makes your baby bear look pretty small," he smiled. "Maybe this was the father."

"Incredible," Henry exclaimed. "How far did you have to drag it?"

"A long way," Feathers answered.

"The meat?" Henry wondered.

"Two Lenape hunters came by, and we gave it to them," Feathers replied. "Can we nail to your barn?"

"Sure, let me get the ladder; this hide is huge."

When finished, Feathers turned to Anna and began. "The hide is my gift of friendship. Now, what is your reply?"

"We can ride to Philadelphia, Shickellamy, but not until Monday morning."

"Good, do you want one of my braves to ride with you?"

"We've taken the trip before," Henry replied. "Do we need one?"

"Some of the Indians are restless, and the French are encouraging them to kill British settlers like you," Shickellamy replied.

"We'll take the brave," Anna declared.

"He'll be here Monday morning." Like before, Fifteen Feathers slipped out the door so quietly and effortlessly that Henry and Anna were startled when he was gone.

"The man is all business," Anna declared.

"So am I," Henry replied. Closing the door and locking it, Henry pulled down the window curtain and dimmed the lamp. "Come here, Anna, love me."

"A bear got into our mill this past week," Henry began in the Franconia Mennonite log meetinghouse on Sunday morning. "It pretty well tore the place apart, and it has taken me the past two days to clean up the mess."

"Sometimes our lives get messed up," Henry continued, "just like my mill did. But God directs his love to us in the day, and in the night his song is with us." Speaking from the forty-second Psalm, Henry encouraged his people. "Lift your prayers to the God of life."

Anna's baby kicked, while an older man yawned and dozed, having worked hard the previous week. Not falling asleep in the warm church was hard for the man, Henry knew. "Don't preach too long," Anna had told him often. "A short sermon is better than a long one," she had counseled him.

"Please pray for Anna and me as we travel to Philadelphia this week," Henry continued. "We hope that our talk with the governor will result in the return of Abraham and Annie Beth Swartz to our community."

"God is our rock," Henry concluded, "and he has not forgotten us. Put your hope in God, and praise him, your Savior and God."

"Short and sweet today," Anna remarked on the way home. "Just the way I like your sermons best. That old man wasn't asleep very long before you finished preaching."

On Monday, October 18, 1725, the necessary factors for Anna and Henry's Philadelphia trip came together. Henry's father came to run the mill for a few days. He would live in the stone house to watch out for the place and feed the animals.

A Mohawk brave showed up right on time, and three travelers left for the capital city.

"This old saddle is uncomfortable," Anna complained.

"Take it easy and you'll figure out a way to manage," Henry replied.

Henry took along Logan's horse and saddle. Henry decided to hand the reins to the Mohawk brave and give him the job of leading Logan's horse to Philadelphia and return it.

"It might help Judge Logan agree to our request," Henry told Anna.

It had been such a mild October that Anna and Henry hadn't planned well enough for the arrival of cold weather. About halfway down the road toward Freedom Inn, the temperature dropped fast. The wind picked up and blew hard, leaves swirled, and in only a matter of an hour icy gray skies moved in, and it started to snow. Winter had arrived.

Anna pulled her coat in tight, but it wasn't enough to keep her warm. Henry soon put his coat on her, which left him freezing. The Mohawk had a blanket which he wrapped around himself.

They hurried toward the inn while the snow fell hard, covering them and their horses. Bull and the horses and their riders had snow all over them. Henry kept looking for lights in the inn window ahead, hoping that it was open, and that they had a bed for him and Anna.

The inn keeper opened the door when Henry knocked, brought Anna inside, and directed her toward the fireplace for warmth. "The dog, Indian, and horses go in the barn," the manager said. "You can have the guest room in the back."

Around the fire, Henry heard a sordid story from the manager of Freedom Inn. The French were stoking the fears of the Indians who had gone on the warpath looking for British settlers to kill. "You might want to keep your hat on your head," he told Henry.

When Henry explained the deal they were trying to arrange to get a brave out of jail in Philadelphia in exchange for the Swartz couple, the manager laughed. "You may not get very far with Logan. These days he's cracking down on Indians."

By noon the next day, the snow stopped falling, and it looked like Henry and Anna could resume their trip. At least one other party of horses had gone ahead of them, so they had a bit of a path through the snow. "Can I buy an extra blanket for Anna?" Henry asked the manager.

"Borrow it, but bring it back. A blanket is hard to replace."

The ten mile ride to Philadelphia was uneventful though difficult. The proprietor at their usual inn in the capital was glad to see them. "Staying for a few days?" the innkeeper asked Henry.

"Yes," Henry replied. "We need meals and a room. Any news on who set fire to the courthouse?"

"Interesting that you ask," the owner replied. "Tomorrow morning at the crack of dawn, a man accused of helping to start the fire will be hung. Logan caught one of them, and he's going to make an example out of him. Did you see the scaffolding set up in the square?"

"I hadn't noticed," Henry replied. "It appears that Logan's not in much of a bargaining mood these days."

"If you came to work with Logan, good luck. He's meaner than a cornered pole cat right now," the owner replied.

Henry got up early the next morning to see the hanging. Noticing that the sentenced man had worked on his mill, Henry confronted Logan at the platform. "This man is a good worker—what good will it do to hang him?"

"We have to set an example," Logan replied.

"Do you have evidence that he set the fire?"

"All the stories I've heard point to him," Logan answered.

"Do you have a witness that he started the fire, because if not, I know someone who saw the men who started the fire," Henry responded.

"Who are you talking about?"

"Your slave, Logan, who's escaped to the western part of the colony, is a witness," Henry replied.

"Sampson saw who started the fire?" Logan queried.

"Yes, and maybe you should wait on hanging this man until you hear from him," Henry suggested.

"Just why are you here in Philadelphia?" Logan asked.

With a crowd around him who had gathered to see the hanging, Henry decided to declare his purpose, standing in the snow in the middle of the town square, where the courthouse had once stood.

"Anna and I have come to ask you to release the Mohawk in prison in exchange for Fifteen Feathers releasing the Swartz couple from their New York captivity. You'll get a productive farming couple working the land and earning tax dollars for you, and you'll no longer have to feed the Indian."

"I'm not in much of a mood to bargain," Logan replied.

The man in the wagon, tied until orders were given to put his neck in the noose, sat motionless, while his wife sobbed loudly and pleaded for his release. The man's children shuffled around. His fate lay in James Logan's hands.

"How about if this man," Henry pointed at the somber man who was about to hang, "comes to work for me. I need help in the mill and the farm," Henry continued. "Then you go find Sampson and ask him what he saw." Henry hoped the Lenape and Sampson were so far to the west that Logan would never find them.

"If it was this man," Henry continued, "then you do what is necessary, but after a fair trial. Every law in the British judicial system demands that you have a witness for a capital crime."

"My, haven't you suddenly become wise about British law," Logan growled. "Meet me in my office at mid-morning. Is 'Shick' in town?"

"I don't know," Henry replied.

"Ask that Mohawk with you to get him and bring him in with you."

"I'll try," Henry answered.

"Guard, take this man back to his cell," Logan ordered.

When Logan vanished, the man's sobbing wife came to Henry and declared, "He's innocent. Thank you for saving his life."

Turning, Henry saw several members of his Junto group in the crowd who were disappointed not to see a hanging. In the crowd he spotted Ben Franklin, and he made his way across the snowy space to talk with the reporter, still with pen and note pad in hand. The tall young reporter was unhappy that he would have to wait a little longer for a hanging story.

29

Discovery

October 1725

"Do you really want that man to work for you?" Franklin asked Henry.

"I was only trying to get him released," Henry replied, "but I could use him on the farm and in the mill. What good does it do to hang a man who has a family?"

Other members of the Junto gathered around to listen. "Logan should have followed through to set an example," Franklin countered.

"Why are you in Philadelphia?" the surveyor asked Henry.

"I'm trying to get the Swartz family home from New York."

"What do you have to bargain with?"

"If Fifteen Feathers gets his Mohawk out of jail over there," Henry motioned, "he'll send a messenger up the trail with orders to release Abe and Annie Beth."

"Have you had to defend yourself against Indians?" Franklin asked.

"No," Henry replied. "Both the Lenape and the Mohawk have treated us well."

"You're lucky," the surveyor responded. "Others haven't been so fortunate."

"The Funks treat the Indians fairly," Franklin replied. "That's how they've survived. The Indians don't attack unless there's a reason."

Turning around, Henry noticed the Mohawk patiently waiting. "I have to send that brave to find Shickellamy, who's around here somewhere," Henry stated. "Meet me at the inn at noon. I'll tell you how it went with

Logan."

As Henry figured, Fifteen Feathers wasn't far away and by mid-morning the Mohawk brought him to the meeting.

Anna, however, who was trying to stay warm and rest at the Inn, took a while to get ready.

"Can you meet Logan with me?" Henry asked.

"You don't need me," Anna replied.

"Logan likes you and I think having you there would help. If you can come along this morning, you can do whatever you want the rest of the day."

In the rented courthouse office on Second Street, James Logan stoked embers in a fireplace that a city worker had lit earlier in the morning.

"The snow and cold started early this year," he grumbled.

Around the big table, Logan welcomed Anna. "When are you due?" he asked.

"At Christmas, or whenever this baby decides to come," she smiled.

A city recorder sat at the table with Henry, Anna, and Logan, in order to write down details. Shickellamy soon entered and took a seat, eyeing Logan but acknowledging the others.

The arrival of Governor John Penn and Lieutenant Governor Keith surprised Henry, but it meant that it was time for the bargaining to begin. The meeting had been Fifteen Feathers' idea, but Logan had agreed and the chief justice made it his meeting, acting as if he had called for it.

"What you want, Shickellamy, is for me to release your Mohawk, and in exchange, you'll get the Swartz couple out of Fort Orange and safely back to Indian Creek," Logan summarized.

"Agreed," Fifteen Feathers replied. The recorder wrote the details on official Pennsylvania letterhead.

"Our prisoner tried to burn the Swartz house down," Logan replied.

"Why is this deal so urgent to you?"

"He is a son of an Iroquois Nation chief," Shickellamy explained. "Iroquois loyalty to the British Crown and Pennsylvania government will be maintained when he walks out of your cell. Someday this brave will be a chief," Feathers informed him.

The unexpressive Mr. Penn interjected that the colonial Pennsylvania government would not need Iroquois protection for its survival and growth in the future. It was a somber but realistic statement, and even Fifteen Feathers could comprehend what the governor had just said.

"Some of the western Indians are on the warpath, being paid good money for English deaths," Shickellamy explained. "It is our Mohawk warriors, scattered throughout the woods of Pennsylvania, who shield your unprotected settlers."

This even the solemn and unexpressive governor understood. "I recommend we release the Mohawk," Penn concluded.

Turning to Anna, Logan asked if she wanted to say anything. "The man in your jail did try to burn Annie Beth and Abe's house," Anna remarked, "and he was one of the warriors who took me to the Iroquois Council in August. He should be released, however, because my people believe in the way of peace and nonviolence."

Henry was surprised at Anna's sudden adoption of Mennonite values. She had kept the peace teachings of the Mennonites out of her vocabulary and speech, until now.

Asserting himself, and trying to remain relevant, Lieutenant Governor Keith urged that the Swartz family be returned before the release of the Mohawk.

"That's not what we came to bargain for," Henry replied. "I trust Shickellamy to keep his word. If he says he will release our minister from Fort Orange, he will. The other day," Henry explained, "Fifteen Feathers crept up behind me while I scraped a bear hide. He and his braves could have killed me, but they did not. My German ears didn't hear them coming." Everyone around the table laughed. "You British officials have your documents, and your seals, but we German settlers make deals with a hand shake. We judge a man by the strength of his grip. I felt the power and trustworthiness of Shickellamy's hand at our farm for the first time at my wedding in March. His word can be trusted."

Logan paused, not sure if anything else needed to be said. He looked at everyone around the table. "Are there any further questions or comments?"

When there were none, and all appeared to be in agreement, Logan asked the recorder to read aloud the bargain, after which he put a Pennsylvania seal on the document. Logan, who always had his gavel, banged on a block and said, "Meeting adjourned."

On the way out, Governor Penn spoke to Henry. "I'm leaving tomorrow at noon for England," he explained. "I want to spend the winter in a place that can be adequately heated—your buildings here are not built for warmth."

"True," Henry replied. "We build functional buildings, and we're often cold in the winter."

"My ship leaves tomorrow afternoon, but I'll host a lunch in the governor's mansion for just a few folks I've come to know. Please bring Anna and come for food and greetings."

Glancing at Anna, Henry indicated that they'd be pleased to come to the mansion and see him off.

"Bull will have to wait outside, right?" Anna smiled.

"That would be best," Penn replied.

Turning to Logan, Henry told him his saddle and horse were at the inn where he and Anna were staying. "You can pick them up there. They were taking up room in my barn," Henry smiled.

"You'll need to build a bigger barn," Logan replied, "with all that money you're making at the mill."

"I have taxes to pay," Henry responded. "A bigger barn will have to wait."

Henry kept an eye on the jail from the inn. About an hour after their meeting, Henry noticed the Mohawk prisoner walk out of the building, where he was met by the brave who had come with them to Philadelphia. The two soon vanished.

Anna had visited Andrew Bradford's print shop before, but on this snowy and cold October Wednesday morning, she met Mr. Bradford's wife Margaret. "Margaret's Print Shop," Anna exclaimed! After the initial pleasantries, Anna told Margaret the story of her four-time great-grandmother Margaret Beck, from Strasbourg, Germany.

"She printed many books," Anna gushed. "We even had one of her books in our log house, but it burned in the fire."

"Your house burned?" the silver-haired Margaret asked.

"Yes, in June. We lost everything."

"Except each other," Margaret motioned at Henry.

"Oh, and Henry had the deed for the farm in his pocket when the house burned."

"Your parents are printers, aren't they?" Margaret asked.

"Yes, how did you know?" Anna wondered.

"I met them when they came into our shop in January, looking for you."

"I miss our print shop," Anna confessed.

"I'm so glad to meet you," Margaret stated.

"You must come to our farm and visit me. Andrew came to our

wedding."

"I knew he had gone to your wedding," Margaret added. "When is the baby due?"

"Around Christmas," Anna answered.

"Who will deliver the baby?"

"I'm working on that," Anna confessed. "Perhaps my mother-in-law. I'm not sure."

"I'm a midwife," the middle-aged Margaret explained.

"You are?" Anna exclaimed. "Would you help deliver my baby?"

"Well, possibly," Margaret replied. "How far is it to your farm?"

"Thirty-five miles," Anna answered. "You can ride it in a day."

"I can come, but we need to set up a way for you to let me know when the baby's about to come."

"How will I know that?" Anna asked.

"You'll know," Margaret replied, "and Henry will know it, and when that happens you send someone to get me, and I'll come right away."

"Ben Franklin," Anna replied. "I bet we can hire him to bring you to the farm, since he's been there several times—did you know he's fallen for a pretty girl who lives near our farm?"

"No, tell me," Margaret encouraged.

"The girl's only fourteen, but she's pretty, and not only has Ben noticed her, but so has Governor Penn."

"Oh my, keep the girl away from the governor," Margaret warned. "He's a strange man."

"Yes, the girl's father had to tell the governor to leave his daughter alone."

"Good for him," Margaret commented graciously.

After Anna had inspected Margaret's print shop they walked down the street to purchase a second dress for her to wear until after the baby came.

Henry had entered a discussion with members of the Junto. Margaret and Anna walked toward their meeting place at the inn.

"Anna, did you know the Junto met in our print shop when Henry came earlier this month?" Margaret asked.

"Were there pretty women who tempted him?" Anna asked.

"Yes, they always have young women serve the men food and drinks," Margaret answered with a frown. "Andrew knows I don't like it when he goes to the Junto meeting."

When Margaret and Anna came to the inn, Henry, Ben Franklin, and a few other men had already assembled around a table, discussing a new book for sale in the city. Henry had purchased a copy of John Bunyan's recently published *Pilgrim's Progress*. The book had only arrived in Pennsylvania a few weeks earlier, and many had already read it, including Franklin.

"It's a sloppy religious tale about Bunyan's warped view of the Christian's journey to ecstasy and heaven. The book won't sell," Franklin predicted.

"Looks like Bunyan's already sold quite a few of his books here in Philadelphia," the merchant from the Junto Club stated. "You may not like the book, but it's selling."

"The ink of the scholar is worth more the blood of martyrs," Anna interjected. "That's what my grandfather said all the time."

The men turned to look at Anna. "My grandfather, Jan De Visscher, said that when people write books, it advances the cause of civilization."

Taking the book, Anna said, "This book sounds interesting, and I'm guessing I might even read it. Henry, where did you get it? I want a few more for Christmas presents for folks in Indian Creek—maybe five copies."

"I bought it across the street. Giving it as a gift is a good idea."

The merchant concluded the discussion with, "Some of us are religious and some of us are skeptics—right, Ben?"

"Look, this is not the time to go after each other," Henry concluded.

At the mid-week evening prayer meeting at the Germantown Mennonite Church, Henry discovered that others had already purchased copies of *The Pilgrim's Progress,* and it was all the talk of the meeting, before prayers and after. Folks wanted to hear from Henry, and they wanted to learn about things at the Franconia Church.

Henry was happy to report that Minister Abraham Swartz should soon be coming home, with his wife and son. "And Anna and I are expecting our first child in December," Henry beamed.

The next morning, James Logan came looking for Henry at the inn. Having taken their time to get up from bed, Henry was eating breakfast when Logan barged in the front door.

"I want to get rid of the man who is accused of helping to start the fire in the courthouse," Logan declared. "Will you take his family to your farm? If not, I'm going to put them on the same ship the governor sails on today, sending them to Britain and out of here!"

"Sit down, Logan," Henry encouraged.

"I don't have much time," Logan grunted. "If you don't want them on your farm, I need to get them passage to England, where with his attitude and lack of skills, he'll end up in the poorhouse or worse."

"What has he done for a living?" Henry asked.

"All kinds of things," Logan said. "Just day labor, picking up jobs wherever he could."

"Let me ask Anna," Henry replied.

After a discussion in their room, Henry returned and said, "Yes, we have room on the third floor of the mill for the family. How many children do they have?"

"Two boys," Logan replied. "They'll be ready to travel with you, I'm assuming, right after the send-off for the governor at noon today?"

"Yes, tell them to be ready. Do they have a horse?"

"One horse and one cart, and one trunk of goods. They are a poor, undesirable family, Henry. Good luck with them," Logan concluded.

The Governor's Mansion on Second Street, near Bradford's print shop, had a large greeting room, where a nice buffet of food had been laid out for the invited guests. Anna and Henry got food and tried to make small talk with other guests. Bull waited patiently outside.

"Here's a toast to the governor," William Keith announced. All joined in to celebrate the man, even though very few in attendance actually liked him. He was, after all, a son of the venerable William Penn, founder of the colony.

Not all joined in with the toast. Henry avoided alcohol and he found something else to drink at the going-away party. Anna had noticed, but didn't share his convictions.

"Thank you," the governor responded. "I hope to return in two years."

"I hope Agnes has found a man by then," Anna whispered to Henry. "Come with me," she whispered again.

"Ben, I want to hire you to help me," Anna said, with Henry listening. "When I need Margaret Bradford to come and help deliver my baby in December, will you bring her to our farm?"

"I can do that," Ben replied. "If you help me get a favorable visit with Agnes."

"I can't promise that," Anna answered. "But she'll likely be at our house helping with the baby. You'll get to see her," Anna smiled.

"The man who almost hung will come for you and Margaret," Henry stated.

Outside the Governor's Mansion, Bull began to bark. He would not stop, and Henry went to see what the trouble was. Returning, he informed Anna that Bull was barking at one of Penn's travel trunks.

By the time Anna and Henry arrived, others had gathered to see what the dog was agitated about. Anna talked to Bull, looked at the trunk, and tried to calm him, but nothing worked. The dog kept barking, loudly.

A small crowd of curious gawkers had gathered, and Governor Penn finally came out to see what had drawn such attention. "Why's that dog barking at my trunk?" Penn asked.

"We're not sure," Henry replied. "Any chance we could open it and see what's inside?"

"Open it? Because a dog is barking?"

The crowd's curiosity was rising, so Governor Penn gave in and ordered one of the servants to climb on the wagon and open it.

Henry and Governor Penn looked in the trunk. "May I reach in?" Henry asked. Penn balked but saw little alternative. "Yes," he answered.

Bull pointed to the spot he wanted Henry to reach for, underneath a bunch of boxes. Henry felt what he was beginning to suspect. At the bottom of a storage trunk, that was going back to the Penn mansion in London, was the long lost gold medallion.

It gleamed in the sunlight when Henry held it up, with a turtle on one side and a cross on the other side. "This is what the Lenape princess Tender Vine received from the Dutch three generations ago," Anna remarked. "You've had it all along, Mr. Penn," Anna glared.

"I've never opened that trunk before," Penn remarked. "It's been in storage for years. Keep the silly medallion."

To his servants he barked, "Get these trunks loaded on the ship."

30

Restitution

October 1725

Anna tucked the medallion in her pocket and turned to Henry. "We should leave soon. I want to get home by evening."

"Agreed. Let's get our things and find the family that's fallen into our care."

The four poor souls Henry had agreed to take home were easy to find in the city square. They had slept in an open barn the night before. Just as Logan had said, they had only an old horse, a cart, and a small trunk with all their possessions.

Russ, the man who almost hung two days earlier, had a hound dog. It took a little while for Bull to accept the friendly mutt, but he did.

Russ walked while his raggedly dressed wife and boys rode in the cart.

"Does your dog hunt?" Henry asked.

"Shep hunts anything—give him a scent and he'll follow it, Mr. Funk. Do you have something in mind?"

"Indians," Henry replied. "I have to find a chief and return something. If your dog Shep can hunt, we'll go on an expedition. You and me and our dogs. Do you have a gun?"

"No, I do not."

"Then mine will be enough. Let's get to the farm by dark."

Henry left Philadelphia with a resolve to return the medallion to Lapowinsa. Whether or not Anna would agree with his goal, and whether or not it would be possible to accomplish it, remained to be seen.

At the start of their trek home, Henry asked about the family's story. "London dregs," Russ explained. "We were poor, had no one to speak for us, and no chances, so we got pitched out like refuse."

"Who pitched you out?" Henry asked.

"A judge who wanted to clean up the streets and get himself reelected because he was tough," Russ replied.

"Who paid for your fare to Pennsylvania?" Anna inquired.

"We were indentured to the ship's captain, who sold us when we arrived at port. Like slaves."

"Have your boys been to school?" Anna asked.

"Not a chance," Russ replied. "We can't afford it."

"Keep the pace moving," Anna urged. "I want to get a fire going at home tonight, not at some campsite or even the Freedom Inn. We've been away too long."

Russ explained further about their plight, walking fast to keep up with the horses and cart. "A plague hit London a few years ago, and we got swept out like trash, so they could stop the dying. The thought was that people like us living in the streets were somehow responsible for what was killing the rich in their nice homes."

At the turn north toward home and Indian Creek, Henry changed the subject. "Anna, I want to find Lapowinsa and return the medallion."

"What makes you think you can find him?" she asked.

"Because this hound can hunt," Henry replied confidently. "Russ says Shep can trail anything."

"They could be on the other side of Pennsylvania by now," Anna responded.

"Or just a day or two travel away," Henry answered. "No one knows."

"How long have they been gone?" Russ asked.

"A week," Henry said.

"Show my dog where they camped, and he'll pick up the trail. We can find them. The dog's part rabbit hound and part blood hound, so be ready to ride fast when he picks up the trail, because he'll be gone."

"Restitution," Henry stated to no one in particular. "That's what we need to do with the medallion."

"Explain the word, Henry. I don't understand," Anna replied.

"It means to give something back to its proper owner, to make something right," Henry stated.

"Okay, I get that. You want to make things right with Lapowinsa," Anna replied.

"Was the chief treated badly?" Russ asked.

"Yes, kind of like you and your family when you got kicked out of London," Henry explained. "The medallion belongs to the Lenape who are getting pushed west by English settlers and the Iroquois."

"Where did you get that big word, Henry?" asked Anna.

"I've been reading the book of Exodus. In the Bible. Moses gave the Israelites instructions about making things right when people got wronged. It's called 'restitution.' "

"You know, Henry, you're a pretty smart guy. I actually read your big word this morning in that new book by John Bunyan, but didn't understand it," Anna replied.

"Are you a teacher?" Russ asked.

"Not a chance," Henry replied. "Teachers don't make any money."

"We pay Chris Dock," Anna added.

"We pay him a little bit, but he makes money to live on from the produce he grows on his farm," Henry answered.

Walking on in silence for a time, Henry shifted the discussion.

"Russ, we need to get your boys in a school so they can learn to read and write."

"I don't see why," Russ replied. "Not knowing how to read and write hasn't much hurt me."

"If you could read or write, you could get a job and support your family," Henry explained. Glancing back at the cart with the downcast mother and her two boys, he continued. "I went to school in Germany. It gave me the skills I need to farm and make a living."

"I went to school in Aruba," Anna chimed in. "We can pay Chris Dock to teach your boys. Maybe someday they could work in a shop or help to run a mill."

"Henry," Anna suggested. "You should write a book about that fancy new word."

"That's a great idea," Henry replied. "I just might. But first we have to make restitution with our former neighbors, the Lenape."

Henry's father was glad to turn the farm back over to Henry and Anna when they tied up outside their house.

"You had a few customers at the mill this week, but nothing very eventful to speak of," Mr. Funk told Henry. "It looks like you have new tenants to live in the mill."

"We do, but first thing in the morning, Russ and I will leave and try to find Lapowinsa. We found the medallion. If you could work in the mill for two more days, I'd be grateful."

"I can do that," Mr. Funk replied. "But next week it's your mill again."

On Friday morning, October 22, Henry and Russ left at sunup to return the medallion, with Russ riding Anna's horse.

Anna spent her day helping Russ' wife and boys make a home in the third floor of the mill. They needed baths, and Anna looked for materials to mend their tattered clothing.

Russ was right. Shep picked up the scent at the Perkiomen Creek settlement and took off running with a howl.

The men rode hard, following the dog, while Bull easily kept up, wondering what they were chasing. At times the men completely lost the dogs up ahead who ran faster than the horses. Shep's howling signaled the direction to ride. By the afternoon, they caught up and reached the Schuylkill, a wide river that presented a problem.

"Could the Lenape have crossed this river?" Henry asked Russ.

"I don't see how—you said there were fifty of them. They probably turned upstream and followed the river. Look, Shep just picked up their trail. Follow him."

By nightfall, the men were tired, their horses were exhausted, and the dogs welcomed a chance to recuperate beside a fire. Henry dug in the saddlebags for grain, meat scraps for the dogs, and biscuits and dried meat slabs for the men. Next to a strong fire, they talked about their lives.

Henry had grown up with enough to eat and clothes to wear on a farm in the heartland of Germany. He had been schooled and given every opportunity. Russ, on the other hand, hadn't known his parents and grew up as an orphan on the streets of London. He never went to school, and lived from one temporary job to the next, until he got sent to America in order to clean up the king's streets.

Before going to sleep, Henry decided that if he couldn't write a book about "restitution," someone in the Mennonite church should write such a book.

Early the next morning, after the fire had died out, Henry and Russ awoke and moved quickly to get warmed up. Speaking little as they mounted their horses, the two men urged Shep to recover the trail, which he soon found.

Shep followed a foot trail north along the Schuylkill. There hadn't been a good place to cross anywhere, and the discouraged Lenape kept walking until either they found a low enough place to walk across, someone with enough canoes to help them, or they settled in one place long enough to make their own.

The hound started howling louder. They were getting closer. By evening of the second day, Henry and Russ spotted the Lenape ahead, camped at the river's edge.

Riding into the clearing, the Lenape offered little resistance or concern when the two men hopped off their saddles. Their spirits were low, Henry could tell. They had been chased from their home, and now they couldn't get across the mighty river in their path.

"Mr. Funk, what brings you here?" Chief Lapowinsa greeted.

"Greetings," Henry began. "We bring good news to you and your people."

"Come sit next to the fire," Lapowinsa encouraged. "Who is your companion?"

"This is Russ. He owns the hound that helped us find you. Let me feed the horses and the dogs, then I will sit with you."

Some minutes later, with both Henry and Russ seated next to the fire and Chief Lapowinsa and the braves listening, Henry started, "We bring very good news."

"You did not bring Anna?" Lapowinsa replied.

"She is very much with child," Henry answered. "We rode hard today and yesterday, and we just got back from Philadelphia. We made a bargain with James Logan to release a Mohawk warrior in exchange for getting Abe and Annie Beth Swartz out of New York."

"You have been busy," Lapowinsa answered. In the light of the fire, the chief's black peace marks on his forehead glistened.

"Chief Lapowinsa, I have some very good news for you and your people. Look what I found in Philadelphia." Pulling the medallion from his pocket, he showed the Lenape around the fire the long-lost gold medallion.

Examining it, Lapowinsa could see the turtle and cross, and he exclaimed to his people: "Our long lost medallion, once with Tender Vine, has been found. Tell us the story of where it was hidden."

In the warm glow of the fire, Henry told the story about the trunk and the way Bull had detected the medallion. "It most likely had been placed there by the 'Great Miquon' himself, William Penn. Apparently his inept and dense son did not know it was in the chest. Fortunately, the unpopular governor has departed for England," Henry stated. Lapowinsa knew enough politics to get the humor in Henry's comment.

With his braves watching, Lapowinsa rose and faced the east, and then turned to look toward the west. But then he turned and seemed to bow in the direction of Bull. Continuing with the ancient ritual, as he had recited just over a week earlier, the group chanted again: " *'We carry the spirit of Tamenend in the land of the Dawn.'* "

"How will you cross the river?" Henry asked.

"Only the Great Spirit knows that answer," Lapowinsa replied. "We will camp here until we find a way to cross." Though discouraged, Henry noticed that every brave held the medallion in the firelight and examined the turtle first, and then the cross on the other side. When each man had held it, the women were each able to hold it, and then the children. It seemed that the resolve and strength of the Lenape began to rise in the presence of the medallion.

"I know how to build a canoe," Russ offered.

"Where did you learn?" Henry asked.

"It was one of my jobs in Philadelphia. If you loan me a couple of tools from your farm, Henry, I can come back here and help the Lenape build a birch wood canoe that can cross this river. We'll ferry them across a few at a time."

Turning to Lapowinsa, Henry asked: "Chief, do you want this man to return with tools and build you a canoe?"

Lapowinsa was embarrassed that desire for the devil's rum among his braves had left them with no tools to build their own canoe. "The Indian name of this water means 'Turtle River,'" Lapowinsa replied. "We would welcome 'Turtle Man' to build us a canoe." The braves nodded in agreement. Russ stood, understood what had just been agreed to and declared, "I will build your canoe. Today Mr. Funk taught me a new word, 'restitution,'" Russ explained. With puzzled looks around the fire he said, "Mr. Funk saved my life three days ago and kept me from hanging." The braves understood when Russ put his hands around his neck.

"I will return in three days and work for you," Russ declared. "I owe a debt to Mr. Funk, and I will help you navigate across Turtle River. Until I return, find the biggest birch tree available and bring it here." The braves rose and chanted again, "*We carry the spirit of Tamenend in the land of the Dawn.*'"

Late on the same Saturday afternoon, Abe Swartz knocked on Anna's door. When she opened, Little John leapt into her arms. Looking up, Anna was thrilled to see Abe and Annie Beth standing on her front step.

"Come in," Anna squealed. "Welcome home!"

"It's good to be here," Annie Beth replied.

"You must be hungry," Anna commented.

"We're famished," Annie Beth answered. "We haven't eaten much since we left New York two days ago."

"I'll make something right away. Please be seated."

"Has anything happened at our house?" Abe wondered.

"You had a fire, but the structure is still standing," Anna replied. "Little John has grown so much since I last saw him."

"As soon as I get a bite to eat, I'm going to check on our house," Abe replied.

"Here, start with some deer jerky. Can you come to church tomorrow morning? Everyone will be so glad to see you!"

"Yes, we'll be in church tomorrow," Abe replied.

Hardened by the sun and the cold, another line or two had crossed Abe's forehead. Not tall, but sturdy as a tree trunk, Abe was determined to fix up his house and resume life on his property. Annie Beth, pretty and petite, exuded a confidence that came from the difficulties of life in a far distant fort for several weeks. Annie Beth had worried about the men in the fort taking advantage of her, but no one had. "Anna," Annie Beth confided, "I'm pretty sure I'm pregnant."

"It's only been a little over two months since your wedding," Anna replied. "Are you sure?"

"I'm not sure, but it sure seems like something's different."

"Then we need a real meal for the four of you," Anna smiled. "Annie Beth, did you ever hear the story in the Bible of what happened when Mary went to visit her aunt Elizabeth who was pregnant?"

Annie Beth smiled, "Yes, Elizabeth's baby leapt for joy! Did your baby jump when we came to the door?"

"Yes, that's why I told you the story," Anna beamed.

Only four days after Henry had met with Fifteen Feathers in Philadelphia, the Oneida chief stepped out of the woods and greeted Henry in front of the Lenape Indians. Camped along the Schuylkill for the last two nights, Henry and Russ were ready to return home on Sunday, and they hoped to make it in one day.

"I understand this man is going to build a canoe for these people," Shickellamy stated.

"How did you know that? And how did you know where I was at?" Henry asked incredulously.

"I am a chief in the Iroquois Nation. We have a network of trails and roads that your people know little about. I have scouts everywhere in these woods. When you rode north, I had you tailed. I want to assist you. What can I do to help bring this man back to work for the Lenape?"

Looking around, and still wondering how Fifteen Feathers could possibly have known where he was, Henry told the chief that Russ' horse was old, lame, and not worthy of the trail. "These are my horses," Henry pointed.

"He needs a horse?" Feathers asked.

"Yes," Henry replied. "He wants to bring his wife and boys back with him for the winter and teach his boys some skills with tools," Henry stated.

"A horse will be delivered to your farm for him," Shickellamy replied. "Two days from now."

"He also needs a gun," Henry added.

"He'll get one."

With that, the chief slipped into the woods, and he and his men were gone.

Henry turned to the Lenape, then back to Russ, and said to Lapowinsa, "I have no idea how Fifteen Feathers knew where I was at, but Russ should be back in about four days."

The trusted horses headed south when Henry and Russ flicked their reins, with Shep and Bull trailing them.

31

Arrival

December 1725

Eight weeks after leaving the Lenape at the Schuylkill River, Sampson the slave rode fast toward Philadelphia to bring Margaret Bradford to Anna's side to deliver her baby. It was Sunday, but the ride was urgent.

Sampson had kept hidden in the forest two months prior when Henry and Russ had visited the Lenape, worried that Henry's traveling partner might be an informant or a spy for James Logan.

When Russ had loaded the wigwam on his cart at the Funks, along with his wife and boys in October, Henry had sent along three bags of flour and two bags of corn for the Lenape to eat during the winter. When the last of the Lenape had been ferried across the mighty river in Russ' newly carved birch canoe, rowed by the strongest braves, Sampson and Pretty Leaves had decided to return to Indian Creek and seek work on the Funk farm. Russ had promised to return Henry's tools, which Sampson delivered to the farm. Russ's family, with little to lose, chose to join the Lenape and travel far away to the western part of Pennsylvania.

Accepted by Anna and Henry and given a job, no sooner had Sampson started work in the mill, when Henry put him on his best horse, sending Sampson on a gallop to Philadelphia to bring the mid-wife to the farm. Anna had begun her contractions before church.

When Sampson arrived at Margaret Bradford's print shop on Second Street in Philadelphia after dark, Ben Franklin came out from a back room to meet the anxious slave. "Where's Mrs. Bradford?" Sampson asked.

"Upstairs," Ben replied. "I'll get her."

When Mrs. Bradford came down the steps, Sampson informed her that Anna's contractions had started and that Anna had asked for her to come immediately.

"We will leave in the morning," Margaret replied.

"Mrs. Bradford, can we ride tonight? It is urgent. The baby may come without you if we delay."

"You want me to ride right now?" Margaret asked.

"Yes, the moon is bright and there are stars out. It is clear and I know the way very well. Can we go now?" Sampson asked. With Margaret's husband Andrew listening, Margaret hesitated about riding at night.

"I'll go along," Ben offered.

"Why do you want to go along?" Andrew asked.

"Because there's a pretty girl at Indian Creek I want to see again," Ben bluntly replied. "I need to get to her house again if I'm going to have any chance with Agnes."

"The three of us can make it to the farm by morning," Sampson pleaded. "Anna needs you."

Monday morning, after Andrew Bradford had helped load up his wife's saddlebags with provisions for the journey to Anna Funk's house, and she and Sampson and Franklin had ridden into the cold night, Bradford opened his print shop for business.

A couple walked in his door whom he had met once before, in January, when they came to purchase a newspaper and inquire about their daughter. Cornelius Meyer began the conversation, having remembered Bradford's name from *The American Weekly Mercury* masthead that he had purchased eleven months earlier. "We're looking for our daughter, Anna," Cornelius inquired.

"You folks are from the Caribbean, aren't you?" Bradford replied.

"Yes, from Aruba," Grietje De Visscher Meyer responded. "We have learned that our daughter has married Mr. Henry Funk from Indian Creek. Can you help us get to their farm?"

"You must have arrived on yesterday's cargo ship," Bradford tried to stall.

"Indeed, now can you or someone you know lead us to the Funk farm?" Mr. Meyer insisted.

When Bradford hesitated, Mr. Meyer offered money. "We will pay you fifteen pounds to take us to the Funk farm."

The money appealed to Bradford, as well as the opportunity to follow his wife and visit the Funks again. Bradford stated that the Meyer couple would need to rent horses, which would cost another fifteen pounds for a week. "We will do that," Mr. Meyer replied.

"How did you know Anna has married Henry Funk?" Bradford asked.

"Bentura and Cool Water came to Santa Cruz and told us about the wedding and that Anna is pregnant," Mrs. Meyer answered.

"All right, you have a deal," Mr. Bradford concluded. "Down the street two blocks is where you can rent horses. We will leave first thing tomorrow morning."

"We are very grateful," Mr. Meyer concluded.

After three months of hard work in Elkton, Virginia, Dorothy Miller started a fire in her own log cabin fireplace. Crude but solid, the small house would protect them from the winter that had closed in on her and Adam.

"What will Christmas be like without any family around?" Dorothy asked.

"We have each other," Adam responded. "And in the spring two more families will join us and build their own cabins.

"I do have two books to read," Dorothy replied. "Remember, you told me I could bring them along when we moved."

Both heard strange sounds outside their door. Adam pulled open the one small window shutter he had cut into the cabin wall. Peering out, he told Dorothy that the curious bear had returned. "It's looking for food," he concluded. "I'm going out there to deal with it."

"Be careful," Dorothy replied. "I've got a Christmas gift to tell you about when you get back."

Picking up Dorothy's gun, the wedding gift from her father, Adam stepped out the door. Within moments he fired the gun, and the bear let out a roar, collapsing into a bloody heap in the white snow.

Back inside, Adam reached for a knife to begin skinning the annoying beast, but Dorothy stopped him. "You're going to be a papa next year, Adam. Merry Christmas."

Flexing his muscles and smiling just a bit, Adam told Dorothy he was glad that someday he may have help to skin out the bears that bothered his family. "Keep this gun loaded, Dorothy. If wolves come poking around while I work, wanting some of our bear, you may need to use it."

Sampson, Ben Franklin, and Margaret Bradford rode up to the hitching post at the Funk farm and quickly hopped off their horses. Mrs. Bradford knocked on the door, and Henry opened it.

"Come in quickly," Henry greeted. "Anna's contractions are getting closer and closer, and we need your help."

"Get me a basin of warm water," Margaret directed. "Also bring towels and a clean knife," she instructed.

Anna noticed but didn't much care who had walked in the house. Preoccupied with birthing pains, Anna gripped the side of her bed when the pain grew intense. Mrs. Kolb and her daughter Agnes realized that an experienced mid-wife had just come to help them, and they were relieved. With almost no introductions or formalities, the three women directed all their focus on helping Anna give birth to her baby.

Henry stoked the fire and kept the house warm, helping in any way he was needed. With Anna's condition stabilized, Margaret warmed herself by the fire and ate a bite from the soup that Henry offered.

The men at the mill eagerly ate the soup. They had tied up the horses in the barn and would spend the day working at whatever needed to be done away from the house.

Anna's contractions had been coming with greater frequency during Sunday and all night. By mid-morning Monday, she was exhausted and sweating, saying things in incoherent ways that were normal for a young mother who had never experienced childbirth before.

It was going to be very white Christmas at the Funk farm on Indian Creek. Not only on Indian Creek, but all across the eastern part of Pennsylvania a major snow storm blew in, and it snowed hard on Monday afternoon, into the night, and until noon the next day. A foot of new snow slowed pretty much everything down to a crawl.

West of the Schuylkill, the Lenape hunkered down in whatever shelter they had. Russ put his family inside the wigwam from the Funk farm. Braves fought to keep a fire going, but the snow came so fast their fire nearly went out. In spite of the snow, Russ went to shoot something for the group. The gun which the Mohawk had given him proved to be a vital means of survival for the entire group, and never so much as during this storm. It did not take long for Russ to shoot a large buck and haul the meat back to camp. Several women worked hard with Russ to cook the deer for their hungry people.

Andrew Bradford watched the snow pile up on Second Street and wondered if he and the Meyer couple would be able to ride in the morning. With a foot of new snow on the ground by Tuesday morning, their departure might be delayed at least one day, possibly longer.

Henry dug a little path from the house to the mill, and talked with Ben Franklin about Agnes. "She's working in the house, helping Anna," he stated.

"Looks like I'm going to be here for a while," Franklin replied. "Can you give me a sheet of paper to write on?"

Digging through his records-keeping desk in the mill, Henry found something suitable for Ben. "Here are my pens," Henry pointed. "Help yourself."

With snow coming down hard, Franklin sat at Henry Funk's desk along the east mill window, stared outside at the house and the barn, and began to write: ***"Henry Funk has demonstrated that slavery is an evil which should be eradicated from this Quaker colony. The way he has treated a runaway slave, and the manner in which the slave has responded are exemplary to all in the colony. When a slave is offered freedom and meaningful work, slavery can turn from a draining enterprise that costs the slave owner, to one in which a free man earns a profit from the freed slave, and the slave can earn his freedom in such a way. The German-speaking people of this colony, while not of the caliber of the English immigrants, are still noble, enterprising, and up-building in a way that will make this colony prosper. With the babies these people produce, and their dedication to family values and hard work, they will prosper and acquire great wealth. Others should follow the lead of the Mennonites and help to end the institution of slavery, though it will take several more generations, most likely, before this can happen."***

Franklin folded the paper, tucked it in his pocket, and planned to publish it the next issue of *The Mercury*. When he deposited Henry's quill pen into its holder, Henry opened the door and walked in with Agnes Kolb.

"I'm a father, Ben," Henry beamed. "It's a boy and we've named him John Meyer Funk, in honor of my father's first name, and Anna's maiden name. You've met Agnes before," Henry shifted. "She helped deliver our baby. Sampson, come with me to the house and see baby John," Henry encouraged.

"There's work to be done here," Sampson replied.

"Sampson, you come with me," Henry directed. Seeing Mr. Funk glance at the two young people in the mill, Sampson understood. "I will be glad to come with you, Mr. Funk. Just a minute, let me get something upstairs."

In the living room, with a reddish looking little boy lying in his happy mother's arms, Sampson congratulated Anna on the birth. "Mrs. Funk, with all the excitement of your baby's arrival, I have not been able to deliver an item to you that I was asked to give you from the Lenape."

Anna only smiled, and Henry asked what he had.

"Chief Lapowinsa asked me to return this gold medallion to you, Mrs. Funk. It is the one you gave him. Now that he has the real medallion, from Tender Vine, he wanted you to have this one. It had been a gift to you, he believed."

Henry took the medallion and placed it beside Anna. She seemed interested, but with a baby on her breast, she only smiled at Sampson and managed a weak, "Thank you."

"There is one more thing to tell you, Mr. and Mrs. Funk," Sampson continued. "The brave who wanted to marry Anna came to me before I left the Lenape and asked me to apologize to you for starting your house on fire last summer. He is truly sorry. He now realizes how wrong he was, because you have helped his Lenape people many times. He knows it is dishonorable not to come himself, but still he sent an apology with me."

Pretty Leaves, who had helped the women with Anna's delivery, nodded in agreement. She had been a witness to the apology from the brave.

"Henry, it's your turn to hold your son," Margaret interjected. Sampson left the house and headed to the barn to avoid the mill. Henry took his son, John, and held him, beaming with joy and happiness. Anna noticed, but then drifted off to sleep, something she hadn't done for a while.

By Tuesday afternoon, four days before Christmas, it stopped snowing and Sampson went and shoveled the bridge over Indian Creek. Bull dug through the drifts with Sampson, and stood on the bridge checking out the creek.

Bull barked in excitement when Ben Franklin and Agnes Kolb came to inspect the structure.

"I want a farm someday like my parents have," Agnes told Ben.

"Would you ever consider moving to a city like Philadelphia?" Ben wondered.

"Possibly," Agnes replied. "The city is a nice place to visit, but I don't think I want to live there."

"I'm going to open my own print shop next year," Ben stated.

"In Philadelphia?" Agnes asked.

"Yes, will you come and visit me next spring when the snow melts?"

"I'd like to visit the city and see you," Agnes replied. "That would be nice. Have you courted before?"

"No one to speak of," Ben answered. "I remember seeing you at Anna and Henry's wedding, and I've been thinking about that ever since."

"The wedding?" Agnes asked.

"No, you," Ben replied. "You've been on my mind ever since their wedding."

"My sister got married to a man, and they moved to Virginia," Agnes replied. "Have you ever visited Virginia?"

"No, I have not," Franklin replied. "Would you like me to take you there for a visit?"

"Yes, I would like that very much. Could we go next spring and see my sister?"

"Let me investigate where they moved to and figure out who can guide us there," Franklin replied. "If that's what you want, I'll plan for it. I will look forward to this trip all winter."

"So will I," Agnes smiled.

On Tuesday, in the Philadelphia Court Square, Andrew Bradford noticed Fifteen Feathers walking through the plaza. Catching up to the regal chief, Bradford asked him for help.

"I need assistance to get Anna Funk's parents to Henry's farm on Indian Creek. They have come from warm and sunny Aruba where they never deal with snow, and they have barely ridden a horse before. This snow will keep me and them here in the city for days until it melts enough for us to ride to the Funk farm. Will you help us get there?"

Shickellamy noticed the Aruban couple in the print shop doorway across the square. "You want to me to ride ahead of you and open the path, is that it?"

"Yes, my wife left Sunday night to help Anna Funk as a mid-wife. I would guess the baby has arrived by now."

"Mrs. Funk has had her baby?" Fifteen Feathers queried.

"Yes. Will you help us?" Bradford replied hopefully.

"Certainly. We can leave in the morning."

Two Mohawk braves led the way, opening up a path for Fifteen Feathers, Mr. Bradford, and the Meyer couple. It was a humorous caravan. The Aruban parents had purchased coats which flapped as they rode, and had tried to load their saddlebags with a bit of food, but Pennsylvania was not like the hills of Aruba. The cold and snow made travel difficult, and they struggled to keep up with three Indians.

By evening, the party rode had reached the hitching post outside Anna and Henry's stone house. Bull barked excitedly, recognizing Fifteen Feathers and Mr. Bradford.

"This house is so nice," Mrs. Meyer exclaimed. "I can't wait to see the inside."

"The dog is massive," Mr. Meyer commented. "Is it Anna's dog?"

"Yes," Mr. Bradford answered.

When Andrew knocked on the door, Henry opened it, greeted his friend, and glanced at the party of visitors outside his house. He gulped in astonishment to see Mr. and Mrs. Meyer.

"Come in," Henry welcomed.

Turning into the house, Henry exclaimed, "Anna, you have special visitors who have come a long way to see you!"

Holding baby John, the miller's wife turned toward the door and beamed at the sight of her parents. "Send them in, Henry!"

32

Notes

Chapter One: Announcement

Henry Funk (1690-1760) was an eighteenth-century leader of the Pennsylvania Mennonites. He was a bishop, writer of two books, and helped to get the Dutch language *Martyrs Mirror* translated into German. He and his wife Anna Funk have many descendants in the United States today.

In this book Anna Meyer is a fictional character. The couple from Aruba, Grietje De Visscher and Cornelius Meyer, described on the first page of chapter one as Anna's parents, are an actual Dutch couple, third-generation descendants of Jansen and Griet Visscher, the main characters in *The Black Tulip*, volume two of Legacy Print Series. If the fictitious Anna Meyer, created in *The Miller's Wife*, was historical, she would have been the same age as the actual Anna Meyer. The Dutch character of Anna Meyer, created in this book, was developed to tell a story and connect generations in the Legacy Print Series books.

The actual Anna Meyer (1702-1758) was an immigrant from Germany, the daughter of Christian and Anna Meyer. The historical Anna Meyer, Henry Funk's actual wife, was from Germany, not Aruba.

The American Weekly Mercury was the first newspaper printed in Philadelphia, and was printed by Andrew Bradford.

Adam Miller, a historical character, was one of the first German immigrants to settle in the Shenandoah Valley of Virginia. A memorial stands in his honor in the Elk Run Cemetery, Elkton, Virginia.

Chapter Two: Pursuit

Henry Funk built a mill along Indian Creek in 1725. A building stands on the foundation of the first mill, with a "1725" stone marker in the peak of the building, located at 680 Mill Road, Telford, Pennsylvania.

Chapter Three: Ambush

James Logan was an actual historical leader in colonial Pennsylvania.

Chief Lapowinsa is a historical character, one of the few early eighteenth-century Delaware Indians whose portrait was painted and survives at the Historical Society of Pennsylvania, located in Philadelphia.

Chapter Four: Capture

The story of the gold medallion emerges from the journals of John Heckwelder, Moravian missionary. Its historicity is questionable, though it may have existed as outlined in this book. The best introduction to the gold medallion is found in *Tomahawks to Peace*, Carlisle Printing, 2009, by James G. Landis.

Germantown Mennonite Church had a log meetinghouse by 1708.

Chapter Five: Speech

After William Penn's death in 1718, his wife Hannah Callowhill Penn, and their three sons, John, Thomas, and Richard, acted as proprietary governors of the Pennsylvania Colony, living in England during most of the 1720s. Pennsylvania was administered by lieutenant governors, and William Keith, forty-six, was the lieutenant governor in Pennsylvania in 1725.

Germantown Mennonites and Quakers did write a statement opposed to slavery in 1688.

Chapter Six: Friendship

The heavy influx of German immigrants to Pennsylvania took place in the early 1700s as described in this book.

Henry Funk was instrumental in helping to establish the Franconia Mennonite Church.

Immigrant Abraham Swartz, a historical Mennonite man, did have three successive wives, as described in this novel.

The book written by the first century Jewish historian Flavius Josephus, mentioned in this chapter, entitled *Josephi des hochberümpten ... histori beschreibers Zwentzig bücher von den alten geschichten ...,* is accurate as described in the chapter, having been printed by the Margaret and Balthasar Beck Press in Strasbourg, Germany, in 1539. It is an extremely rare book, though one copy can be found in the Eastern Mennonite University Library, Harrisonburg, Virginia, which in 2007 was donated to the library by the author of *The Miller's Wife.*

Chapter Seven: Petition

Ben Franklin was nineteen years old in 1725, though it is unknown whether he ever visited the Funk farm. He did hold views, found in his writings, that were unsympathetic toward the German immigrants in Pennsylvania.

The place where Adam Miller settled was not called Elkton until the mid-19th century.

Chapter Eight: Wedding

Chief Shickellamy was an actual Oneida leader and worked on behalf of the Pennsylvania government as described in the book.

There are no historical records revealing that Henry Funk heard harmonies from the Indians at his wedding.

Chapter Nine: Negotiation

The deadly effects of rum on the Indians of colonial Pennsylvania are true.

The account of the thirty Mennonite families moving from New York to the Tulpehocken Creek area in Pennsylvania was an historical event.

Chapter Eleven: Mirror

Conrad Beissel immigrated from Europe and helped establish the Dunkers in Pennsylvania, later called Church of the Brethren. Beissel went on to be instrumental in establishing the Ephrata Cloisters. In years following 1725, Henry Funk helped to get *Martyrs Mirror* printed in German at the Ephrata Cloisters print shop.

Henry Funk wrote a book called *A Mirror of Baptism*, completed in 1744, and reprinted as late as the year 2000. It is still offered for sale in some bookstores.

Chapter Twelve: Fire

Smallpox and other diseases, brought by European settlers, may have killed as many as 90% of the native Americans.

The historic seal on Henry Funk's land deed, from Governor Keith, included corn and grapes.

Chapter Thirteen: Stone

The scouting trip of Zook and Yoder to Pennsylvania is fictional, though a few Amish did come to Pennsylvania very early in the eighteenth-century. In 1742, three Zook families and two Yoder Amish families arrived in Philadelphia aboard the *Francis and Elizabeth* ship, among 328 German immigrants. One of those Yoder families aboard the ship are ancestors of the author.

Henry and Anna Funk did build a stone house on Indian Creek.

The Bible verse mentioned in this chapter is 2 Thessalonians 1:11.

The hymnal referred to is the *Ausbund*, the sixteenth century hymnal of Anabaptists, and used by colonial American Mennonites in the early eighteenth-century.

Chapter Fifteen: Feathers

The Bible verse referred to on the first page of this chapter is Exodus 17:14.

Chapter Seventeen: Nation

Estimates of the number of people in Philadelphia in 1725 vary, and numbers are not precise, but the city had approximately ten thousand residents, and the overall population of Pennsylvania was around fifty thousand.

Chapter Eighteen: Council

Ordination by lot to choose ministers was used by most Mennonites in colonial America. The Bible verse usually written on a slip of paper, inserted into one Bible, was Proverbs 16:33.

Abraham Swartz was ordained to the ministry, eventually becoming a Mennonite Bishop.

Chapter Nineteen: Teacher

While Annie Beth Kolb's older sister was Dorothy Kolb, she did not marry Adam Miller.

Christopher Dock would have been in his twenties in 1725, and was the Mennonite community school teacher. The name of his wife is unknown, and the account of his interest in Dorothy Kolb is fictional.

Chapter Twenty: Double

The writings of Benjamin Franklin mentioned in this chapter and this novel are fictitious and are not taken directly from his writings.

Annie Beth Kolb did have two older sisters named Dorothy and Maria, and she had a younger sister named Agnes.

The burning of the Philadelphia court house is fictitious.

Chapter Twenty-One: Underground

Joshua Fry and Peter Jefferson were surveyors and adventurers from Virginia who made a famous map, completed in the 1750s, that showed The Great Road, the original of which is stored with the Library of Congress. Peter Jefferson's third child was Thomas Jefferson, born in 1743, who became the third president of the United States.

Chapter Twenty-Two: Runaway

Daniel Trico was the eleventh child of Joris and Catalina Trico. Joris and Catalina were one of the earliest Dutch couples to immigrate to colonial New Amsterdam. Their first child is the first known child to be born in the New World from Dutch parents. Thousands of descendants in the Americas today trace their ancestry to Joris and Catalina Trico. The story of the birth of their first child, at Fort Orange, is told in chapter twenty-seven of *The Black Tulip*, 2014, the author's second novel in *Legacy Print Series*. It is uncertain where Daniel Trico lived, and it is fictional that he visited the Funk farm.

James Logan owned a slave that he named Sampson. The slave's African name is unknown. It is historical that Sampson ran away from Stenton, Logan's mansion. It is fictional that Sampson visited the Funks.

Chapter Twenty-Three: Tickets

John Penn, one of William Penn's sons, was a proprietary governor of Pennsylvania during the 1720s. It is unknown whether he visited the colony in 1725, and it is doubtful that he ever visited the Funk farm.

Chapter Twenty-Four: Junto

Ben Franklin started a discussion group, called Junto, in the late 1720s. The methods of the group as outlined in this chapter are close to the original pattern of the group that Franklin created. Later this group came to be called the American Philosophical Society.

The description of Chief Lapowinsa's leather pouch comes from the famous portrait of him housed in the Historical Society of Pennsylvania, in Philadelphia. The details of porcupine quills decorating an elk hide pouch come from a mid-eighteenth-century Lenape pouch found in the collections of the National Museum of the American Indian, Washington, D.C.

Chapter Twenty-Six: Escape

The excerpt from Ben Franklin's writing in this chapter is fictional.

The quote from Henry Funk is taken from his book, *A Mirror of Baptism*, originally written in German, and later translated into English in 1851 by Henry Funk's grandson Joseph Funk, from Singers Glen, Virginia. The quote can be found in *A Mirror of Baptism*, by Henry Funk, Gospel Publishers, Moundridge, Kansas, 2000, page 72.

Chapter Thirty: Restitution

Henry Funk wrote a book called *Restitution, or an Explanation of Several Principal Points of the Law*, published in German by his children in 1763 shortly after his death. It was later translated into English.

In the King James Version of the Bible, the word "restitution" is found especially in Exodus 22.

Chapter Thirty-one: Arrival

Henry and Anna Funk's first child was a boy which they named John Meyer Funk. Their second child was also a boy, whom they named Henry Meyer Funk, who moved to Rockingham County, Virginia, and is buried in the Trissels Mennonite Church cemetery, Broadway, Virginia. Henry and Barbara Funk were the parents of Joseph Funk, the renowned Mennonite printer and musician from Singers Glen, Virginia.

Historical Characters
Henry Funk
Andrew Bradford
Chief Lapowinsa
James Logan
Grietje De Visscher
Cornelius Meyer
William Penn
Abraham Swartz
Elizabeth Swartz
Benjamin Franklin
Annie Beth Kolb
Chief Shickellamy
Conrad Beissel
Dorothy Kolb
Christopher Dock
William Keith

John Penn

Adam Miller

Sampson

Alexander Spotswood

Agnes Kolb

Daniel Trico

Catalina Trico

Peter Jefferson

Joshua Fry

Mr. and Mrs. Kolb

Mr. and Mrs. Funk

John Meyer Funk

Tender Vine

Fictional Characters

Anna Meyer

Lenape Mother

Margaret Bradford

Little John Swartz

Jacob Swartz

Bentura

Cool Water

Pretty Leaves

William and Jubilant

Zook

Yoder

Russ and family

Bull

Shep

		Descendants Chart of Legacy Print Series Books, Volumes 1-3
Generations	1	Margaret and Balthasar Beck (1500s) (from *Margaret's Print Shop* book, Volume 1)
	2	Unknown (1500s)
	3	Jan Cornelisz (- 1625) and Anna Visscher (1556-1627) (from *The Black Tulip* book, Volume 2)
	4	Jansen (c. 1605) and Griet Visscher (c. 1606) (from *The Black Tulip* book, Volume 2)
	5	Jan De Visscher (1600s)
	6	Grietje De Visscher and Cornelius Meyer (1600s-1700s) (from *The Miller's Wife* book, Volume 3)
	7	Anna Meyer (ca. 1705-1758) and Henry Funk (1690-1760) (from *The Miller's Wife* book, Volume 3)

www.ingramcontent.com/pod-product-compliance
Lightning Source LLC
Chambersburg PA
CBHW051408170626
46809CB00006B/2069